The Braymyer Saga

By: Dusty Williams

The Braymyer Saga
Copyright © by Dusty Williams; 2016

ISBN-13: 978-1511862301
ISBN-10: 1511862300

Books included:

Braymyer Hill

California Charm

The Road to Braymyer Ridge

Dusty Williams

This book is dedicated to all of my wonderful grandparents. I hope that everyone can be as lucky as I have been to be surrounded with the love they have shown.
Nanny and Pa
(Kim and Larry Williams)
Nana and Grandpa
(Sherry and Wayne Jeffers)
Granny and Poppaw
(Ollie and Sam Edmonds)
Peepaw and Bop-Bop
(Robert Holloway & Carolyn George)

I would also like to thank my parents whose faith in my ability to change the world has brought me one step closer in obtaining my lifelong dream of becoming a writer:
Eric and Pam Holloway
&
Aaron and Karen Williams

Furthermore I could not have accomplished anything in life without the support of my six siblings:
Cody Williams
Aaron Williams, Jr.
Logan Holloway
Kailey Holloway
Shannon Wyrick
Amanda Green

To my wife J Anna and our children, Kalob, Micaiah and Davian who are always my rock and yet my steady wind reminding me of what is important in life.

Lastly I would like to give a special thank you to Mrs. Eloise Swayze whose story of baby by way of a buzzard laying a rotten egg was inspiration for a part of this book. The story was handed down by her mother, Tevis (Williams) Cloud.

Dusty Williams

Part I

Braymyer Hill

Dusty Williams

"A family is nothing without a home to gather in.
It can be a tent, a cabin or the simple shade of a cottonwood
tree,
but there must always be a place where the heart can open up
and rejoice
with those closest to it."

-Rosalee Braymyer, 1879

Dusty Williams

Chapter One

June 20, 2010

Nathan Sanders lay in his bed as another lonesome soul shuffled past his door down the long hallway. There was an occasional moan or grunt heard and the sound that can only be found in a nursing home; the long, high pitched whaling of a voice that cannot be compared to anything natural in this world. It was dark out and it looked as if it were going to be another long night for the few residents who still had their right mind.

The fluorescent lights flickered on occasion, going from dim to bright as if the staff were trying to make their patients go crazy. The new plasma television that hung on the wall hurt his eyes so he rarely turned it on and tonight was no exception.

Mr. Sanders moved an old picture box from his nightstand and placed it on the bed beside him. As he removed the lid, the hallway echoed with that distinct whaling and a tear ran down his wrinkled face.

"Pappy? Are you okay?" I said getting up from my chair, only to have him motion me to sit back down.

"I'm fine, John. Sometimes this place makes me sad is all."

"Well, you know if it was up to me, sir, I wouldn't let you stay here a minute longer. But Grandma Rose thinks it's best and since she's your daughter and all…"

"I know, son, and besides you ship out tomorrow. You can't very well take me to Iraq with you."

"Ha, those Muslims wouldn't know what to do with you around, sir."

We both laughed for a minute and enjoyed a moment together. "Pappy, I hope your court case goes good tomorrow, but I'm sure it will."

"I hope you're right. I don't want to let anything happen to that house, it means too much to me and someday to you."

"Yes, sir. I remember you telling me about it several times, but I need to head home and get some sleep and you better do the same. Grandma will be here early in the morning to get you."

I stood up from the chair and my great grandfather held up his hand for me to shake and as I did he looked me in the eyes, "You take care of yourself over there, don't let them German's get the better of you, you hear?"

"Yes, sir." I said, feeling a bit sorry for him.

Nathan Sanders had forgotten about the photo box and when he was alone again he turned his attention back to it. The first thing he pulled out was an old black and white tintype photo. It was a young, very good looking couple and taped to the back of it was a note that read:

> "Nat and Rosie
>
> 1866
>
> Together Forever"

Nathan continued through the pictures, news articles and letters until he stumbled onto his favorite one. It was a crisply folded cream piece of paper that looked as if it had spent most of its life in an oven. He carefully unfolded it and then began to read:

> To our family of the future,
> November 26, 1874
>
> A family is an important thing, but it is nothing without a home to bring them together. We are living in rough

times, but the Lord has been good to us. We have built our home on sturdy ground, good land and it has seen the births, deaths and someday the marriages of our family. No matter what happens, protect this home, this land and keep it in the family so that long after we're gone, our descendants can continue to live in the home we created and profit from it. Stand strong and never fear the world, but let the world fear you.

Nat and Rosa Lee Braymyer

The next morning, Nathan's daughter, Rose Tyler picked him up and they headed to the old historic, downtown section of Sherman. The town was quiet today and the old buildings stood tall as if they were welcoming him to their old city. A young man was raising the Texas flag in front of the courthouse as they drove by and Nathan thought of his great grandson for a moment.

Driving through the old part of town brought back many memories for the old man, especially when they would drive over a section of the street that was still hand laid bricks, rather than cement or asphalt. Old trees that struggled to overpower the building in height surrounded the courthouse. Nathan felt for a moment as if he were an old tree, being threatened to be cut down from beneath.

He had spent his whole life trying to instill in his only daughter the importance of family, but at times he got the feeling that she would rather him just shut up. It hurt him that his daughter felt this way about their family history and the history of people in general, but he knew there wasn't much he could do about it but tell his family's story over and over and perhaps one day it would mean something.

Rose Tyler was a slim, five foot three, sixty four year old widow who cared more about nice cars than the sentimental value of life. She had once had blonde hair, but had started dying it brown long ago to cover up her grayness. She wasn't a bad person and if given the opportunity she would give the shirt off her back to a stranger, but the everyday things, like her father, she had grown accustomed to seeing so much she didn't feel the need to care as much. After all, they would always be there no matter what.

"Are you going to be okay in here, Daddy?"

Nathan looked down at the photo box in his lap as they neared the municipal building and then over at her. "Yes, Rose, I'll be fine. Are *you* going to be okay?"

The two of them went into the small courtroom and Mr. Sanders began to talk as soon as Rose had pushed his wheelchair close enough that the judge could hear.

"The home sat atop a large hill in a small clearing near Dixie, Texas. Its long driveway was lined with tall aged cottonwood trees that had been planted years before. The house was made of white stone and had four large white columns across the front of it. I remember well going to see this old home on my frequent trips to Dixie.

My mother was a Braymyer and often times she would tell us stories of the old Braymyer home and how it came to be. My mother's name was Jennie Rose and she was the first of the second generation of Braymyer children to have been born in that old house. It was a house of happiness and guarantee, but the blood and sweat it took to make this house cannot be measured by any scale we have in use today.

You call it imminent domain and I guess because not only am I 92, but in a nursing home as well, you think you can just take it for the next large superstore or whatever it is you are wanting to build. I honestly do not see how you can even imagine destroying something with as much history as that old house on Braymyer Hill. Why, I remember hearing the story of when Nat Braymyer and his wife, Rosalee first came to Dixie in 1867. It was early spring and all the Bradford Pears were full of white flowers…

Chapter Two

1867

Nathaniel Braymyer was a quiet man, but when he spoke, everyone listened and obeyed if need be. He was the type of man that others longed to be like and was thought highly of no matter where he went. At just over six feet, he was dark skinned, handsome, smart, strong and had a way about him that brought others near. His family was from eastern Tennessee, but had settled in Walnut Grove, Missouri shortly before Nat was born in 1848.

His father, John Braymyer had ran a successful farm and ranch for the most part of his life and like the Braymyers before him, he put his wife and children front and foremost. John's wife, Mary Anna was half Cherokee Indian, but other than the dark complexion of her skin you could not tell it. So with John's determination to work hard and make the land something and Mary Anna's appreciation of the land and all it had to offer, Nat had a good future laid out before him, built upon the morals of his parents.

Rosalee Burns was not a quiet person at all. She had a tendency of speaking her mind in her own little polite way no matter what the consequence was. Nonetheless, people loved her for it and if ever they needed an honest opinion, she was the first person they went to. She was Missouri's very own southern bell with blonde hair and standing just over five foot four.

Since her brother had died of pneumonia, she was an only child of her parents, Brice and Addie Leona Burns. Brice was a successful Baptist preacher in Walnut Grove and Addie was active in all the community events, often times dragging Rosalee along with her. Unlike the Braymyers who lived out in the country, the Burns family was proud to make their home on Hickory Street, right in the middle of all the happenings of Walnut Grove.

So on Christmas day in 1866, eighteen-year-old Nat and sixteen-year-old Rosalee were married. Even though they were different in many ways, people had foreseen this union when the couple were still toddlers. Nat being the prince of country life and Rosalee the queen of the city and all its events. The two of them lived with his parents for the first two months of their marriage, where Rosalee learned a great deal about country living. Then, one day in late February, Nat came home and announced to everyone that he and Rosalee would be leaving for Texas in a couple of weeks.

Everyone in Missouri dreamed of Texas, but many just saw it as a dream and accepted the fact that they would never see the land of New Hope as people were referring to it. Rosalee was thrilled at the new adventure and wanted nothing more than to be somewhere far away with Nat. Their love had grown in just a short time to such an extent that nothing else seemed to matter anymore except the two of them and making each other happy.

So in two weeks the couple loaded up what little they had into their covered wagon and headed south toward Indian Territory, to officially begin their new life together as husband and wife. The wagon didn't have much in it, so they would be able to travel fast and light toward this unknown land they would soon call their home. As they rode out of town, teary waves and good-byes were behind them and they were on their way.

"Nat, do you think the Indians will try and hurt us?"

"Probably not, most of them in these parts are pretty friendly. Shoot I wouldn't be surprised if we don't even see one."

"Well as long as you think it's safe then I suppose we don't have anything to worry about."

"We'll be fine, darling. I won't let anything happen to you, I promise. And besides my mother has Indian in her and you seemed to get along with her just fine."

"Yes, Nat, but Ma Braymyer's family was civilized. Who knows what these wild men ahead of us will be like. I just cannot bare the thought of one of them trying to take our scalps. I've grown rather fond of mine and prefer it stay just exactly where God put it."

Nat chuckled as he moved the reins up and down to pick up speed by way of the two mules pulling it. "Rosie, you're something else…"

The wagon rode steadily down the dirt road across Indian Territory with Rosalee on constant lookout for the so-called wild men. Luckily, Nat had saved enough money so he wouldn't have to stop and work along the way; they were instead able to travel straight through, stopping only to camp. After two weeks of traveling through unknown territory, they came to the Red River and Rosalee finally felt a sense of relief.

"My goodness, Nat, have you ever seen water so red?"

"Can't say that I have, Rosie."

"Nat, you don't suppose it's red because the Indians swim in it, do you?"

Nat laughed and shook his head as he forded the rushing river.

The water was low for this time of year, but it was moving pretty quickly. Before crossing, they secured all their belongings in case the current became too strong and they were forced to float down the river. Rosalee watched the red water in amazement and halfway expected to see Indians swimming in it somewhere upstream.

A short time after entering the river they were safe and sound on the other side…in Texas. Once on the other side, Nat steered the mules off the trail to set up camp for the night. Their chosen camp spot was surrounded by a group of large trees and looked to have been used by several other travelers who had traveled this path before them.

Nat searched the area for sticks and other things that could be used for firewood, which was hard given the popularity of this spot. After he had gathered up enough fuel, he started a fire and watched as the smoke drifted toward the river. After it had been started, Rosalee began preparing their first meal in Texas.

The two of them sat by the fire as the sun slowly made its way out of the western sky and into the great unknown. Texas seemed perfect to the young couple. The sky was clear and there was even a certain smell about the land that neither of them had ever smelled. The air was fresh and as the critters of the night began to come out, even their voices sounded different than those they had lived with in Missouri all their lives.

"So where do we go from here, Nat?" Rosalee asked as she laid her head on his chest and gazed up at the sky.

"Well, I reckon we'll go south in the morning until we find a nice place to settle. I don't want to venture too far from the river though; you never know when a river might come in handy."

Rosalee was about to respond, but she suddenly felt sick. "Are you okay, Rosie?"

"Yes, I just haven't felt very good today. Probably just need a good nights rest is all and now that I won't have to worry about Indians I suppose I'll sleep just fine tonight."

They slept their first night in Texas under the open sky and dreamt only of their bright future. This would be their life now and thus far, Texas seemed to be the perfect place. The two of them counted more shooting stars that night than they had ever seen and each one was made a different wish by them.

Nat had the wagon team hitched and ready before the sun had risen. Rosalee, still feeling ill, reluctantly climbed aboard the wagon and took her seat next to him. Nat steered the team south with his wife on the bench at his side, the morning was bright and clear and showed all signs that this would be a good day.

It was mid morning when they came upon the small settlement of Sandusky. It wasn't anything but a small community with a church, which also served as the school, a small general store and a few scattered shanty houses. The trees throughout town were already turning green, which Nat said was a good sign for a warm year. Rosalee took his word for it, because she had never paid much attention to trees before, let alone when they turned green.

After the team had been hitched outside the store, Nat went in to get some information about farmland in the area. Rosalee stayed outside to watch their wagon and waited impatiently for him to return. She watched the trees, still thinking about her husbands earlier comment and wondered how a man could get to be so smart as to know how the weather would be for that year just by observing a simple tree. Trees, she thought, were simple things that provided breath and shade, not something that could tell the future.

The sun was out in full force now and warmed the back of her neck as she pondered the subject, while a cool breeze blew upon her front side. This, combined with her worsening nausea, made for a long wait. Rosalee turned her attention and watched as people walked around town. Most of them seemed to just be out exploring what the new day had brought, with no place specific to go. People, she thought, can say a lot about a town just by their actions. This she knew from her town living up in Missouri and supposed that it was probably a lot like trees telling of the weather.

Just as quickly as Nat had gone into the false front store, he came back out carrying with him a brown package. He climbed into the wagon and handed it to Rosalee."What's this, Nat?"

"Well, open it up, silly goose."

Rosalee tore open the package to find three yards of blue calico material, "Nat, this is beautiful. It'll make a lovely dress."

"Well, I can't have the prettiest girl in Texas walk around in an old dress now can I?"

"Thank you, Nat. Did you find some land?"

"No, but I found where to go. There's a land office a few miles ahead in a town called, Dixie."

"Dixie? Well, that's got a nice ring to it. Do you think the trees will be green there too?"

"Of course, silly." Nat said as he drove the wagon out of Sandusky. "Land sure is pretty out here, a man could do mighty fine for himself in this country."

"Yes and it will also be a good place to raise a family," She answered him.

Dixie was larger than Sandusky by several streets and just as Nat had promised, all the trees were green, just as they were all along the trail between the two towns. It was a real nice little town and unlike Sandusky, it had a post office, school house and two churches. There were a lot of houses scattered out on the numbered streets and people were walking around everywhere. Wagons came and went in and out of town, tending to their business and tipping their hats as they drove by.

Rosalee watched all the commotion and new at once she was at home here. There was so much to do here and so many people to meet that she wondered how she would ever get acquainted with them all. Surely the people of this town are good folks, she thought, they all seem so happy and at peace.

They spent two days camped outside of Dixie while they waited to find a decent piece of land. On the third day, Nat came walking up to the wagon with a piece of paper and smile on his face. Rosalee looked up at him as he approached her and knew immediately that he had good news.

"Well, Rosie, we got ourselves some land. It's about three miles west of here."

"Oh, Nat, that's wonderful news! And we'll still be pretty close to town too."

Down by Dixie

April 04, 1867

I'm sure you've all noticed that Dock's bakery is now open for business. I went by there yesterday morning and I have to say it is some of the best apple pie I've ever had, well aside from my wife, Martha's, of course.

Mr. Phelps reported that we have received 4 inches of rain in the past week; crops should do well this year, which will be good after our poor farm year last season.

We've run out of room in our cemetery, so John Knight has graciously donated some additional land to be used as the burying grounds. If you would like to reserve a spot go over to the Baptist church and see Mrs. Huntington as soon as possible.

Anna Belle Brown gave birth to twin boys Saturday last. Both young fellas are in good health, but unfortunately they both look just like their father, sorry Ben, better luck next time.

Our town sure is growing! In the last month, more than four families have arrived. The latest arrival, being two weeks ago, was Nat Braymyer, 19 and his expecting wife, Rosalee age 17. They have settled just west of this town where they will plant cotton this year. Mr. Braymyer hopes to have their new home built in a couple of months, plenty of time before their new baby.

Allen Goldston

Chapter Three

June 21, 2010

"Mr. Sanders, telling us your family history is not going to help your case. If you cannot give me some facts that proves this house and land is of historical value, then there is nothing I can do."

The cocky judge crossed her arms and looked down towards Nathan Sanders, expecting him to make an apology and walk out. She had her perfect brown hair neatly sitting on her shoulders and had no sense of compassion in her eyes or her voice. It had only been a few seconds since her statement, but she continued to stare as if the man was taking too long to respond.

Sanders stood up from his wheel chair, something he hadn't done in almost a year and slowly got his balance. The fragile man walked a few steps closer to the judge, then turned to face the two pimple faced attorneys. Rose worriedly watched and prayed that her father would not fall and make a fool of himself.

"Judge, I take after my great grandmother, Rosalee…"

"I'm sure you do, Mr. Sanders," the judge interrupted while the attorneys made smirk remarks about his age. The judge looked over in their direction and quickly rolled her eyes, not caring if the old man saw or not.

"I tell things how they are. Now, where was I…"

Nat and Rosalee had been in Texas just under two months and the log house was almost finished. It was small, but larger than most cabins and instead of having one large room, it had two rooms, equal in size, with a fireplace at both ends of the rectangular structure. The chimneys were made out of gray rock that had been gathered from the nearby creek and mud had been placed between every one of the logs to keep the wind out.

Nat had cut down the trees himself and hauled them to the home site from the woods at the back of their land. Rosalee had planted a large garden on the north side of the east facing home so they would have plenty of food for the winter. Although she was raised in town, Nat was making a country wife of her yet and she was learning rather quickly.

The creek ran through the west side of the land and it provided an ample supply of clean water, but the walk was too far from the house so Nat dug a well near the cabin. The cabin was in an open field with trees surrounding it to the south and along the creek to the west. So far, the Braymyer's had been blessed with good fortune and they had high hopes for their cotton crop this year.

Nat's father had given them enough money to start their new life in Texas, but it would be up to them to survive and carry on. Indeed things were looking good for the soon to be three of them. The cotton that Nat had planted a month after their arrival had already started to grow and it looked as if the land would prove to be fertile.

By June the log cabin was finished and Nat and Rosalee were home at last. Nat worked in the fields and in his spare time started building the barn, which was almost finished. The Braymyer land was beginning to look more and more like a farm, a home and it would be a proud place to live.

Rosalee often made trips down to the creek to cool off on the hot summer days and found comfort in the shade of the trees. On one visit she gathered up several cottonwood tree seeds and brought them back to the farm with her. She planted several in an open area near the cabin where she hoped a newer bigger house would be built someday and then she planted two parallel rows from the house to the dirt road, which would someday create a shaded pathway to the house.

Rosalee was finishing up all the house chores one day when she noticed that things were growing dark outside, earlier than normal. As she stepped outside with the broom still in her hand and wash cloth across her shoulder, she saw Nat walking toward her before she even noticed the blackish gray clouds moving their way.

"What is it, Nat?"

"There's a storm heading this way, it looks like it's going to be a bad one too."

"A storm? In June?"

"Looks that a way, as strange as it may sound."

Nat placed a hand on Rosalee's growing stomach and made small talk with the unborn child as little drops of rain began to fall from the darkening sky. "Well, we best get you and your Ma inside before you get all wet."

Rosalee went back into the house and straightened up things a little more while Nat went out to the partial barn and ensured that the animals were secured in case the storm got too bad. After she had swept the last little part of the cabin, Rosalee put the broom beside the cast iron stove and went into the main room where Nat was coming in from the front door.

The storm was moving slowly and as it got closer the rain began to come down more heavily. The two of them kind of enjoyed the approaching rain, it offered a sense of excitement from the recent dull summer days of farming. Loud crashes of thunder shook the little cabin, followed by bright streaks of lightening.

Rosalee sat in a rocker near the west window where she could watch the approaching storm and hoped for the best. They were fortunate, she thought, as young newlyweds they had a lot more than most people in their situation and not a day went by that Rosalee did not thank God for it.

The storm looked bad and she began to rock the chair faster and faster, slowly, but steadily as the previous feeling of excitement quickly disappeared. What were they to do if the storm ruined their crop? It was their livelihood and without it there would be nothing left for them. Rosalee thought this over, but didn't dare mention it to Nat; she didn't need him to worry. What about their safety? She got up from her chair and sat on Nat's left knee with him in his rocker near the fireplace.

He put his arm around her, "Are you scared, darling?"
"A little bit, I've never seen a storm like this before in my life, Nat."

"It'll be over soon, besides we could sure use the rain this late in the year."

There was a sudden silence from the growing thunder, but the lightening continued to light up the dark sky, reminding them that the storm was still out there. It remained still, very still and all that could be heard was the pocket watch Nat's grandfather had given him. It slowly ticked as if their time was limited and at any minute the ticking would stop and so would their lives. The two of them continued to listen to the tick, waiting for it to come to a stop when suddenly, and without any warning, large chunks of hail began falling to the ground and smashing onto the thin roof above their heads. The west window came crashing in spreading glass and ice all throughout the cabin onto the floor Rosalee had just finished sweeping.

Now there was nothing to keep the storm out. Nat sat there and pretended to be brave for Rosalee, but the truth was, is that there was nowhere they could go to be anymore safer than they were now. So they sat together in the rocker and waited to see what was next. They waited to see if they would be there in a couple of hours or be blown into the sky and if they did survive the storm, would they be able to survive living in Texas.

What if coming to Texas had been a mistake? Maybe Nat should have taken his father up on his offer and farmed the back 100 acres of his land rather than move off. No, Rosalee thought, the move to Texas was necessary. Like Nat had said, Missouri was getting too crowded and it wouldn't be long until there wasn't any land left at all and what kind of future would that be for their children. Storms happen everywhere, they just needed to be brave and get through this first Texas storm and then everything would be okay.

The hail was growing larger and continued to bombard the Braymyer home with its weight and sharp edges. Nat continued to hold Rosalee, steadily rocking the chair all the while in hopes that it would calm their nerves that had been put on the edge by this storm. The storm took its time as it slowly pushed its way through the country and with every burst of thunder; the cabin shook a little more and offered at any moment to collapse on top of them. Although it was mid afternoon, it looked to be a moonless night outside, visible only when the lightening stretched out across the sky or from the sky to the ground in its longer than usual flashes.

Rosalee held tight to Nat as the house began to rock back and forth, it was as if the ground beneath them would give way at any given second. There was now a loud roar coming from outside and not only was it getting louder, but it was getting closer. It was a noise neither of them had ever heard before, but would be one that they would forever remember as long as they both lived.

In an instant, the roof began to move away from the walls of the cabin, revealing a combination of dirt, wood, rain and hail. It first moved side to side and then slowly, back and forth. For a few seconds, it lifted completely off of the house and then came crashing back down atop the beaten cabin. Pieces of wood from it snapped in half and disappeared somewhere into the dark sky, leaving gaping holes above their heads as the storm pushed its way inside with them.

It wasn't long until the entire roof was gone, lost somewhere in the stormy sky. Nat grabbed Rosalee and moved her to the floor where he lay on top of her to offer as much protection as he possibly could. Rosalee's body shook with fear beneath his as he tried to comfort her with kisses on the back of her neck. He desperately searched for something to grab on to, but there was nothing to be found.

Rain, hail and a fierce wind engulfed the inside of the cabin, throwing anything and everything wherever it pleased. Nat was lifted a couple of feet into the air and thrown to the other side of the room, leaving Rosalee and her unborn child unprotected.

The south wall of the house collapsed outwards, exposing the inside to even more damage than before. Things in the cabin began spinning with such force that Rosalee could not figure out how she was still lying in the same place she was before. "Nat! Where are you?" As she screamed, tears streamed uncontrollably down her face where the wind showed no sympathy and stole away even those before they had made it halfway across her cheeks. There was no reply, not that she could hear anyway and she began to fear the worst.

The storm pushed through swiftly and as it did, more and more of the log cabin was destroyed. Rosalee was soaked in rainwater and had a small cut on her forehead from a piece of ice falling from somewhere above. Nothing was visible anymore, everything seemed to have been sucked into a giant dirt cloud and all was black as everything went round and round.

The loud roaring they had heard just minutes before was now upon them and revealed itself as a large twister as it sat atop Braymyer Hill. The once peaceful place had been overtaken by a storm that very few have had the liberty of seeing in their lifetimes and those who have wish they could forget it. In the midst of her crying, Rosalee was praying and continuously hollering for her husband, but again there was no reply other than the loud noises the storm was producing.

It seemed like she lay there for hours as the storm beat down on top of her, but within twenty minutes of the first hail drops, the storm mysteriously passed, leaving only a light drizzle of rain behind it and a variety of soothing colors. Rosalee pushed some of the debris off of her and quickly jumped to her feet. "Nat!"

She heard a grumble on the other side of what used to be the cabin and rushed towards it as fast as she could. There were things strewn out everywhere and it took her awhile to make her way through the mangled mess to where her husband was. Nat was slowly emerging from a pile of random objects that used to make up their home. As he became more and more visible, bloody scratches were revealed throughout most of his body.

"Nat, are you okay?"

"Yes, darling, I'm fine, just a little scraped up," he said stumbling towards his wife.

Nat held her in his arms and kissed her among all the rubble. A soft wind blew catching Rosalee's blonde hair and her blue dress. The two of them walked away from the pile of scrap to see flattened grassland everywhere, as far as they could see. To their amazement, all of the cottonwood trees that Rosalee had planted were still there, even though they were only little saplings.

They spent the night sleeping beneath the open sky and its many stars, as if it were their first night in Texas all over again. A small fire flickered in the humid Texas wind revealing small glimpses of their demolished home. It had taken over two months to build it and in one afternoon it lie completely flattened atop a hill in north Texas. Perhaps living in Texas would be harder than they had thought, but they both knew that they would never give anyone the privilege of seeing them head back to Missouri with their tail tucked between their legs.

When Rosalee awakened the next morning, Nat had already been to the cotton fields to survey the damage and was heading back.

"We lost half the crop, Rosie. Most of the garden is gone too."

"We'll manage alright, Nat. You can still hunt game for food."

"I know, Rosie, but it won't be as easy on us now and I don't want you to have to want for anything a single minute of your life."

"Nat, life's no fun if everything is easy. And besides, wanting for things makes you appreciate it when you have it."

Nat shook his head and headed back to the fields. "How could she be so calm?" He thought. "They had lost their house and half their livelihood and she was perfectly okay with it. Why did she always have to see the good in things?"

Rosalee spent all day sifting through the remains of their home. Some of the things she came across she did not recognize and had no idea what it once was, but she pushed forward and busied herself with the never-ending task at hand. She was able to find most of their clothes, bedding, food and their most prized possession, their family bible.

The barn Nat had started building was almost done, aside from one small section of the roof and miraculously received little damage from the storm the day before. It stood there and looked towards the remains of the cabin and almost seemed to be frowning for its lost neighbor.

"We'll have to stay in the barn for a little while, Rosie, at least until I can get a new house built."

"That's fine, Nat. At least we'll have a roof over our heads."

"Hopefully what's left of the cotton will be enough to build you a proper house. I don't want you and the baby having to be in a cabin when the next storm like that comes through.

Down by Dixie

July 08, 1867

It is sad news for me to have to report, but Isaac Brumelow and three of his children were killed last week when the storm came through. His house has completely vanished from its previous place, so his wife and his surviving children will be heading north to stay with relatives. Will Kincy said he saw a twister cross over the county line road heading toward the Braymyer place. Braymyer informed us that his house and half his cotton crop are a complete loss.

Mrs. Fannie Jewell passed away two days after the storm. Doc. Ruyle says the storm scared her so bad that she had a heart attack. She was 51.

Joe Riddle celebrated his 91st birthday on Sunday last. Riddle settled near Sugar Hill twenty years ago, but makes frequent trips to Dixie to visit his sister, Mrs. Polly Green.

Reports from Whitesboro say that since the storm last week, the price of almost every crop has went up. Whitesboro reported 3 twisters in the storm last week and the town received most of its damage on the north side.

Allen Goldston

Chapter Four

October brought some cooler weather, which meant it was almost time to harvest the cotton. Rosalee and Nat had spent the last two months living in the barn and they were the hottest months yet. Rosalee didn't mind it, but Nat felt ashamed that his wife had to live in a barn, especially with a child on the way.

Rosalee was able to make the barn feel very much like a home. There was only one window and she covered it with a lace pattern that she had sewn in her spare time. The floor was dirt, but she kept it neatly swept none the less and she also hung up their family pictures along one of the walls.

Nat had moved the old stove that was in the cabin into the barn so they would have heat during the winter and so that Rosalee could prepare their meals inside rather than over a campfire. The barn was built out of simple plank wood and mud was crammed between its cracks to keep the wind and rain out. The mules and two milking cows stayed in a separate section of the barn that Nat had blocked off so that they couldn't wander into their living quarters.

Rosalee was busy preparing their supper when Nat walked into the unusually bright barn. "Well, Rosie girl, it looks like the cotton will be ready to harvest any day now. I'll probably give it one more week in the sun though."

"That's wonderful, Nat."

"Yep, I reckon if the winters not bad, I can start on the new house. I've got big plans, Rosie…, big plans," he said walking out of the open door.

Nat liked to surprise Rosalee so very rarely did he tell her his plans and he hardly ever shared finances with her. It was Nat's job to take care of his wife and that was exactly what he was going to do. He was going to make sure that his wife and child had everything that they could possibly want or need and no matter what the cost they would live comfortably for the rest of their lives.

After a week had passed, Nat began harvesting his cotton and preparing for the trip to Whitesboro, which was about ten miles away, but it had the nearest cotton gin around. He was able to find some field hands to help him pick the cotton, which they did from sunup to sundown. There were about ten people working in the fields, including Nat, there were seven men and three women. Times were tough and everyone was in need so Nat told them he would pay them after the harvest made it to market.

The days were long and although it was cooler than it had been in some time in Texas, it still seemed that they would all drown in their sweat. The cotton bushes scratched them at times, causing their bodies to burn when their sweat mixed in with their wounds. The job had to be done and the only way Braymyer Hill would become a successful farm was through hard work.

Every night he came into the barn with bloody hands and often times, Rosalee would have to feed him his food at night. She begged him to let her help, but he refused her every time she asked. Her only job was to bring them water four times a day and a loaf of bread to share, that was enough he said.

Nat Braymyer had never worked so hard in his life, but he remained in high spirits and at the end of every day would say, "Rosie, that's one day closer to taking the cotton to market."

The group continued to work in the fields for two weeks, stopping only for a few hours on Sunday to rest and worship the Lord. On the last day, the cotton was loaded into five wagons and it was now time to take it to the cotton gin. Rosalee stood beside the first wagon, which was the one Nat was driving, and looked up at him as he smiled bigger than she had seen in a long time. "Be careful and hurry back home."

"I will darling; you take good care and remember Mr. and Mrs. Nelson are just down the road if you need anything. They are going to come by and check on you ever so often while I am gone anyhow."

Nat leaned down and kissed his wife before making haste down the drive to take their cotton to market.

Rosalee stood beside their temporary home and watched as the wagons made their way south. She would be having the baby any day now, but the cotton needed to be sold, she only hoped it would be worth it.

She looked around her and then at the little cottonwood trees sprouting up alongside the drive. Someday, she thought, someday this will be a fine place to live. She went to the well and one by one brought each tree a pail of water before going back into the barn. Once inside she sat in one of the rockers Nat had recently made and began crocheting a blanket for her baby.

Across the room near the stove was a wooden crib that Nat had also made a few weeks before from one of the large cottonwood trees along the creek. It sat there lonely with no one to occupy it as nightfall began to come upon the valley. Rosalee slowly began to fall asleep in her rocker and dreamt of their baby, the cotton crop and their new house that would soon be underway.

The second day was coming to an end and Nat had still not arrived back home. Rosalee was tending to her fall garden when the pain first started. The pain, however, was the second thing she thought of, the first being the fact that she was all alone.

She could scream, but the chances of the Nelson family hearing her were slim. After the pain had stopped for a moment she got off her knees and headed to the barn; the thought had just hit her, my baby is going to be born in a barn. She quickly forced the thought out of her mind, realizing this was not the time.

After getting into the barn she calmly took a drink of water from the dipper and lay down on the feather mattress. The pain had subsided for a moment and she took this opportunity to make herself as comfortable as she could on the bed. She suddenly became very scared, but knew that she must contain herself.

Maybe Mrs. Nelson would come by? She had heard that childbirth could take hours. She longed for her mother now, or any woman for that matter. Had women really done this before? She became angry that women had to bear this pain and it just wasn't fair. Where was Nat? This was half his burden to bear too and he wasn't even there. All because of that stupid cotton!

Her emotions were whirling like the devastating twister that had come through a couple of months before. She wanted badly to just go to sleep and wake up when it was all over. Where was Nat? He should have been here by now.

"I hate that stupid cotton!" She shouted.

What if he was robbed and the cotton was stolen…cotton, cotton, cotton! As much as she hated it, their lives depended on that cotton and what if something had happened?

It was dark now and it took the last bit of her energy to light the kerosene lamp. There were moments that the pain seemed too much to bear and at other times she thought she might take a nap. She screamed, praying that somebody out there would hear her and make this whole mess go away. She prayed, but prayer took too much concentration so she resorted back to screaming as loud as she could.

The darkness faded into the morning light on October 24, 1867 and she knew she didn't have much time. A shadow covered the sunlight in the doorway. "Rosie?"

She was too weak to call out his name so she answered him with heavy breathing.

"Hold on Rosie! I'm going to go fetch Mrs. Nelson!"

Before she could attempt to beg him to stay he was already riding towards the Nelson farm. The pain had grown so strong that she was mostly numb in some areas and she was almost completely convinced that she was not going to make it through this miracle alive.

Twenty agonizing minutes later Nat came rushing through the door with Mrs. Nelson. Things grew foggy and soon everything was black…

When Rosalee awoke, the sun was struggling to stay in the sky and Nat was standing beside her holding the baby. "How's the baby?" She asked.

"Rosie, he's great. Here, hold him."

Nat carefully handed the baby to her, trying not to wake him up while Mrs. Nelson came over to check Rosalee for a fever.

"You seem to be healing up just fine," she said, "I'm going to leave you two alone for awhile. You be sure and call on me if you need anything."

Rosalee moved her hand over his soft, blonde head. Nat leaned down and kissed her on the forehead, "You okay, Rosie?"

"Just a little tired is all."

"Just stay here and rest, take all the time in the world. I love you so much, Rosie."

"Well, did you sell the stupid cotton?"

"Oh, Rosie! You won't believe it! I got over two thousand dollars for it!"

Her mind went blank, she had never even dreamt, let alone ever seen that kind of money before.

"I'm gonna' build you the finest home in all of the Red River valley."

"My goodness, Nat, that's wonderful. Looks like that old storm didn't get the better of us after all."

The baby started to move around a little and a small yawn was expressed across his face. Rosalee held him close, "What should we name him?"

"Well," Nat said scratching his hairless chin, "What do you think?"

She looked down at the baby and then thought of how good their lives were going to be now that the cotton had been harvested. Things would never be the same and as much as she hated to admit it, it was all because of that stupid cotton…

Chapter Five

June 21, 2010

The court had taken a fifteen-minute recess and Rose Tyler had excused herself to the ladies room. Her father remained in the courtroom where he said he was fine and didn't need to leave for anything. She stood in front of the mirror and put powder lightly across her tan skin.

She had heard this story many times, but why did it seem so different now? It was the same thing she had grown up listening to, but now for some reason it was as if she was understanding it better, or learning something new. She looked into the mirror and for a second it wasn't her that she saw, it was Rosalee Braymyer. She watched in amazement and before she had time to convince herself that she was going crazy, her cell phone rang.

"Hello?"

"Hi grandma, it's John how is everything going?"

"Hi, John. I'm afraid it's not going so well. The judge doesn't seem to care one way or another about your Papaw's story or of the house for that matter. Not that I can really blame her…"

"Grandma, you know how much that house means to him. It's not only a part of him, but it's a part of us as well."

"I know, John. I think I am starting to realize that myself…"

There was a loud screeching sound over the phone.

"John, what was that?"

"Grandma…I'll…"

The call was dropped and Rose just assumed it was turbulence from the plane I was on. She gathered up her things and made her way back to the courtroom where Mr. Sanders was waiting for her, unaware that I was about to be on an adventure of a lifetime.

I put my phone in my pocket and held tightly to the arm rail on my chair as the oxygen mask fell in front of all the other passengers and myself. The plane shook and seemed to be going from higher to lower as it flew through the Texas sky. An announcer came over the intercom and announced there was some turbulence and to please remain buckled until instructed to do otherwise.

But why is there turbulence? I thought. The sky was perfectly clear and there was something about that voice that came over the intercom that seemed uncertain. Something wasn't right…

I had been on very few plane rides in my life, but I knew enough to know that there was something wrong with this situation. One of the stewards was heading down the aisle way and I flagged her down.

"Excuse me, maim, but what's the real problem with our flight."

She hesitated for a moment and then in the brightest face said, "Why it's only turbulence, sir, that's all."

Horse crap, I thought. Something wasn't right.

Down by Dixie

March 03, 1871

By now we have all noticed that our small community is getting crowded. I wish I could write to you all and say that it is new homesteaders coming in to join us, but it is with sadness that I cannot. It seems as though more and more outlaws are moving into this territory from somewhere beyond the Red River. Just yesterday a wagon pulled up carrying nothing but whiskey and was unloaded at the old bank building. I'm afraid our peaceful days of living in Dixie are coming to an abrupt end. Sheriff Jackson confirms this and tells me that there are too many for him and his deputy to handle.

This morning I received unfortunate news of what happened to our neighbor city of Sandusky. The entire town was burned down when a group of arrogant drunks got into a fight. At present, nothing remains of the town and I have to say that it scares me to think that something like that could happen here in our precious Dixie. Be safe my fellow citizens…

Allen Goldston

Chapter Six

1871

"Cotton Braymyer! Get back here this instant! Don't make me get your Pa!"

It was no use; Cotton was running as fast as his little legs would let him, hands full of blueberries from his mother's kitchen.

Before he could make it across the yard, Nat scooped him up in his arms. "What do you have there, little fellow?"

"Buebewwys," he said through berry stained teeth.

Rosalee came walking up with Mary Lee Braymyer on her hip with every intention of ringing both their necks. "Nat, if you want your blueberry pie you had better have a talk with your son!"

She tried to act serious, but Nat could see a smile trying to form at the edges of her mouth.

"I tell you what," he said, "How about we all eat blueberries now and then later I'll take us out to get some more from the fields for a pie?"

"Yeah!" Cotton shouted hysterically.

Rosalee's face was now gleaming with a smile as she walked up the steps of the house with Mary Lee. "You're going to spoil that child to the devil, Nat Braymyer...mark my words."

It was spring again and the two-story house stood tall overlooking the cotton and wheat fields. The four large white pillar-like columns ran from the porch all the way up to the second story roof. The outside of the house was all whitewashed wood, but Nat assured Rosalee he was going to stone the house with his next good crop money.

Indeed the Braymyer's days of living in a barn had long passed. Nat built the house shortly after Cotton was born and now it was considered one of the finest homes around. The cottonwood trees Rosalee had planted were now small, but healthy trees along the drive and around the house, laying the foundations for a beautiful farm someday.

There were six rooms upstairs and seven rooms downstairs, which provided plenty of room for the family of four, soon to be five. To the south of the house was the small barn that they had lived in their first year in Texas and just to the right of it was a larger barn which was also used as a cotton gin. In fact, it was the first cotton gin in the area. Nat had cleared out an additional four hundred acres for wheat and corn and thus far the farm had done nothing but prosper.

On a small hill overlooking the Braymyer farm in the southwest corner was the Braymyer Cemetery. It had been created a year before when Mary's twin sister, Jennie Rose died at the age of one. But death was apart of living here on the Texas plains and the Braymyer family pushed forward into the future.

After Rosalee's father passed away the fall before, her mother, Addie Burns joined the family in their large home. Rosalee was glad her mother was there so she would be able to help her with the delivery of her unborn child sometime next month.

Nat now had a total of five horses, three milking cows, one steer and two heifers; he was considered by most in the area to be one of the most prosperous farmers around and he had the house to prove it. Lunch had ended a few hours before and it would soon be time to start preparing dinner. Rosalee busied herself cleaning the house while her mother played with Mary and Cotton in the backyard. Rosalee was sweeping the main entry when she heard a wagon pull up outside. She walked out onto the front porch to find two men sitting on the wagon seat.

"Maim," one of them said as he tipped his hat.

"Can I help you, sir?"

"Yes, maim, is your husband around?"

Nat was already heading to the front from the barn out back, "I'm her husband. Nat Braymyer, what can I help you with?"

"I don't mean to scare the lady," the driver motioned towards Rosalee, "But we've come to get the help from as many men as possible."

"Help with what," Nat asked putting his hands on his hips.

Rosalee did not like the situation. The two men were rough looking and looked like the type that had killed people, more than once. She was glad they were discussing this in her presence.

The one driving the wagon, and the only one to have said anything thus far, was tall and dark with a black moustache that looked to have last nights dinner still caked in it. He wore a black cowboy hat that had seen better days and he had traces of chewing tobacco stuck between his teeth.

The one sitting next to him seemed to be younger, but still had a dangerous look about him. Unlike the driver, he was light complected and had dirty blonde hair, almost down to his shoulders. She also noted that both wore gun belts, however they were both empty.

"Well, sir, my name is James Cunningham and this here is Rex Souther. We're from out Dexter way. You see, yesterday morning a posse of about seven men came through the country up there, robbing and killing several people, including my wife and boy.

We're trying to get some men together to go after them. They headed north into Indian Territory. A group of us are meeting in Rock Creek tomorrow morning to go after them. We'd be much obliged if you could come along, we need every man we can get."

"Well, gentlemen, I'll think it over and if I'm able I'll see you at Rock Creek first thing in the morning."

Rosalee interrupted. "Nat, you'll do no such thing…"

"We'd be much obliged; maim," the driver said looking toward Rosalee. The second man just grinned at her.

The wagon drove out the same way it had come and headed towards the Nelson farm. Before Nat could even get a word out, Rosalee was talking his ear off.

"Nathaniel Braymyer! Don't even think about it! You could be killed and the baby will be here soon!"

"Now, Rosie, what if those outlaws had came here for you and the children?"

"Nat, I don't like this one bit. There was something strange about those men and besides where was that man at when his wife and son were killed?"

"Rosie, you're overreacting, I'm going to go see Alex Nelson in a little while and see what he thinks. A man has to protect his family, Rosie. What if the outlaws come back? Then, what?"

"Nat…"

"Rosie, darling calm down…you don't want to let your temper get the better of you." Rosalee turned and stormed back into the house.

The next morning before the children had awakened Nat Braymyer and Alex Nelson rode north towards Rock Creek. Rosalee sent him away with both looks of anger and understanding.

Rosalee went about her business after Nat had left, but the thought never left her mind that something might be terribly wrong. She paced the floors of the entire downstairs and every five minutes looked out the front door to see if her husband was riding back yet. A couple of hours after he had left, Rosalee was sweeping the front entry for the third time that morning when she heard gunshots coming from the Nelson home.

She stepped outside and looked in that direction and there was a thick cloud of dark smoke arising in the distance. She immediately knew something was wrong and her mind jumped to the worst; someone had shot the Nelson family and burned their home.

She threw the broom down and ran into the house. "Momma! Get down here!"

"For lands sake, Rosalee, what is it?" Addie said walking down the narrow staircase.

"Trouble's coming, Momma. Get the children and take them to the cellar out back! Hurry! And keep quiet." Addie hurried as quickly as her near fifty-year-old body could. Once she had stopped Cotton's endless questions with a handful of blueberries, she gathered the two of them up into the cellar and shut the door behind her.

Addie was a petite woman with graying hair that she always kept in a bun. She wore a black lace dress as she was from the old ways, which meant wearing black to demonstrate mourning for her deceased husband.

The three of them sat on a bench in the cellar while Addie continued to feed Cotton blueberries and tell them stories in a whisper to keep them quiet. Cotton listened intently, but was constantly looking up toward the cellar door through the dim candlelight as if he was planning an escape.

Rosalee frantically shut all the shudders on the downstairs windows as fast as an eight month pregnant woman could. After she had finished she took one last look towards the northeast and just as she had suspected, there were riders, maybe four or five, heading toward her home.

She ran back into the house and shut the double doors behind her. She gathered all the guns up that she could find and put them in the entryway. There were two colts, a shotgun and two rifles. She had never killed a man before, but if it meant doing so to protect her family then she would. Kneeling down by the door, Rosalee prayed. She prayed for strength to kill a man, which she knew she would most certainly have to do and she prayed for good aim.

No sooner had she said amen the sound of galloping horses could be heard from outside. She grabbed one of the colts, wiped the tears from her face and patiently waited for whatever was next.

- - - - - - - - - - - - - -

When Nat Braymyer and Alex Nelson arrived outside of Rock Creek, they were surprised to find that only the two men they had seen the day before were there. Cunningham and Souther both rode black saddle horses with a flying W brand burned into them.

Cunningham was the first to speak as they approached the two men. "Mr. Braymyer, Mr. Nelson, so glad you could join us," he said spitting tobacco on the dusty road beside him.

Nat looked the two men over for a minute and thought about what Rosalee had said about the men. They were about a half-mile outside of Rock Creek and it was just the four of them. "Where's everyone else?"

Souther gave a sour look in his direction, which he must have done often because the wrinkles on his face fit it perfectly. "Oh, they'll be here soon enough."

Nat noticed on a hill in the distance there was a rider sitting amount a colorful paint horse. The rider in the distance made no sudden movements and just sat there as if there was a situation to observe.

"Don't move!" Cunningham said drawing a gun on Nat as Souther did to Nelson.

Cunningham, whom seemed to be the ring leader, had both Nat and Nelson dismount their horses, while Souther took away their guns. When they were both on their knees, Souther hog-tied them and tightened the rope as tight as he could.

Nat continued to keep a steady eye on the man in the distance with quick glances so that the two gunmen would not notice. Nat was sure it was an Indian and unless his eyes were playing tricks on him, he was slowly getting closer now.

Alex Nelson was a dark complected tall man with blue eyes and given his unusual height, being hog-tied was not comfortable for him at all. He spit some of the dust out of his mouth before he spoke, "What do you want from us? I thought you needed our help, what kind of sick joke is this anyhow?"

Cunningham shifted his aim to Nelson, "Well, right now my brothers are robbing your homes and as for your women and children, well, I don't know about them." The man laughed and followed suit by coughing, hinting that chewing tobacco wasn't his only friend.

Nat struggled as hard as he could to break free from the rope and get to his feet, but he was stopped by a bullet in his right thigh. It went straight through his leg since it was shot at such close range and just missed the bone by a few centimeters.

"I wouldn't try anything like that again," Cunningham shouted, or the next bullet will find its way between your eyes."

Souther began to laugh in an unbearable high-pitched cackle, almost as if he were a drunken woman. He walked over to Nelson and kicked him in the face. "Can we kill them, James? Can we?"

"Hell, why not. They ain't any good to us anyhow. We already got their women and homes."

A million and one things went through Nat's mind. Mostly thoughts of his wife, children and his unborn child he would never get to meet. He hardly noticed the growing puddle of blood around him and at this point he didn't care. Everything he cared about in life was being threatened to be taken away and there was nothing he could do about it. Why had he fallen into this stupid trap?

He and his wife had worked hard to create the home they had and now it would be gone, probably burned to the ground and carried off with the wind. He held his head down low as he drowned in sorrow and guilt. "I'm a Braymyer," he thought, "We don't give up that easy." He lifted his head up again and held it high. "If I'm going to die, it'll be with a proud face," he thought.

Souther took a steady aim with his gun and moved it back and forth between Nat and Alex, like he was playing some kind of game. "Now which one should I shoot first…"

Alex couldn't stand it any longer and he threw his body towards the man. There was a loud crack that filled the air and Alex Nelson fell forward, staining the dirt road even more with his blood.

Immediately after the gun was fired, there was a strange whistling sound, as if something was cutting the air with a knife. The noise came to an abrupt end with a loud thud that caused Rex Souther to fall face first between Nat and Nelson's body. Souther's body hit with such force that it shook Nat a little bit and when he looked over at him there was a an arrow in his back.

Cunningham turned quickly and began firing shots at the approaching Indian. Nat struggled quickly once again to break free and this time was able to loosen the rope around his hands. Souther may have tied the rope tight, but the drunken fool was no expert when it came to knots.

After freeing his hands, he grabbed the dead man's gun and turned it quickly toward Cunningham who was still turned firing at the Indian. Nat didn't even take time to aim because he was so angry and after pulling the trigger twice Cunningham fell off his horse with two holes in his head.

Nat's leg continued to bleed and by now he had lost too much blood and he knew something had to be done. Things started to spin around him and he suddenly became both thirsty and hungry. He easily rolled to his side and lay softly onto his back with one hand holding his wound.

He gazed up into the vast blue sky, waiting for whatever was next. A shadow appeared over his face, followed by a shirtless Indian peering down at him. He was tall and dark, as any Indian would be. He had a painted red marking across his right shoulder and wore his black hair braided over the left shoulder with cream colored beads strung through it.

"Do you speak English?" Nat struggled to spit out.

The Indian chuckled a little bit and then somewhat clearly said, "Yes, I speak English."

"Then please don't kill me."

He laughed again, "Do not worry, my friend. I not kill you. I take you and fix your leg."

"I need to get home! My wife and children are in trouble!"

"All in time, my friend. We fix your leg. I am Two-Feathers."

"Na… Nat Br…" his eyes closed and he entered a dark sleep beneath the hot Texas sun.

- - - - - - - - - - - - -

"Come out, maim. We know you're in there."

"What do you want?" Rosalee shouted from behind the front door back at them, "Go away!"

"Aw, now that's not very polite," another voice said as she counted *two* in her head. "We just wanna' talk is all."

"Go talk to my husband, he's in the barn."

"Your husband!" *Three* Rosalee thought. "'Why your husband is on a wild goose chase with my brother up in Injun land. Then again, I reckon he's dead by now anyhow."

"I knew it!" She thought, as she became angry. "Cowards! You couldn't come when there was a man here!"

"That would take all the fun out of it now wouldn't it? Besides without a man around it makes things a whole lot easier.

Four

Rosalee moved up the stairs carrying all the guns at once. When she had reached the top she went into a front bedroom which had windows looking out. Very slowly and careful not to be seen, she peeked out the window. There were only two of them, the other two had disappeared.

One of the men out front cleared his throat. "You know, maim, it would make this a whole lot easier if you would just come on out here. Why, if you cooperate I might just make you my wife now that you're a widow and all."

Where were the other two men? She quickly listened to her surroundings, observing every little noise she heard. There it was. She could hear the cracking of the stairs as someone walked up. She had her back against the wall between the two front windows and from where she was sitting she could see through the doorway directly in front of her and into the hallway where the top of the stairs emerged.

She carefully took aim in that direction, ready at any minute to shoot an intruder, to do the unthinkable thing for a Christian woman to do, kill someone. But it must be done; her family was depending on her.

Whoever was coming up the stairs was trying to be sneaky, there was very little noise. Suddenly she saw a dirty hand emerge on the stair rail at the end of the stairs. It moved slowly along until the man's body was in full view.

He was short and dirty. He looked like he had been rolling around in a pile of ash. His hat was weathered and looked to be missing pieces from it. She steadied her aim and in one quick motion fired the revolver.

The bullet struck him in the head and she could hear the man's body fall down the staircase, banging up against the wall as he did. One of the men outside shouted, "Huck! Was that you? Did you get the woman?"

When there was no reply, the two men outside became uneasy. Rosalee concluded that the other missing man was in the barn. That meant he was close to the cellar…she must act quickly.

Since the two men outside were now nervous, she decided to use it to her advantage. She peeked out of the open window again and carefully took aim at her second target.

He was taller than the first one she had shot, but by no means was he considered tall. Like the other he was dirty and by the sound of his voice he was probably missing several teeth.

He, along with his partner stood there facing the front door, a revolver in both of their hands. They were completely unaware that she had moved upstairs and was now watching them from above, but that was about to change.

She shot.

The bullet hit him in his stomach and he immediately fell forward. The second man started firing in the direction of the window, not caring where the bullets went and cursing out words to Rosalee.

"Jake! Get over here," he shouted. "She's shot Dave and probably Huck too!"

Again there was no reply.

The lone gunman out front stood there with guns in both of his hands, steadily scanning the house up and down for any movement.

Rosalee moved to the back of the house and looked out one of the windows. The missing man was walking out of the barn, unaware of what had just happened to his partners. He was heading directly for the cellar.

Luckily the window in the back room was open too and without giving it a second thought, Rosalee shot the man in the head, stopping him in his tracks.

There was more cursing coming from out front and a few gunshots echoed throughout the house. She knew she had to get rid of this last man, but how could she with him watching the house like he was? She needed a distraction of some sort to get his attention so she could finish the job. If he were to leave, he would only come back with more gunmen.

She went into her bedroom and grabbed a candle stick holder. Re-entering the hallway she threw it as hard as she could toward the other end of the house and then darted back to the front window.

As soon as she reached it, she began firing without hesitation. Two shots were fired back at her, but both missed. The man had to reload his gun and Rosalee continued firing until he was struck in the chest and fell to the front steps of the porch. She fired one more bullet into him to ensure he was gone and then the pain in her stomach started and she went into labor.

Down by Dixie

March 19, 1871

Yesterday morning a group of outlaws attacked the Braymyer and Nelson farms, shooting and killing Mrs. Nelson and two of their four children. The bandits left the younger two children for dead, but they are both recovering well at their aunt's house in Dexter.

After leaving the Nelson farm, they traveled the short distance to the Braymyer home, where Mrs. Braymyer, aged 20, shot and killed all four men. Shortly after killing the last man, Rosalee Braymyer gave birth to a son whom she named after her father, the late Rev. Brice Burns. Both Mr. Braymyer and Mr. Nelson have still not returned from a trip to Indian Territory where they were allegedly tracking outlaws, however it is now believed that it was a set up to get the two men away from their homes.

Mrs. Nelson, aged 28 will be buried in the Braymyer Cemetery this afternoon, along with her two children, Jack 12 and Nancy 08.

Dixie continues to grow. We had another wagon full of no goods show up three days ago and they show no signs of leaving. Lord help us…

    Allen Goldston

Chapter Seven

When Nat awoke from what seemed like a months sleep, he noticed that the sun was barely visible in the sky as it made its way into the night. He slowly sat up, not forgetting the throbbing pain in his right thigh, which had seemed to have spread to his entire right leg.

After he had managed to sit upright, he noticed that his wound had been bandaged and was packed with an herb of some sort. He looked around for a moment and saw Two-Feathers standing nearby with a tin cup in his hand. "Where am I?" Nat mumbled.

The tall Indian walked closer, "We camp here two moons tonight. You sleep one sun."

"I've got to go, my wife and children are in trouble."

Nat began to try and get to his feet, but was stopped by Two-Feathers. "Here, you drink water."

Nat took the cup and drank until it was empty and then proceeded to try and get up. "I've got to get home to my wife and…"

"You're wife is beautiful woman. I ride to your house this morning and watch from big hill. You're children play outside, baby crying inside."

"Baby?" Nat's mind filled with regret, he had missed the birth of his child. Rosalee would never let him go anywhere again and he would never hear the end of it.

"You're wife sit in chair on big porch and wait for you to come home."

"How do you know where I live?"

"I, Two-Feathers, watch white people. I watch you many times. You good man."

Nat was shocked that a complete stranger had been watching him and he had never even seen him." I appreciate your kindness, Two-Feathers, but I've really got to get home."

The sun had almost shone its last ray of light over Texas and things were slowly getting dark. "You sleep here tonight and I take you home tomorrow."

As bad as he wanted to be home with Rosalee, he knew there was no way he would make it there in the dark with a wounded leg. Two-Feathers had a nice fire going that kept them warm on the cool March night, unlike the hot day that had just passed them by.

The stout Indian had killed a deer earlier that day and now the two of them feasted on it as the night continued to take over the land.

"Where is your tribe, Two-Feathers?"

"My people hate white man, my friend. I think there are some good white men and some bad ones, like with all men."

"That's a good philosophy. But don't you ever miss your family?"

"If my people, my family choose to live a coward life than I cannot miss them, my friend, it is their choice."

"Hey, Two-Feathers, you didn't by chance learn your English from a Mexican did you? You sure say *friend* a lot."

The Indian smiled, "No, it was a Spanish man, brown like my people, but different than us."

Nat couldn't help but let out a laugh, "Well I reckon it don't matter how you come to learn it anyway."

"It is a hard world to live in without speaking it and I can call you my friend because you are a good man, my friend."

"The way I see it, Two-Feathers, you're a good man too. You saved my life you know."

"You would save many lives too, Brameer, you good man."

Nat slept comfortably under a buffalo hide that the generous Indian had given him that night. When the sun started to come up the next morning, Nat and Two-Feathers were already headed in the direction of the farm, with Alex Nelson's body thrown across Nat's horse. They were within sight of the large house just before noon and Two-Feathers stopped.

"Come on, Two-Feathers. Have Lunch with us." Nat said motioning toward his home.

"Go be with your family, my friend, I come visit you soon. I must go for now."

The Indian turned his paint horse and rode in the direction they had came from while Nat went forward to his home.

"Strange man," he mumbled to himself as he neared the house, "but good man."

Rosalee was sitting on the front porch rocking Brice when Nat rode up.

"Nat!" She screamed. She wanted badly to get up and run to him, but she was still too sore from the delivery of the baby.

Nat slowly made it off his horse and up the porch stairs to Rosalee and the baby, "Hello, darling."

"Nat, you're hurt. Are you okay? What happened?"

"It's nothing much, Rosie," he said leaning down to kiss her. "Who's this little fellow?"

"Nat, this is your son, Brice." She said handing the baby to him as he sat down in the rocker beside her.

Nat looked in amazement at the small baby and noticed there was a sense of mysteriousness written across his face, much like the Indian he had spent the last two days with.

Nat ran his fingers down one of Brice's arms and then tickled his stomach a bit. "Brice Two-Feathers Braymyer," he said looking over at Rosalee.

"Two-Feathers! Nathaniel Braymyer are you out of your mind!"

"It's a long story, Rosie darling, I'll tell you in a little bit."

"Pa! Pa!" Cotton said running onto the front porch with his grandmother and Mary Lee trailing close behind. "Pa! Ma killed bad men!"

The Braymyer family sat very contently on their front porch, happy that each one of them was alive. They shared their stories of what had happened over the last couple of days and vowed never to leave each others sides again. Cotton listened anxiously to the story about the Indian as Two-Feathers himself sat atop his paint and watched from afar.

Chapter Eight

July 04, 1976

Sixteen year old Peter Riddle drove his car down a country road northwest of Dixie with two of his buddies, Ralph Davidson and Jimmy Berry. It was dark outside and the last of the fireworks had just finished illuminating the air across the north Texas sky.

Ralph sat in the front with Peter and looked over at him as they continued down the rock road. "Why are we going out to this old house again?"

"Geez, Ralph, how many times do I have to tell you this story?"

Jimmy spoke up from the back seat, "Come on Pete, tell us again. You tell it the best."

"Okay, every year when the family that lives in this house goes on vacation this time of year, a group of ghost move in while they're gone…"

"Where did they come from?" Ralph interrupted.

"Do you want to tell this story? Anyway, a long time ago there was a bunch of outlaws that attacked this old place. Supposedly a blonde-headed woman who used to live there long ago killed them all. According to the story all these men were buried up in the woods somewhere behind the house in unmarked graves, never to be found again.

Every year when the house is empty, they all walk up from the graves and into the house where they were killed. Some people say they are just lost, but other people think that they are out looking for revenge because they were killed so quickly. Back in the fifties, a blonde headed boy came out here looking for the ghost and he was never heard from again.

They say that the ghosts will only go after people with blonde hair and when they get them they take them back to their graves and stay there until the next year when they come out again."

Ralph looked around the car and suddenly got a cold chill as he looked at all three of their blonde heads. "Are you *sure* this is a good idea?"

"What, are you too chicken? I can pull over and let you wait here for us."

"No…uh, that's ok. I'll go with you."

The car turned into the driveway and drove down it towards the old house with the giant cottonwood trees hanging above their heads. Once they had pulled up in front of the house, Pete turned the car off and put the keys on the dashboard. "Are y'all ready?"

Jimmy threw open the back door and jumped out while Ralph took his time, forcing his shaking body to exit the car. Pete held up his flashlight and shined it in the direction of the house with the other boys on either side of him. They slowly walked toward the steps of the front porch, all the while observing their surroundings.

Once at the steps, they walked side by side up onto the front porch. There was a scratching noise coming from the end of the porch to their right and all three boys stopped in their tracks. "Wh..wh..what was that?" Ralph said shaking even more.

Pete shined his light in that direction, "Awe, it ain't nothing but an old farm cat."

The cat's green eyes reflected in the bright light and then it jumped off the porch into the darkness. They made their way toward the front window step by step as the wooden porch cracked beneath them with every step they made.

Once at the window all three boys looked into it and into the dark front sitting room. As they looked around the room with the light of the flashlight they saw a figure move across the room in their direction. It seemed to disappear and reappear until suddenly it popped up right on the other side of the window. It was a blonde headed woman looking straight at the three of them.

"AHHH!" They all shouted, Ralph being the loudest, and ran as fast as they could back to the awaiting car. Once inside, Pete struggled to find the keys and struggled even longer to force the key into the ignition.

Ralph glanced back at the house and on the front porch where they had just stood was the same woman in a blue dress looking out at them with a cat sitting at her side. Pete threw the car in reverse and sped out of the driveway, barely missing the trees on his way out.

Chapter Nine

June 21, 2010

The plane continued to shake and seemed to be everywhere across the sky other than on a straight path. I sat in my seat in my Army uniform, buckled as tightly as I possibly could be, wondering what in the heck was going on.

One of the stewards slowly made her way down the aisle and stopped at my side. "Excuse me, sir. I couldn't help but notice your uniform and was wondering if I might talk to you about something."

"Sure go ahead," I said as she sat down in the seat next to me.

"I would appreciate it if you would not say anything to anyone about this, we don't want people getting frantic over nothing."

"Ok…?"

"Well, we were wondering if perhaps you knew how to fly a plane?"

"Fly a plane!"

"Shhh…"

"Not so loud, sir. Yes, fly a plane," she said, now in a whisper.

"Why would you want to know if I can fly a plane? What's going on?"

"Well, it appears our pilots have been poisoned. Neither one of them are responsive right now and none of the flight attendants know how to fly a plane."

"Well how in the hell are we flying right now?"

"We are on auto pilot right now, sir. So do you know how to fly a plane?"

"I have no idea how to fly a plane. In fact this is only my third or fourth time on a plane myself."

"Well, don't they train you for these kind of situations?"

"I'm not sure how my training is going to help me fly a plane! Isn't there anyone else on board who can fly it?"

"I'm afraid not, sir. Won't you at least take a look and see if you can possibly land us?"

I don't get scared easyily, in fact there are very few things that do scare me. But being on a plane with two poisoned pilots would be towards the top of my small list of situations I'd rather not be in.

I followed the middle-aged woman toward the front of the plane and just before getting to the cockpit, the two pilots were laying on the floor outside the door. I stepped into the room and sat down in the seat.

"Good, God…we're going to die if I'm suppose to fly this thing."

Chapter Ten

When Nat and Rosalee rode into Dixie on the morning of June 05, 1871, they were shocked to see how busy the town had become. Two-Feathers rode in the back of the wagon and watched the people of the town in amazement.Nat had hired the Indian to help him out on the farm not long after he had saved his life. The middle-aged Indian slept in the barn except on some occasions when he would make a camp nearby.

Cotton was amazed at the brown man and wanted to spend every second of his time with him. Two-Feathers had proved to be a great asset to the Braymyer farm, he was probably one of the hardest working men in the county, whether he was an Indian or not.

As they turned down Main Street, Rosalee was becoming nervous as she saw all the strangers gathering throughout the town, most of whom were men who seemed to be drunk. "Nat, what's happening to this place?"

"Nothing good, Rosie, nothing good."

Nat drove the wagon down the street until he came to Allen Goldston's newspaper shop and home. "Here, Rosie, you stay here and visit with Martha while Two-Feathers and I go get all the supplies for the farm."

As they pulled up, Rosalee's good friend, Martha Goldston came out of the front door. "Rosalee, how are you?"

"Hi, Martha…"

"Never mind that, come on let's get inside. These streets are no place for a lady."

After Rosalee had made it inside, Nat and Two-Feathers continued down the street until arriving at the general store. Dixie's store was almost too large for the small town, but it made it a convenient meeting place for some of the locals. It had a large false front and two green glass paned doors leading out onto its long narrow front porch.

When the two of them had secured the wagon they stepped up onto the large porch and went inside. There were a bunch of local farmers and business owners gathered near the register discussing Dixie's fate.

Jim Tuley was the owner of the store and never was there a man merrier than him. He was a short balding man with a potbelly and he always wore a black apron across his body.

"Morning, Nat," he said as they came in, "What can I do you for?"

"Oh, just here to get a few supplies for the farm."
"Well, I am sure you will find everything you need in here…somewhere."

There was a loud commotion outside in the street that was followed by breaking glass. A woman let out a yelp and before any of the men could react, Two-Feathers was already outside.

Nat followed suit and when he stepped out of the store, a fat man with a long tobacco stained beard had a gun pointed at the Indian. "What's going on here?" He asked, cautiously stepping closer.

"This ain't none of your concern, get back about your business, mister."

"I'll ask you again. What's going on out here?"

"Mister, do you have a death wish or something?"

"Maybe I do, or maybe I just don't like seeing guns pointed at my friends."

"Well, if you're friends with this here Injun, mister, then you ain't no better than him. Maybe I'll just shoot you both."

The drunken man turned the gun on Nat and looked him up and down. Nat noticed behind the man, a broken whiskey bottle and a girl who looked to have been hit across the face lying nearby.

Nat's blue eyes turned into a deep shade that can only be seen in rare parts of the world. He looked at the man and lifted up his cowboy hat a little to get a better view. Nat was twenty-two and was a strong attractive man that feared very few things. He was always nice and good to others, but Nat Braymyer had had enough of the renegade outlaws taking over this part of the country.

There was a certain coolness about him that could be compared to no other man. The other men stayed in the store for fear that a mark would be placed on their head by other outlaws around town. Nat took a step forward, making the obese man nervous.

"Maybe I'll shoot you first."

"Mister, you don't know whooo…"

The unmistakable echo of a gunshot filled the air.

Nat had no gun on him, he had merely planned to wrestle the man's gun away from him and chase him off. Two-Feathers remained standing in the same position he was in for fear that the unknown gunman would strike again.

The large man tried to stay up on his feet, but alas it was no use. He fell to his knees first, followed by landing face down in the dirt. When he had fallen to the ground, Rosalee appeared holding a shotgun behind where he had once stood.

"Rosie!" Nat yelled running toward her, "What are you thinking! You're supposed to be inside!"

"Maybe I should be, or maybe I just don't like seeing guns pointed at my husband."

Nat grabbed the gun and held her in his arms and kissed her a long kiss beneath the morning sun on Main Street. There was another gun fired somewhere across town, followed by screams and laughter.

"Come on, Rosie darling, let's get you inside the store. Where's Martha?"

"She'll be along shortly, she's getting some things together."

Down by Dixie

June 05, 1871

Well friends, I am closing up shop.

The unlawfulness of this town has become too much to bear for my family and I. We will be staying at the Braymyer home until things settle down here in town. My prayers are with the better citizens of this town that they might find safety. This morning both the Methodist and the Baptist churches were burned down. God speed my friends and good luck.

Allen Goldston

Chapter Eleven

It had been a week since Allen Goldston and his family had come to stay with the Braymyers. Allen and Martha had two children, Abigail, who was Cotton's age and Henry who was Mary's age. The small family of four had made their home in Dixie for the past ten years and it was hard to just walk away, but their safety depended on it.

The children enjoyed playing with each other and were glad to have each other's company on the hot summer days. Rosalee, Martha and Addie spent their days tending to the children, housework and when they were able to, they sat in the front room and knitted. It was almost as if they were all long lost relatives who had at last found one another and now valued their time shared together.

Martha was a pretty plain woman, but she was not ugly by any means. Her features were strong and for a woman she was taller than most. Her eyes seemed to be set back in her head deeper than most people and her black hair was darker than many a night's sky. Her husband was short and although he was only in his mid thirties, he was already balding. He was slender and wore glasses over his unique green eyes, which stood out more than anything else on his body.

Allen helped Nat and Two-Feathers on the farm wherever he could, but it was obvious he was not accustomed to farm life. Like Cotton, he was intrigued by Two-Feathers and observed him very carefully as if he were planning to write a book about him or something. Nat looked at the Indian and understood him and just saw him as he was.

The women were sitting in rockers in the front room knitting some clothes for baby Brice and talking about past times. Rosalee had made a fresh loaf of bread that morning, so the house smelled delicious. The children were in the front yard playing, with the exception of the baby who lay on a blanket near his mother. The loud thud of boots stampeded up the front porch steps and through the double doors. All three women nearly fell out of their rockers at the commotion.

Nat stood there with his thumbs through his suspenders and looked wild eyed at them. "Come on ladies, what do you say we go for a swim and eat blueberries all day long?"

"Yeah! Boobewwys!" Cotton said running up to Nat from behind. He was swooped up into his father's arms and was turned to face the women.

"Well," Nat said, "I got one vote!"

All the women looked around at each other not knowing what to say. Addie was the first to laugh, "Nathaniel Braymyer, I do d'clare."

She stood up and was heading toward the staircase when she turned back to Rosalee and Martha, "Come on girls, I think it's high time we have some fun, even if it means watching the men drown!"

They gathered up some food to take along, including the freshly cooked loaf of bread and after everyone was ready to go, they all walked across the field to the creek. Cotton walked proudly alongside his father, trying to match him step for step.

When they reached the creek, the children were the first to get in. They were all scared to venture too far into the water except for Cotton who dove right in. Mary, Henry and Abigail stuck their feet in and splashed a little, but refused to go too far from the safety of the bank.

The water was only about a foot deep along the bank and when the others realized this; they slowly made their way deeper into the water. The women sat on a red checkered blanket near the creek shore and watched as the men dove in like wild horses. The farther out into the creek they went, the deeper the water got and once in the middle it was up to Nat's shoulders.

The afternoon sun made the day warm and the fresh water felt good to their bodies. Allen, Nat and Two-Feathers played with the children while the women continued to watch from their blanket.

For the first time since her husband's death, Addie did not wear black. Her time of mourning over the past was over and it was now time to move forward with her life. Since the death of her son, Stephen, Rosalee was all she had left.

"You know," she said to the other women, "I think I'll go for a swim myself."

"Mother!" Rosalee protested, "That isn't lady like!"

Addie looked at her daughter and with a sly smile responded to her, "Neither is killing a man, Rosalee."

Addie waded out into the water in a green dress while Martha and Rosalee laughed among themselves.

"Grandma! You're swimming!" Cotton yelled splashing his way toward her.

The swimming adults made a large circle in the middle of the creek and the children swam from one to another. Mary was the first to get out of the water when her brother threw a frog on her, followed shortly by Abigail.

The day had brought some much needed peace to the Dixie valley for two families and their Indian friend. They feasted on the loaf of bread and blueberries and swam the day away not worrying about anything. When the sun started to grow weaker the group of tired people headed back in the direction of the farm with Cotton following reluctantly behind.

When they reached their home they were surprised to see that a rider was approaching them from down the long driveway. As he got closer they realized it was fourteen year old Charlie Knight. The Knight family were good friends to the Goldston's and Braymyer's and were one of the few remaining families that cared about Dixie's future.

Allen approached the boy with the rest of the group close behind. "What are you doing out this far, Charlie?"

"Bad news, Mr. Goldston. My Pa sent me out to tell you and Mr. Braymyer."

Nat stepped up to the horse, "Come on, Charlie, come in and get some water."

After Charlie had gotten some water and was able to catch his breath, everyone gathered around him in the front sitting room.

"Mr. Goldston, a group of drunks burned your shop to the ground and the café too."

Martha was fighting back tears as she learned their livelihood was destroyed, but in order to keep the children calm she held them in.

Nat put his hand on the boy's shoulder, "Is that all, son?"

"No sir. There's more. It's cholera, it's spreading through the area like wildfire! Seven people are dead in town, including the Sheriff."

"Where's the doctor, boy?" Allen asked in a panic.

"Doc. Ruyle left town a few days ago, sir. Said this place was being taken over by the devil. Pa said he went to Gainesville."

"You did good, son," Nat said looking over at Rosalee and then back down at him, "Now hurry back home before it gets dark."

In a few days, Addie was in bed with a fever, followed shortly by Rosalee. Martha tended to them night and day, doing everything she could to get them well. With his mother in bed sick, little Brice was not getting enough to eat and it would only be a matter of time before he was sick as well.

Nat tried to get him to drink milk from the cow in the barn, but it only made the baby sicker than he already was. Nat didn't sleep any; he was always worrying about something. During the day he worked the farm to keep his mind busy and watched after Cotton and Mary. Seven days after they had gotten the news of Allen's shop and of the cholera outbreak, the Braymyer home was slowly crumbling to pieces.

The men were in the barn one morning, trying to figure out what they could do, or if there was even anything that could be done. "Braymeer," Two-Feathers said looking over at his friend, "I take baby to white town. Someone feed him there."

"I don't know, Two-Feathers it would be awful dangerous. I mean, an Indian showing up in town with a white baby?"

"Nat," Allen said, "It might be Brice's only shot to make it. He's hardly eaten anything in the last week and unless something is done, he won't stand a chance."

Nat decided to let his Indian friend take his son to town so that he could find a nursing mother to care for him until Rosalee got better…if she even got better. That same day, Two-Feathers mounted his paint horse and with the baby tucked in the crack of his right arm he rode off towards Dexter.

Nat didn't know what to do anymore. His wife and mother in law both lie in bed with little hope of surviving and now his son was being taken off somewhere to be tended to by strangers. He prayed for a miracle every day and night as he sat beside Rosalee's bed. He watched her sleep and was mad that there was nothing he could do. He was suppose to protect his wife, but how could he.

The days seemed to drag on and it was by far the hottest summer in Texas since their arrival. Mosquitoes filled the sticky air and the ground was so hot that it looked as if there was steam coming from its surface and the large cracks throughout the dark soil.

It had been two days since Two-Feathers had left with Brice and there was still no word from them. Martha and her son were the next to take ill with the crippling illness. Allen and

Nat did all they could to take care of the sick, while trying to also manage the three healthy children.

Martha and Henry did not last long with the cholera. Only three days after they had became sick, they were both dead, leaving Allen in a great depression. They were buried up on the hill with Nat's deceased daughter and the Nelson family. The Braymyer cemetery was growing in size and continued to do so on June 30, when Nat dug a grave for Addie Burns.

Allen occupied himself with his daughter, but the thought of his wife was always on his mind. He would spend hours at her grave up on the hill and sometimes stay throughout the night.

It wasn't in Nat's blood to give up, but he was growing closer and closer every day. Cotton and Mary spent their days out in the Texas heat, not understanding why their mother wouldn't get out of bed or why their grandmother was put into the ground. Nat pushed himself to carry out the farm duties, but he didn't see how he would be able to make it without Rosalee.

Chapter Twelve

The judge folded her hands beneath her chin and for the first time that day showed a little hint of compassion. "Ok, Mr. Sanders, although I still don't see where this story is going, I'm going to allow you to continue after we take a fifteen minute recess, okay?"

"Yes, your honor."

The aged Nathan Sanders walked down the aisle and into the lobby with his daughter Rose, who was surprised that he had denied his wheelchair. He had been revisiting his family's past and had a great sense of melancholy as he looked around him.

Rose held his hand as they walked toward a soda machine. "You're doing great, daddy, just keep telling the story like your grandpa Cotton told it to you."

"I will, Rose darling, but there are things I just cannot remember no matter how hard I try."

"I know, daddy, but like I said, you're doing great."

Rose got her father a soda out of the machine and then sat with him while they shared it. She tried calling her grandson, but there was no answer.

"Daddy, do you think Nat and Rosalee ever regretted coming to Texas?"

"Absolutely not! Nat and Rosalee became Texas and it became them. Rose darling, a place can only be as good as the people that call it home and the two of them put their sweat and blood into not only that community, but to the entire state of Texas, just like so many others did. If it hadn't been for Nat and Rosalee and all those other brave pioneers who came to Texas and endured the wild frontier, why you and I wouldn't be here today."

Rose could hear the distinct voices of the two young hot shot lawyers they were battling in the courtroom. They were now walking toward Rose and her father, strutting themselves about in their fancy suits.

"Give it up, old timer. Your precious family home is coming down and our money making country club is coming up!" They laughed as they continued past them.

Nathan looked in their direction and shook his head with sympathy for them, while Rose fought the urge to get up and deck them. They finished their soda and slowly made their way back to Judge Dawson's courtroom where she was already waiting for them. "Have a seat, Mr. Sanders and you may continue."

"Yes, now let me think. The creek water was cool…"

"Rosalee was sick, daddy," Rose whispered.

"Ah, yes, Rosalee was very ill…"

- - - - - - - - - - - - - - - - -

The streets of Dexter were jammed packed with wagons and horses the afternoon that Two-Feathers rode in with Brice. The town looked promising and it seemed that it would grow to surpass every town around in size. It had three dirt roads and all of them were full of buildings. There were all sorts of people in town, from common farmers to slender women dressed in elegant dresses. As he rode down the main street of the bustling town, most of them stopped what they were doing to look at the Indian carrying a white baby.

Two-Feathers tied his horse up on the only available hitching post in front of the general store and then walked up onto the platform to enter the store. Before he could enter, a small balding stout man that wore overly large round glasses came out of the double doors to him.

"Hello, Injun. I'm sorry, but we don't allow your kind inside, but if there is something you are in need of, I will be happy to bring it out to you. Say, is that a white baby you have there?"

"Yes, my white friend baby. He needs milk, he getting sick."

"Why can't his mother give him some milk?"

"Mother very sick, she sleeps always."

"Wait right here, I'll go fetch the sheriff, he's just next door."

The storekeeper walked next door and shortly after came back with the sheriff, whom looked the situation over. Luckily, Two-Feathers had no problem getting the two men to believe his story and shortly after the sheriff arrived, Brice was being taken over to the hotel where the school teacher stayed. The men had Two-Feathers wait outside the store until Brice had been taken care of.

The widowed schoolteacher had just lost her baby prematurely and was glad to help Brice; it made her feel useful in a strange way. After about an hour the sheriff was walking back across the wide street toward Two-Feathers, holding Brice in one arm and a glass bottle of milk in the other.

After Two-Feathers had mounted his paint, the sheriff handed Brice and the bottle of milk to him. He assured him that he would be out to the Braymyer home to check on the baby and if he needed more milk to be sure and bring him back. The Indian made his way through the crowd of people and horses and started the journey home.

"This was easy, almost too easy," he thought to himself as Dexter disappeared behind him. When he was about two miles out of town, he got the feeling that he was being watched and sure enough he was.

The Indian was struck in the back by an arrow of his own people. His sympathy and compassion for white people would be the cause of his death. He struggled off of his horse before another arrow had a chance to hit him and placed the baby on the ground, leaving him in God's care. He turned to face the approaching riders where another arrow was implanted into his chest. He fell to his knees and everything went black, Two-Feathers was no more.

There were only two riders approaching them and once they had scalped their brother who lie dead on the ground, they scooped up the baby and headed north into Indian Territory.

Dexter News

July 06, 1871

Just outside of Dexter last week an Indian called Two-Feathers was killed by his own people. He was carrying Brice Braymyer, a white baby whom he had brought to town to get milk for him while his mother was ill. The whereabouts of the baby are unknown, but there are several groups of men who have ventured into Indian Territory in search of him.

It seems that more and more farmers are coming into Dexter for their business needs. This is probably due to the fact that Dixie is completely abandoned except for a group of outlaws who have taken over the city. Texas living sure can be tough.

The cholera that spread out around Dixie seems to be dissipating. It is estimated that more than thirty people lost their lives to this recent outbreak, our thoughts and prayers are with the families of those affected.

Giles Baum

Chapter Thirteen

It had turned out to be one of the worst months for the Braymyer family as their loved ones disappeared. A plague of bad luck had settled in on the Texas frontier until Independence Day of 1871 when Rosalee's fever finally broke and like a baby, her first words were "I'm hungry."

Nat was beside himself that there was a chance that his wife might live, but full of worry about his infant son. Even Allen, although still grief stricken, seemed to be a little happier that day.

Nat waited on her hand and foot and by that evening, she seemed to be making a full recovery. Her first questions after she was fully able to speak were of the baby. For the first time since his life had fallen apart, Nat broke down as he told her the fate of everyone and that he would have to leave her side tomorrow to go and get Brice from Dexter.

The next morning before Nat saddled up to head to Dexter, Rosalee asked him to take her up to the cemetery so she could say her goodbye to her mother. They stood on the tree-covered hill and looked at all the stones, one by one, remembering them all. The Nelson family and their two children, Martha and her son and Addie Burns.

Nat put an arm around Rosalee and a hand on Cotton's shoulder who stood beside him. "I reckon we'll be resting up on this hill soon enough, Rosie."

"Hopefully not for a long while, Nat, a long while."

Rosalee was weak for the rest of the year and while she was recovering, Nat was scouting Indian country for any trace of his son. At one point, he went all the way to Colorado looking for him, but there was no sign to be found anywhere. Nat and Rosalee convinced themselves that Brice had most probably been killed by the tribe that had taken him and there would be no hope of finding him. Posters were posted as far away as California, but there were never any leads to his whereabouts.

Nat made his last trip in search of his son in November and by Christmas time he was home for good.

Allen and his daughter were still staying with the Braymyer family because things in Dixie had not gotten any better. Occasionally they would see smoke rising from the town as another building was burned to the ground. Most of the families in the area had left because of the outcome of Dixie, but there were a few that remained behind to fight the storm of outlaws and settle the land no matter what the cost.

December was busy in the home as everyone prepared for Christmas. Everyone needed something to get their mind off all the bad things that had happened that year and of what had happened to Brice, so they used Christmas to get the job done. Nat had taken Cotton with him to the woods near the creek where they cut down a large cedar tree and hauled it back to the house.

The two of them mounted the tree in the front sitting room and the bushy greenery filled the house with a scent of cedar. Although it had been a rough year for the family, they remained confident that things would turn out better. On Christmas morning Rosalee was busy preparing their dinner, which would consist of a chicken and a ham. The smell of the food combined with that of the cedar to make the entire house smell like Christmas, which helped to lift their spirits even more.

Cotton, Mary and Abigail anxiously waited in the front room near the tree to see what they would get for Christmas. They huddled around the fireplace and snacked on peppermint sticks that Nat had gotten them from Dexter.

It had started to snow two days earlier, so the Braymyer farm glistened in a white blanket of ice. The snow continued to steadily fall down to the farm, slowly getting thicker and thicker atop the muddy ground. A small stream of smoke rose out of both of the chimneys and drifted away into the white sky somewhere unknown to man.

Nat and Allen were in the barn tending to the animals and gathering up the children's presents they had hidden there. After everything had been taken care of in the barn, they pushed their way back through the snow toward the house. As they stepped up onto the snow-covered porch, Nat looked in the direction of Dixie, there was smoke rising into the snowy sky.

"Looks like something else is burning," he said hitting his boots on the side of the house to rid them of snow.

Cotton was the first to run toward the men as they stepped into the house, "Pa! Where's our presents, Pa?"

"Easy son," Nat said handing him a package wrapped in brown paper.

It didn't take him long to shred the package of its paper which revealed a wooden revolver that Nat had carved himself and a small cowboy hat. Cotton immediately ran through the house chaotically shouting and hollering and making occasional gun noises with his mouth.

Abigail and Mary patiently waited as their fathers brought them their identical packages. Both girls took pride in carefully opening their gifts and placing the paper neatly to their side so that they might find use for it later. Once they were opened, the girls held up matching dolls, except Mary's had blonde hair like her and Abigail's brown like her hair.

Rosalee walked in to announce that dinner was almost ready, where she was met with a kiss from Nat. The entire house was merry, but there was still a sense of loss at the Braymyer home. Everyone gathered in the back dining room and joined hands as Nat blessed the food. He mentioned all those that they had lost that year and that the next year would bring good fortune.

When he was finished, everyone began to eat and talk and share stories of Christmas' in the past. There was hot cider and sweet tea to quench their thirst and for a moment they were all happy again. The children anxiously waited to be dismissed from the table and when Rosalee finally excused them, they all took off up the stairs to play with their new toys.

Nat sipped his hot cider and let it flow slowly down his throat. "You know, Allen, it seems to me that all the outlaws are starting to get more frequent out here near the farm."

"I've noticed that too. I dread the day one of them knocks on the door."

"I sure hate to see this nice land being overrun by rebels."

"Yes, if only there were something we could do…"

"Well, maybe there is…"

"What did you have in mind, Nat?"

"Well, I'm pretty good with a gun, but there are a lot of men running around Dixie right now. Maybe we could see if some of the other farmers want to form a posse and take back Dixie?"

"Well, that could work, but there are not a whole lot of farmers left around here."

Rosalee put her napkin down on the table. "Nat Braymyer, why must you go out and look for trouble? It seems trouble is going to find us here anyway and besides, things are finally calming down and we are perfectly content."

"Rosie, what are we going to do when a group of those men show up at our farm?"

"Probably the same thing we would have done had you been here when those outlaws showed up last time. Now, let's enjoy Christmas and talk about this some other time."

The conversation changed to talking about the weather and the children. They ate off and on all day, in no hurry for Christmas to end. When the sun had finally gone away, the two families gathered in the front room while Rosalee read from the book of Luke. Everyone slept nice and warm in their beds that night, thankful that they had each other.

Chapter Fourteen

The snow had almost completely melted in one day shortly after the New Year had begun. The days were shorter, but they seemed to last a week at a time as there was nothing to do at the farm during these colder months. Against Rosalee's will, Nat had started planning his attack on Dixie to occupy his time.

Every Sunday afternoon the local farming families that still remained in the area would come to the Braymyer house. The women and children visited and played in the house, while all the men met in the barn to come up with a plan.

They all knew that they had to do something or it would only be a matter of time until their own homes were taken over. Hank Webb, Levi Gordon, Jasper Knight, Thomas Riddle, Bill Turner, Hardeman Tyler, Allen and Nat sat among the hay bales and scratched their heads as they thought.

"There's got to be something we can do," Knight said, "But there is just too many of them."

"That's why the law refuses to help us," Riddle answered.

Nat looked around the room for a moment and sized everyone up. "Well, men, we're all good with a gun, but you're right, there is a lot of them and only a few of us."

"You have an idea or something?" Hank Webb asked.

"Yeah, I do, but it's dangerous and I'd understand if some of you wouldn't want to do it."

Knight scratched his head a little harder, "Well, let's hear it."

"Well, we could try and attack them at night, but they would still have the upper hand on us. We need to make some kind of a distraction to separate them and lower their numbers."

"Unless you've got a wagon full of whiskey, you're not going to get any of them anywhere," Riddle said thinking the situation over.

"True. Jasper you live the closest to town, what's the latest happenings down there?"

"Same thing as it always is. Once or twice a week a building is burned and then they celebrate by tearing something else up. Last week a group of them rode out to Seth Houston's place and took all his livestock. After they shot Seth, they took off with his daughter. I imagine she's dead by now."

From outside the barn a rider could be heard approaching them. Almost all at once all the men stepped out of the barn. It was a slender shaggy man with holes in his clothes. "Well now, what do we have here?" He said looking the men over.

Nat stepped up to the man, "Something I can do for you?"

"Yeah, we've been noticing all you men meeting up here every Sunday and we don't like it. So I come to see what you're up to."

"We?" Knight asked.

"Yeah, Mack Dillon's gang."

"Who is Mack Dillon?" Allen asked.

"Why hell, man, he's the one running your town you fool. And he don't like you all meeting up here like you're doing."

"You a friend of this Mack Dillon?" Nat asked stepping even closer.

"Ha, only his number one."

"Well, good then. Now listen up. Rather than sending you back to him with a bullet hole in your head, I'm going to give you a message for him."

"Ha… you're awful cocky now ain't you, son?"

Nat was getting more and more aggravated. "Shut up and listen you idiot. Tell Mr. Dillon his days in Dixie are numbered and he'd be smart to get out now, or else."

"Ha, what are *you* going to do?"

"Just give him the message before I change my mind about putting a bullet in your head!"

"Alright, but Mack won't be happy about this. Hell, he'll probably send some men out here to kill every one of you worthless farmers."

Nat pulled out his revolver and pointed it at the man, "My mind is starting to change…"

"Hiya!" The man said kicking his horse… and he was gone.

"Well," Nat said, "Looks like we've got our distraction."

"I'd say so," Allen said. "So what now?"

"Well, men, I think it would be best if you and your families stayed here. We'd be making it easy for them if we split up."

All the men agreed. The house was full of children playing and women gossiping when they went back in. It was going to be a long night and they all knew it.

Two men at a time stayed up for a three-hour lookout shift. The night was cold and quiet and the drunk noise was so loud from Dixie that they could hear it all the way out at the farm. Nat and Allen had the first shift. Nat kept a steady eye towards the town, listening to everything that echoed through the valley. "They're celebrating."

"Celebrating what?"

"They'll try and attack us here sometime tomorrow morning, mark my words."

"What are we going to do then? Do you think we're ready for them?"

"If we play our cards right I think we can handle them. We'll wait in the trees alongside the road and ambush them when they head this way."

Each man passed the plan on to the next when his shift was over. By the next morning, every man had his gun loaded and plenty of extra ammo at hand. They kissed their women and children goodbye and side by side headed down the drive with the little cottonwood trees at their side. After walking about a mile down the road towards Dixie, they scattered into the trees on both sides where they patiently waited.

Rosalee and Beth Knight took charge of the women and children. They had the other women gather up blankets and food just in case they had to make a run for Dexter.

Everything was quiet at the house after the supplies had been gathered, even the children made no sound. Cotton stood by the front door with his wooden gun and watched in the direction his father and the other men had gone. The air in the house remained thick with worry; only the steady tick of the clock could be heard.

The men continued to wait for an hour until riders could be heard coming up the road. They checked one last time to ensure their guns were ready for battle. There were fourteen of Dillon's men riding toward the eight of them. Since it would be an ambush, the odds were not bad.

The riders rode by the hidden farmers slowly, in no hurry. As soon as the last rider had passed, all the men jumped out and began to fire their weapons.

A thick cloud of gun smoke engulfed the area, helping the farmers who were afoot by hiding them. Bullets whizzed by Nat's head, but he continued to pursue the gang with the other farmers close behind him.

The gunfight lasted only a few minutes and then all was quiet. Nat cautiously observed his surroundings to ensure that he was safe. When the cloud of smoke had finally cleared it revealed that none of the farmers had been hurt and all fourteen of the gang members lie dead in the road.

It was a good victory, but the men knew things would only get harder. Dillon's men in town were sure to have heard the gunshots and when his men did not return, he would only send more. Nat pointed his gun into the air and fired three times so that Rosalee would know they were okay. The farmers gathered up some ammo from the dead gunmen and were able to find enough horses that had not been shot so they could ride the rest of the way towards town.

When they got within a half a mile of town, they once again hid themselves in the trees on both sides of the road. If they could get rid of one more group that rode by, then they might be able to make a successful attack on Dixie.

- - - - - - - - - - - - - - -

When Rosalee heard the three gunshots she began to worry all over again, for she knew that now the men would be heading even closer to town, to more danger. Cotton continued to stand guard at the door. He rose up his wooden gun and pointed it toward the porch. "Pow, Pow," he said.

A man with a gun came through the door and picked him up in his arms. "Hey! I shot you! You're dead!" Cotton protested paying no attention to the real revolver pointed at his head.

Rosalee screamed and in an angry motion pointed her shotgun in that direction.

"Put the gun down, woman," the man said, "Or the boy dies."

Rosalee hesitated for a moment and then followed the man's direction, placing the gun on the floor in front of her. The man looked to be in his thirties and had a distinct scar across his right cheek. He looked through the room, moving his gun from one woman or child to another.

"Is this the Braymyer Boy?"

The room remained silent.

He put the gun to Cotton's head and shouted. "Someone better answer me or I swear to God I'll blow his head off!"

"Yes," Rosalee said, "He's my son. Now put him down!"

The intruder chuckled, "Sorry, maim, I can't do that. The boss wants me to bring him into town." He moved his gun around the room again, threatening them one by one. "Now, I'm going to get on my horse and ride away. If any of you give me any trouble, I'll kill the boy."

Rosalee was fighting back tears of both worry and anger. "Mister, don't you dare…"

"I mean it," he interrupted, "Any problems and he dies."

The gunman carried Cotton outside and hopped up onto his horse with Cotton fighting him the whole way, but it was no use. Once atop his sickly looking animal they rode off. Rosalee ran after them screaming and shouting, but the rider paid no attention to her as he rode off.

She flew open the front doors and grabbed her coat. She could not let anything happen to another one of her children. She went up to her bedroom and grabbed a revolver, rather than taking the aimless shotgun. After she had gathered everything up, she rushed back out the door and into the barn where she saddled a horse and rode off in the direction of her son.

Chapter Fifteen

Sally Houston had been taken away from her farm northwest of Dixie just three days earlier and her life would never be the same. When the attack happened, she was upstairs in her room knitting a new blanket for her father. Since the death of her mother it had only been the two of them and she did everything she could to take care of him.

Sally was seventeen and was growing into a beautiful young woman with auburn hair and the brownest eyes anyone had ever seen. The three riders she was now sitting with around a small campfire were the same three who had killed her father and taken her away south. She had been raped by all three of them and if she even tried to fight them off she was quickly slapped across the face and forced to do what she was told.

All her life she had tried to do the right thing and live by society's standards no matter how hard it was at times. Now, as she sat among the stench of the men, she was regretting her entire life. What had she done so wrong to deserve this? No matter what she did, she would never be the same and no decent man would want her for a wife after she had been ruined by these three.

Her life was pointless, she thought. What was her purpose for living now, nothing good could ever come from her now, not now that she had been violated and not once, but several times. Her dress was torn and tears ran down her dirty face as she sank into a depression. She wanted badly to run toward the western sun and never stop, hoping that by some miraculous way the sun would cleanse her of this filth she had had to endure.

Maybe, she thought, maybe sometimes we have to rise above society's expectations and do something we were taught all of our lives not to do, kill a man or three. Sure it was a sin, but then again wasn't raping a woman and killing her father no worse a sin? She looked over at the men who were getting close to becoming drunk, which would mean it would only be a matter of time before one them advanced on her, followed suit by the other two.

They were somewhere on the north side of Fort Worth and she had overheard one of the men say something about selling her once they got to town. Said people would pay a nice penny for someone like her and they could just go out and find another girl for themselves. She couldn't let that happen, not to her and not to the next girl the men would go after.

She reached her hand out and grabbed one of the careless drunk's guns who had left it sitting nearby her. All three looked up at her, but their attention span was slow due to the alcohol and none of them realized what had happened until she shot one of them in the head, the same one that had killed her father. She quickly turned the gun on another and killed him while the third man threw himself on top of her.

With the gun between them, she pulled the trigger and the bullet struck into the man's chest before coming out of his neck and entering into hers. She lie there in a growing puddle of blood and prayed for forgiveness. The man atop her rolled off to her side and she gazed up into the darkening sky, hoping that soon everything would be full of light.

Chapter Sixteen

Nat and the other men didn't have to wait long before another group of riders were approaching them from the east. Snow had started to fall pretty heavily, but once again the men prepared themselves for another ambush.

This group only consisted of about ten men and was being led by the shaggy man that had come to the farm the day before. Levi Gordon sneezed and at once the riders fired their guns into the trees in his direction. A bullet struck him in the head, four feet from where Nat was; the battle was on.

Shots echoed across the dirt road as bodies began to fall to its surface along with the snow. It was less than a minute when the day grew silent and Nat Braymyer found himself standing alone with only Allen Goldston, Jasper Knight and Thomas Riddle.

The four of them had made it through alive, but their number had been cut in half. "What are we going to do now?" Allen said looking at his fellow townsmen on the road.

Nat put a hand on his shoulder, "Allen, we've made it this far, we might as well try and finish the job."

The four men hesitantly agreed to move forward with their plan and their next stop would be Dixie. The snow was getting thicker with every minute that passed and with it came colder air. They rode at a steady pace, in no hurry to get to Dixie. Nat thought he heard a rider behind them, but the snow made it impossible to see.

As they neared the town, they could hear men talking in the distance when suddenly a rider flew by them from behind and was heading toward Dixie.

"Pa!"

Nat heard Cotton's voice holler from the horse that had just flown by. "Hiya!" He yelled at his horse in pursuit of the rider with the other men close behind. When they entered Dixie they had almost caught up with the rider, but now they were in enemy territory.

The fast moving horse stopped in the middle of Main Street where Allen Goldston's shop had been and dropped Cotton to the ground in front of a man.

"Cotton!" Nat said dismounting his horse.

"Hold it right there," the man in the street said pointing a gun in Nat's direction.

He was slightly overweight and his chaps moved a little as the winter wind blew up against him.

"Leave my son out of this!"

"Oh but why?" The man said, "Why shouldn't I kill the son of the man who wants me and my men to leave town?"

"You must be Dillon," Nat answered.

There were now four other men walking up behind him and the dismounted rider who was standing at Dillon's right side. They all had their guns drawn and pointing in the direction of Nat and his friends.

"That's right," Dillon said grabbing Cotton by the arm.

The snow was now coming down with such force that it hurt when it smashed into Nat's face. It was obvious that this snowstorm would soon turn into a blizzard, which could last for days.

"Let my boy go, Dillon. He's not apart of this."

There was a shot fired from somewhere behind Dillon and his men. Dillon and his gang looked around at each other puzzled, hinting that it was only the six of them left.

"Go see what that was," Dillon ordered, motioning to one of his men.

The chosen man walked away into the snow and shortly after hollered back. "I don't see anyone, Mack!"

"Well a gunshot don't come from nowhere!"

"Please," Nat calmly said, "Just let my son go."

Another shot was fired from somewhere in the distance. "Simon! Was that you?" Dillon shouted, never turning his head away from Nat. "You had better hope this isn't one of your tricks, Braymyer, or else…"

There was still no answer from beyond the snow. Dillon's remaining men were getting nervous as they looked into the snow. One of them looked over at Dillon, "Maybe we should just leave town, sir. It's only the five, I mean six of us left here anyway."

"Shut up!" He snapped back, "We're not going to be defeated by a group of farmers!"

The man's arm around his neck was agitating Cotton and he wiggled unsuccessfully to free himself of the grip. Dillon continued to look in Nat's direction, with his gun now to Cotton's head. Cotton started to complain and demanded the man let him go. "Shut up, boy, before I put a bullet in your head!"

Cotton was able to slightly turn his head and when he did, he bit Dillon on his forearm, causing him to curse into the air and release his hold on the boy. Cotton ran towards his father and shots broke out on Main Street. Dillon was struck in the shoulder by a bullet from Nat's gun and he took off running into the snow.

Knight and Riddle had both shot a man and Nat turned his gun to one of the two remaining. Cotton hid behind his father, wrapping his arms around Nat's left leg. Nat was hit in the left arm by one of the man's bullets before he put one of his own in the shooter's head. Allen had killed the other remaining outlaw with a shaky hand. Knight stepped over to Nat, "Are you okay?"

"Yeah, I'll be fine," he said leaning down to check on Cotton. "Let's find Dillon and finish this."

Nat kept Cotton close to his side and the men walked down the street in search of their final target. "Dillon!" Nat yelled, "Come out and be a man!"

A dark shadow was forming in the snowy air in front of them and was slowly moving closer. The men aimed their guns in its direction and patiently waited as the shadow drew nearer.

"Drop your gun, Dillon!"

"Nat?"

Out of the snow in front of them was Rosalee carrying a revolver.

"Rosie?"

They met in the middle of the street where he met her with a kiss in the same spot they had kissed on their last trip to Dixie.

"Nat, you've been shot!"

"I'm okay, darling. Here, take Cotton and go wait in the store, you'll be warm there."

"Nat, I want to stay with you. You're hurt!"

"I'll be fine, Rosie. Now go on, it will be safer for Cotton anyhow. Allen, will you go with them and keep an eye on them?"

"Yeah. No problem," he answered, relieved to be getting out of the cold.

"Nat, be careful," Rosalee said looking up into Nat's eyes, "And hurry back to us."

He kissed her again and roughly rubbed his hand across Cotton's head before they headed in the direction of the store. Nat, Riddle and Knight continued down the street in search of Dillon. Knight turned to Nat as they neared the end of the street, "Do you think he went into one of the buildings?"

"Possibly," Nat answered stepping over the man's body that Rosalee had shot in the head, "It's getting colder and I shot him in the shoulder."

As they passed a building, they would go in and check for Dillon, but they had no luck. Just before reaching the end of the street a shot was fired and struck the snowy road next to Nat. The three of them put their backs together and began searching around them as far as the snow would allow them to see.

"Come on, Dillon!" Be a man and show yourself!"

From across the street a voice answered. "Come find me, but come alone."

Nat looked at the other men and nodded his head for them to stay back before heading in Dillon's direction. He slowly crossed the street to the east side where the wounded man was waiting for him, hands at his side.

"You think you can out draw me, boy?" Dillon said laughing.

Nat put his gun in his gun belt and looked the man in his eyes, the same man who had threatened the life of his son. "You're nothing, Dillon. It's going to be a pleasure getting you out of this town and giving it back to its rightful owners."

Dillon reached for his gun, but Nat beat him to it by a second and stopped him with a bullet to the chest. Dillon fell to the ground and as he fell, the town of Dixie began to rise once again.

Chapter Seventeen

March 30, 1873

The Knight farm was one of the oldest farms in the area, just a short distance away from the busy streets of Dixie. The home sat down in a small green valley with a few pecan trees surrounding it. It was a small two story house made out of wood from the lumber yard over on Second Street and only had three rooms downstairs and two above. It had seen many years and changes of its surroundings, but it stood tall as if it had just been built.

Jasper Knight had been brought to the area by his parents when he was just a small boy and was proud to call this land home. For the past twenty years since he had turned eighteen, he made his living as a wheat farmer. He was short and solid and every feature on his body was dark, due mostly to working out in the hot sun all his life.

His wife, the former Beth Clements, was light skinned and about an inch taller than he was. The two of them had been blessed with six children, all boys and only losing one as an infant. In the wintertime it was crowded in the small home with the large family, but there was a sense of togetherness none the less.

Charlie was their youngest son at sixteen and since it was late March, Jasper and all the boys were out working the fields in preparation for the upcoming farming season. Beth was inside the stuffy house doing her annual spring cleaning now that the boys would spend most of their time outdoors and it was during this time that she felt a great sense of relief after the long winter months.

There had been a fire in the fireplace the night before and the hot ashes were still flickering on occasion as she carried a shovel full of them outside one at a time. On her third trip out the door, a small piece of red coal fell to the floor and went between the cracks of the wooden floor. Unaware of what had happened she continued to clean out the fireplace until it was completely empty.

After finishing, she went upstairs to gather some of the boy's quilts so that she could take them outside and wash them. As she emptied one of the beds, she noticed that the house was becoming very hot and just assumed that it was going to be a hot day. When she had gathered an armful of the material she headed back toward the stairs where she was met with a thick cloud of dark smoke coming up after her.

Trapped on the second floor she panicked, not knowing what to do. She quickly ran to the east window in the upstairs bedroom and opened it to look out toward the wheat fields.

"Fire!" She shouted, "The house is on fire!"

All six of the men dropped what they were doing and ran as fast as they could toward their burning home. Beth paced back and forth, trying to figure out a way to get out of the burning building. Once the men had arrived they made a steady line from the well to the house and passed buckets of water down the assembly line to try and fight the growing flames that had now engulfed the staircase inside.

Jasper ran around to the side of the house to see if there was any way he could climb up and enter into one of the windows, but there was nothing for him to grab hold of. Meanwhile, thickening smoke that continued to rise up onto the second floor was choking out Beth. She put one of the quilts up to her face to try and block some of it out, but the smoke was getting too thick.

Her eyes burned as she looked around her and tears started to force their way out of the small holes in the corners of her eyes. The smoke was causing her chest to burn and even when she tried to lean out of the window, there was too much smoke exiting out into the fresh air. She looked around her one last time and she suddenly became weak, slowly lowering herself to the smoky floor.

Outside, all the boys continued to work as hard as they could to put out the fire, but they seemed to be getting nowhere. Jasper searched desperately for a way to make it to the second floor and finally, using a hammer to dig into the old wood he slowly made it up the side of the house. Once to the open window, he threw himself into the smoky mess to find his wife lying on the floor.

He scooped her up into his arms and headed back toward the window. As he neared the square window, the floor began to give way and he fell. With one of his hands, he reached for the window seal to grab hold of, but as he did his wife's body fell into the roaring flames as he hung above her.

He screamed as loud as he could for his wife, but he knew there was nothing he could do now, she was probably already dead when he had scooped her up. He pulled himself back up through the window and threw himself out, breaking one of his legs and arms. He laid there and didn't care about the pain, he deserved it he thought.

There was no way to fight the fire, it had gained too much strength and soon the entire house was falling to the ground on which it had been built so many years before. When there was nothing but ash left Beth's sons searched the mess for any sign of her and all they were able to find was the blue broach she had been wearing that day.

Chapter Eighteen

June 21, 2010

I sat in the cockpit and looked around at all the buttons and levers as the steward took a seat next to me.

"Sir, does any of this look familiar to you?"

"Uh, sure, I think my friend played a game on his PlayStation that looked something like this."

I could finally see the worry on her face as she realized I was telling the truth when I said I knew nothing about planes. I looked out of the windows in front of me as we sliced through the white clouds in the blue sky, hoping this wouldn't be the last scenery I would ever see.

"Here," she said handing me a pair of headphones, "Put this on. The air traffic should be able to talk to you and walk you through what you need to do."

I put them on my head and buckled up as tight as the safety belt would allow. A voice came through the headset telling me to remain calm and that everything was going to be ok and that they appreciated me stepping forward and taking charge.

What was I supposed to do? I thought, *let the plane crash!*

"Pull the red lever back, this will take it off auto pilot."

"Uh, do I want it off auto pilot?"

"Yes, sir, that is the only way you will be able to land..."

I reached for the lever and as I did my knuckle punched in a yellow button.

Over the intercom a computerized voice said, "Please remain buckled, we are crash landing."

Oh Crap. I could hear people throughout the plane start to shout and scream. "Oops, wrong button?"

"It's okay, sir, just pull the lever back and follow the instructions I give to you. We will have this plane landed in no time."

Yeah, but in one piece, I thought. The steward next to me had her head down and started praying, often times repeating the same sentence over and over, "Please God protect us…"

I placed my hand on the lever and hesitated.
One…Two…Three… I pulled.

The plane wobbled and rocked a little bit and I was now in control of not only the plane, but of the lives of everyone on board. *Oh boy, it's going to be a bumpy ride.*

The voice on the headset continued to direct me to do different things and said we would be landing shortly, once we got into a rural area. I looked over at the steward who had taken a break from her prayer. "So, how exactly did we get into this mess?"

"Someone poisoned the pilots before they boarded the plane. According to their symptoms, it was some kind of delayed release chemical. At least that's what the nurse on board said."

The headset was becoming overtaken by static and I could barely hear what the man on the other end was saying.

"Go…take…pull…down…up…over…"

"Ah great," I muttered out loud, "This day just keeps getting better."

And the praying continued…

Chapter Nineteen

April 07, 1875

Charlie Knight rode steadily along the dirt road towards Preston, a small settlement that had once been a trading post along the Red River. At eighteen, he was probably one of the stoutest boys from Dixie, but hidden behind his farmer's muscle he had a heart of gold.

He only stood about five foot seven, but there was no doubt that he could handle his own if need be. He had bright red hair and freckles scattered across his face among his green eyes. He was handsome in his own way, but had no interest in settling down and marrying, this made him different from almost every other boy his age.

He was heading to Preston to visit with his mother's sister and her family and to help them out on the farm since they had no sons of their own. It would be a nice change for him to get away and see a little bit of the world, even if it was only a few miles away.

The sun was brightly shining down upon him and his black mare as he neared Basin Springs, a small farming community in the middle of no where. A breeze slightly shook the tops of the nearby trees alongside the rode, but it was not strong enough for him to feel it as he rode down the old trail. When he was about a mile away from the town, he heard a voice shouting, "Help! Please Help me!"

He tightened up the reins on his horse and turned to his right to see what was going on. A young teenage girl was running through the wheat field heading his way, shouting as loud as she could. She couldn't have been more than sixteen and her brown hair was flowing every which way as she ran toward Charlie.

"Please, sir, please help me," she said as she walked up to him.

"Easy there, little lady. Calm down. What's the matter?"

"It's my Ma and Pa. They're stuck in the well! Please help us!"

Charlie helped the young lady up onto his horse and rode swiftly through the field toward the distressed farm. "How did they get in the well?"

"Pa was digging it and he passed out so Ma went in after him, but the rope fell in with her. Please you've got to do something."

"Just hang tight little lady, we'll get them out just fine. Which way?"

"Straight ahead over on top of that hill over there among the trees."

When they arrived at their destination, Charlie could vaguely hear a woman's plead for help. He quickly dismounted his horse and grabbed the rope from the side of his saddle and headed toward the hole in the ground. "Can you hear me down there?"

An echoed whisper replied softly, "Yes…please help."

"Hold tight, I'm going to get you out."

Charlie tied one end of the rope around a nearby tree and the other end around his waist. He tied a bandanna around his face to keep from breathing in the carbon monoxide as he slowly lowered himself into the dark hole. His boots stuck to the muddy walls and the back of his shirt became sticky and wet as he neared the bottom.

Once he had reached the bottom he could feel two bodies in the darkness. He had no light and didn't want to use a kerosene lamp for fear of causing an explosion. He nudged at the bodies, but there was no response. He scooped up the woman first and threw her across his shoulder as he gasped for fresh air.

He gradually made his way up the hole, which took three times longer than the decent. Once he had emerged in the sunlight once again he pushed the woman's body onto the surface and stopped for a moment to get some air before descending back into the hole.

The young girl ran over to her mother, terrified at the blackness of her body. Charlie proceeded back down into the well for the last victim. He took small steady breaths, forcing his lungs to accept every bit of power the oxygen provided. When he reached the bottom again, he struggled to put the man's body across his shoulder, which took all of what little breath he had out of his body.

 He strained to shimmy his way back up the hole with the large man on his shoulder. As he neared the light he pushed the man's body with all his might out of the hole and onto the ground somewhere above him. Using the rope to pull himself up out of the hole, he slowly emerged into the light, but then things went terribly wrong.

The rope had had too much pressure on it and just in front of the tree where it was tied off, the rope snapped sending Charlie Knight back into the dark hole one last time. His body twisted and turned and banged up along the walls as he flew down to the bottom of the pit. Just before reaching the bottom his ankle twisted along the muddy walls and he could hear it snap. He was in excruciating pain, but because of the way it twisted, he was stopped just before hitting the bottom. He was sitting straight up in the air, his back along one side of the wall and his twisted ankle and good foot on the other.

He tried to gasp at the pain in his ankle, but there was no oxygen to be had anywhere. He resorted back to small breaths, which seemed to intensify the pain he was having. Using his back and one leg he shimmed his way upward along the muddy walls towards the girl's voice that was shouting for him.

He didn't have the breath to answer her so he concentrated on making it out of the well alive instead. With each step he made upward, the pain got a little worse and his small breaths became more and more frequent. The voice was getting closer above him, but he didn't even bother to look up. He looked straight ahead at the muddy dirt across from him and focused on slamming his boot as hard as he could into the wall as he moved upward.

It seemed like days that he pushed himself up out of that well. He continued onward and upward with more adrenaline pumping through his body than he had ever experienced. As he continued through his pain, he felt a hand on his shoulder and was relieved that he had almost made it to the top. With one last kick of his good foot, he threw himself onto the grassy ground beside the two dead bodies he had just pulled out, thankful that he was not the third.

Chapter Twenty

August 15, 1880

Indian Territory

Nine year old Brice Braymyer had been renamed long ago by the Comanche Indians that had abducted him. White Indian Boy had been brought up by a well respected couple, Runs with Sticks and Cloudy Star, who could not have children of their own. They were good to the boy, but most of the other members of the tribe treated him poorly.

Brice knew no English and for the most part knew nothing about his white family. All he had ever been told was that a lone Indian had taken him and when the Indian was killed, the baby was brought to the tribe where he was adopted. He had turned out to be a great hunter and helped supply the tribe with all sorts of food, which especially helped them during the wintertime when game was scarce.

Brice, like most of his tribe members, rode a tall paint horse and knew that without his horse companion, he would be nothing. The sun shone brightly down on him as he rode across the prairie, observing his surroundings to see if there was anything he could gather up that the tribe could use.

As he topped a hill he came face to face with four army riders who were as startled as he was upon their approach. "Hey, Dave," one of them said to the leader, "That Injun's white!"

White Indian Boy turned his horse and flew off toward the eastern horizon, hoping his people would hear him whooping and yelling. The four officers were hot on his trail as they rode bigger and faster horses and within 5 minutes of chasing, the white Indian was wrapped in a rope from the youngest of the riders.

They pulled him down to the ground and hog-tied him to keep him from getting away. "Do you know English, boy?"

The Indian looked at them with his blue eyes, puzzled at their noises. "English! Do you know?"

He continued to stare at them.

The young rider looked at him puzzled and then turned to the captain of the gang, "Where do you think he came from?"

"He was likely kidnapped when he was younger and probably doesn't even know he's white."

White Indian Boy remained silent, wondering what these pale skinned riders were going to do to him.

Another rider spoke up next, "Dave, do you know of any children that are missing?"

"Only, one. But hell that's been almost ten years ago. I think the name was Braymyer or something of that sort."

The young one took a closer look at the Indian, "What do you think we should do with him? Take him to town and see if a family can identify him?"

"That would probably be the worst thing we could do for the family. Even if he was their child and we returned him, he would just run away and hurt them more. He's been wild too long, it's better off if the family just assume he's dead."

The group of men looked down on White Indian Boy with sympathy and shook their heads. The captain cut the rope away from him and the lone White Indian took off across the prairie.

Down by Dixie

June 28, 1884

Well folks, it's been another hot week here in Dixie and it seems that the temperature just continues to rise. My daughter, Abigail will be having her 16th birthday party this coming Saturday at the Baptist church. I hope you can all make it out, even if you are of the Methodist faith. There will be plenty of lemonade and Cotton Braymyer has agreed to play some tunes on his fiddle.

Mr. George Knight was married Friday last to Mrs. Peggy Riddle. The nineteen-year-old groom a son of Jasper Knight and the eighteen year old bride a daughter of Tom Riddle. We wish the two of you all the best.

If you haven't had a chance to make it over to the store be sure and stop by and see them. Henry Wilcox, storeowner, has just received a new order of fabric.

Sheriff Nat Braymyer informs us that things are looking mighty fine in Dixie. He says he has not had to make an arrest in two months, the last arrest being that of Margaret Gordon who threatened to shoot her husbands private parts off if he didn't wash his hands before supper.

The Dixie Methodist church will be putting on a play next month about the founding of America. I hope to see you all there.

Allen Goldston

Chapter Twenty One

Cotton Braymyer walked down the country road heading towards Dixie. He was barefoot and wore his signature straw hat while chewing on a piece of wheat. He was by far the most popular sixteen-year-old in that part of Texas. He was strong, good looking and was not shy in any way, shape or form. All the girls around wanted to spend time with him and most dreamed about one day becoming Mrs. Cotton Braymyer.

His parents, Nat and Rosalee had become admired by everyone around and were respected by anyone that knew them. After his father had ran Dillon's gang out of town, he became not only one of the most successful farmers around, but the sheriff of Dixie.

Nat and his wife now had two more children besides Cotton and his sister, Mary Lee. Seven year old Nathaniel John, Jr. and five year old Addie Leona. Nat had modified their house by building the outside out of white limestone, strengthening it against the spring storms.

Cotton continued down the road with the July sun beating down on the back of his tan neck. His father was at the sheriff's station and his mother had sent him to tell him that dinner would be ready early. It wasn't important news, but Rosalee knew how much Cotton liked going to town so she gave him any reason she could.

When he arrived in Dixie, the town was bustling with people of all sorts, most of whom stopped to talk to Cotton. It was Friday, so Main Street was filled with everyone as they visited with each other and went about their business. Cotton watched everyone as he took the long way to his father's building.

"Cotton!"

Abigail Goldston was running up to him. Abigail was one of the prettier girls of the town and she was head over heals when it came to Cotton.

"Hi, Abigail. How's everything going?"

"Cotton Braymyer, don't talk to me like I'm a stranger. What brings you to town?" She said as she walked alongside Cotton.

"Ma sent me to fetch Pa and tell him dinner will be ready soon."

"Oh I see. Well, are you still going to come over to the church tomorrow and play your fiddle for my birthday party?"

"Yes, maim. Any special tunes you want to hear?"

"Well, I like Oh! Susannah and Dixie land, but Happy Birthday will do just fine."

Cotton continued to watch the people of Dixie, barely hearing what Abigail was saying. "Cotton, are you listening to a word I'm saying?"

"Huh? Oh, yeah, Abigail, I hear you…"

She laughed and knew he didn't mean to ignore her. "Well, Cotton Braymyer, I've got to get home so I can get supper ready for Pa and I."

"Oh, okay. Bye Abigail."

Cotton was nearing the sheriff building when Abigail left his side. He stepped up onto the small platform in front of the building and went in. Nat was sitting behind a desk with his feet propped up on top of it. "Hey son, what are you doing here?"

"Hey, Pa, Ma sent me to tell you that dinner will be ready soon," he answered as he looked around the room.

"Sounds good to me."

"Oh, Pa. I saw two hogs on my way to town today and yesterday when I was at the creek I saw a bunch of tracks. I thought maybe we could go hunting on Sunday on account that tomorrow is Abigail's birthday party."

"Sure, son. That sounds like a good idea to me."

Cotton picked up one of the rifles from the gun rack and sized it up. "Pa, when can I become one of your deputies?"

Nat laughed a little bit, "Well, son, maybe next year when you turn 18. You ready to head to the house?"

"Sure, Pa, but I need to run by the store and get some liquorice for Nathan and Addie."

"Ok, you run and do that and I'll meet you outside and we can walk home together."

"Ok, Pa. See you in a minute."

Cotton went to the store and got the candy for his brother and sister and then met his father outside his office. The sun was halfway hidden behind the horizon when they got to their house.

The next day Cotton put on his good clothes and boots, grabbed his fiddle and saddled up his brown mare. He was off to Abigail's party and most everyone in town would be there.

It was mid morning when he rode into town and up to the Baptist church and people were already starting to gather in the churchyard. A group of his fishing buddies were standing in a circle talking and he quickly joined them where he became the center of attention.

All the boys, both his age, younger and even a little older looked up to Cotton and wanted to be like him in every way possible. At first, it was mostly the younger people who had shown up, but shortly before noon adults and families began rolling in, including the Braymyers.

The people of Dixie were always looking for a reason to get together and celebrate and Abigail's birthday would allow them to do just that. With the exception of very few people, almost everyone in and around Dixie was there. The town's population had been steadily increasing ever since Dillon was killed and the total population was now estimated to be somewhere around 300 bodies.

As Cotton continued to stand in the circle of friends, an occasional girl would stop by and tell him hi. At exactly twelve o'clock, Allen Goldston stood up on a small wooden platform that had been created for the event to get everyone's attention.

"I want to thank everyone for coming out today and I want to thank the Lord for this fine weather we're having."

Allen motioned toward Cotton, who began making his way to the makeshift stage.

"And now, the finest fiddle player in the Dixie area, at only sixteen years old, Cotton Braymyer. Who'll be playing us some tunes!"

There were claps and cheers as an unbashful Cotton stepped up with a smile and a special wave to his younger siblings and Abigail. The sun reflected off of his dirty blonde hair and his blue eyes stared out to the crowd.

At a little over six feet tall, Cotton stood over the audience and began to play. He started with Happy Birthday, where everyone sang along, followed by his made up second verse:

> And Abigail Goldston's getting older,
>
> Look out boys here she comes,
>
> For the finest woman in Dixie,
>
> Is almost marrying age.

There was another round of applause before Cotton started his next tune, Oh! Susanna:

I came from Alabama, wid a banjo on my knee.

I'm gwyne to Louisiana, my true love for to see.

It rain'd all nigh the day I left, the weather it was dry.

The sun so hot I froze to death; Susanna don't you cry.

Oh! Susanna, Oh don't you cry for me,

Cos' I've come from Alabama, wid my banjo on my knee.

Before giving the crowd a chance to applaud him, he jumped right into Dixie land:

I wish I was in the land of cotton,

Old times they are not forgotten;

Look away! Look away! Look away! Dixie Land.

In Dixie Land where I was born,

Early on one frosty mornin,

Look Away! Look Away! Look Away! Dixie land.

Then I wish I was in Dixie, hooray! hooray!

In Dixie Land I'll take my stand to live and die in Dixie.

Away, away, away down South in Dixie,

Away, away, away down South in Dixie.

After Cotton finished playing, the crowd gave him a final long applause. He bowed down, enjoying every bit of the attention and then jumped down from the stage where he was met with a hug from Abigail.

"That was wonderful, Cotton, thank you so much."

"Awe, it was nothing, Abbie." Cotton replied looking down at her five foot six body.

"I like that," she said.

"Huh? Like what?"

"You called me, Abbie. I like it."

Cotton laughed a little, "Well, Miss. Abbie Goldston, might I share your birthday lunch with you?'

"Why, Mr. Braymyer, that sounds like a swell idea to me."

The two of them made a plate of food and then searched for a place to enjoy it. They walked over to one of the few crowdless areas of the churchyard where Abbie laid out a quilt for them to sit on.

The sun was warm and everyone at the birthday party seemed to be having a good time. Occasionally Cotton would get a glimpse of one his buddies making a funny love face in his direction.

Abbie sat as close to Cotton as she could without being unlady like. They took their time eating the Texas barbecue and enjoyed every bit of each other's company. "Cotton," Abbie said, breaking the silence, "Do you ever think about marriage?"

"Marriage?"

"Yes, silly. Marriage as in a man and…"

"I know what marriage is, Abbie, but no I don't guess I've given it much thought. I think more about running Pa's farm or becoming one of his deputies."

"Well, those are all good things, Cotton, but don't you think you'll need a woman to take care of you? To cook and clean and such and of course to have children with someday."

"Well I guess so. I just haven't really thought about it."

"Well, Cotton, I think you'd make a good husband. You're smart, hardworking and I haven't seen you lose your temper not once."

A small breeze blew through, making Abbie's brown hair flow like waves in the sun. The breeze also helped relieve some of Cotton's discomfort over the subject that they had been discussing.

"And you'd make a good wife, Abbie. I reckon you would make any boy happy. Say, isn't Phillip Thomas kind of sweet on you?"

"Cotton Braymyer! Don't you ever mention that name in my presence again! Why, he is the absolute rudest, hateful and most unclean person I have ever met!"

Cotton couldn't help but laugh a little, but quickly stopped when Abbie gave him a serious look. "Awe, sorry, Abbie. I was just fooling."

Abbie let a small smile slip from her closed lips. "So, who are you sweet on these days, Cotton? Seems like every girl around wants to spend time with you."

"No one in particular. Like I said, I haven't thought much about it."

The churchyard slowly became emptier as the streets of Dixie began to fill up once again. Everyone walked by Abbie to give her birthday wishes when they left until it was only the young people again.

Abbie moved a little closer to Cotton. "Cotton, do you want to come have supper with Pa and I sometime?"

"Sure, I'd love to," he said a little confused as he frequently ate dinner with them, but this invitation seemed different somehow.

"Well, I've got to get going. I am meeting some girls at my house for tea. Thanks again for playing your fiddle today."

"Sure, it was no problem," he said with his hands hanging over his bent knees. "Here, I'll help you get your quilt."

"It's okay, Cotton. You sit on it for awhile an you can bring it when you come for supper."

"Gee thanks, Abbie."

As Abbie was getting up she leaned in and kissed Cotton on the cheek. Before he had a chance to say anything, she was gone, somewhere across town. Cotton's insides grew weak and he didn't know what to think. He hadn't thought of any girls in that special way, he was just having fun, but if he were to choose, Abbie was just as good as any of them.

She may even be better, he thought. She could cook, clean and she had been taking care of her father since she was young. So at sixteen he had been kissed and the only thing on his mind was a burning question, "What do I do next?"

Chapter Twenty Two

Nat Braymyer sat in his office early on a Wednesday morning and enjoyed a hot cup of coffee as the citizens of Dixie began making their way out into the open streets. Their voices began ringing out throughout town and cutting through the peaceful silence of the morning time.

He finished the last bit of his drink and then hopped to his feet. Standing in front of a large mirror, he straightened his badge, put his suede cowboy hat on and positioned his gun belt just right to where it hung down slightly. Once he was satisfied with his appearance he stepped out into the warm morning sun and made his way south down Main Street.

He stopped at every other building he passed as people talked to him and asked about his family and such. As he approached the lumber yard the smell of freshly cut pinewood filled the air and caused him to stop for a moment and take in the relaxing scent. From the other side of the building he thought he heard a man and a woman arguing over something.

When he made it to the small alleyway where the commotion was coming from he saw Felix Adams holding a knife in the direction of Marietta Brawl who was standing directly across from him. Nat rushed up on the scene, "Hey, what's going on here?"

"I'm gonna' cut this woman, she done stabbed me in the hand!"

Marietta Brawl was focused in on Felix's eyes and showed no sign of fear. Dixie had no Saloon, but if it had had one you can guarantee that Miss Brawl would have been the girl upstairs. She had been orphaned as a young child and had basically raised herself just outside of town. She had brown hair and a combination of blue and green eyes.

"Marietta, is this true," Nat said stepping closer.

"Sure is. The pig tried to get frisky with me and if you ask me, pigs and sheep should never mix."

Felix Adams stood there with his left wounded hand down to his side and his shaky right hand in the air with the knife still pointed at now both Marietta and Nat. The smell of whiskey could be smelt twenty feet away as it rose off of his body.

"Felix, let's say we get you to Doc. Ruyle and let him have a look at your hand?"

"No! I'm gonna' cut me this woman!"

"Now, no one is cutting anybody today. I will take Miss Brawl to the Sheriff building with me and have a little talk with her.

Felix was getting mad and his whole body began to shake. "I said, NO!"

At this point, Marietta was getting a little uneasy at the drunken man's refusal to put the knife down. She slowly pushed herself in Nat's direction who was standing just to her left. Once close enough she put herself behind Nat slowly so that Felix wouldn't lose his temper again.

"Now, Felix," Nat said, "Just put the knife down and let's go see Doc."

"I said NO, Braymyer!" In a quick motion, Felix threw the knife at the slim shoulder of Marietta's that was sticking out from behind Nat. The knife flipped through the air as it made it's way toward them and embedded itself into Nat's right shoulder.

Down by Dixie

August 15, 1884

Our beloved sheriff was stabbed in the shoulder when Felix Adams threw a knife at his estranged lover, Marietta Brawl. Sheriff Braymyer tells us that Miss Brawl was standing behind him when the knife was thrown. Luckily Braymyer's wound was not bad enough that Doc. Ruyle couldn't fix him up. The Sheriff took Adams to the jailhouse and he is still there until they can figure out what to do with him. Marietta Brawl left town shortly after the incident and has not been seen since. Good job, Sheriff and get well soon.

We have a new neighbor over here on Main Street. Anna Belle Brown has started her own restaurant because she said the food at the current one is just too greasy. She says that if you would like some healthier food then to come on over and see her, she promises it will not make you spend an hour in the outhouse like the food from her competition. She also says to tell Oscar Turnbourgh, the current owner of the restaurant on Riddle Street, that she means no offense by opening up a new one, but men should stick to the fields and stay out of the kitchen! Oh Ben, what are we going to do with your wife?

The widower, Jasper Knight married yesterday to Keziah Cook. We wish you both the best of luck.

Allen Goldston

Chapter Twenty Three

The next two months flew by for Cotton and Abbie as they spent every extra moment they could together. Most of the time they would spend their days swimming and having picnics at the old creek that ran through the Braymyer farm.

Occasionally Cotton's younger siblings would join them and they would spend the entire day down there. Now that Cotton had shown a special interest in Abbie, all the girls were jealous, but it didn't stop them from trying to spend some time with him.

Abbie was not a jealous person, in fact it made her feel good that Cotton had chosen her. It was a perfect match since their fathers were friends and the fact that Rosalee was like her mother.

When October came they were not able to spend as much time together. Since his father was busy in town as sheriff, Cotton was in charge of overseeing the farm and October was harvest time. He worked day and night to ensure everything was done perfectly. Nat had hired some laborers to help out and even though Cotton was only about to be seventeen, he was in charge of them.

After a few weeks the harvest was over and Cotton felt a great sense of relief. There would be a good profit that year and most importantly, his father would be proud. Of course, Abbie was glad that she would now get to spend more time with Cotton again.

It was a Saturday morning and Abbie was in the kitchen with Rosalee preparing as much food as the kitchen could yield. Tonight would be the annual Braymyer Harvest party, which would also celebrate Cotton's birthday. Nat had not gone to town that day and instead stayed home so him and Cotton could go hunting.

The two of them walked along the creek bank with their rifles over their right shoulder. The weather had slightly gotten colder, so all the animals were on the move.

"You did a good job on the harvest, son. Looks like we'll make a good profit this year."

"Thanks, Pa."

"You know, you're seventeen now and you've become a good man."

"Thanks, Pa. So does this mean I get to become one of your deputies?"

Nat grinned, "Maybe, son. So how about you and Abbie?"

Cotton blushed, "Me and Abbie?"

"Yes, *you and Abbie*. How are things going?"

"Okay I guess, Pa. She keeps talking about getting married and stuff though."

"Ha. Son, women talk about getting married their whole lives. Besides, why wouldn't Abbie make a good wife?"

"Oh no, Pa, it's not that. She'd make a fine wife, but where would we live? I don't have any land of my own or a job. I wouldn't be able to support her is all."

"Well, son, I wanted to talk to you about that. Your Ma and I have been thinking about moving into town…"

"Into town? But what about the farm?"

"Well, when you settle down and get married, we want you to take over the farm and keep it in the family."

"Really, Pa?"

"Yes. Being the Sheriff doesn't leave much time for farming, son, and you've proved yourself worthy."

The two of them continued hunting for wild game, but Cotton's mind was lost in a dream. Now he had a future, a plan and he thought of nothing else. It was late afternoon when they arrived back at the house. Nathan and Addie were playing in the yard and the smell of good food Rosalee, Abbie and Mary Lee were cooking could be smelled clear outside.

Wagons began driving up a couple of hours before nightfall and the party began. There was lots of music and couples turned the front yard into a dance floor, including Cotton and Abbie. There were people everywhere and they all seemed to be having a good time. Laughter and good times from the Braymyer farm could be heard miles away.

Cotton grabbed Abbie's hand and led her around the back of the house. Once they were alone he held her in his arms and gave her a long kiss.

"Abbie, do you still think I'd make a good husband?"

"Of course, Cotton. Why?"

"Because if I can get your Pa's permission, I'd like to marry you."

Abbie leaped into his arms and kissed him again. "Oh, Cotton! Really?"

"Of course, Abbie. I love you."

"Come on, Cotton. Let's go find Pa right now and ask him," she said taking his hand and leading him in through the back of the house.

Allen Goldston was standing in the dining room with a small group of men when Abbie walked in, leaving Cotton in the hallway. "Abbie, what are you doing in here? You should be out having fun."

"Pa, can I see you in the other room for a minute?"

They stepped out into the hallway where Cotton was waiting. He stood there tall and didn't seem to be nervous at all.

"Pa, Cotton has something he would like to ask you…"

"What is it, Cotton?"

"Well, sir. My Ma and Pa are going to be moving into town and I'm to run the farm now."

"Well that's good news, Cotton my boy."

"Yes, sir, Mr. Goldston, it is. Sir, if it'd be alright with you, I'd like to marry your daughter."

Allen looked at the two of them and then over at Abbie. "Is this what you want, Abigail?"

"More than anything, Pa."

Allen smiled and then reached out to shake Cotton's hand. I couldn't think of anyone better. You have my blessing."

"Thank you, sir."

Abbie ran up and hugged her father and then took Cotton by the hand once again and went back outside. Abbie first drug Cotton to all her friends to tell them the news. Word spread fast throughout the party and soon everyone was talking.

"Hey, Abbie," Cotton said stopping her, "Don't you think we should go tell Ma and Pa?"

"Oh, of course! I can't believe I didn't do that first!"

Nat and Rosalee were on the front porch enjoying the music when the young couple approached them with the news. They were both thrilled and Rosalee and Abbie hugged for a long time.

The Texas sky was clear and full of stars as the party continued into the night. Braymyer's Hill was full of joy and it seemed that life would continue to bless the place with life.

Cotton and Abbie's parents, along with the two of them at their side stood atop the front porch and looked out at the crowd. Allen ordered the music to stop and got everyone's attention.

"I don't mean to interrupt the party, but the Braymyers and I have an announcement we would like to make. Our children, Cotton and Abbie are now engaged to be married!"

People started cheering and hollering and more music erupted into the night sky to celebrate the beginning of a couple's new life. The celebration continued on into the night until it was interrupted by a shot fired from the front porch.

Nat, Rosalee, Cotton and Abbie were on the porch beside each other with another man holding a gun that no one recognized. He held the gun to Abbie's head.

"Now," he said, "If any of you want to see this couple wed, you're going to do exactly what I say." He turned to Nat, "I want all your money from the harvest you just had. People over in Dexter say you did mighty well."

Before Nat had a chance to tell him that he would give him the money, an arrow struck the man in the stomach. He fell to the porch and everyone turned to see a white Indian boy who had approached them from behind.

Everything remained quiet until he struggled to spit out a few English words. "That…bad man."

Nat stepped off of the porch with Rosalee close behind, but by the time they had neared the peculiar Indian, he was already amount his horse. And although they didn't know it, the lone white Indian that had just saved their lives was in fact their son whom they had thought died as an infant. White Indian Boy rode his horse in the direction he had come from, never to be seen by them again.

127

Down by Dixie

November 01, 1884

Mystery Man

What appeared to be a "white" Indian showed up at the annual Braymyer Harvest Party. He was responsible for killing the man who held my daughter at gunpoint. If you have any information about him, please let us know. The Braymyers and I would like to thank him.

Julius Gibson was in Dixie the other day from Sherman. He was here visiting his brother, John.

Sandusky has built them a new store and they report that thus far business couldn't be any better. This will help a lot of folks who live out that way so that they will not have to travel so far to get supplies any more.

Bachelor, Charlie Knight has just moved out to the old Nelson farm to run his own farm. Ladies, I would say he would be quite a catch for your daughters, especially since the esteemed bachelor Cotton Braymyer is now off the market.

Allen Goldston

Chapter Twenty Four

June 21, 2010

"So you're telling me that the town of Dixie was almost destroyed and Nat Braymyer stopped it?"

"Yes, your honor," the elder Nathan said adjusting himself in his wheelchair.

One of the young attorneys seemed to be getting agitated that the judge was showing interest in the man's story. "Your honor, haven't we heard enough of this old man's story?"

The judge looked in his direction, "Mr. Donihoo, this house and this family in particular were very instrumental to the town of Dixie, whether its citizens know it or not. Mr. Sanders, did Nat and Rosalee ever move into town? I mean, why would they want to give up their successful farm and a large house to just move three miles away into town?"

"Because it was their son, your honor. Nat and Rosalee thought the world of their children and wanted to supply them with everything they could."

"What about their other three children? Did he not give them any part of the home place?"

"Cotton was the oldest son. It was his responsibility to carry on what his father began. When his other children married he provided for them accordingly. His younger son, Nathan had no interest in farming. So rather than giving him some land, he bought him a house in Whitesboro where he became a successful lawyer."

"I see. So did Nat and Rosalee move to town or did something happen?"

"Oh, heavens yes. Now let's see if I can remember correctly…"

Down by Dixie

November 17, 1884

Well, my fellow Dixie neighbors, the town is a lot safer than ever before. Sheriff Braymyer and his family have moved into town over on First Street. His son, Cotton Braymyer who married my daughter, Abbie, Saturday last, will be running the farm. Welcome to town Sheriff!

The temperature sure is getting colder for this time of the year, looks like we may be in for a hard winter this year. I haven't seen a bird in the sky for some time now, it looks like they've all gone south.

I was sure sorry to get the news yesterday that the elderly mother of Jasper Knight passed away. Tabitha Knight was 96 and had been a long time resident of Dixie. She will be missed greatly.

The town continues to grow. Tom Riddle's nephew, George Peters has opened up a photography studio on Riddle Street. I went by yesterday and got my photo taken, he did a real fine job.

Allen Goldston

Chapter Twenty Five

The first snow fell in early December and it lasted almost two weeks. It had been a long time since people had seen snow like that in the area. Everything was covered in a thick blanket of white and occasionally the wind would blow so hard that it made it impossible to go outdoors.

Cotton and Abbie stayed warm in the front sitting room of their home as they watched the second round of snowfall in mid January. They passed the slow winter days by discussing their plans and their future together. It didn't take long for the two of them to grow accustomed to married life. They would be parents sometime that summer, so there was a lot to do in preparation.

Cotton got up from his chair and walked towards Abbie. "I've got to go feed the horses and cows, I'll be right back," he said kissing her on the forehead.

He stepped onto the back porch where the northern wind rushed upon him. The barn was only thirty feet or so from the house, but the blowing snow made it impossible for him see.

The week before he had tied a rope from the house to the barn so he wouldn't get lost in the white out conditions like he was seeing now. He grabbed a hold of the rope and slowly made his way through the thickening snow. When he finally reached the barn, he had ice frozen to his ears and eyebrows. Once inside he paused for a moment to blow his breath into his hands.

He quickly took care of the animals and gave them enough hay for two days. After everything was finished and he was satisfied, he went back out into the cold towards the house. The wind was howling and blowing with extreme force when he stepped out of the barn. Everything, including the air around him was solid white, making it hard for him to see even his hands. He moved slowly, clinging to the rope with both hands.

The wind continued to push against him, knocking him down to his knees at times. He used the rope to pull himself back up and as he did, he felt the rope loosen. He knew immediately that the rope had come untied from the house. He went back to his knees, letting the rope fall to the snowy ground.

On his hands and knees, Cotton followed the rope toward the house. He only hoped that it had not fallen too far away. It seemed like hours that he crawled through the snow, sinking deeper and deeper into its depth. He finally reached the end of the rope, but there was no house.

In a moment of desperation he fell into the snow, fully aware that he would probably freeze to death. Then, somewhere in the howling wind, he thought he heard his name being called, but he couldn't be certain.

The rope was still attached to the barn somewhere behind him so he grabbed it and stood up. He started walking to his right with what little energy he had left, knowing that the tightened rope would only go as far as the house. He continued searching for the house and the voice he thought was calling his name, but there was nothing. The rope was as tight as it could possibly be and it was the only thing holding him up until finally giving way.

Cotton fell face first into the snow holding a useless piece of rope in his hands. Adrenaline pumped through his body with every beat of his heart and it forced him to get to his feet and push forward. He walked in the direction that he thought the house was supposed to be in, but he couldn't find any sign of it.

As the snow continued to take over his body, he wandered the land that he knew like the back of his hand, but he was getting nowhere. Suddenly he came to a stop when he hit his head on something. He swayed back and forth in the roaring blizzard for a minute and then put his hands on the object that he had hit. It was one of the cottonwood trees that his mother had planted lining the driveway.

Like the land, he knew every detail of every tree around his house. He ran his hands up and down and back and forth along the tree, feeling for anything that might give a hint as to which tree this was. With his hands as high as they could possibly go, he felt a small knot protruding out of the trunk. Just as he had thought to begin with, this was the third tree away from the house on the opposite side.

He took in a deep breath of the chilling air and gathered just a little bit more strength so that he might try one last time to get out of this storm. He moved very slowly and cautiously across the driveway and found the tree directly across from the one he had just observed. He moved west, knowing that the knot on the other tree faced east, toward the road. Within a matter of seconds he reached the next tree and then the next where he stopped for a moment.

Once at the last tree he used his hands to observe its trunk. He was looking for a small bald spot where he and his father had carved "B R A Y M Y E R" a few years before. It should be about eye level, he thought and continued to feel for it. He wrapped is arms completely around the tree and sure enough he felt the inscription on the other side, which meant he was on the west side of the tree.

With his back to the tree he placed both his hands behind him, flat against the trunk. In one swift movement he gave himself a hard push to keep the wind from swaying him and took off running northeast toward where the house should be. He continued to run as his eyes began to collect ice in all their small cracks. At last he hit the front porch with his right shin at a full run. He fell to the ground, but quickly got to his feet as he knew he was almost there. He climbed up onto the porch and went straight ahead where he hit the wall of the house.

Following the house with the guide of his hands he made his way to the front door and threw both of them open. He pushed himself inside and instead of everything being white, it all went black.

Cotton woke up in his bed with several quilts on top of him. He slowly opened his eyes and saw Abbie sitting in a chair near the fireplace.

"Abbie?"

"Cotton! You're awake!" she said jumping out of the chair.

"How long have I been asleep?"

"Just since yesterday. Are you feeling okay? Do you need anything? Oh, Cotton, I thought I lost you."

"I'm okay, darling. I'm mighty hungry though."

Abbie hurried down to the kitchen to get him some food and was right back upstairs by his side. Cotton stayed in bed the rest of the day with Abbie at his side. "Abbie, won't you bring me my fiddle?"

She went over to the other side of the room to where his fiddle was and brought it back to him. Cotton began to play:

When I left my eastern home, a bachelor so gay

To try and win my way to wealth and fame,

I little thought that I'd wind-up burning twisted hay

In the little old sod shanty on my claim

Oh the hinges are of leather and the windows have no glass

And the board roof lets the howling blizzard in;

And I hear the hungry coyot' as he slinks up in the grass

'Round my little old sod shanty on my claim

The couple slept nice and warm that night and didn't wake up until the next afternoon when the snow had already begun to melt.

Chapter Twenty Six

June 21, 2010

Two middle aged surveyors arrived at the old Braymyer home just after noon and were setting up their equipment. The two attorneys Mr. Sanders was fighting had hired the two men to come out and survey the land since they were sure to win their case.

They took their measurements and walked around the old farm looking at all the old buildings. "You know," the older of the two said, "It's a shame their gonna tear down this old place. As old as this house is, it looks about as good as the White House."

"Yeah, but people want stores and country clubs, not old houses."

They continued to walk around the peaceful place and took more joy in looking around than they did writing down all their data. The older one walked up to the cottonwood nearest the house along the drive and ran his fingers across what looked to have been something written. He used is pointer finger as if it were a pen and tried to rewrite whatever had been written so that he could determine what it was.

"Hey, Joe, what do you think this says over here on the tree?"

"Not much telling, it looks too weathered to tell anymore. Probably two lovers' names or something."

"I don't know, it feels like it was all one word."

He looked out across the welcoming fields in front of the house and then up at the sky. It was a clear day and the sky was completely empty, not even a bird made its mark across the vast blueness.

Down by Dixie

January 23, 1885

It looks like the snow is finally melting away. For a while a person could not see clearly across the street and there was hardly anyone out of his or her house. It's sad news for our friends in Sandusky because their new store collapsed with the weight of the snow. No word yet on if they plan to rebuild.

Rachel Stephens, owner of the tailor shop over on Riddle Street passed away last week. Doc Ruyle says she suffered from consumption and that she was only 34. She leaves behind a young son.

Things seem pretty peaceful in these parts lately and I think that we are all due for some pleasant living. The Methodist church will be putting on a play next Saturday about how the Mack Dillon gang was defeated and removed from our very own Dixie. Nat Braymyer and myself will both be in the play, portraying none other than ourselves.

Make sure you go by the café over on Main Street, they said that because of all the snow they have too much food and they don't want it to go bad so everything is half price. I think I'll be eating there every day this week, you can't beat that price.

Allen Goldston

Chapter Twenty Seven

Oddly enough, the rest of the winter was mild with little snow and in March Cotton began plowing the fields while Abbie busied herself with Spring-cleaning. It was a peaceful time for the newlyweds and they were perfectly content with their lives.

Cotton was out in the fields plowing and Abbie was on the front porch cleaning some of the rugs when a horseback rider approached her. He wore an old brown hat with longer than usual hair sticking out behind it. He was missing a few teeth and had large indentions across his face.

"Hello there," Abbie said looking toward the man, "Something I can help you with, sir?"

He pulled out a revolver and pointed it at her. "Shore is. Keep your mouth shut."

Abbie was terrified and nearly fainted. She did not budge from the position she was in and didn't speak a word. The man dismounted his horse and walked up onto the porch toward her. He looked her up and down and made a slow circle around her.

He grabbed her hands from behind and yanked her off the porch. "What do you want?" She asked struggling with the man.

"I said no noise!" He snapped at her as he backhanded her across the face. He tossed her up onto his horse and rode off towards the north as fast as he could.

Cotton stopped the plow horses for a minute to wipe the sweat from his forehead. He looked in the direction of the house and smiled knowing that this was all his and Abbie's and that their life here would be good.

- - - - - - - - - - - - - -

Rosalee sat somewhere near the Red River with her hands tied behind her back with a group of other women, whom were not required to be tied up. She had been the one to give them the biggest fight for her freedom when she had been captured and in a way the kidnappers feared her.

Five men sat on horseback surrounding them when the sixth rode up to join them. He had a young girl on the back of his horse and Rosalee's heart sank when she saw them. Abbie was thrown to the ground with the rest of the women and struggled to sit up right.

"That's a good one, Zeke! She'll bring a pretty penny," one of the men said.

Abbie wiped her face off with her hands and looked around her.

"Abbie!" Rosalee said.

Abbie looked in her direction and for a small moment was relieved. "Rosalee." She moved toward her. "What's going on? What do those men want?"

"I don't know, but it can't be good. Is Cotton okay?"

"Yes. I mean, I think so. He was plowing the fields when that man got me. What about Nat?"

"He's fine. He probably doesn't even know I've been taken. I was on my way to your house when I was gunned down by that man over there on the right."

There were six men and five women and all the men looked like they could use a gun, and well. The leader of them appeared to be in his late thirties and had black hair. He was dressed a lot nicer than everyone else in the gang and seemed to take better care of himself. The only other man in the gang that interested Rosalee at all was the one who had taken Abbie, he would not take his eyes off Rosalee.

The leader walked over to the group of frantic women. "Okay, ladies, we're about to cross the river and I want everyone on their best behavior. I'd hate to leave a body in the water if you know what I mean."

All the women were scared, but Rosalee wasn't afraid to speak up. "What do you want with us you ignorant coward?"

The man leaned down to Rosalee, "Well, maim, there's a group of Comanche that are looking to repopulate themselves and, well, they need all the women they can get."

The man laughed and Rosalee spat in his face where her face was met with the backside of his hand. Five of the men each grabbed a woman and mounted their horse. The dark leader of the group grabbed Rosalee and mounted his stallion. They crossed the Red River and entered into Indian Territory just before sun down, but the men didn't stop. They rode straight through the night, putting as much distance between them and Dixie as possible.

- - - - - - - - - - - - - -

Cotton was just about to come in from the fields when he saw his father riding towards him. Cotton laid the reins down and stepped away from the plow.

"Hey, son, it's looking good out here."

"Thanks, Pa. What are you doing out this way?"

"I came to see how much longer your Ma was going to be and see if she wanted a ride back to town."

"Oh? I didn't know she was here."

Nat helped Cotton put the plowing team in the barn and then they went into the empty house through the back door. They called out their names and searched the entire house, but found no one. The two of them met out on the front porch after they had finished going through the house.

"Where do you suppose they went," Nat said rubbing his chin.

"Beats me, Pa. Abbie wouldn't go anywhere far without telling me first."

Nat looked at the ground near the porch entrance. "Whose tracks are those, son?"

Cotton stepped down to take a closer look. "Never seen them before, but they're only a few hours old."

"I don't like this, son. Go get your horse, we'd better follow them."

They followed the tracks north on the dirt road and hadn't gone very far when they spotted a piece of white cloth in the road ahead. When they got close enough Cotton got off his horse to pick it up. "Pa! That's Abbie's handkerchief!"

The father and son team rode as fast as they could toward the north with the unknown tracks. When nightfall came, they continued onward.

Chapter Twenty Eight

Just before sunup the group of men and kidnapped women stopped to rest. The women could barely keep their eyes open, except for Rosalee who was wide awake. Her and Abbie sat with the other three women around a small campfire about twenty feet away from where the men were. All the women looked to be the prettiest ones from their community, aside from one, Charlotte Ferguson.

Her features were very plain and she was thinner than most wild birds in the wintertime. She didn't say much and mostly kept to herself. When she did talk, in her quiet feminine voice, it was mostly about church and praying that these men would be forgiven.

Rosalee went to church every Sunday, but she believed that sometimes God expected you to handle a situation with the tools he gave you, rather than sit around and pray about it all day.

"Lord, please forgive these men of their sins! They know not what they do, oh Lord…"

Yes indeed, Rosalee had had enough.

"Good Lord, woman! Shut up!"

Her soft voice sent chills through Rosalee, "That wasn't very polite."

"Well hell, neither is being kidnapped and taken away from our homes. No, Charlotte, these men know exactly what they're doing and I hope they rot in hell for it!"

"Lord please forgive her…"

"Charlotte, perhaps you should pray silently for awhile," Abbie interrupted.

She put her head down and began to pray to herself. Docia Williams was in her late twenties, a tall dark headed woman who looked to have come from money. Aside from Rosalee, she was the brave one among the group. She carried herself with grace and looked at the men as if they were dogs.

She was, in some ways like Rosalee, so she stayed as close to her as possible, knowing that if anyone could get them out it would be Rosalee. "Mrs. Braymyer, do you think there's any hope of us getting out of this mess we're in?"

"Oh there's hope, Docia. We just have to wait for the right time."

"Well, what exactly are you planning on doing?"

"Well, ladies," Rosalee said looking around at them all, "The only difference between them and us is guns."

Betty Taylor, a thirty-year-old widow piped up, "Yes, but how are we to get a gun?"

"We have to take one of theirs, that's how."

Docia said, "Do you think we can kill enough of them with one gun before they kill us?"

Charlotte became hysterical, "Thou shall not kill thy brother. Oh, Lord! Please forgive them! Please oh please oh, Lord..."

"Well I reckon we could use Mrs. Ferguson as target practice."

Docia and Abbie laughed a little while Charlotte became quiet.

At mid morning, Lee Osmond the dark headed boss of the gang rallied his men together over bacon and cowboy coffee. "Boys, we're due to meet up with the Comanches today, but don't I think it'll go smooth."

The short ignorant man that had taken Abbie from her home let out a yawn, revealing several missing teeth and the ones he did have were brown and soggy. He was a classic hobo of the eighties, only he'd been given a gun. "Whetchya mun, boss?"

"Just what I said, Zeke. The Comanches are going to out number us and they're gonna' figure they can just take the women free and clear."

"Boss, cain't we's keep a few of thems womens fer us? I's sweet on tha blonde one."

"No! And quit asking or I'll give you to the Comanches with them!"

Luke Simco was a tall dark complected man and wore mostly black to show his personality. "So what's your plan, Lee?"

"Me and you will ride up with the women, the rest of you hide out and watch. Shoot em' one by one if they give us any problems."

The men were around their own fire and paid little attention to the women at the moment, except Zeke who couldn't take his eyes off of Rosalee who busied herself watching the men and studying their habits. "I think we'll have the best chance to get the gun from the stupid one."

"Our father who art in Heaven…"

All the women at once said, "Shut-up!"

"Anyhow, I think he'll be our best shot."

Docia looked over at the men, "I think you're right and besides he kind of fancies you so you would have a better shot at getting close to him."

Rosalee thought about a plan and then acted. "Excuse me! Can someone take me to take care of some business?"

Zeke's face lit up. "Can I boss? Pleeeese can I?"

"Hurry up and keep your hands off her!"

The short man waddled over to the women and lifted Rosalee up by the rope binding her hands. He smelled of old whiskey and poor man cigars and for a moment, Rosalee thought she really would have to take care of some business.

They walked off into the woods, him just a half a step behind her. She stopped and so did he.

She turned around and was almost face to face, "What's your name?"

His face turned red, "I'z Zeke, mum."

"Well, Zeke, do you think you can untie me?"

"O's no mum, boss man wudn't like that."

"Oh, Zeke, we could have much more fun if you'd untie me for a minute. You see, I don't really need to take care of any business. Well, the truth is, is that I'm awful lonely for a man…"

"Awz, Miz. Rozale, I'z kept you company. I reekon a minute or's so wudn't hurt none."

He slowly untied her, all the while looking into her eyes. Once she was loose he leaned forward to kiss her. She turned and threw up in her mouth as he licked her cheek. She put her arms around the mucky man and slowly, very slowly reached for his revolver that was stuck in the crack of his rear.

She carefully put her hand around the butt of the gun and prepared herself to rip it out of his pants. As she slowly made the first tug, her finger slipped…

POW!

"Awwwwwwwz! My ballz! You's shot my ballllllz!!!"

Rosalee and Zeke had ventured about fifty yards into the woods, but after the shot was fired she could hear plain as day, "Oh Lord! Jesus! Bless these violent devils!"

Zeke fell to the ground and when he did the gun remained in Rosalee's hand. "You'z done shot my ballz you…"

150

"Zeke! I don't want to kill you, but I will. Now you stay quiet," she said pointing the gun at him.

He was quiet, other than the moans and groans of a man who had just lost his manhood. Rosalee moved quietly towards the camp, knowing the other men would be upon her soon. She heard horses behind her and turned around quickly, gun ready.

"Nat! Cotton!"

"Hello, Rosie darling."

"Ma, where's Abbie?"

Back this way, there's five more men."

"Rosie, you stay here, come on, son!"

Nat and Cotton rode about ten feet until they came upon two men. The first, a fat double chinned balding man Nat took out with a bullet between his eyes. The second, a boy no more than twenty Cotton shot in the chest. Two more riders came up, including Lee Osmond.

Cotton easily took out the young one at Lee's side, but Lee planted a bullet into Cotton's right shoulder. Nat pointed and fired, bringing Lee to the ground with blood shooting out of his neck. "Are you okay, son?"

"Yeah, Pa, it don't hurt much."

"That's four, your Ma said there were five."

They rode the rest of the way into the camp where they found the remaining women.

"Oh, Jesus! Lord! Not more murders!"

Cotton ran up to them and took Abbie in his arms. "Abbie are you okay?"

"I'm fine, Cotton. You're shot!"

"It's nothing, really."

"Your Ma, she went into the woods with one of them, we heard a shot."

"Ma's fine, Abbie. We left her back on the trail."

As Nat and Cotton untied the women, Luke Simco approached them afoot from behind, holding a gun to Rosalee's head. "Put your guns down!"

They turned to see Rosalee struggling to break free.

"Let my wife go!"

"I said put your guns down!"

Rosalee lifted her leg and kicked the man in the crotch. He cursed into the air, reaching for an escaping Rosalee. Nat and Cotton both fired bullets into the dark man's chest, but before he fell to the ground he sent a bullet in Rosalee's direction.

It struck her in her lower back and she fell to the ground face first. Nat, Cotton and Abbie all ran to the heart of their family, Rosalee Braymyer. Nat turned her onto her back, allowing her head to rest in his lap.

"Rosie! Stay with me! Don't close your eyes!"

"Nat, I'm shot…"

"Rosie, you're going to be okay!"

Cotton and Abbie gazed down upon her, fearing the worst. They both took one of her hands where she used what little strength she had to squeeze them. There was a trail of blood appearing from beneath her body and slowly flowing away like a smaller version of the Red River.

"Nat, I'm so sorry for dying…"

"Rosie, don't be sorry, everything is going to be okay! I promise!"

For the first time in his life, Cotton saw his father cry. The tears from Nat's face streamed down and entered into the growing river of his wife's blood. He held her tight as the life was slowly leaving her pale body. There was nothing he could do and no way he could make this all go away.

"Rosie, I'm so sorry, I should have protected you better…I…"

"You were a fine husband, Nat and I'm so glad I got to share my life with you…"

Her eyes slowly started to grow heavy and threatened to close at any moment, never to be seen by this world again. "Rosie! Stay awake! Don't leave me!" It was no use. Within a matter of seconds the weight of death was too heavy and her eyes gave way, taking with them one of the finest women to have ever called Dixie home.

Chapter Twenty Nine

June 21, 2010

There was still no sound on the headset and the passengers continued to shout and scream as I steered the shaking plane downward. I could see the ground a little clearer now and could definitely tell that we were somewhere in the country.

The plane made a loud roaring noise as we drew nearer and nearer to the earth's surface. "Hey miss," I said to the lady next to me, "Would you mind saying a prayer for me too?"

She continued to pray, only opening her eyes occasionally to check and see if perhaps this had all been a dream, but it wasn't. I searched for buttons on the console that said anything about landing, but there was very few. I push one that said landing gear and I only assumed that it dropped the wheels.

I felt as though I were playing a video game, only this one I would have to win or it would be the last one I ever played. We continued to fall further and further and I had both hands on the steering stick in front of me, hoping that by some rare chance I had been a pilot in some past life.

I looked down at the landscape and suddenly everything became very familiar. *This can't be,* I thought.

It was Dixie and our plane was heading straight toward the Braymyer home that my Papaw had so often talked about. *This can't be good...*

As bad as it may sound, my life and the lives of the others on board suddenly didn't matter. The only thing I cared about was avoiding that house, or else my Papaw would be devastated.

I turned the plane sharply right as we were now just above the ground. It moved slowly and crossed over the old farm at the very end of the long driveway, just next to the street. As it crossed, the bottom of the plane hit one of the large cottonwood trees and the front of the plane jolted upwards.

The plane came crashing down into the front pasture and slid across the old cotton fields, belly first. Dirt and other debris flew up making it impossible to see out the windows. It came to a stop in the open field and everything was quiet. I looked over at the steward next to me and was relieved to see that she too had made it through alive.

Cops, ambulances and fire trucks were at the scene before we had even exited the plane and they watched as we all stepped out unharmed. It was a miracle that no one was injured and it wasn't until later that the authorities told me that had we not hit that old cottonwood tree then we would have went nose first into the ground and the plane would have probably blown up.

So in a strange way, I owe my life to those cottonwood trees on Braymyer Hill, or more importantly to my ancestor, Rosalee who planted them there years before. It's funny how many uses a tree can have; they can help you find your way in a snow storm, save a crashing plane and who knows, maybe they can even predict the weather.

Chapter Thirty

February 16, 1889

Mary Lee Braymyer folded her hands across her chest as her small classroom slowly made their way out of the front double doors beneath the school bell and headed home. She shivered as a cold draft swept across her small body and caught a piece of her blonde her.

She grabbed the broom at the front of the classroom and started to sweep the main aisle so that she would not have to do it in the morning when she arrived. She had been teaching for almost a year and enjoyed very much being around the children. There was a sense of innocence about them that made her wish she too were still a child.

"Hurry up, Mary!" Nat junior said, "It looks like a snow storm is coming!"

"I'll be along shortly. Take Addie home and wait for me there."

She continued the light cleaning throughout the schoolhouse until she heard steps coming onto the front porch. She leaned herself against the broom and watched in that direction until a man appeared in the doorway.

Charlie Knight had been watching Mary Lee for quite some time and had just now gotten up the nerve to speak to her. "Afternoon, maim."

"Charlie, you don't have to call me, maim. I'm not an old maid yet. What are you doing here anyhow?"

"Well, I come to see if you would like any help before the snow gets here. It looks like it's going to be a bad one this time."

"Why thank you, Charlie. Here take the broom and I'll start cleaning the blackboard."

Mary Lee watched as Charlie attempted to sweep and couldn't help but laugh. She walked over to him and put her hands on his and proceeded to show him the proper way to do it. When she touched him, her body was immediately warmed and she couldn't help but look up at him.

She looked into his soft green eyes and got lost somewhere within them. Charlie began to blush and Mary Lee quickly contained herself and went back to the blackboard. As she continued to clean the board, she would glance back at him occasionally, not to see how well he was doing the job, but to observe him in general.

After they had finished, Charlie walked her to her house on First Street and then headed out of town towards his farm before the storm arrived. Mary Lee watched him from a front window as he walked away…she was in love.

Chapter Thirty One

August 15, 1895

White Indian Man, his Comanche wife and their twin boys sat around a campfire in northern Oregon as the sun made its way beyond the horizon. They were on their own and would now try and live by the white man's ways since the tribe continued to treat them differently than everyone else. There was no future for them there and something in White Indian Man's gut told him he must set out to make a life for himself and his family. It was as if it were a trait handed down to him from an unknown source as Indians rarely left their tribes.

He had slowly begun to learn English on his way to Oregon and could carry on a conversation with a white man with little to no accent. He cut his hair and was able to stake a claim on a piece of land in Oregon where he would attempt to farm. His name was changed to John White and he took pride in his new namesake. Before he had left Indian Territory he had heard brave stories about a father and son named Nat and Cotton, so when his children were born he named them after those unknown men because they sounded like good white man names.

The sun was now almost gone and he knew he must force himself to go to sleep, because tomorrow was the start of their life in a new place and tomorrow he would start building their "white man home."

Chapter Thirty Two

June 23, 2010

Before the judge could make her ruling in Mr. Sanders' case, the two attorneys received a phone call from one of their clients. They were told of the news of what had happened with the plane crash at the future home of their country club. The two child like men walked away from the courtroom and didn't even bother to tell the judge.

There was no way they could build a country club there now. It would take months to clean up the plane mess and even then the land would probably be protected as a memory to those who walked away from the crash. They were like children who had just lost their favorite toy, but they were soon after some other old timers land and if they thought Nathan Sanders was a tough one to beat, wait until they met Charlie Knight's grandson.

The judge seemed satisfied that the two of them had just walked out. Although she was one of the toughest judges in Grayson County, she had almost been moved to tears by the old man's story. It was a lucky thing too that the case was dropped, because since there was no written documentation to verify the man's story, there would have been no way for the judge to rule in his favor.

So in the end, by way of a plane crash, Rosalee Braymyer ensured that her family home would remain forever standing for her future generations; not too bad for a city girl.

Three days after the courtroom incident Nathan Sanders and his daughter, Rose Tyler were heading out to the old farm. Nathan had refused to go back to the nursing home and insisted on moving back to the big house. Rose reluctantly agreed, but made him promise that she could have someone come out once a day and check up on him.

When Rose's new box car pulled into the drive, the cottonwoods were there to greet them, aside from the one closest to the road. "Rose, darling, drive on past the house will you? I wanna' go see the cemetery."

The small car drove past the house and onto a trail lined with grass taller than it in the back pasture. Normally, Rose would be frantic, but things like cars didn't seem so important anymore. Rose parked the car at the foot of the small wooded hill and the two of them got out. With her help, Nathan walked up to the old graveyard.

The grass and thorn bushes had grown up thick, hiding most of the stones among the trees. Nathan looked around in a melancholy gaze, "I sure wish I could get up here and clean this place up like I used to."

"Daddy, you know that's too much work for you. Maybe I can get my grandsons up here one day."

"That's a swell idea, Rose. I guess I'll be resting up here before too much longer."

They walked through the cemetery until they came to the largest stone Rose had ever seen. She wiped it off with her fingers and read:

Rosa Lee Burns Braymyer

August 04, 1851-Polk County, Missouri

March 23, 1885-Indian Territory

A woman too good to be here long

Next to hers was Nat's and their infant daughter and directly behind them was Cotton and Abbie.

Nathaniel John Braymyer
March 25, 1848 – September 21, 1908

Cotton Nathaniel Braymyer
October 24, 1867 – June 17, 1948

Abbie Braymyer
July 31, 1868 – June 28, 1954

Jennie Rose Braymyer
January 11, 1869 – April 29, 1870

Allen Goldston
July 03, 1841 – December 08, 1886

Charlie & Mary Lee Knight
January 01, 1857 – January 11, 1869
March 22, 1923 – January 27, 1932

Nathan closed the old rusted cast iron fence as they left and headed down to the car. "You know, Rose. I bet this year would be a good year to plant cotton."

"Daddy, don't be silly!"

"I'm just saying is all."

Three weeks later, Rose's grandsons cleaned up the cemetery and a week after that, Nathan Sanders was buried beside his grandpa Cotton, and he was right it was a great year for cotton. Rose moved into the old Braymyer house up on Braymyer Hill and lives there to this day.

Chapter Thirty Three

June 20, 1907

When Rosalee died, people looked as if they had had their heart taken away from them. The town fell quiet for almost six months, wondering how this could happen to their Rosie.

Nat was devastated, but he still had three children to take care of. He continued to push himself forward, knowing good and well that that is what Rosalee would want and slowly the days got a little easier.

Allen Goldston died the year after Rosalee and was buried next to his wife and son. He went to work one day and collapsed shortly after walking through the door. The town got a little quieter that day as well.

Abbie gave birth to a girl, Jennie Rose and no one spoiled her so bad as Cotton. There were also three other children born to the couple, Cotton John who died a few years after he was born, Brice Nathaniel and Martha Abigail. Year after year the crop continued to yield good profits and the Braymyer family slowly marched their way into the future.

Cotton was sitting on the front porch whittling at a piece of cedar wood when the thought struck him. "What would Ma think if she could see her family now?" He reckoned she'd be mighty proud at the outcome.

Mary Lee married Charlie Knight, who was quite a bit older than her, but they had a good marriage blessed with three children who all reached adulthood. Nat junior married Polly Ann Riddle and lived in Whitesboro where he ran his own law office and raised their four children. The youngest, Addie Leona married Alfred Green and moved out to Rock Creek where they also had four children.

Nat had retired as sheriff and had moved back out to the farm with Cotton. The elderly man stepped out onto the porch and took a seat next to his son. They looked out over the land as the sun slowly made its way out of the dark. It shone down rays of every sort of yellow, revealing the Braymyer land and all the hard work it had taken to make it what it was.

"Looks like a storm will be rolling in a little later, son."

"Yeah, Pa, it sure does. We better get everything settled down before hand."

Nat looked over at his son, "Ah, can't be no worse than the ones we've went through in the past."

The huge cottonwood trees that Rosalee had planted lining the drive rustled as a morning breeze swept through. Pieces of cotton blew up onto the porch with the men. They continued to sit there in their rockers, everything was peaceful, and everything was just. The Braymyer family had made their mark on Texas and Texas had become apart of their blood. Everything was good.

The End

Down by Dixie

September 03, 1921

It seems every day another family is moving out of the area. Ever since the fire in '94, Main Street has just disappeared. I can't say that I blame folks for leaving, times are hard and unless you're a farmer there's not much work around here.

I remember my mother in law always saying, "Dixie is a fine place to live, it just needs to be civilized is all." Now that most of the civilized people are moving on, I'm not sure what's going to happen around here, I guess it'll be up to the few of us left behind.

I went over to see Doc. Stubblefield in Whitesboro about my hand pain and by and by he said I needed to quit writing so much. So I guess this will be the last paper for a while. It's sad to see this place dying like it is, but I guess towns are a lot like people, they live and they die. I'll always remember the good times though.

So if you ever wanna' hear about how Dixie used to be or all those courageous people who helped settle it up, well then come on up to Braymyer Hill and I'll tell you all about it over some fine Dixie tea.

Mrs. Abbie Braymyer

Part II

California Charm

"Life is about endurance and testing to see how strong you will allow yourself to become. I don't want much out of this life, but what I do desire I intend to get…no matter how hard I have to fight."

Dottie Braymyer

Chapter 1

March 03, 1874

"Mary Anna! Mary Anna! Hurry up! Will's fixing to leave!"

Rachel Lloyd, the colored maid of the Braymyer home frantically ran about the kitchen packing the last bit of food for Will Braymyer who was about to leave for California.

"Calm down, Rachel dear. He can't very well leave without food."

Mary Anna Braymyer was standing at the door of the kitchen watching as Rachel packed everything into a small metal tin. She stood there in a red silk dress that only the finest women in Missouri wore, with her black hair pinned up into a perfect bun.

Twenty eight year old, Will Braymyer stood beside his elegant brown mare and took one last look at his two story childhood home. It stood atop a large hill overlooking a natural spring that had provided the freshest water he had ever had the liberty of drinking. The house was whitewashed wood with a large wrap around porch extending all the way around it. It would always hold a special place in his heart and he would always have fond memories of Braymyer Ridge.

A few years before, his younger brother, Nat had left and headed for Texas because Missouri was becoming over populated. Now, Will was doing the same thing for the same reason, only instead of heading south, he was heading west… California bound.

Rachel and Mary Anna ran outside before he climbed atop his horse. Rachel handed him the tin, while the short body of Mary Anna grabbed the six-foot body of her son in both her arms.

"You take care of yourself, Will," she said as a tear escaped her heavy eyes.

"Awe, come on, Ma. Don't cry, it's not like you're never gonna' see me again."

"You don't know that, Will. What if something were to happen?"

"Just don't think like that, Ma. Everything will be just fine, I promise."

He wrapped her up in his arms and gave her one last hug before turning to his father.

John Braymyer stood there in a proud stance and looked his son over. "Well, son, be careful out there and don't trust anyone, you hear?"

"Yes, sir. You've taught me well, Pa. I reckon I'll manage just fine."

The two of them shook hands just before Will rode off into the early morning western horizon. The only life he had ever known was behind him along with the rising sun and he didn't dare look back for fear that he would turn around. He had lived an exceptional life so far, but he knew if he wanted to amount to anything he would have to take a chance and travel to a new land where a man still stood a chance at survival.

He was a handsome man, with blonde hair and the bluest eyes most anyone had ever seen. But at twenty-eight years old, he was still single and had no intention of settling down any time soon.

It wasn't that girls hadn't tried to get him to court them, because there were a handful of them that wanted desperately to marry him. Will was too much a man though, he would rather spend all day fishing and hunting instead of being drug on romantic picnics and such.

Missouri girls were just missing something, he thought. Some small quality that every girl, in his opinion, should have. He couldn't place his finger on it, but he was sure he would know it if he ever saw it.

His mother had sworn that he would be the death of her and that he shouldn't be so picky when it came to women. It was partly her own fault, however, in that Will had a bad habit of comparing women to his mother and there was no one out there that could be compared to Mary Anna Braymyer.

She had been born and raised in Georgia by her wealthy grandparents. Her mother, Anna Walker, had fallen in love with a Cherokee Indian and bore two children with him, Mary Anna and a son, Walks. Shortly after Mary Anna was born, her Indian father died and her mother followed soon after by way of a broken heart.

She was raised as a white woman and the only trace of her Indian ancestry made its presence in only her dark hair and brown eyes. It made her unique and a rare breed and she had the million-dollar personality to go with it. At a young age, she met and married the blonde headed John Braymyer and had since been devoted to her family.

Will thought about all of this as he continued to ride westward and had to fight away the melancholy mood that was trying to take him over. "I've got to do this," he thought, "A man can't accomplish much staying in the same home he was born in all his life. California… here I come!"

The Walnut Post

March 03, 1874

Well friends, it's time to say goodbye to another one of our fellow comrades. That's right, Will Braymyer left this morning for California. This comes just seven years after his brother, Nat Braymyer left for Texas. It seems as though the respected family is branching out.

D. L. Burns has resigned as the mayor of our fine city of Walnut Grove and has moved into his late brother's home, Brice Burns, over on Hickory Street. There is no word yet on who will take his place. It looks like we will be without a mayor for a short time.

Next weekend will be the annual Walnut Grove Memorial Day picnic. There will be skits and speakers to tell us how this little city of ours was founded. From what I hear, there will also be a pie baking competition, so gentlemen come hungry!

G. B. Lowe

Chapter 2

March 31, 1874

When Will rode into Denver, he was surprised to see how busy the town was. None of the towns he had ever been to back in Missouri had been as lively as this one. There were people of all sorts walking about and the cheerful chattering noise could be heard all throughout town.

Will had never been more hungry in his life, so as soon as he arrived at the bustling town he went straight to the café. Every street in town was lined with businesses of all sorts and as he made his way in the direction of his next meal he passed three general stores, all promising better deals.

The café sat between a photography shop and a tailor store. He tied his horse to the hitching post and stepped up onto the long wooden walkway that ran in front of all the buildings. As he approached the double red doors, he could smell the scent of good food and his mouth began to water.

Once inside, he hung his trail beaten cowboy hat on the hat rack and made his way across the room to an empty table. He passed several tables full of people, but they were all preoccupied with their food to look up and notice him.

He took his seat and a young lady was immediately at his side. She wore a green dress and had her auburn hair in braided pigtails that came across her shoulders and down to her chest.

The greenness of her eyes almost matched her dress perfectly and her slenderness could have swept almost any man away. She was no more than a half an inch over five feet and looked to be in her early twenties.

Will took notice of all of this, but like the rest of the hungry customers he was more worried about getting his food.

"Hi, there," she said, "Would you like our special today? It's only twenty-five cents. You get steak, grits and a slice of apple pie…"

"Yes, maim. Why that sounds delicious," he interrupted her.

"Alright then. I'll be right back with your food."

The small attractive waitress headed back toward the kitchen, leaving Will at the table alone. Certain tables were now finishing up their food and the sound of gossip and laughter was filling the room.

Within five minutes the waitress was back with his food and large cup of coffee. The smell of the steak almost overwhelmed him to the point where he thought he would just pick it up with his bare hands and eat it.

"Here you are, sir. And I got you a larger than normal piece of pie on account that you look awful hungry."

"Will…please call me Will," he said with a mouth full of steak.

"Well, Will, my name is Dorothy. It's a pleasure to meet you."

"Same to you, Dorothy," something about saying her name sent chills down his back. "The food sure is good."

"Thank you, I'll give the cook your compliments. Are you here for long or are you just passing through?"

"Oh, no maim. I'm heading out to California. I was gonna' see about finding a wagon train to join up with, you know…for the company and all."

"Well, there's one leaving tomorrow morning in that direction. In fact, my parents and I will all be on it. I can take you to see the Captain after lunch if you'd like."

"Oh, I'd be much obliged, maim."

"Well, you sit here and eat a while before your food spoils."

"Yes maim, thank you."

She looked down at him and smiled before walking to another table. There was something about him she couldn't place her finger on, but then again she had never seen the Braymyer charm before.

Will watched her walk away briefly and then dove back into his food, barely remembering to chew. After he had finished his plate and an additional three slices of apple pie, he leaned back in his wooden chair and stretched his arms up as high as they would go.

As Dorothy was walking toward him, she was putting a red shawl over her shoulders. "Are you ready to go Mr…"

"Braymyer, Will Braymyer."

"Alright then, Mr. Braymyer, I'm Dorothy Travis. Shall we go see the Captain now?"

"Yes maim. That sounds like a fine idea to me."

Will led his horse behind him as he and Dorothy walked side by side down the dusty road. People were walking in all directions as they approached a group of wagons in an open area between two buildings.

"Captain Perkins?" Dorothy shouted as they walked closer to them.

A slender middle aged man with brown leather looking skin appeared from behind a wagon. He was slightly taller than average and his clothes looked like they had traveled many miles.

"Dorothy," he replied, "How are you?"

"Hi Captain, I'm doing well. This is Will Braymyer. He's looking to join a wagon train and head to California."

The Captain turned to face Will and stuck out his hand, "Is that right? I'm John Perkins, I'm the Captain of this here wagon train."

"Will Braymyer, sir."

The Captain looked Will over and then observed his horse. "Can you use a gun?"

"Yes, sir. Never had a problem before."

"Well," he said scratching his head, "It's fifty dollars a head and you'll be expected to pull your weight. Think you can handle that?"

"Absolutely, sir!"

"Alright then. I'll see you tomorrow morning."

They shook hands again and then the Captain walked back to the wagon he was working on.

"Come on, Will," Dorothy said, "I want you to meet my parents."

Will followed her across the small opening to another wagon where an older couple was sitting beside a small fire. "Poppa, Ma, I want you to meet Will Braymyer. He's going to be on the wagon train with us."

The man stood up to shake his hand. He was tall and in his younger days he looked like he was probably a successful cowboy. He had gray hair and between the wrinkles on his face were a pair of green eyes.

"I'm Henry Travis. Glad to hear you'll be coming along with us."

"Thank you, sir. I look forward to it."

"This here is my wife, Margaret."

Will tipped his hat in her direction, "It's a pleasure, maim."

"How do you do," she answered looking in her daughter's direction.

Margaret Travis was a very attractive woman and looked to be several years younger than her husband. She was short and had a very thin figure. She had the same auburn hair as Dorothy, only hers had been faded over her lifetime.

"Well," Will said, "I reckon I'll ride outside of town after I go get some supplies and set up camp for the night."

"Nonsense!" Henry Travis said. "You'll camp here with us tonight. Go fetch your supplies and dinner will be waiting for you when you get back."

"I'd be much obliged," Will said.

"Don't mention it, we'd love to have the company."

Dorothy looked over at Will and blushed a little bit before he headed in the direction of one of the stores.

Chapter 3

Just before the sun came up, the wagon train of four wagons went west on Main Street and didn't turn back. There were six men on horseback, including Will and they were being led by Captain Perkins. Four riders rode in front of the wagons which consisted of the Captain, Will, James Goodnight and Ben Sutherland, while Marshall Wilcox and Abner Douglas brought up the rear of the eager travelers.

James Goodnight looked as if he had made this journey several times and he kept a constant eye on all of his surroundings. He was a scout by blood and had probably been one of the first white men to have ever laid eyes on the western frontier. He was a tall dark mysterious man, but had a sense of compassion written across his dark face. He was forty-eight and rode like a young boy who thought he could force his horse to fly into the western sky.

He was an original cowboy and wore the weathered trail beaten clothes to prove it. His spurs were unpolished and lacked that special shine that the rich folk' back east insisted on having. He had a black moustache above his hidden upper lip and the shadow of his black cowboy hat made it near impossible to see the upper portion of his face.

Goodnight rode directly in front of the first wagon and a little to the right while Ben Sutherland was directly to his opposite. Ben was in his mid thirties and looked to have lived a life of luxury at one point or another. He was short, but very stout and a man would have to be crazy to go up against him in a brawl. His features were light and like Will, he had a set of blue eyes that could calm even the fiercest of storms. Unlike Goodnight, he kept a steady eye on the trail ahead of him, rather than observing all his surroundings.

Will rode between the two men next to the Captain and studied each one of his fellow scouts so that he might learn everything he could. He would copy Goodnight as he looked

181

around the horizon in all directions and then focus his attention back to the trail ahead.

The first wagon was the Travis family and occasionally Margaret would go lie in the back and take a nap while Dorothy took her place on the wagon bench. When she did, Will had a hard time scouting the landscape for danger for he was too busy scouting what was sitting on the wagon behind him. He would have to struggle to keep up with the captain on these occasions and often times found himself slowly getting closer and closer to the wagon and farther away from Captain Perkins.

The second wagon was Rev. Pippin and his large family. He always wore a black suit and was constantly brushing off the trail dust from his small plump body. He wore glasses and had a slightly balding head atop his fifty-year-old body. His wife, Hannah sat at his side with her small gentle figure and most times kept her back as straight as possible with her hands folded in her lap. There were seven Pippin children, four boys and three girls. The oldest was Charlotte who was in her mid twenties and the youngest being Ann Marie who was twelve. The children would take turns riding in the wagon, limiting the number to only two at a time to prevent too much weight on the wagon, while the others walked along side.

The Pippin's were good people and were some of the kindest folks Will had ever had the liberty of meeting. Ann Marie had had Will's heart from the moment they were introduced. She had adopted him as another one of her older brothers and wanted to know everything about his life. Occasionally, her twenty-year-old brother, Sam would walk alongside Will and help him scout for trouble. The family had traveled far, coming from Wisconsin three years before and just now making it to Denver because of several stops along the way.

Third in line was Andy Williams, his wife Mahala and their four children aging in range from three to thirteen. Andy had once been a famous fiddle player back east and had made a great name for himself, even being invited to play at the White House once. But when he turned thirty, he decided to settle down and marry his wife and shortly after their first child was born. After their marriage they moved to Tennessee where he owned a general store and now they too were heading west in search of something better.

The last wagon consisted of the Turner siblings, Beth who was nineteen, Travis who was sixteen and the twins June and April who were both fifteen. Their mother was a sister to Henry Travis and since both of their parents had been killed in a house fire they were venturing to California with their uncle. It was written on their faces that they had lived through great pain since the death of their parents, but even stronger was the feature of strength. Beth had been forced to take control of the family and had put herself last and her younger siblings first.

About twenty feet behind the Turner wagon, Marshall Wilcox and Abner Douglas rode side by side. They were best friends and had been raised on adjoining farms in Mississippi. Marshall was twenty-three and had sandy blonde hair that was covered beneath a, top of the line, beige cowboy hat. His clothes were nicer than most people of the area and he seemed to get agitated when the dust from the wagons in front of him settled on his nice clothing.

Abner on the other hand lifted his nose up and enjoyed every scent the west had to offer. He was on the adventure of a lifetime and was in the best of moods with every day that they continued on. He had brown hair, green eyes and a combination of light and tan skin across his tall twenty six year old body. As he rode down the never-ending trail he was constantly whistling a merry tune up at the blue sky.

The farther west they went, the more desolate the land became. Will would look out across the land and wonder if he was making the right decision, he only hoped that as they continued westward, the land would soon become green again.

After three weeks of traveling and small, short lived camp sites, the Captain announced that tonight they would camp early and feast on the deer meet that the scouts had hunted down that day. The tired travelers had a little spark of hope appear across their faces when they heard the news, for they could all use some much needed rest.

About four hours before sun down, the wagons rode off the hard packed trail a little ways and made a circle with their wagons to offer some protection from the outside. In the middle of the circle, Will and some of the other men made a overly large fire pit and lined it with the brown sandstone rocks that were so popular to the area.

Dorothy Travis stepped out of her father's wagon wearing an elegant yellow dress with her beautiful auburn hair flowing down her back, except a small piece which was held up a little higher with a matching yellow ribbon. She looked as though she had just walked off the streets of a booming eastern city and showed no sign that she had been apart of the unending journey they were all on.

Will glanced over at her and then quickly turned back to his fire pit duties. "What is it with her," he thought, "Why her? Why must I be so drawn to her? No girl had ever caught my attention like her and I just don't understand."

His thoughts were interrupted by Abner Douglas who was helping him. "Now that, my friend, is a fine piece of woman. God made very few of them...yes sir."

Will blushed a little, but moved his head back down out of view as he continued to stack rocks. "Oh, yeah?"

"Oh come on, Will. You think I don't notice you head over heals for her? Hell, anything she needs, Will Braymyer will be right there at her side to go fetch it for her."

"What? I'm not like that, I mean I don't do that. I mean..."

"Easy, Will boy, ain't a darn thing wrong with it. Shoot, if I thought she would pay me half the attention she pays you, why I imagine I would be all over her too. Nah, I've got my hat set for her cousin, Beth." Abner turned to face the Turner wagon as he said it and then headed in that direction. Before he left, he turned back toward Will, "Don't wait too long, Will. A woman like that don't stay available long. Shoot, if she makes it to California without a beau at her side, why them western boys will be all over her and she'll have the pick of the lot."

Will watched as he walked away and then turned his face back toward Dorothy's direction whose dress was flowing into the westerly wind. He knew everything Abner had just said was true, but what if he wasn't good enough for her? Why her? There had been so many other girls who would have married him at the drop of a hat, but why was he so consumed with her? Perhaps he enjoyed the chase and preferred a woman who didn't come easy. He wasn't sure, but whatever it was he knew he never wanted it to end.

Dorothy returned the quick glances in his direction and after she was able to get away from the other gossiping girls, she made her way towards him. His palms became an instant ball of sweat and he felt as though his head would pop off of his body due to the increasing pressure in his throat. What should he say? Was he presentable enough to be in the presence of such a woman?

As his head whirled around the subject, he almost took off running toward the open horizon to escape the embarrassment of not being good enough for her. "I'll just get it over with," he thought, "I'll ask her if she wants to go on a picnic. No, that's ridiculous, who would want to go on a picnic out here? I'll say she has nice hair. Nice hair? No, what if she took it the wrong way."

Dorothy was almost upon him now and he thought he felt sweat run down his backside. "Marry me."

"Marry you? Will are you okay? You don't look so good?"

"Uh, yes, I mean marry me, like a joke. Um, like..."

"Will? Are you sure everything is okay? You don't seem the same."

"Yes, I mean, I'm fine. Your hair looks nice."

"My hair? Thank you Will..."

This was going nowhere and Will was just about to head for the hills and never look back. Dorothy looked into his eyes and lost herself somewhere beyond the sparkle of their blueness. She could see a trickle of sweat come from somewhere beneath his cowboy hat and make its way down the side of his face.

"Will Braymyer, would you like to go on a walk with me?"

"Um, sure, Dorothy. Do you want to go now?"

"Yes, that would be lovely."

The two of them walked side by side beyond the protection of the wagons and into the open field. As they got farther and farther away from the wagons, Dorothy took his hand in hers. Will looked down at their connected hands and wondered if there was something that he was supposed to do.

Dorothy had never been more attracted to any man than she was to Will Braymyer. Sure they hadn't spent much time together, but from what she could tell he had all the makings of a fine husband. It wasn't just his personality that swept her off her feet and kept her attention at all times, but it was also his remarkable good looks.

186

She dreamt of being held in his tall muscular arms as the sun set somewhere behind them and she longed to feel his lips next to hers. He was tall and she enjoyed every minute of looking up into his sea blue eyes. She didn't know what it was that kept her so occupied with thinking about him, but it was something she knew she would never feel again.

She didn't understand how a man could be so attractive and have a heart of gold to go with it. Any time she ever needed anything, he was right there to do whatever he needed to for her. How many other men out there could be as good as Will Braymyer she would often think to herself, and how is he not taken?

Will forced the lump in his throat down to somewhere within his gut. "Dorothy, I'm sorry if I made you uncomfortable back there. I'm not rightly sure what I was thinking. There is something about you that makes me act funny and I've never felt anything like it before. Any time I see you, I have to remind myself to breathe before I turn blue in the face."

"Oh, Will. You didn't make me uncomfortable. And besides you were just joking weren't you?"

"Oh, uh, absolutely. I mean, I don't rightly know what come over me back there."

Dorothy let out a sigh and she began swaying their hands back and forth.

"You sound disappointed, Dorothy. I mean, if you wanted it not to be joke then I reckon it wasn't. I mean, if you wanted?"

"Well, Will, I don't want you to ask me to marry you if you're doing it just because I want you to if that's what you're getting at."

"Oh, boy. You see, Dorothy, the thing is, is that I don't

honestly know anything when it comes to you. You make me feel so clumsy and yet so sturdy that I don't know what to think. It's a feeling that I've never rightly felt before and honestly it's something I don't want to ever lose."

"You mean to tell me, Will Braymyer, that you've never felt this way over a girl before?"

"No, not at all. I don't know why, I guess I just had no interest in any of them. Or maybe, just maybe, God was telling me to hold off so I could meet you. I don't know Dorothy, I don't know what it is... I just can't figure nothing out anymore."

"Well I suppose I should stop you from going on and on about how you feel about me for my own personal pleasure, Will. The truth is, I can't stop thinking about you either and whenever I look out of the wagon and don't see you up ahead, my heart sinks for fear that something has happened to you and I wasn't there to help you. I want to be by your side, Will, I don't ever want to leave and whatever future you have planned in California, Will, I want to be apart of it."

"You really mean it, Dorothy? Do you really mean all that?"

"Of course, Will. I don't ever want to lose this feeling I have inside for you. It is more real than anything I have ever felt in my entire life."

Will turned to face her and brought her closer. She looked up into his eyes, enjoying every minute of her now very real fantasy. Will leaned in and kissed her and the two of them were lost in a land that neither one of them had ever had the pleasure of visiting. It was an island of paradise with just the two of them and they both knew that even though they had barely known each other, they wanted to spend the rest of their lives trying to figure the other one out.

Will held her close in his arms and breathed in the sweet flowery scent of her body while her head was against his manly chest. The wind came through and pushed against their bodies as they gazed at the setting sun to the west, but their love was strong and no wind out there could move them from beside each other, they were both right where they belonged.

"Dorothy?"

"Yes, Will?"

"Will you marry me?"

"I would be honored, Mr. Braymyer." And they kissed again.

- - - - - - - - - - - - -

When they arrived back at camp, the food was almost ready to eat and their fellow travelers were walking joyously around the campfire. Andy Williams got his old fiddle and sat on a wooden barrel where he began to play:

"List all you California boys, And open wide your ears,

For now we start across the plains with a herd of mules and steers.

Now bear in mind, before you start, That you'll eat jerked beef, not ham

And antelope steak, oh cuss the stuff! It often proves a sham.

You cannot find a stick of wood on all this prairie wide;

Whene're you eat you've got to stand or sit on some old bull-hide."

Everyone feasted on all the deer meat, salt pork and biscuits that the women had prepared while Will and Dorothy were on their long walk. Will went directly to Mr. Travis to ask for his blessing in marrying his daughter and much to his surprise, he said yes without hesitation. He had feared that once in California he would not be able to keep boys away from his daughter and that she had been much too picky in the past.

Will told him of his plans to run a fruit plantation and a small ranch of horses and Henry seemed to be pleased with the idea. Since Dorothy was an only child, Henry insisted that they have as many children as possible to keep the Travis blood flowing strong. His wife's face lit up when she heard the news and she was probably more excited about it than her daughter. The two of them had liked Will from the moment they first met him back in Denver and they couldn't be happier in their daughter's choice.

After everyone had eaten, couples threw themselves out onto the dance floor and began to dance around the large fire. People clapped and cheered and made drum sets out of the wooden barrels that had carried flower and other dried goods. Abner Douglas and Beth Turner danced merrily around with Will and Dorothy not far behind.

When there was a break in the music the Rev. Pippin whistled clear out into the night sky to get everyone's attention. "Listen up, people! We have a special ceremony that will be taking place now! That's a right folks, we have two marriages! Abner Douglas and Beth Turner and also my own daughter, Charlotte and Marshall Wilcox.

The two couples made their way over to the reverend holding hands with their partners. They were all so happy and were glad that some good was coming out of this never ending traveling. Will and Dorothy watched from nearby as the happy couples repeated their vows to each other and couldn't help but laugh when the reverend made a stern face toward

190

Marshall as he said, "Repeat after me!"

Dorothy laid her head on Will's chest and watched them as they finished up their marriages. "Will," she said, "Do you think it would be too soon for us to get married now?"

"Dottie, I don't want to spend another minute without you."

"Dottie... I like that, Will. Let me go talk to Poppa and Ma," she said kissing him.

She walked the short distance to where her mother and father were sitting and talked with them for a minute. Will watched as she leaned down and kissed them both and then ran back in his direction.

"Will! They said it would be a swell idea! Poppa's going to go tell Rev. Pippin and I'm going to go change. I'll be right back!"

Will stopped her with one of his arms around her stomach and swung her back in his direction. "Come here, you. Let me kiss you one more time."

After they had kissed, she hurried back to her wagon where her mother was waiting. Henry Travis walked over to Will and handed him a cigar and a small glass of whiskey. "Son, here, take this it will calm your nerves."

"Oh, really sir, I'm okay..."

"Nonsense, now here take this and relax a little bit."

Will took the glass of whiskey, too embarrassed to tell him that he had never drank before, but he was pretty sure Henry got the idea when Will made a horrible face after downing the drink. "How... how exactly is this going to calm my nerves?"

"Ha! Just give it time, son. It will work its magic! Now here, take this cigar and smoke with me. After all, it looks like I'm about to get a new son and that's something to celebrate!"

Will took the cigar, hoping desperately that it would somehow get the awful taste of whiskey out of his mouth and smoked it with his soon to be father-in-law. They watched as the newlyweds began to dance to more tunes coming from Andy's fiddle. Ann Marie Pippin ran up to Will and threw her arms around him.

"Will! Is it true you're getting married too?"

"That's right, little bug. You want to stand up there next to me?"

"Will! I wanted to marry you!"

"Awe, come on now. You will find the right guy out there when you're marrying age. Besides, you're much too pretty for me."

"But Will!"

"No, buts, little bug. So what do you say, do you want to stand up there next to me?"

"Fine, I guess so. But I'm not going to say one word to Miss Travis!"

"Ha, suit yourself, but I bet if you talk to her you two could be best of friends."

"Well...we'll see, I guess."

Margaret Travis left the wagon that Dottie was in and made her way over to the three of them. She had a special glow not only on her face, but over her whole body that only a proud mother could have.

"Will, she's almost ready. You had better go stand over next to the preacher."

"Come on, Ann Marie," he said, "I can't go without my best little bug."

She rolled her eyes and reluctantly followed him. Rev. Pippin ordered the music to stop and everyone sat there in silence. Andy played a soft tune on the fiddle and as he did, Will Braymyer's future wife emerged from behind a wagon.

She was wearing a white dress with a silver necklace that Will had noticed her mother wearing a few days before. For a girl who was living in the west, she sure had a sense of style and he knew immediately that his mother would like her very well. Her auburn hair glowed in the light of the fire as it sat atop her head in a perfect bun with a few jewels scattered throughout it.

Everyone gazed at her as if they had never seen anyone look as good as she did that night. She looked like a queen that had somehow been thrown off her throne and into the vast western landscape of America. Will watched in amazement and couldn't figure out how he had gotten to be so lucky as to get a wife like Dorothy Travis.

When she reached Will, they joined hands just above Ann Marie's head and Dottie looked down at her and gave her the most understanding, kindest smile a person could give anyone. Ann Marie looked up at her, removed her hands from her hips and smiled back, realizing that Miss. Travis might not be half-bad.

The music stopped and the preacher began to read from his weathered bible. "Do you William Charles Braymyer and do you Dorothy Elizabeth Travis..."

Everyone continued to look at the two of them as they made their life long promises to each other. Will's blond hair sparkled between the fire and the moonlight and his eyes had never been as blue as they were that night. Rev. Pippin finished the ceremony and Will leaned in and gave her her first kiss as Mrs. Dottie Braymyer.

Claps and applause once again filled the night air and the music erupted once more. The three couples danced the night away, with Ann Marie stepping in occasionally for Dottie. The weary travelers were all at peace with their lives for the night, but tomorrow they must get back on the trail and head to California.

Will held his wife close and wondered how in one day, he was able to admit he had fallen in love, express his feelings for the first time in his life and end the day by marrying the love of his life. He was a happy man, and he slept like a king that night beneath the open sky with Dottie at his side.

Chapter 4

The next day, the wagon train got a late start, but was back on the trail by mid-morning none the less. They were somewhere in Utah and the sun was beating down upon them as they continued westward into the great unknown. Will took his place alongside the Captain at the head of the group while Dottie sat in her parent's wagon with Ann Marie at her side.

Captain Perkins said that everyone needed to be on extra lookout now for the desert Indians and to keep the guns loaded at all times. Will could tell the Captain was nervous as they rode on, he couldn't keep his eyes focused in one area very long, but rather he danced across the landscape with his vision.

A part of Will wanted to be in the back with Abner and Marshall so they could all talk about their new married lives, but when he thought about it enough, he was thankful that he was allowed to be up front with the more mature men. Sutherland and Goodnight kept to themselves mostly and now that they were on high alert, the Captain also said very little.

Will wondered what his Ma and Pa were doing back in Missouri and how life was treating them since he had been gone. He wished they could have been there to see him get married, but knew they would be proud and would have most definitely approved of his decision.

From all the way up front, Will could hear Abner Douglas whistling away at the warm day. He must have known a million songs, for he never whistled the same tune twice and Will often wondered if perhaps he was making up some of the tunes.

The wagons rode into a valley that was surrounded by giant red cliffs on all sides except for behind them. As they traveled through, the rocks got closer and closer together until only the small wagon trail ran through it and the mountains of rocks were right at it on both sides.

The rocks forced the front riders to ride one behind another as they went through the pass, rather than side by side. Abner continued to whistle and it echoed throughout the entire pass and then made its way back to the travelers. When they were about halfway through, there was a sudden return whistle coming from somewhere within the rocks.

"Hold up!" The captain shouted, turning his horse completely around and then ending up back in the same direction he had started in.

"What is it, Captain?" Will asked.

Abner had stopped whistling, but there was still a faint short whistle here and there and it seemed to be coming from all around them.

Dottie and Ann Marie stuck their heads out of the front of the wagon and looked ahead in Will's direction, both checking to make sure he was okay. Everyone remained quiet, listening ever so carefully for that short chirp of a whistle that would make its occasional presence around them from somewhere within the red rocks.

"There's Indians somewhere out there," Capt. Perkins said. "They're scouting us out, they whistle to each other as a way of talking."

"You think they'll attack us here?" Will asked.

"I'm not sure, but we best move along in case they do decide to attack. We would be trapped here for good if they move in on us now."

The riders and wagons cautiously moved forward through the pass, the whistle following them all the while. Even the horses seemed to be a bit on edge by the man made whistle and they would let out an occasional grunt to remind their riders of the impending danger.

Just before reaching the opening of the pass, an arrow was shot into the Pippin's wagon, going straight through the canvas top and striking the newlywed Charlotte in the chest.

Shots rang out with such force that the walls of the pass threatened to cave in at any given moment. The women and children were shouting and screaming while all the men fired up into the rocks at moving targets.

Dottie and Ann Marie, along with Margaret leapt out of the wagon and took cover beneath it where they were less likely to be shot by an arrow. The other wagons soon followed suit, but again the Pippin's wagon had run out of luck.

As the family climbed out of the wagon, all five of the remaining children were shot by an arrow somewhere on their bodies. Hannah ran to her children where she too was met with the point of an arrow and all of them slowly drug themselves beneath the protection of the wagon.

Will jumped off his horse and used the animal as his shield as he took aim into the rocks and shot every time he saw a painted face emerge from behind a rock. He had fired eight times and all eight times had been a success. Sutherland was brought down with an arrow in the neck, leaving only Will, Captain Perkins and Goodnight at the front of the line.

After about five minutes of their attackers picking them off one by one, the wild men charged down the side of the rock wall in their direction. There were about ten of them and every one of them shot arrows at the white settlers as they approached them.

Will continued to fire, praying that enough of them would be dead soon so that the others would run back into the desert. Goodnight shouted out cuss words at them and with his rifle in hand he ran toward them like a mad man, shooting two of them down before he fell to his knees.

At the Travis wagon, the women continued to stay beneath the wagon while Henry Travis stood up on his wagon seat and shot at another group of Indians that were coming down at them from their right. Slowly, one by one he and Andy Williams brought them down the cliff with bullets inside of them.

As Henry continued to fire, arrows whizzed by his body on all sides until at once, three struck him in his abdomen. He struggled to stay afoot for a moment, but then a forth arrow hit him in the shoulder, forcing him to fall backwards off of the wagon seat.

He landed directly next to his wife, Margaret who screamed hysterically at her husband and at the blood pouring out of his mouth. She left the cover of the wagon and threw herself on top of him begging for life to re-enter his body. Dottie remained under the wagon with Ann Marie and watched as an arrow struck her mother in the back and went all the way through into her father, pinning the two of them together.

Margaret struggled to get up and was able to stand up on both of her feet, the arrow still protruding through her body. She turned toward the Indians with a look of pure disgust and anger and pointed her husband's gun in their direction.

She was choking on her own blood and her vision was becoming more and more blurred as she struggled to stay on her feet. She fired once and shot one of the men in the legs before another arrow hit her in the chest. She fell down beside her husband and looked up into blue sky.

Dottie reached out and grabbed for her father's gun. "Ann Marie! You stay here and don't move! Do you understand!"

Ann Marie was in tears and couldn't even spit out a word, but she shook her head yes and then buried her face back into her palms.

Dottie now had the gun in her hands and looked over at her parent's bodies to make sure she wasn't dreaming. She wanted desperately to cry and run to Will, but she knew that this wasn't the time for emotional outpour, even if she had just witnessed her parents being murdered.

She ducked her head down below the side of the wagon and caught her breath while telling herself that she could do this. In a swift motion she threw herself up onto the wagon seat and fired at the approaching attackers. She didn't care if she got shot, she didn't even care if they kidnapped her, she was out to kill for vengeance.

She jumped down from the seat toward the Indians and continued walking toward them, sweat and tears pouring down her face. The butt of the gun never left her shoulder and her finger was attached to the trigger. As she continued walking and firing, she noticed that someone was beside her, walking and firing right alongside her.

She didn't dare look for fear that it would give the Indians an upper hand and she would be shot, instead she focused in on her targets, fearing her luck would soon run out.

The mysterious gunman at her right was now almost directly beside her. "Hello, Mrs. Braymyer."

"Will!"

"Keep firing, darling. I'm going to walk ahead of you and when I do I want you to get behind me."

That was all the talking they did as they continued toward the Indians. What had started as eight attackers in front of them, was now down to two and as Dottie stepped behind the protection of her husband's body, the last two of them fell to the ground.

The rocky pass grew quiet as the smoke lifted from the air. Will turned to Dottie and took her in his arms, not knowing what to say as he looked over at the bodies of her parents. She pushed her head as deep into his chest as it could possibly go and cried uncontrollably.

Ann Marie emerged from the wagon and ran over to her family's wagon where she found her entire family dead, slaughtered by the Indians. She let out a loud high-pitched scream that echoed throughout the rocks louder than the gunfire could have ever thought about being.

Dottie turned to face her and forgot all about her parents as she ran to the girl and took her in her arms. Will looked around and was shocked as he saw the bodies of several of his fellow travelers on the ground. When it was all over, only him, Dottie, Ann Marie, Beth, Abner and Beth's younger brother, Travis were left standing in the pass.

- - - - - - - - - - - - - - - - - - - -

Will, Abner and Travis loaded all the bodies onto the Pippin wagon and drove out of the pass with the Turner and Travis wagons following behind them by way of Dottie and Beth. Once out of the pass, Will steered the wagon off to the right of the trail and stopped.

The three men took shovels and began digging holes atop a small hill while the women sat and watched, unable to believe what had just happened. Just before nightfall, the last body was covered in the Utah dirt and the last cross was hammered at its head.

Will held Dottie in his arms, while Ann Marie wrapped her hands around his waist and cried. All of them stood on top of the hill while Abner recited versus from the bible. A warm breeze blew upon them as the sun turned bright orange in the western sky and the hungry travelers turned and headed back toward their wagons.

Dottie and Beth gathered up enough strength to prepare a meal of salt pork on the fire that the men had made while they stood nearby and talked amongst themselves.

For the most part, they stood in silence until Will spoke up. "Well, boys. Do you reckon we should push forward?"

"We've come this far," Abner said, "It'd be a shame to turn back now."

"And besides," Travis said, "There's nothing for me back east except for more graves to visit. I say we keep going, it'd be kinda' disrespectful to the bodies up on the hill if we turn back now."

"Well then it's agreed. We'll leave out first thing in the morning," Will said, "Travis, why don't you take the Captain's horse. I think you deserve it."

"You mean it, Will?"

"Man needs a horse and you've proved yourself today, son."

The fire went out just after they had all finished eating and no one bothered starting it up again, they were all too tired and something about the light depressed them. They said very little to each other that night and slept in the pitch dark as the coyotes howled in the distance.

The next morning, Will drove the Travis wagon with Dottie at his side and Ann Marie in the back while Abner and Beth drove the wagon behind them. Travis proudly rode the white stallion in front of the wagons, leading them west.

Three days after burying the majority of their crew, they came upon an old desert shanty that had been abandoned for some time. They pulled up to it and anxiously went in to explore the intriguing structure.

It had three rooms in it and every room had a fireplace. The main room served as the kitchen and living area, while the room directly beside it and the one behind it were both bedrooms, which still had feather mattresses in them.

They had come through a small trading community about four miles back and the man at the general trading post had told them about this place. There was a small creek that ran behind the house and the land was open as far as they could see. It had slowly started to look greener as they had been traveling on and this place looked as if it would make good farmland.

The women went in and began preparing their meal while the men took the animals to the old barn out back after watering them in the creek. When they had finished, they joined the women inside where they saw them smiling for the first time since the Indian attack.

They had been talking about their lives back east and all the good times that they were blessed to have endured. They spoke only of their happy memories and forced the recent slaughter out of their minds.

They stayed in the house for two weeks, not wanting to get back onto the westward trail and travel on. They relaxed and lived off of the game that Will and Abner were able to hunt from the area.

Will walked into the house one night after tending to the animals, "Well, I reckon we should probably hit the trail tomorrow morning, no sense in staying on here forever."

"Will," Abner said, "Beth and I have been talking and we think we're going to stay on here, permanent like."

"Are you sure, Abner? We're not too far from California."

"Yes, we've talked it over and the land is good here. Travis, you'll be eighteen soon so we'll leave the decision up to you. You can stay on here or if Mr. Braymyer will allow it, you can travel on with him."

Travis looked at his sister who looked back with understanding eyes and then over to his cousin and then at Will. "Mr. Braymyer I'd sure like to keep on going. This farming is just not for me, sir."

"That's fine, Travis. You're welcome to come with us." Will reached out his hand to Abner, "Abner, good luck to you and

202

if you ever need anything, just head west you'll know where to find us."

"I appreciate it, Will and who knows, we may make it out to California someday yet."

Dottie hugged her cousin, Beth and they shared a few tears together as they knew that tomorrow they would have to say goodbye. It had been a long journey and neither Will or Dottie blamed them for wanting to stay on.

When the sun came up, Will, Dottie, Ann Marie and Travis got back onto the dusty trail and headed west. Abner and Beth stood outside of their new home and waved them off as they continued on, drawing closer and closer to California.

Chapter 5

It had been almost three weeks since they had left Abner and Beth behind and just as Will had hoped, the land was indeed becoming more promising the further west they went. Dottie continued to ride atop the wagon and they would have to make frequent stops when she became sick.

Will had held up his promise to his father in law and the young couple were expecting their first child. Ann Marie had become like their daughter and she had turned out to like Dottie very much.

Ann Marie was remarkably good looking for as young as she was. She had the prettiest smooth brown hair and cool aqua eyes to go with it. When they had started on the trip, she was more of a tomboy and didn't care if she was dirty or not, but now that she had been around Dottie, she carried herself with a little more grace.

Travis continued riding his horse near the wagon eagerly waiting to get to that far off place they were headed. He had taken after his mother's side of the family and had been blessed with good looks as well. He was average height, blonde headed and green eyes that showed more compassion than anything else.

One afternoon as the wagon continued along the trail, they came across a wooden sign that read; "California." They all stopped and took a moment to enjoy themselves and everything that this long journey had meant. Dottie ran her hand across the letters of the sign as a tear fell from her face.

Will put his arm around her and looked past the sign into California. "You okay, Dottie?"

"Yes, Will. I am just happy that we finally made it and I just wish my parents could be here to enjoy it with me."

"Well, Dottie. I reckon they're looking down on us right now. Seems to me that they probably beat us here. I hear angels can travel a lot faster than people…that's what I hear anyhow."

"Oh, Will," she said laughing a little bit, "You're full of it!"

"Hey look here!" Travis yelled, "I've got one foot in California and one foot over yonder! How do ya' like that. I'm in two places at once!"

The rest of them laughed and shook their heads at him. "Travis," Ann Marie said, "You don't have the brains God gave to a buzzard!"

More laughter erupted, even Travis couldn't help but laugh at the joke intended for him. The four of them stood there for a moment longer gazing out over the California land and knowing that it wouldn't be much longer now before they were able to settle down for good.

Ann Marie took a small splinter from the wooden sign, wrapped it in a piece of white cloth and put it in the back of the wagon. After everyone had taken their last look ahead of them they loaded up and continued onward.

The wagon rode a little more joyful into this land of opportunity and even the horses had their heads a little higher as they breathed in the fresh California air. It had been a long hard journey, but they had finally made it to that far off place people in the east only dreamed about.

They traveled five more miles past the California border and came to a small town called Texia. Will drove the wagon to the general store and the group of newfound Californians went inside.

Will stocked up on supplies and bought some fabric for Dottie to make her and Ann Marie a new dress, a California dress as he called it. When they had finished in the store they drove outside of town and set up camp.

"Will," Dottie said as they sat around a campfire, "How much longer do you think we'll be traveling for?"

"Well, I reckon we'll go on for three more days and get ourselves right into the heart of California and that's where we'll build our home."

Just as Will said, they went on for three days and about ten miles out of Yuba City they pulled the wagons up to a group of trees. Will held up the land deed he had gotten back in town and shouted, "California! You're all mine!"

They had arrived at their homestead in mid morning and they spent the rest of the day setting up a permanent camp. Travis wandered the hills for firewood while Ann Marie and Dottie unloaded all of the food and kitchen stuff.

Will took the canvas off of the wagon and using some long sticks, he made a tent. He had two extra canvas tops in his wagon so he was able to make three tents. The camp sat on top of a small green hill that had a few trees scattered across it.

To the north of it there was a large creek that ran east to west and it offered plenty of water for anyone around. Standing on top of the hill, a person could see for miles across the land and they all knew that it would make a great place for a home.

The next day, Will and Travis began cutting down trees from a nearby forest and hauling them to the future home site. Together, the two of them stacked them up one by one and slowly a log cabin was emerging. After two weeks of non-stop work, all the walls were standing and a small barn was partially behind the house.

Since they had arrived at their new home, they had not seen a single person until one day Will was on top of the house getting ready to build a roof. As he sat on top of the eastern wall, in the distance he could see seven or eight riders heading in their direction.

"Travis," he shouted, "Go fetch me my pistol."

Travis ran toward Will and Dottie's tent and brought his pistol to him, carrying the rifle for himself. Will climbed down from the roof, took the pistol and waited next to Travis.

Dottie and Ann Marie were down at the creek gathering up some grapes and fresh water for them. As the riders got closer, Will noticed they were all Mexicans and wore overly large hats. They all looked to be armed.

"Aye Gringo," the leader said pointing his gun at the two of them. "Give me your denero or I kill you."

"I don't have any." Will answered.

The Mexican rider clicked his pistol into firing mode and began to laugh, "Give me your denero or I kill you and your Senorita over at the creek!"

All eight of the riders began to laugh and Will could tell that they had been drinking.

Will stood there looking in their direction trying to figure out a way to avoid giving them the money he had saved up. If he were to lose it, there would be no way that they would be able to survive in California. "Travis," he said, "Go fetch me my saddle bag."

Travis returned to the tent as everyone watched him. He came back with the bag and handed it to Will. Will reached into the brown leather bag and pulled out a small pouch, which had all his money inside of it. The Mexican fired a bullet into Will's stomach and he fell backwards.

Travis threw up his gun and shot the leader in the head, but before he was able to take out another one he was lying on the ground with a bullet in his upper right shoulder. Travis fell backwards and he bled so badly that the Mexican's thought that they had shot him in the heart.

One of the riders jumped down and grabbed the sack full of money, kicking both Travis and Will before getting back up onto his horse. The now seven riders headed back east riding as fast as they possibly could.

Dottie and Ann Marie returned to the campsite about twenty minutes after they had heard the gunshot and found the two men lying on the ground. Dorothy frantically ran through the camp looking for something to pull the bullets out and pack the wounds.

She started with Will who let out an occasional grunt as she used a knife to dig into his stomach for the bullet. The deeper she dug, the more the blood poured out of his body.

Ann Marie sat with Travis who was still fully conscious and had only been playing dead in front of the attackers. He had his head propped up in Ann Marie's lap and watched as Dorothy removed the bullet from her husband who was now making no noise at all and had his eyes completely shut.

About thirty minutes after she started she pulled the bullet out of Will's stomach and packed the wound with some of the fabric he had bought her to try and stop the bleeding. Dottie threw herself on top of her husband crying uncontrollably. "Will, don't you dare leave me here alone! Please God, please don't take him from me!"

Chapter 6

The next morning, with Dottie still by his side, Will opened his eyes and gazed up into the blue California sky. Dottie was sleeping after being next to him all night, but Ann Marie jumped up and shouted for Travis to come out of his tent.

The noise woke Dottie and when she saw that Will was awake she began to cry again. "Will, I thought I lost you! Don't you ever do that to me again!"

"I'm alright, darling. Just a little sore is all." Will tried to sit up, but the pain in his stomach stopped him.

"Stay there, Will. You rest and I'll get you something to eat."

Ann Marie was at his side and holding his hand, refusing to leave. "Will, are you going to be okay?" She said crying.

"I'll be fine, little bug. Don't you cry over me."

"Will, I shot the one that got you," Travis said walking over with his arm in a sling from the same fabric that was in Will's stomach.

"You did good son. Now go fetch me my gun. We've got to get my horse saddled so I can go get our money back."

"Will!" Dottie protested hysterically. "You are to hurt! You mustn't go after them! What if you get shot again?"

"Dottie, I have to! There's no way we can make it without the money. A man can't just sit around and get robbed and not try and do right by it."

"But, Will, please don't go!" She said throwing herself back on top of him.

"I have to, there's no other way we can make a life for ourselves here. If I leave now, chances are I'll be able to catch up to them tonight. Hopefully, they haven't spent all our moncy yct."

Dottie couldn't argue with Will and she was heartbroken just the same as if he had already died. "Travis, you stay here and look after the women while I'm gone. You're in charge, you hear?"

"Yes, sir. I'll watch over them real good."

"Good boy."

Will forced himself off of the ground after Dottie had changed his bandage. He swayed side to side once he had made it up onto his feet. "Little bug, you be good and help out Travis, okay?"

"I will, Will. Please don't go." She said wrapping her arms around him.

"I'm afraid I have to, Sweetheart."

Will took Dottie in his arms who continued to cry. She held on to him like it was the last time she would ever feel the warmth of his body again. He turned to his brown mare and used the last of his strength to pull himself atop her. Once in the saddle, Dottie handed him up his rifle and his pistol as he hunched forward to cause as little pain to his wound as possible.

Will followed the Mexican's tracks east, in too much pain to turn back and wave goodbye. He could smell the deer meat in his saddlebag that Dottie had packed him and for a moment it drew his attention off of his pain. He didn't know how he was going to get their money back, but he knew he must at least try.

Dottie watched as her injured husband rode away and placed a hand on her growing stomach. Tears continued to fall across her cheeks as he disappeared into the California landscape.

She turned back to their farm where Travis and Ann Marie looked at her as if she was about to do something crazy. She cleared her throat, "Travis, you're still weak, go rest up while Ann Marie and I tend to the farm."

"Dottie, really I'm…"

"Travis go on now. I only have time for one stubborn man today and he just rode off. Please, just go rest."

Travis threw out a quilt beneath one of the trees and tried to take a nap, but all he could think about was Will and how badly he wanted to be there to help him.

Dottie tore down the tents and gathered up the canvas from them. She had no idea how to build a roof, but she figured a wagon canvas would work just fine for the time being.

She climbed up onto the top of the cabin as Ann Marie threw up the canvas to her. With hammer and nail in hand, she secured all three canvases on top of the cabin, allowing them to overlap and hang down over all the walls.

When she was finished she climbed down and just like that the cabin was finished. "Well, Ann Marie, looks like we got ourselves a cabin."

The women hauled everything into their new home, which only had two rooms and one fireplace and then began cooking supper. Travis sat in a rocker near the women and not a word was said about Will.

After they had eaten, Dottie started knitting the first piece of clothing for her new baby, mostly to keep her mind busy. Everyone sat in silence and the only thing that could be heard was the steady rock of the chairs.

For two months the Braymyer home was almost completely silent and there had still been no word of Will or his whereabouts. Dottie had received a letter from his mother and she replied to it, telling her everything except what was going on with Will. A mother shouldn't worry unless she knows for sure her son is dead, she thought.

In late October, Dottie left the house and went for a walk across their farmland that had sat dormant that entire year. She crossed several fields until she came upon a meadow that was surrounded by trees except the area she had entered through.

She walked to the middle of it and threw herself down into the golden grass. She had hit rock bottom and didn't know what else to do. They were running low on food, being saved only by Travis hunting for them every day and the baby would be here soon and she had still not heard from Will. Dottie didn't know what to do anymore, it had been the hardest year of her life and she didn't think she could bare another one like it.

She sat there in the meadow and prayed as she wept and yelled up at the sky. After she had cried all she could and tears refused to come out anymore she stood up. A wind from what seemed like directly above engulfed her. It was almost as if it were blowing away all of her worries and problems that life had dealt her and for a moment she felt completely free.

Her dress flapped into the wind along with her hair and the only thing that held her down was her large stomach that had a steady thump coming from inside of it. She raised her hands up into the air, fully prepared to ascend into the clear sky and leave everything behind.

She lowered her hands back down and placed them on her stomach as she continued to look up. The wind slowly started to shift and move to the right. Since Will had left, that wind was the closest thing she had to hang on to aside from her unborn child.

She ran after it as it continued to move away, "Wait!" She shouted, "Take me with you!"

She continued to run into the trees after the wind, she didn't care how far she had to go, she was going to catch that wind. It continued to twirl and twist in front of her as she ran through on an old foot trail.

She continued down the trail as it turned left and right and then made its way downward where she was forced to stop as it came upon a creek. She stood on the bank and watched it as it spun on top of the water, moving so fast that it caused the dirt beneath the water to scatter about making the water brown.

It continued to do so and then within a matter of seconds it shot up into the air so fast that it looked as if it went beyond the blue sky. Dottie watched as it flew away and then looked back down at the muddy water.

She sat down and was about to start crying some more, thinking that she had completely lost her mind. She lifted her head out of her hands and gazed into the clearing water. Something caught her eye as she watched the dirt settle to the bottom.

In the muddy mess there was a gold colored rock forming at the bottom. She stepped into the cool water and reached in after the object. It was so heavy that it took both of her hands to pull it out and she nearly fainted when she realized what it was.

She had pulled up out of the water a large chunk of gold, too heavy for her to carry alone. After she rolled it up onto the bank she sat down to catch her breath. "I thought the gold days were over," she said out loud.

She couldn't believe what she was seeing and she knew without a doubt that she would never have to worry about anything again as long as she lived, but more importantly her baby would have a good life. Excitement overwhelmed her as she searched for a place to hide it.

She rolled it away from the trail and hid it beneath some brush next to a nearby tree. She stood back up and brushed herself off and then went as fast as she could back to the cabin to fetch Travis.

She had been so excited that as soon as she got within a hundred feet of the farm she began shouting for him. Both Travis and Ann Marie followed her back to her hidden treasure, both unaware of what exactly it was she was leading them too.

Neither one of them had seen her this excited since Will had left so they knew it had to be something big. She led them to the tree and the large chunk of gold was right where she had left it.

"Dottie! Is that gold!" Ann Marie said putting her hands over her mouth.

"Yes, we're rich!"

Travis leaned down to take a closer look, "I've never seen anything like it before, where did you find it?"

Dottie, who was almost completely out of breath pointed over to the creek, "Over there in the creek. Do you think you can carry it back to the house?"

"I reckon I can," Travis answered. "What are we going to do with it?"

"We need to take it to Sacramento and cash it in. I don't want people in these parts knowing we have money, or worse, gold on our property."

Chapter 7

Travis took the gold into Sacramento and cashed it in. When he rode back to Dottie, he had fifteen thousand dollars… more money than any of them had ever seen. Everyone was happy inside the little old log cabin, their only regret was that Will was not there with them to enjoy it.

Dottie wasted no time and by early January she had hired enough workers that her new elegant two-story home was finished. She was careful to pay all the workers in bank drafts so that they would think she had no money at her farm.

The house was made out of white stone and like the house at Braymyer Ridge, it had a porch going all the way around it with a larger balcony on the second floor above the column filled front porch. There were seven bedrooms and 4 fireplaces, it was by far one of the nicest homes in the area.

The three of them lived happily in the new home and were excited to see what the future would bring, but they always remained hopeful that Will would return to them. Ann Marie was now doing most of the housework as Dottie drew closer and closer to having the baby.

Just before sun down on January 23, Dottie went into labor. She was in the kitchen when the pain first started and she drug herself up to her bedroom with the help of Travis and Ann Marie. After she had made it to her bed, Travis went outside the bedroom and waited just in case Ann Marie needed anything.

Childbirth was no place for a man and even though he loved his cousin very much, he had no intention of being apart of this miracle, especially when he heard the screams coming from beyond the door. Ann Marie did everything she knew how to for Dottie and never left her side until the next afternoon when the baby was born.

"Travis!" She shouted running out the door, "It's a girl! Dottie had a baby girl!"

"Great," he answered, "Another girl…"

"Oh hush now. Come on, you can come in now."

Travis reluctantly followed Ann Marie back into the bedroom where Dottie was sitting up holding the baby. "Travis," she said, "Say hello to your cousin."

Travis looked down at the small baby and couldn't see what the big fuss was about. He had seen puppies that looked prettier than a newborn baby. But he reckoned for a baby, she was mighty handsome.

Ann Marie walked around the bed and stood on the other side of Dottie. "What are you going to name her?"

"Well, I've been thinking about it for awhile now and it seems that there are two things that have forever changed my life. California and Gold. So, I think I'll name her California Gold Braymyer."

"California Gold!" Travis protested.

Ann Marie and Dottie both laughed. "Well, Travis, we can call her Callie."

"Well I figure Callie ain't half bad."

"Isn't Travis," Ann Marie corrected him.

Dottie looked down at her child, "So Callie it is."

- - - - - - - - - - - - - - - - - -

When Will Braymyer left for town that day in search of his money, there was no way even the strongest man could have made it with the kind of wound he had. He made it half way to Yuba City and then fell off of his horse and watched the buzzard's gather above him.

He thought for sure he was dead, there was no hope and now who knows what would happen to his wife. As he continued to lie there the life slowly exited his body into an unknown

218

plane. Just before he closed his eyes for the last time, a Mohave Indian stood above him.

When he woke up three days later, he was in one of their villages being tended to and nursed back to health by some of their woman. It had taken him a month for his wound to completely heal up and even though he was still sore he was almost ready to head back to his farm.

Will Braymyer had started his life in California with a string of bad luck, which is why he was a prisoner in Mexico when his daughter was born. The day before he was set to leave for home, a group of Vaqueros attacked the small tribe and took several prisoners to use as slaves in their home country.

Will was now working alongside the same Indians that had saved his life and was spending all day and half the night mining for silver. His clothes were rags and he hadn't had a good shave since he had been shot outside of his home.

There was no way for him to escape the country without being noticed by someone, so there was little hope for his survival. The prisoners were kept in several shanties and there was always at least four or five guards on duty for the thirty of them.

It could be an easy victory for the prisoners, but even if they were to kill guards and escape they would be gunned down before traveling a mile. Will was ready to give up and thought about killing himself as he picked away at the rocks.

As these thoughts filled his mind, he was reminded of what his Grandma Alice had once said; "Being a Braymyer is special and it is most certainly different. We aren't like most people…we're survivors."

Will put the pickaxe down and thought for a moment. There had to be a way to get out of here. He had to get word to someone so that they could send help. It was doubtful that the Army would come down to rescue one white man and a bunch of Indians…it had to be something else.

It would have to be someone smart too. This kind of escape would take special planning and only a certain type of person could do it. Suddenly it hit him. His younger brother, Nat who was now a sheriff over in Texas was the wittiest person he knew and if anyone could get him out of this mess it would be him.

Now he just had to figure out a way to get a letter sent out. When the sun had went down and all the Mexican's of the camp were having a fiesta, Will snuck out of the back window of his one room shanty that he shared with nine other men. He had dressed himself in a sombrero and wrapped a large Mexican blanket around him.

Keeping his head down he walked around the crowd and headed to the back door of the post office. Once inside he grabbed an ink pen and paper and wrote a note:
Dottie,
I'm alive.
Send for brother, Nat in Dixie Texas.
Prisoner in San Luis, Mexico.
Love Will

Will addressed the letter and placed it into the outgoing mailbox that had already been sorted through. He made sure to hide it among all the other letters so it would not be seen by anyone around there. After everything was in order, he went back out the back door and into his shanty… now it was in God's hands.

Chapter 8

Dottie was sitting on the front porch rocking Callie when Travis rode up to the house on his white stallion yipping and shouting for her. With the baby in her arms, she stood up and watched as he drew nearer.

"Travis, what is it?"

He was out of breath and between the few short breaths he did have he managed to say, "Will…he's alive!"

"What!"

"Here, here is a letter from him."

Dottie took the folded piece of paper from him and opened it up. "Ann Marie!" She shouted, "Come quick!"

Ann Marie came out onto the front porch to see what all the commotion was about. "What is it?"

"It's Will! He's alive! Hurry, go fetch me a pen and paper I've got to send for his brother in Texas."

She hurried back into the house and in no time she had brought back a pen and paper. Her face was lit up as bright as it possibly could be and she watched over Dottie's shoulder as she wrote a letter to Texas.

Mr. Nat Braymyer,
Your brother needs help. He is in San Luis, Mexico as a prisoner. Please help.

Your loving sister in law,
Dottie Braymyer

Travis took the letter and rode as fast as he could back into town to see the letter off. When he returned the anxious tension in the house was so great that he couldn't bear it. After everyone went to sleep he sat on the front porch, wishing there was something he could do himself to save their Will.

He could go after him himself, but then the women would be left unprotected and if something were to happen to them, he could never forgive himself. No matter how bad it hurt, he knew he must stay on at the house like Will had asked him to.

_ _ _ _ _ _ _ _ _ _ _ _ _ _ _ _ _ _

Abner and Beth stood beside the shallow grave that now held their infant son. Their lives had been hard since they had decided to stay behind and in fact Abner had completely given up farming. He took to the hills and became an animal trapper, selling their skins for rock bottom price at the nearby trading post.

Beth was left at the house by herself most of the time and usually there were three or four wagons a day that would stop and beg for food. Life had been unfair to them, much like it had been to Will, but they were happy and content in having each other to lean on.

They walked side by side back to the house, slowly on account that Beth was still sore from the childbirth. They held their heads low as they continued down an old dirt trail to the home they had made.

"Beth?"

"Yes, Abner?"

"What do you say we give California a try?"

"Oh, Abner… I thought you'd never ask."

_ _ _ _ _ _ _ _ _

March 1875

The Braymyer home was still full of anxious people as the days drug on and turned into night. Dottie was relieved to find out that her husband was alive, but was more worried now than ever before. She busied herself with the baby and the housework while Travis tended to the animals and had started plowing up some of the land to the east.

Dottie had decided that Will was coming home no matter what and she didn't want him to come home to a desolate farm. She had placed an order in Yuba City for grape seed and once the fields were ready she planned to fill them with grapes.

She forced herself to not think about all the bad things life had thrown her way and instead looked brightly into the future, which would include her husband. Her and Will were one of the richest families in the area and no one even knew it. She kept her money a secret and had the majority of it hidden beneath the house in a wooden box that could only be accessed through a trap door beneath the dining room table.

It was early morning as she swept the front porch while Ann Marie made biscuits in the back kitchen. The air was like breathing in fruit juice and the wind reminded her of that day she had stumbled onto the golden rock.

Dottie looked up and noticed that there was someone walking down the path to the house. She studied the figure as it drew nearer and was about to go get the gun when she realized it was a woman heading in her direction.

She was walking through the growing grass, wearing a bonnet and a flower patterned dress. She was colored and looked to be in her thirties, her dark skin reflecting brightly off of the sun.

"Can I help you with something?" Dottie asked her as she approached the porch.

"Yes, maim, I sure hope you can. I's looking for work, I can do most anything I swear I can."

"Don't you have a family somewhere?"

"No, maim, They's all killed on the way to California. We come from Mississip you see and some Indians killed them off. All but me and one white family that is. They brought me

223

over to Yuba City and I's been there for two weeks. Then the gentleman at the store told me if I's looking for work I should come pay you a visit."

Dottie looked down at her with sympathy and understood what it was like to lose your family under those circumstances. "Do you have a name?"

"Oh, yes, maim. My name is Keziah Underwood, but you can call me Kizzie."

"Well, Kizzie, I'm Dottie Braymyer. Do you have a bag or clothes or anything you need to get."

"No, maim. Just what I got's here on my back."

"Very well, then. You can stay upstairs in the guest bedroom."

"Oh no, maim. I don't mind sleeping out in the barn, being that I'm color an all. "

"Nonsense. Just because you're black don't mean you have to sleep in the barn. Besides, you'll be spending most of your time in the house anyway so you might as well sleep there too."

"Oh thank you, maim, thank you."

"Well, come on then. We've got work to do."

That night after everyone had gone to sleep, Dottie sat alone in the dark at the dining room table with a cup of hot tea. She was glad Kizzie had come to the house that day, Lord knows they could use the help, especially with planting season coming up. It would be nice if she could hire workers to plant the fields, but she knew she couldn't do that without people finding out she had money and then every outlaw in the country would be knocking at her front door.

The night was quiet and she enjoyed the peacefulness that it brought her. Before she went up to bed, she said a prayer for her husband just as she always did and then looked back on her life. It had only been a year ago that she was a waitress in a Denver café and now she was quite literally sitting on a fortune she was too afraid to touch.

The next morning she took Callie and Ann Marie for a walk along the creek that had given her fortune. They stuck their bare feet in the cool water and talked about their lives.

"Dottie," Ann Marie said, "When do you think I'll find love?"

"Well honey, that's hard to say. Usually you don't find love, but it finds you."

"Well, I'm fixing to be fourteen and I've been a woman since last August. Do you think people see me as a woman?"

"Well I don't see why not. I certainly do."

"What about Travis? Do you think he looks at me like I'm a woman?"

Dottie looked over at her, now realizing where this conversation was going. "Honey, Travis is a smart boy, but when it comes to women he wouldn't know what to do if you wrote it out for him."

"So, how's he ever going to learn?"

"Well, he's going to have to have a girl, I mean a woman, to take him by the hand and force him to open his eyes."

Ann Marie looked out into the water and thought about it for a moment. "So, say I were that woman… I just need to take him by the hand and…"

"Oh, Ann Marie." Dottie said laughing now, "Just ask him on a picnic or bring him down to the creek for a swim. Whenever you take him water while he's plowing, stay and talk for awhile. Things like that get a man's attention. The only time a man realizes anything important in life is when he's having fun. You'll do good to remember that lesson."

"So… do you think Travis is at all interested in me?"

"I don't see why he wouldn't be. You're a beautiful young lady. The only problem with Travis is that he's so used to seeing you that he probably doesn't realize how beautiful you are."

"So what do I do?"

"Put on a dress you haven't worn in awhile. Wear your hair a little different, things like that."

Down by Dixie

February 1875

Friends, our town will be without a sheriff for a little while, but fear not because Mr. Charlie Knight will be filling in. Sheriff Braymyer will be heading to Mexico where his brother has gotten into a pickle. We wish you the best of luck Sheriff and pray for your safe return.

Anna Belle Brown had another baby last week. This makes number eight and wouldn't you know it, just like the last seven, this baby boy looks just like the father. Poor poor kids… just kidding Ben.

Over on Riddle Street there is a bunch of old rockers that Tom Riddle made. He is selling them for two dollars apiece so be sure and check them out.

Allen Goldston

Chapter 9

Nat Braymyer, the good looking Texan, watched from a nearby cliff as his older brother was forced to chisel away at some rocks. It had taken him awhile to recognize his brother, he didn't look at all like he used to.

He was just a pile of skin and bones with a long blonde beard beneath his chin. It made him sad to watch as he lifted and dropped the pickaxe and then he became angry when the Mexicans shouted in his direction, threatening something in an unknown language.

Nat was over six feet tall and although Will was good looking, Nat outdid all the Braymyer boys when it came to looks. He had tan skin like his mother and a rare color of blonde hair. His blue eyes matched Will's exactly, only Nat's were a little deeper and clearer.

He had gone to Texas seven years before where he now owned a successful cotton plantation just outside of Dixie Texas. Three years ago, the town had been taken over by renegade outlaws and thanks to the efforts of Nat and a few of his friends, they were able to take the town back. Nat was elected sheriff and had served as so since.

Nat took off his cowboy hat to prevent anyone from seeing him and he continued to steady his eyes on the camp below. He noticed that aside from his brother, there was only one other white man and the rest of the prisoners were Indians.

There were about fifteen buildings scattered throughout the fly infested clearing below him and he could smell tequila rising into the air from where he sat. Mexicans were scattered about, holding old civil war guns with bayonets on the front of them.

He scratched his head as he tried to come up with a way to save not only his brother, but the other innocent prisoners as well. There were too many Mexicans for only him and his brother to defeat and the only way they stood a chance was if they could get the Indians to attack them as well.

When nightfall came, Nat lowered himself down the cliff and just outside the small clearing. He slowly crept along the rock wall that went through the western part of camp. He went around the partying Mexicans and made his way to the shanty that he had seen his brother go into.

When the coast was clear he went around to the back of it and looked through the window. He could see Will sitting on the floor, as there were no beds, looking off into space.

Nat tapped on the window and Will immediately snapped out of his gaze and looked in his direction. He ran to the window and unlatched it.

"Nat," he whispered, "You made it."

- - - - - - - - - - - - -

Ann Marie and Travis sat on a blanket beneath an oak tree beside the house. They were feasting on turkey and ham with a cold pitcher of lemonade at their side. It was a nice day outside and Ann Marie had convinced Travis to take a break from the fields and have lunch with her.

"Travis?"

"Yeah Ann Marie," he said with a mouthful of turkey.

"Do you see me as a woman?"

"Umm, sure I do. Why do you ask?"

"Just wondering is all. I think you're a fine man, Travis Turner."

"Gee, thanks Ann Marie. Are you feeling okay?"

"Of course I am. I just thought you should know I think you're a good man."

"Thanks… this is real good turkey."

"Travis! Are you not going to say anything nice about me!"

"Huh… wh…"

"Ugh!" She said standing up, "I should have never said those nice things about you!" She stormed off into the house.

Travis sat there and watched in disbelief, not knowing what had just happened. He thought about it for a moment and then dug into the turkey again. Shortly after Ann Marie went inside, Dottie came out and joined Travis.

"What's wrong with Ann Marie?" He asked.

"She has a crush, Travis."

"A crush? On who?"

Dottie looked at him and started to laugh. "You, silly!"

"Me, wha… why me?"

"Well I don't know, but I don't think she just intentionally picked you."

"But, it's Ann Marie!"

"Travis, open your eyes and take a look around you. Take a good look at her and what she's becoming… someday Ann Marie is going to do great things."

Dottie got up to leave Travis with his thoughts and as she walked toward the house she saw a wagon heading in their direction. It was riding fast as it made its way toward them and when it got closer, she realized it was a stagecoach.

It stopped directly in front of the steps that Dottie was standing on and the side door opened. A beautiful slim blonde-headed woman emerged from the wagon wearing a blue dress. She was about the same height as Dottie and had her hair tied with a blue ribbon.

After she had stepped out, two small children struggled out of the wagon. One was a seven year old boy with blonde hair like his mother and sea blue eyes and the other was a girl, a little younger with blonde hair as well.

The elegant looking woman looked over at Dottie and smiled. "Are you Dottie Braymyer?"

"Yes, I am…"

"Hi, I'm Rosalee Braymyer. We're sisters I suppose. I'm married to Will's younger brother, Nat. These are my children, Cotton and Mary Lee."

Dottie put her arms around her and hugged her. She was glad to see another Braymyer, it was the closest thing she had to Will since he left. She began to cry and Rosalee comforted her by rubbing her hand across her back.

Cotton and Mary Lee ran out into the yard and began to play tag with Travis, while the women went inside to see what Kizzie was cooking. They sat around the table and drank tea while they got acquainted with one another.

"Where is your husband?" Dottie asked.

"He put us on a stage to come look after you and he headed straight for Mexico to fetch Will."

"Oh that's wonderful news! I only hope he is able to bring him home to me."

"Well, Dottie, I reckon if anyone can bring him home, my husband would be the one to do it. That man's so stubborn I have a hard enough time getting him in for supper on time!"

The two of them laughed over the subject and Dottie filled her in on everything that had happened, even the gold which she made sure to whisper to her.

"Dottie, you done the right thing hiding that gold like you did. People hear that you've got money and trouble will find its way to you. So how are things in general around here? You have a real nice house, but how's the everyday wear and tear going?"

"We manage pretty good, some days are harder than others. Travis works real hard in the fields, but I know he wants to take off for Mexico and help Will. The only thing holding him back is the fact that he doesn't want to leave us unprotected."

"Ah, I see. That's a good man. You know, there's four of us women here now, I reckon we can hold down the fort if he wants to go on down to Mexico. In fact, I'd feel a lot better off knowing my husband had someone to help him."

"He would love that, Rosalee, but you're going to have to be the one to tell him. He's too stubborn to listen to me and doesn't want anything to happen to us."

"I'll take him on a walk after while," Rosalee said standing up and taking the baby from Kizzie. After she had Callie in her arms she sat back down in her chair.

"Rosalee, won't you and Nat consider moving out here to California? I'm sure Will would be delighted."

Rosalee looked down at the baby and smiled, "Afraid not. I'm a Texas girl now and don't think I could ever give it up. Besides, I've got a baby at home waiting on me to get back just as soon as we get you your husband home."

Kizzie served them some apple pie and they sat and talked all afternoon as if they had known each other their whole lives. There was an instant connection between Dottie and Rosalee and they were glad they had gotten to meet one another.

Kizzie prepared a big supper that night and everyone in the home sat around the large table and enjoyed themselves while they feasted.

"Hello the house!"

Travis jumped up and grabbed his gun and headed for the front door with Rosalee not far behind him, gun in hand as well. They walked out onto the front porch and Travis immediately lowered his gun.

"Beth! Abner! Dottie, come quick!"

Travis jumped down and wrapped his arms around his sister and then turned to shake Abner's hand. "What are you doing here?"

"We decided to give California a try after all."

Dottie came out of the front door and ran down to greet them. She was so excited that she began to cry. The two of them joined them at the dining room table and they were filled in on what had happened to Will. Dottie looked around the room at everyone and was half way at peace, now if only the Braymyer brothers were here.

Chapter Ten

Abner and Travis crossed into Mexico three days after leaving the Braymyer farm. Travis reluctantly went, finding it hard to say no to Rosalee and besides, this would give him time to think about what Dottie had said about Ann Marie.

Once in Mexico, they made their own trails several feet from the main one until they veered off and went up a steep cliff that overlooked the camp. They tied and hid their horses behind some boulders and on their bellies they slowly scooted to the edge of the cliff.

They watched as the Mexican Vaqueros shouted at their prisoners and pushed them to work harder and faster. When a prisoner refused there was a simple solution, kill them and that is exactly what they did.

"Do you see Will?" Travis whispered.

"No, not yet. Keep your eyes open though… this has to be the right place."

They continued to scan the prisoners in search of Will, but all they saw were tired and beaten old Indians with skin hanging loosely from their bones. They watched for thirty minutes until their attention was turned to a gun behind them.

"Don't make a move boys or I'll shoot you both."

Abner and Travis put their hands on the ground beside them and barely remembered to breathe. "What business do you two have up here?" The voice asked from behind.

Travis spoke up, "We're looking for our friend, now are you going to shoot us or what cause I'll be damned if I'm gonna' let you put me down there in that camp."

"Does this friend got a name?"

"Will Braymyer. What's it to you?"

The gun was lowered and the two of them rolled over to their backs to where they could see who the voice was coming from. "Will Braymyer is my brother, I'm Nat."

Travis rolled away from the edge of the cliff and stood up to shake his hand. "Mister, you sure had me scared there for a minute. I'm Travis Turner, a cousin of his wife's. This here is Abner Douglas, he's married to my sister, Beth."

Abner stuck out his hand and shook Nat's.

Nat looked back down in the direction of the camp. "I'm sure glad you boys showed up, I was getting awful nervous about tonight."

"Tonight?" Abner asked, "What's tonight?"

"The escape. I've been sneaking guns into the prisoner's shacks the past few nights and last night was the last time. Tonight, the prisoners are going to run for it and Will and us will be heading on our own trail back north."

"Do you think we can make it past all of them?" Travis asked.

"You ever seen an Indian with a gun, boy?"

"No, sir."

Nat laughed, "You give an Indian a gun and he darn near thinks he's God. I figure them Indians will give em one heckuva' fight."

The three of them hid out on top of the cliff and waited for nightfall, when hopefully they would all escape Mexico. They ate beef jerky that Nat had in his saddlebag to prevent them from starting a fire and besides it would give them plenty of energy for later that night.

"Why are women so complicated?" Travis asked looking dumbfounded over at the two of them.

Both Abner and Nat started to laugh. "Well, son," Nat answered, "I don't rightly know. I guess God figured he needed to make something complicated so he picked women I reckon."

"Ha, and us men are the ones paying the price," Abner said answering again.

"Well, the other day, Ann Marie said I was a fine man and I said thank you and that the turkey sure was good. Well, next thing I know she stormed off into the house and said she wished she'd never have said a nice thing about me. All on account that I didn't say something about her."

"That sounds about right. Women can be moody," Nat said, "Yes sir they can. You've just got to be patient with them is all."

Abner looked over at Travis, "So are you sweet on Ann Marie?"

"I don't rightly know. I've never really thought about it, but Dottie said to me that Ann Marie was crushing on me or something."

The two older men laughed again. "You're in trouble now, son," Nat said, "You might as well bow down and do what you're told."

"But how do you know if you've got the right woman?" Travis asked, still completely confused.

"You just do, Travis my boy," Abner said putting a hand on his shoulder, "You just do."

They took turns taking naps off and on all day until finally the sun had disappeared. The Mexicans gathered around their large campfire as they did every night and began drinking tequila.

The three men made their way slowly down into the hollow and followed the rock wall to the shanty that Will was in. Will was by the window watching for them and as soon as he spotted Nat he crept out of the back door.

"Will!" Travis said in a loud whisper.

"Hey, boy. You taking good care of Dottie and Ann Marie?"

"Yes, sir. And your daughter too."

"Daughter?"

"Come on," Nat interrupted, "We haven't got time now. We've got to get out of here before we get shot at."

The four of them carefully made their way back to the cliff and climbed to the top where their horses were waiting. Just as they had done earlier that day, they lie on their bellies and watched the partying camp below.

Within five minutes after getting up there, Indians began flying out of the shanties yipping and yelling while firing their stolen guns at the drunken Mexicans. The four of them began firing shots themselves down towards them and when the Mexicans figured it out, they returned fire up to the cliff.

Bullets continued to ring out and echoed off of the cliff walls along with the continuous yelling of the angry Indians. Mexican bodies fell everywhere and it wasn't long until they were defeated. The only task left to complete was to make it to the border without being killed.

After the Indians had killed the last Mexican they ran north like they were a pack of hungry wolves and didn't turn back.

"I'm shot in the shoulder," Abner said as he rolled over.

Nat looked his wound over and grabbed a piece of cloth from his saddle. "Here put this on it to stop the bleeding. We'll get the bullet out when we cross the border."

The four of them mounted their horses, Will getting on an extra horse Nat had brought along and headed north. They followed the Indian's trail only a short time and then turned north west so that they had less of a chance of being discovered than they would have behind the loud Indians.

Will was week and he looked even shaggier than he had when Nat had first found him. His weathered body was frail, but his blue eyes shone like they had never shined before as he kept a constant eye toward California.

They rode fast and hard and didn't say one word to each other until they had arrived back in California just before sunup. Once across, they stopped their horses beneath a tree and all four of them threw themselves onto the ground except Nat who went directly to Abner and began digging the bullet out.

Luckily it had ricocheted off of a rock before striking him so it wasn't very deep. After he got the bullet out he went over to his brother. "Will, how's it feel to be a free man?"

"Ha, it feels mighty fine. It'll be even better when I get home. A daughter?"

"Yes sir, Will," Travis said, "And you'll never guess what she named her!"

"What's that, son?"

"California Gold Braymyer!"

"What! California Gold! Has she lost her mind!"

Everyone was laughing uncontrollably. "Well," Travis said, "If it makes you feel any better we all call her Callie."

"Where in the world did she come up with that name?"

"Well she got California on account of the trip to California and she got the Gold part because, oh yeah…"

"What is it, boy?"

"Well, you're rich now. You see Dottie went on a walk and she found gold."

"Gold? How much?"

"Oh it's a might much. She even built a house."

Will looked around at them all wild eyed until he came to Nat's shining face. "You're just enjoying all this way too much aren't you, Nat?"

"Hey, it's not everyday someone saves his older brother's life…well then again I reckon I saved you a time or two from Pa's whip growing up," he said slapping his hand on Will's knee.

Travis cooked all the food they had and Will ate every bit of it and was still hungry. Nat went to a nearby town and got him a razor and a fresh pair of clothes and before they left their camp the next day, Will looked like his old self, only skinnier.

Chapter Eleven

The women sat in the front room knitting listening to the steady tick of the clock. Ann Marie sat nearest the window and watched desperately for Travis to return. She had felt so ashamed of her little fit she had and now she may never see him again.

There was very little talk, for they all knew that the men had all had plenty of time to make it to Mexico and now they patiently waited to see if they would be returning or not or if they would have to go down there themselves and deal with the Mexicans.

"Miz Braymyer! They's riders coming up the drive!" Kizzie said coming in from sweeping the front porch.

Dottie and Rosalee were the first ones at the door as the group of four riders approached them. "Kizzie, go fetch the guns! Hurry!" Dottie shouted to her.

She brought the guns back and handed them to her. "Now go upstairs with the children!"

Rosalee, Ann Marie, Dottie and Beth all walked out onto the front porch with rifles across their shoulders as the riders drew nearer. Side by side they all four stepped off of the porch and into the front yard and walked towards them.

A wind blew through and caught all of their dresses and pieces of their hair, pushing them to the east. When they were half way into the front yard they stopped as the riders stopped no more than six feet in front of them.

"Hola!"

Dottie took one step in front of the other women. "Where I come from, it's hello."

"Oh, mouthy white woman. That okay, I like em' mouthy."

The four Mexican Vaqueros all began laughing among themselves. They looked to be brothers because they all had the same features and were all almost the same height.

"What do you want?"

The leader began to laugh again before he spoke up, "Well we come to rob you, but now I not so sure. There are four of you and four of us, you can all come with us and be our wives."

The three women behind her lifted up their guns as Dottie spat up into his face. He looked shocked at first and then as he wiped it out of his black moustache he became angry.

"I'm going to cut your throat for that you loco white woman."

Ann Marie was getting nervous and she looked around at the other women who had their eyes steadied on the riders in front of them. She followed suit and turned her attention to the one closest to her, aiming her gun towards his head.

Dottie was getting angry. She was tired of fighting so hard to live. She was drained of energy and just wanted to live a peaceful life as a wife and a mother, but if California wanted to deal her this hand, then she was going to give it her best.

Dottie kept her eye on the leader who was directly in front of her. "I'd like to see you try you smelly tequila drinking scum bag."

Ann Marie nearly fainted at the words. Dottie had always been the nicest, sweetest woman she had ever met, even sweeter than her own mother who was a preacher's wife. To hear those words come from Dottie meant that she'd had enough and there was no stopping her now.

The leading Vaquero looked down at her and laughed again, "Ha, it's going to be a pleasure killing you!"

Dottie shot him in his right arm causing him to drop his gun to the ground. The other men lifted up their weapons in the direction of the women where Rosalee stopped them. "Put the guns down! Now!"

They all hesitantly dropped them. Dottie walked closer to the injured rider. "Get out of here! Tell all your *amigos* not to come here no more. A crazy white woman who's had enough of your kind lives here. Now get!" She shouted as she shot the gun towards the ground near the horses causing them to take off.

The riders rode off in the direction they had just come from, making frequent glances back at the dominant women. Rosalee stepped up to Dottie who was fighting back tears and put her arm around her. "You did good, Dottie, real good."

"Oh, Rosalee, I've never been that mad before in my life. I don't know what came over me. I feel so horrible and dirty, I just don't know what to do."

"Don't you be sorry one minute," Beth said, "Those men woulda' killed and raped us and then tortured the children. You did the right thing, now don't you be ashamed."

Ann Marie put her arms around Dottie and buried her emotional face in her dress. "I love you Dottie, don't you ever die. You're like my Ma and I don't ever want to lose you."

Dottie leaned down and held her in her arms. "Don't you ever worry about me dying, darling. I'm a California woman now and I don't intend on going anywhere. And Ann Marie, you became my daughter a long time ago so don't you fret none over that either. Now let's get inside where we can all settle down."

The four of them went back up onto the porch together and headed into the house. Before going inside, Dottie turned and looked toward the southern horizon where the riders had gone, "I dare you to come back," she said.

- - - - - - - - - -

The next day all the women sat on the front porch drinking lemonade and laughing at the look on those men's faces the day before. It had been a small triumph for Dottie, but there would probably be many more to come before the land was tamed.

They all sat in rockers, Dottie and Rosalee in the middle with Beth and Ann Marie on the outside. "How come women don't get as much respect as men do?" Ann Marie asked them.

"Oh Lord," Rosalee said, "Wouldn't we all like to know the answer to that one!"

They laughed, except for Ann Marie who seemed aggravated over the subject. "I mean it, it just doesn't seem fair that they have more rights than we do. All we get to do is have children, housework and chase Mexicans away from our homes. What if I wanted to vote or something like that, I don't think it's right we can't do stuff like that."

"Well," Beth said, "A wife has an awful lot of control over her husband's thoughts. Say I want a certain person elected, well all I have to do is go on and on about all the good that person has done and sure enough, by way of my husband I've done voted!"

Dottie was smiling at her cousin's comment, "Now if only we could get them to mend the fence when we need them to!"

They sat there all morning talking the day away until early afternoon when they once again saw four riders approaching them. "Jesus, not again," Rosalee said standing up with her gun as the others followed her lead.

They made the same walk they had the day before only instead of stopping in front of four Vaqueros, they all stood in front of their men. Dottie flew into Will's arms when he had gotten off his horse and they kissed the longest kiss they had ever had.

Dottie cried as she was swept away with love in his arms, the same arms she had fallen in love with so many months ago. She was glad to finally have that feeling back that she had first experienced when she met Will for the first time.

"Hello, Dottie, did you miss me?"

"Oh, Will, oh, Will… you've come back to me. Were they absolutely horrible to you? Oh, Will are you okay? You're so thin."

"I'm fine, darling nothing a little bit of good cooking won't cure."

Ann Marie stood beside Travis' horse as he dismounted. "Hello, Travis."

He took his hat off and let the sun beat down upon him, "Hi Ann Marie, did you miss me?"

"Well, it depends… did you miss me?"

Travis smiled and looked over at Nat who was looking in their direction. He then turned back to Ann Marie, "Yes, maim I sure did."

Her face lit up and she wrapped her arms around him and gave him a hug. Travis stood there like a bump on a log while the other men laughed at the scene.

Ann Marie let go and looked back up at him, "Now there is one thing you need to know, Travis. After we get married and it's time to vote you are going to have to vote for who I say, do you hear me?"

"Married? Vote?"

"Why, Travis, you don't want to marry me! Ugh, fine!" Ann Marie turned to storm back to the house.

"Ann Marie, wait!" He said grabbing her arm. "I would love to marry you, but we will have to decide equally on the voting."

"No Travis, it's what I say and that's final! If you can't accept that then you cannot marry me." She folded her hands across her chest and looked up at him.

"Come here, you," he said pulling her back into his arms.

Land of Lebanon

April 14, 1892

Jim's tailor shop just opened up over on Georgetown Street, he's got some real nice deals on clothing over there so be sure you go and check it out.

Last Saturday my husband, Travis and I were on a buggy ride and we came across a group of outlaws just east of here… folks, be sure you keep an extra eye out, we don't want any of them in our nice little town.

The election for Mayor will be held this coming Saturday, the day before Easter. The candidates this year are our former Wiley Franks and a new comer, David Styles. Be sure you go and vote and ladies make sure your men know what they're doing when they cast their ballot.

Callie Braymyer won the title of Miss Lebanon last weekend, a reward well deserving for the beautiful daughter of Will and Dottie Braymyer.

Ann Marie Turner

Chapter Twelve

April 15, 1892

As Callie Braymyer walked throughout the busy streets of Lebanon, the new up an coming town just two miles away from her father's plantation, she admired the elegant dresses that some of the women were wearing. She continued down Main Street until she came to her Aunt Ann Marie's bookstore.

She stepped up onto the long wooden platform that stretched out in front of all the false front buildings and went inside. As she closed the door behind her, a little bell rang on the backside of the door.

Ann Marie looked up from her desk. "Callie, good morning! How are you?"

"Hi Ann Marie. I'm doing good, how are you?"

"Oh you know, holding down the fort while Travis patrols the streets behind that sheriff badge he is so proud of."

"Ha, that sounds about right."

Callie took a seat across from Ann Marie at her desk. Callie had grown into a beautiful woman, carrying both traits of her mother and father in her appearance. She had dark blonde hair stretching down to the middle of her back and green-blue eyes, that no one had ever seen before.

She was seventeen and by far the most eligible woman in the area. She had taken after her mother and always wore the most stylish clothing whenever she made visits into town.

"Who do you think will win the Mayor election, Ann Marie?"

"Well, I don't rightly know… I sure hope we get to keep Mr. Franks cause I sure don't fancy the idea of having a out of towner come in and take over. There's no telling what will happen."

"Have you gotten to meet him yet?"

"No, but I heard that he has killed people down in Texas. I wanted badly to run the story, but Travis told me not to on account that it might bring us trouble."

"Really? However did you come across that story?"

"Well about a week ago there was a gentleman by the name of Thomas Riddle who was passing through. He happened to see one of the voting posters hanging outside and he turned to me and said, "Hmm, I wonder if that is the same Mr. Styles that killed that family in Dallas.""

"No!"

"Yes, and what's worse is that Mr. Riddle said there had been more murders that he may have committed."

"Why on earth wouldn't Travis let you run that story?"

"Well he said we didn't know for sure and since Mr. Styles has that big ol' gang working on his farm outside of town, Travis said they might come make trouble with us if I were to run that story."

"Do you know where Mr. Styles came from?"

"No, but I tried asking him once in an interview... all he said was in a great big bear of a voice, 'Same place everyone comes from, back east.'"

"I sure hope he doesn't bring trouble into our town, it was bad enough getting it this settled up around here."

"You and me both, Callie, but a lot of folks around here want change and they figure Mr. Styles will give them that change."

"That's terrible, Mr. Franks has been here so long."

"I tell you one thing, I got a bad feeling about this one and most times when I get a feeling, it's usually right. But I already told Travis to vote for Mr. Franks and of course he will on account that I told him to."

Callie started laughing, "Ann Marie, do you really think Travis will vote for him just because you said so?"

"Absolutely, that was our agreement when we married, I said to him, Travis, now until women get the right to vote you will vote for whoever I say, do you hear me?"

"And he agreed?"

"Oh heavens yes, I was quite a charmer when I was younger, just ask your Momma and Poppa, they'll tell you."

"Speaking of Momma, you should have seen her the other day. Lord, Kizzie went after them chickens again with an axe."

"Oh no…"

"Oh yes, she got the head off one and she brought the chicken inside, well as usual it wasn't fully dead yet and as soon as she plopped it on the kitchen table it flew through the house. Momma was in the front room sewing and goodness you should have seen her when that headless chicken flew across her lap!"

Both women were laughing hysterically, "Oh Callie, your Momma is a piece of work… what did she do? I may have to print this up in the paper!"

"Don't you dare! Momma would die! Anyway, she flew up out of that chair like it was the Second Coming of Jesus. She ran out of the house just a shouting and screaming that Poppa thought the house was on fire!

Well, Poppa he came up from the barn directly to see what all the commotion was about and here comes Kizzie out of the house with that axe and instead of chasing the chicken she started chasing Momma!"

"No way!"

"Yes, maim. Poppa finally got that axe away and when he asked her why in the world she was chasing Momma, she looked Poppa in the eye and with the straightest face said, 'Why Mr. Braymyer I couldn't tell the difference in the two. They's both covered in feathers and trying to fly away so I figured I'd go for the bigger one… to get more meat and all.'"

"Oh Callie! You're kidding!"

"Nope, you should have seen Momma's face, I didn't think she'd ever go back into that house!"

"Do you think Kizzie was kidding around?"

"I don't rightly know, Ann Marie… she sure has done some crazy stuff here lately, but you never know when it comes to colored people. They are the nicest people in the world, but sometimes they do some crazy stuff. Poppa said he thinks she is losing her mind so every morning he gives her a glass of whiskey to drink to try and straighten her out. He can't bring himself to send her to the poor farm."

"You're joking right?"

"No, only thing is, is that it doesn't straighten her out right away. Why for the first hour after she's drank it, she walks sideways all through the kitchen trying to fix breakfast. The past three mornings the eggs have been nearly completely raw!"

"Oh Callie, how I do miss all the happenings at your house. I've had some of the best laughs up on that hill than I have anywhere else."

"You're telling me! The other day I was telling Momma she ought not let Poppa give Kizzie that whiskey and she said to me, 'Callie if Kizzie doesn't get that whiskey than I'm going to be a headless chicken!'"

"I do declare, Callie! Your Momma is something else!"

They sipped on their tea to try and calm their laughter but often times found themselves thinking back on the story and by the time their cups were empty most of the tea had been spit onto the floor.

Ann Marie had become the older sister that Callie had never had. Will and Dottie had had five more children, but none of them lived past the age of two at the most. There had been some sad times in the Braymyer home, but at the end of the day the family settled down with a bowl of good laughter and pushed forward.

The gold that Dottie had found would last them the rest of their lives, but they hardly ever touched it. Will had went ahead with the grape plantation and it had yielded profit every year since his return from Mexico. Although they were not blessed with a large family, they counted their blessings everyday and devoted themselves to their daughter and their home.

When Callie had finished visiting with Ann Marie, she said her goodbyes and headed back out onto the busy streets. Lebanon had been created just four years before and had already acquired four streets full of businesses and town homes. The west side of town consisted mostly of saloons and such, while the east side was kept more proper with hotels and boarding homes.

Callie wore a bright green dress around her small figure and as she passed through town, people couldn't help but stop and stare. She kept a slight smile on her face and made small glances at the people she passed. She was approaching the west end of town which she dreaded, but it was the only way she could go to head towards her house.

As she passed one of the three saloons she could hear the drunken quarrels of men inside. The saloon business had sky rocketed ever since David Styles and his crew had settled up just outside of town. There were always rough looking men wondering around town now, making Callie's visits less frequent in town.

She ran her finger through a strand of her long hair as she neared the saloon, trying to calm her nerves as she passed through. When she was even with the double swinging doors, a man was thrown out into the street knocking Callie backwards.

It had startled her so bad that she let out a scream of terror before she even realized she had landed in the arms of a man. The man slowly lifted her back up to her feet and away from the drunken man who lie on the street.

She brushed herself off, quickly removing the dirt that had plastered itself onto her dress, not daring to look and see whose arms she had fell into, after all this was the west side.

The young man stood there in a suit and watched her as she busied herself cleaning up. He had dark brown hair and freckles scattered across his nose and high cheekbones. He was slender and stood near six feet tall, towering over Callie's five foot three body.

He removed his cowboy hat and held it with both hands near his stomach. "Pardon me, maim. Are you okay?"

For the first time Callie looked up at him and was almost taken away by his remarkable looks. "I'm fine, thank you." She said in a short tone.

"Might I assist you further? You look to be shaken up a bit."

"I don't think that will be necessary, sir. Besides I would much rather not associate with anyone mixed up with Styles and his men?"

"Styles? Oh no, maim. I think you have me confused. I just rode into town this morning. I've come from Alabama."

"Oh," she said in an apologetic voice, "Well, what brings you out here?"

"Just thought I would make a fresh start for myself."

"Did you come out here alone, Mr....?"

"Russell, Matt Russell and yes, maim I sure did."

"Well, Mr. Russell, anyone who comes out here alone is most likely running from someone or something, so if you'll excuse me..."

Matt was intrigued by her spunk and wanted desperately to dive deeper into conversation with her. "Now that's not fair, maim. You know my name but I still only know you by your distinguished good looks."

Callie looked at him, puzzled a bit by his word choice, "Callie Braymyer, now If you don't mind, I'll let you get back to running."

Matt laughed, but quickly stopped himself when he realized it slightly offended Callie. "I'm not running from anything, Miss Braymyer. You see I am an only child and both my Ma and Pa died earlier this year. Didn't see much reason for me to stay back in Alabama. So after the estate was settled I headed west."

"Oh, I see," Callie thought about apologizing for a moment, but quickly deserted the thought.

"And what about you? Are you a native of this fine territory?"

The two of them began walking beside each other down the street. "I was born shortly after Momma and Poppa settled here. I'm an only child as well so it seems we have something in common."

"Well, I do hope that we find we have much more in common than that. I must say Miss Braymyer, you are one of the finest ladies I have ever had the pleasure of meeting."

"Mr. Russell, were you born with that flirtatious talk or is it something you acquired in the saloon back yonder?"

He looked over at her and almost let another laugh slip, "No maim, saloons are not my type of company to keep."

"Well then, what are you doing on the west end of town?"

"Well, it's like I said, I just arrived here this morning. I was out exploring and such. Guess I ended up in the wrong place, or in the right place for your sake."

Callie looked at him, irritated that he would think she would depend on someone. She was perfectly fine on her own. She ignored the comment and continued walking.

Matt waited for an answer, but when there was none he went on. "So do you have any advice for a newcomer like myself?"

"Well, other than staying away from the west side of town, I would say stay away from Styles and his men in general."

"Who is this Mr. Styles you keep talking so much about?"

Matt's southern accent was warming to Callie as she continued to walk by his side. "He's running for mayor. He's been here a couple of months and started a ranch outside of town. Since he's been here there has been more drunken men in these parts than ever before."

"Well now, I hate to hear such depressing news about a place so lovely as this one. Do you think he'll get the vote?"

"I hope not, but he has a lot of men who will vote for him and a lot of people around here are looking for a change. What do you plan on doing? Will you be staying around here or moving further west?"

"Well, Miss Braymyer, I have to admit the land is beautiful here and if I am able to find work I think I just might stay on awhile, especially with a beauty such as yourself running around these parts."

Callie blushed, "Mr. Russell, what kind of work is it exactly that you do?"

"Well, I've always been a farmer, miss. Been working in the cotton fields since I was knee high." He motioned with his hand down to his knees.

"Know anything about grapes, Mr. Russell?"

"No maim, but I reckon I could learn just about anything. Why do you ask?"

"My Poppa owns a grape plantation just west of town. I'm sure he would give you work, that is if you could prove yourself."

Matt stumbled over one of his boots and nearly fell into Callie, "I… I reckon I would be up for the job. Where might I find your Poppa?"

Callie laughed at his clumsiness, "Come along Mr. Russell, I'm heading there now."

Chapter Thirteen

April 20 1892

Polk County, Missouri

Mary Anna Braymyer had been a widow for four years and since all of her children had moved away she was left only in the company of her maid and her friend, Rachel Lloyd. It was early morning as the two of them loaded the last few items onto the wagon outside of the home on Braymyer Ridge and then the two of them stopped and looked back at the house.

Mary Anna had aged with grace and although her hair was still very dark, there were streaks of silver scattered about it. Her once dark brown eyes had now turned to a lighter shade and the wrinkles of age made their presence across her face.

Rachel was short like Mary Anna and although she was only a few years younger, she had no gray in her hair. For a colored person of the time, she was very well educated and as many years as she had spent with the Braymyer family she had grown to be apart of the family herself.

They stood there looking at the house and reminisced about past times and people of long ago. "You know," Mary Anna said, "A lot of things have happened in that house, Rachel. It sure is sad to leave it behind."

"I know Mary Anna, but there's so many new comers around here that we don't hardly belong anymore. Say, do you remember that day when Jesse James came up to the house and had dinner with us?"

"Ha, of course I do! He was a sweet boy, that one. A true confederate. I still don't think he was actually murdered, I think they just buried some other poor ol' boy in his place if you ask me."

The two of them started laughing as they continued to share stories about the house and all the people who had come and gone. "It's hard to believe they're gonna' turn it into a boarding house, Rachel," Mary Anna said as she stepped up to the side of the house. "Here help me with this."

"What are you trying to do?"

"I may have to leave the house behind, but I can at least take part of it with me. Help me take this piece of wood off from below the window."

"Shoot, you are crazy, Mary Anna!"

The two women struggled and after about five minutes of pulling they ripped off a piece of the wooden siding and loaded it into the wagon. They both stopped and sat on the end of the wagon to catch their breath.

"Rachel dear, I swear I don't feel old inside, but boy does my body act old."

The two elder women continued laughing as they climbed up onto the wagon seat, Mary Anna being the one driving. Rachel turned to her friend and said, "A lot of folks say we're crazy, Mary Anna. Two women traveling to Texas alone and having to go through Indian Territory. You sure this is a good idea?"

Mary Anna whipped the reins at the two white stallions and smiled, "I reckon two old ladies have the right to one more adventure before they die. What do you say?"

"Well as long as it's with you then I look forward to every minute of it."

The wagon rode south heading for Texas where Mary Anna's youngest son, Nat lived…and she was right, it would be one heck of an adventure for two old ladies.

Chapter Fourteen

"Callie! Come downstairs! Hurry honey!"

Callie ran down the stairs to find her mother waiting for her in a plaid dress. "What is it Momma?"

"Shhh, follow me," Dottie said whispering and leading Callie to the kitchen door. She cracked it open and motioned for her daughter to come closer. "Callie peaked in where she saw Kizzie standing on the table chanting something."

"Momma, what on earth is she doing!"

"I don't know, honey, I think your father gave her too much whiskey this morning. She's been up on that table for near an hour."

"Well, shouldn't we get her down?"

"Callie, look closer. She's got a knife in her hand."

"My, God. What are we going to do?"

"I need you to go get your Poppa, he's out in the fields with Mr. Russell. You must hurry though, I don't know what I'm going to do if she decides to chase me with that knife."

"Okay, Momma. You keep an eye on her and if she gets down you run outside."

"Okay, honey, now run along."

Callie went out the front door and ran towards the fields. She could here Kizzie inside chanting something in a foreign language and knew that she had really lost it this time. The afternoon sun was beating down upon her as she approached her father and Mr. Russell.

"Poppa," she said, gasping for air, "You better come quick, Kizzie's really gone off the deep the end this time. Momma is just having a fit."

Matt Russell made quick glances at Callie as she did him.

"Callie," Will said, "What is she doing?"

"Why Poppa, she's on the kitchen table dancing around with a knife and chanting in some foreign language."

Will looked over at Matt, come on son, we had better go see what this is about."

When they had arrived back at the house, Dottie was still outside the kitchen door spying on Kizzie. "Will, hurry, come over here," she said as Will walked up behind her.

Will looked into the kitchen door with Matt right beside him. "How long has she been doing this, Dottie," he asked.

"Well over an hour now, Will I told you to quit giving her that whiskey! Now look what she's doing!"

"Oh, Dottie, the whiskey helps calm her nerves."

"Will Braymyer! Do you call this calm nerves!"

Matt and Callie looked at each other and exchanged smiles.

Will turned back to the door and flew it open and walked toward Kizzie. Matt cautiously followed behind him while the women waited at the door. "Kizzie! What are you doing?"

"Hiya!" She shouted as she turned on the table, swinging the knife through the air. "Humma humma goodya! Hiya!"

"Kizzie! Snap out of it! What is wrong?"

"I can't stop Mr. Braymyer, they's bad spirits in this house, bad bad spirits. I got's to cut them out with this here knife."

"Now, Kizzie, what makes you think there is bad spirits here?"

"Cause, I was sweeping the kitchen floor, shortly after I had my drink and something bumped into me. I swear it's true, God's honest truth something bumped into me."

"Will was trying not to laugh, "Kizzie for God's sake, give me that knife and get down from there."

Kizzie looked at him wild eyed and slowly handed over the knife and stepped down off the table. "Now," Will said, "Why don't you go lie down for a little bit, no more whiskey for you for a little while."

Kizzie held her head down and slowly made her way out the door and up the stairs. "Callie," Dottie said, "Would you and Mr. Russell mind going outside while I have a word with your Poppa?"

"Oh boy," Will said, "I'm in for it now."

As Callie and Matt stepped out onto the front porch she could hear her mother scolding her father. The two of them walked out into the yard, laughing to themselves.

"Callie, I don't mean to offend you or anything, but your family sure can make a man laugh… in a good way you know."

Callie laughed a little, "Oh trust me, I know. Those two can keep anyone on their toes and with Kizzie acting the way she does, why it's like a carnival in there."

"You know, Callie, I've been working for your Poppa for two weeks now and I haven't hardly gotten to spend any time with you, other than dinner of course. Anyway, I was wondering if you would like to go on a buggy ride with me some time."

"Well, as long as Momma and Poppa says it's okay, then I don't see why not."

"Excellent, how about tomorrow afternoon?"

"That sounds like a swell idea to me, maybe those two can get along long enough for me to get permission."

They both continued to laugh as they walked up to a swing that hung from a tree in the front yard. Callie sat down and Matt began to push her into the westerly wind.

"So, Matt, what do you think about California?"

"Well, I think it's a fine place, especially with you here."

"Matt, you mustn't flatter me so much."

"Why not? I'm only speaking the truth."

"Still, I don't deserve half the nice things you say to me. I was horrible to you that first day in town."

"Awe come on now, it's not your fault. You thought I was apart of that Styles gang."

"Well, it wasn't right and I do owe you an apology."

"Don't mention it, Callie. Besides you're going to make it up to me tomorrow by going on a ride with me. So what do you think about Mr. Styles winning the election."

"Don't be silly, Matt. He is already threatening to remove Travis as sheriff so he can put one of his drunken men in his place. I fear the town will be overrun by thieves and bandits."

"Well I haven't been here long, but I have to say I have seen a change in the town since he was elected and I wouldn't necessarily say it is a good one."

"And poor Ann Marie, she speaks her mind so freely on such causes that it will only be a matter of time before Styles closes her shop down. I fear that day, Matt, because Ann Marie will not be moved easily."

"I got that feeling when they were over for dinner last night, she sure has a way of speaking her mind, but there is nothing wrong with that."

"So Matt, are you happy here in California, I mean are you really happy?"

"Of course I am, there's only one thing that would make me happier."

"Oh? And what's that?"

"You already know the answer to that, silly, I want you to be my wife someday."

"Now why on earth would I choose you over all the California boys who have been after me for most their lives?"

"Because, Callie Braymyer, I'm different and you know it. You and I are a lot alike, there's no questioning that."

"Ha, and what do you suppose it is that we have in common?"

Matt gazed into her colorful eyes and tried not to get swept away in her California charm. "We both have a passion for life that very few others experience. We can be the nicest people in the world, but when we see something we want, nothing can stand in our way until it is ours. Callie, we're both out to conquer the world and do whatever it takes to be happy and successful."

"Matt, you make me sound so spoiled and arrogant!"

Matt was laughing and didn't care if it made Callie furious or not, "It's okay to be spoiled and arrogant, Callie, as long as you do it with grace and grace, my dear, is something you have an abundant supply of."

Callie glared over in his direction but inside she knew he was right and it gave her comfort in knowing that there might be someone else out there just like her. She wasn't a bad person, this she knew, but Matt had a point when it came to her determination and he was right, nothing ever got in her way when she wanted something.

When Will and Dottie had things settled down in the house, Callie and Matt went back inside to join them. They all had a good laugh over Kizzie's incident earlier that day and much to Dottie's pleasure Will had promised not to give her anymore whiskey.

After dinner, Callie laid in bed drown by thoughts of her future. She wanted to be married someday, but not a single ounce of her being wanted to be burdened with the responsibility of a household and children. She wanted to serve a grander purpose in life than stay at home and tend to things. She wanted to rise above society's expectations and prove to the world that she could do great things.

She had been raised by her mother and Ann Marie's opinions and being an only child didn't help her situation. Matt Russell wasn't a bad person, she thought, and he would probably make a fine husband. With his southern charm and her California charm, there's no telling what they might accomplish together.

Matt had a head on his shoulders and she knew he would go far in this world, now if only she knew where he stood on women's rights. Would he be telling her to mind her own business all the time, or would he listen to what she had to say and consider her opinions?

"Well," she said out loud, "If I am meant to marry Mr. Russell then so be it, I shall not fight the urge to be wrapped up in his arms any longer. Besides, all great people need someone at their side… even me I suppose."

Land of Lebanon

April 30, 1892

Well, just as I suspected our town has gone to the wolves ever since Mr. Styles took over. The saloons are now unable to keep their customers within their walls and the drunken fools are making their presence in the better half of town. There's not much the sheriff can do about it because he no longer has the mayor's support.

Mr. Mayor, I think you need to come by my bookstore and read a book on how to run a town, I declare, most of us women could do better than you. No sir, I will no longer keep my mouth shut and I dare you to utter my name. Why come on over and bring all the torches you can find, I've got plenty of water in the pail and enough sass and spit to put out any flame you throw my way.

Doc. Yale headed to Yuba City yesterday, said he had a higher purpose than to take care of drunks. Not that I blame him for it, but it is a sad shame that we are all having to suffer for our new mayor. Good job mayor, I hope you are proud of yourself and next time you head upstairs to see Fannie Albright, maybe I'll show up for an interview, you ruthless pig.

Ann Marie Turner – The should have been mayor

Chapter Fifteen

"Ann Marie, you've really done it this time. What are we going to do when the mayor reads this?"

"What do you mean, what are we going to do? Travis, we're going to stand up for what is right, that's what."

Travis Turner had a worried look on his face, the same look that always made its presence when Ann Marie spoke her mind. He sat in a wooden rocker near the fireplace in their two-bedroom house on High Street while Ann Marie prepared supper.

He looked over at his wife with a pleading look in his eye, "Darling, I know what you said is right, but do you realize what could happen to us now?"

"What? They'll run us out of town? The same town you and I helped settled up? No, Travis, I'll shoot as many of them as possible before that happens. At least then I'll sleep in my grave with a little peace of mind."

"And what about Callie? You know how much she looks up to you? What good are you to her if you're dead?"

The thought just struck her that if she were dead she wouldn't get to see the Braymyer family anymore. "Well, it's just a sacrifice I'm going to have to take for the greater good. I will not stand by and watch this town ruin."

"Oh, Ann Marie, what am I going to do with you?"

"You're not going to do anything with me, Travis, maybe you should think about doing something for this town."

"Darling, I think it would be best if you go stay with Will and Dottie. You will be safe there."

"Travis, this is my home and I am not going anywhere. It's Styles who needs to seek shelter."

Just as Ann Marie was finishing up supper, there was a growing thunder of voices gathering outside their home. "Come out woman! I've got a special flame just for you."

The two of them immediately recognized the voice as Mayor Styles.

Travis grabbed his rifle, "Ann Marie, go to the back bedroom and wait there."

"I'll do no such thing, Travis. Give me a gun."

Travis knew there was no arguing with her so he reluctantly handed her a pistol. "Stay behind me."

The two of them made their way to the front door, taking small steps as they went. "What do you want, Styles," Travis shouted from the other side of the door.

"I want an apology from that no good woman, or else…"

"You'll get no such thing from me you ignorant pig!"

"Ann Marie," Travis whispered, "Please… let me do the talking."

"I'm sure we can work something out, Mayor. We'll come by your office tomorrow morning."

Ann Marie looked at Travis as if she were going to slap him. "Travis, I won't do it," she whispered.

"I don't think so," the mayor shouted, "Why don't the two of you come out here. We need to discuss some things."

"We won't come out if there are guns pointed at us," Travis shouted back.

"You'll come out here, Turner or we'll burn the house down."

The two of them slowly stepped out onto the front porch where Styles was waiting with three men. Styles was a tall muscular man and very few people dared challenge his word and the few who had usually disappeared.

He was in his early forties and had thinning blonde hair atop his hatless head. There was not a single ounce of human compassion anywhere about him and had the devil had an angel in Lebanon it would have been Styles.

The three men with him were all in their twenties and had the drunken arrogant look of youth about them. Every one of them had tobacco stains on their faded clothes and dirt embedded beneath their finger nails. They all wore gun belts and each one of them rubbed their filthy hands across the butt of their pistols.

Styles stepped up to the porch and got in Ann Marie's face. The smell of his body nearly made her vomit in her mouth. "Woman, I aim to get an apology from you if it's the last thing I do."

"Well, Mr. Styles if it's an apology you're seeking you're wasting your time. I don't apologize for speaking the truth."

"That's Mayor Styles to you, you stupid woman," he said as he drew even nearer to her face."

Travis stepped closer, "Styles, I'm only going to ask you once to get out of my wife's face."

Styles pulled his gun out of its holster and slung the butt of it into Travis' face, bringing him unconsciously to the ground. Styles quickly turned back to Ann Marie and pulled the gun out of her hand, throwing it back behind him. He grabbed both of her hands and pulled her closer.

"Apologize woman!"

Ann Marie looked up into his cold dark eyes as an angry vengeance took over her body. She spat into his face and lifted her knee, kicking him in the crotch. He let out a great moan and then backhanded her across the face, bringing her to the ground beside her husband.

Styles leaned forward and walked away holding himself while his gang gathered up the Turner's and took them to the jailhouse. Styles walked the short distance to the bookstore and threw a lit lantern through the front window, sending the building up in flames.

- -

Callie sat beside Matt on the front of the wagon as they drove out across the fields of California early in the afternoon. It was the first day of May and the weather had been overly pleasant the past few days.

"Well, Callie, what do you say we ride in to town and see what's happening... I promise to stay away from the west end," Matt said laughing.

"That would be lovely, can we stop by and see Ann Marie?"

"Well I don't see why not."

"Thank you, Matt. I must tell her about Kizzie's latest outbreak, I just know she'll get a good laugh out of it."

"You know, Callie, I had a talk with your Poppa last night."

"Oh?"

"Sure did, we talked mostly about you."

"Me? Matt, why did you talk about me?"

"Well, I just told him that I had my hat set for marrying you someday."

"You didn't!"

"Sure did."

Callie looked at him and admired his boldness. "Well, what did he have to say about that?"

"Good luck."

"Good luck?"

"That's right. He said if I could convince you to marry me then it was alright by him but I had better be ready for one helluva' fight."

Callie couldn't help but laugh. "Did he really say it was alright by him?"

"Sure did. And you know what else?"

"What?"

"I heard him talking to your Momma this morning and she said if we were to marry that I would be the best thing that ever happened to you."

"You mustn't flatter yourself, Matt. Perhaps I would be the best thing that ever happened to you."

"Oh no doubt about that, Callie, no doubt."

Matt drove around the outside of Lebanon to avoid going through the west side of town and entered onto Main Street from the east. There were people walking along the streets, mostly drunks and those of ill reputation, which was strange for this part of town.

"Matt look!" Callie shouted as they approached Ann Marie's bookstore. "They've burnt down the store!"

Matt stopped the wagon and Callie ran up to the charred remains. She walked to where the front door had once been and found the word "P I G" written in red paint across a piece of wood with a paper nailed nearby.

Callie picked up the piece of paper and read Ann Marie's latest paper. "Matt," she said climbing back into the wagon, "Hurry we've got to get to Ann Marie's house!"

Matt cracked the horsewhip at the two black stallions pulling the wagon and headed toward High Street. "Oh, Matt, I hope nothing bad has happened to Travis and Ann Marie!"

"It will be okay, Callie, I'm sure they're fine."

"I hope so, I don't know what I'd do if something happened to them."

Matt reached his hand over and held Callie's in his to try and comfort her. The people along the street flew out of their way and hollered curse words in their direction as they sped by.

When they reached the Turner house they were relieved to find that it was still standing, but everything was quiet. Callie flew off of the wagon with Matt right behind her and ran into the empty house. She ran through, checking all the rooms and met Matt back in the front room.

"Matt, they're not here. Where do you suppose they are? What if something happened!"

"Calm down, Callie, we'll find them."

They went back out of the house where they found a neighbor of the Turner's walking up to them. It was Betty Reeves, the elder widow of the former sheriff. "Betty!" Callie shouted running up to her, "What's happened to Travis and Ann Marie!"

"Calm down, sugar. The mayor had them thrown in jail yesterday."

"Jail? Why would he throw them in jail?"

"Well, Mayor Styles doesn't need much of a reason to throw anyone in jail. I suppose Ann Marie's latest paper is what done it in for them."

"Oh no, Matt we've got to go get them!"

Before Matt could say anything, Callie was already running back toward Main Street to the jailhouse. Matt rushed off after her, having to stop and pick up his hat as it flew off his head.

He caught up with her just as she rushed into the doors of the jailhouse. Ann Marie and Travis were in a small jail cell together and when Callie ran in, they both rushed up to the jail bars.

"Callie!" Ann Marie said.

"Ann Marie! What happened," she said running up to them.

"That's far enough!" A man wearing a sheriff's badge said standing up from a chair. "These two are not allowed visitors."

The man was one of the three that had been with Mayor Styles the day before at the Turner home. He had acquired more tobacco stains on his shirt and smelled as if he had been up drinking all night, no doubt celebrating his new position.

Callie stopped in her tracks and turned back toward him, "You let these two go! They have no business being here!"

"Oh yes they do. They threatened the Mayor's life yesterday."

"How much to get them out? I'll pay you!"

"Maybe you didn't understand me, miss. These two are not going anywhere. In fact, the Mayor has a right mind to see them both hanged, you know, to use them as an example and all."

"That's ridiculous! You'll hang a couple just because a woman speaks her mind!"

"You bet, it's time the women in these parts start showing the men some respect."

Matt walked up closer to Callie, rubbing his hands along his colts on either side of his gun belt. He looked over at the new sheriff, sizing him up in every way possible. "These two have done nothing wrong, now you let them go."

"Easy, son, or I'll throw you in there with them!"

Callie looked quickly at Matt and then back to the sheriff, "On what grounds?"

"On the grounds that he's threatening the sheriff of Lebanon!"

"Sheriff? Why you're nothing more than a drunken mule!"

Ann Marie let out a small laugh as Travis hung his head even lower and whispered to himself, "Lord help us."

"Miss, if you're not careful I'll…"

"You'll what? Hit me? Throw me in jail? Why I wouldn't let the likes of you get close enough to lay a finger on me you floundering idiot!"

"Ok miss, you asked for it."

He drew out his gun and pointed it in Matt's direction as he stepped closer to Callie. She backed up until she was against a wall. She placed both of her hands palm down onto the wall and desperately felt for a way out. As she continued to search the wall, her right hand brushed across a horsewhip.

She quickly yanked it from the wall and flung it in the man's direction with a loud crack. It struck him across the face and he let out a loud yelp as he turned the gun on Callie. Matt quickly threw himself onto the man and pushed him to the floor where he landed on top of him.

He got the gun away and shoved the man's bandana into his mouth so he couldn't yell for help. "Callie, go fetch me that rope over there!"

Callie ran to the other side of the room and brought the rope back to him where he proceeded to tie the man up. As Matt was doing this, Callie grabbed the keys off of the desk and quickly unlocked the jail cell that held Travis and Ann Marie.

"Callie!" Ann Marie said throwing her arms around her, "You were wonderful!"

Travis helped Matt tie up the sheriff and then threw him into the cell they had just exited. "Callie," Matt said, "You stay here, I'm going to go fetch the wagon and bring it around back. We've got to get out of town as quickly as possible."

Matt ran out of the front door and across town to get the wagon while the rest of them waited inside. "Ann Marie," Callie said turning away from the door and toward Ann Marie, "Are you okay?"

"Yes, we're fine. That was so brave of you to horsewhip him!"

"I was just caught up in the moment I suppose."

"Callie," Travis said trying not to let a smile slip, "I swear between you and my wife I don't know how I'm still alive."

"Oh Travis," Callie said, "There's nothing wrong with a little spunk in a woman."

"A little!" He said laughing, "My God, between the two of you there's enough spunk for everyone in California!"

They heard the wagon pull up out back and Travis cracked the door open to ensure it was Matt. "Come on," Matt said, "We're all clear."

The three of them got into the wagon with Matt who drove the wagon as fast as he could out of town. "Matt," Callie said, "Don't you think Styles and his men will come after us?"

"Probably, we'll have to take to the woods after we see your Momma and Poppa."

"I hope we don't cause them any trouble? Do you think they'll try and hurt them?" She said worriedly.

"Don't you fret none over your Momma and Poppa," Ann Marie said leaning up to the front of the wagon where Callie and Matt were sitting, "They can handle their own, believe you me."

Chapter Sixteen

May 03, 1892

Indian Territory

Mary Anna and Rachel had been traveling for thirteen days and were right in the middle of Indian Territory. They had passed many other settlers as they continued south and every person that they passed looked at the two women as if they were crazy.

There had been a few small settlements along the way as they ventured deeper into the territory and the few Indians that they did see were always friendly to them. As they continued down the trail they saw up ahead a lone Indian sitting amount a beautiful paint horse looking in their direction.

"Look at that horse," Mary Anna said, "Have you ever seen one that looked so beautiful?"

As they approached the rider they both realized that although the man was dressed as an Indian he was very much white. The fearless Mary Anna pulled the wagon to a stop right beside him as Rachel's palms began to sweat.

"How do you do?" Mary Anna said.

The White Indian said somewhat clearly, "Hello."

"Fine weather isn't it," she said trying to prolong the conversation.

"Yes, good weather."

"Say, are my eyes playing tricks on me or are you white?"

"I White Indian Man. I white man, raised by red man."

"Well isn't that something. Well, we better be on our way we're heading to Texas!"

The man smiled at the old ladies excitement and nodded his head. The wagon continued on for about five minutes when Mary Anna suddenly stopped the wagon. She turned to Rachel who had still been laughing at Mary Anna's boldness with the Indian.

"Rachel, don't you remember Nat's son, Brice who was taken by Indians... you don't suppose..."

Both women turned around to where the white Indian had been standing but he was nowhere to be seen. Although Mary Anna didn't know it at the time, the man she had just spoken to was in fact her grandson who had been missing since he was an infant.

They continued southward for three days talking the ears off of anyone they passed along the way. On the third day, Rachel became sick with fever and they were in the middle of nowhere.

Mary Anna helped her into the back of the wagon and made her a little bed as she continued to drive the wagon. Later that evening Mary Anna spotted a cabin in the distance and drove the wagon towards it.

When she went in to investigate she found that the cabin had been abandoned and she struggled to get Rachel inside and onto one of the deserted beds. After she had caught her breath from moving her friend she began boiling water and doing everything she could to get Rachel better.

The days turned into nights and Rachel's fever continued to show its presence as the sweaty chills occupied her body. Mary Anna cooked soup every night and forced her to eat it, but she was still not gaining any strength.

Chapter Seventeen

Beth Douglas busied herself in the kitchen of her home just outside of Los Angeles. She stopped for a moment and gazed up at a hill in the distance, which had a single stone sitting atop it. Her husband, Abner had died the winter before of pneumonia and she was now left alone to raise her four children.

As she aged, her beauty became more and more apparent and although she was raising four boys alone, she had no gray hair. The eldest son, Abner Junior, or Aj as they called him, had taken over the farm since his father had died and at sixteen he had more than proven himself worthy.

He had taken his father's death the hardest and soon accepted the fact that life was not going to be easy and if he needed to toughen up then that is exactly what he was going to do. He spent his days in the field and as much as Beth tried to hold up a conversation with him he would often times just ignore her.

The second child was Turner who was fourteen and was almost a complete opposite of Aj. He had his mother's kindness and his father's determination. He would much rather spend his days beneath the shade of a tree engulfed inside of a book than face the realities of life. He had courage, however and often times he would wind up with a bloody nose for standing up against his older brother.

The twins, Sam and Eli were eight and were more boy than anyone had ever seen. They were always sneaking some kind of critter to the supper table, almost giving Beth a heart attack most of the time. They passed their days down by a nearby creek and looked for innocent bugs to torment.

Beth continued rolling dough for a loaf of bread as she thought about how her life had turned out and wondered if things would turn out all right in the end. She continued to stare up at her husband's monument, recalling past times of their long trip to California.

She knew her boys were not perfect, but then again who was. She was just thankful that she had them and was not left alone. She doubted very seriously that she would ever find a husband again, there was no way a man could get to her from behind the shield of her sons.

Abner had been a good father to them and all four of them would jump right on a task if he had asked them to. It wasn't that they didn't listen to her, but there was a lack of respect when they viewed their mother. What happened, she wondered, to the days when children respected their elders? Times are changing, she thought, who knows what this world is coming to.

Turner and the twins were off exploring some new adventure while Aj sat in the front sitting room whittling away at a stick. The house smelled like blueberry pie in the warm May sun and for the first time in a long time, everyone seemed relaxed.

Beth left the loaf of bread to rise and took a seat near Aj where she proceeded to knit at a blanket she had started last year but had not found the time to finish. She slowly rocked in the rocking chair, creating a steady creak with every forward motion, intentionally trying to get her son's attention.

"Aj, what do you think about going to see your Uncle Travis sometime?"

"Oh, Ma. There is absolutely no way I will have time. Someone has to tend to the farm you know."

"We can manage it, son. Besides I think you could use a break and time to relax."

"I'm fine, I'm a man now and men don't need breaks."

Beth let the silence take back over the room until it was interrupted by the sound of horse hooves outside. Aj quickly jumped up and grabbed his father's rifle. "Ma, you stay in here and let me handle this!"

"Aj, calm down. Show a little hospitality."

"It could be trouble, now you just stay here."

Aj went out the front door and Beth peaked out the nearby front window. She saw a dashing man who looked to be in his mid forties sitting atop a white stallion, the most beautiful horse she had ever seen. He had blonde hair that had grown darker because of age and blue eyes she thought she had once seen somewhere.

"Mister," Aj said, "I don't know what you've come here for, but we don't need no trouble from the likes of you."

The man tipped his hat and looked down at the arrogant youngster. "No need to get yourself all wound up, son. I don't come here for trouble. I'm only looking for a warm meal."

"This here ain't no boarding house. If it's a meal you want you'll have to keep on riding into town. Now get on!"

Beth came out the front door, "Aj, you mind your manners."

The rider looked down at Beth and took in her beauty, "Howdy, maim."

"How do you do?"

"Just looking for a warm meal, maim. Been on the trail a long time. Names John Braymyer, but folks call me, Johnny."

"Braymyer? Are you any kin to Will Braymyer?"

"Yes, maim. That's my brother. I intended to see him, but I took off in the wrong direction. You see I'm headed to Los Angeles to join up with a cattle drive. I reckon I'll backtrack when I'm done and go see my brother up near Yuba City."

"Why, Mr. Braymyer, we're practically family! Will's wife, Dottie is my cousin."

"You don't say, maim."

"I'm Beth Douglas. Won't you come inside."

Aj looked at his mother in disbelief and then turned around and went back inside. Johnny Braymyer dismounted his horse and then looked in her direction, "Quite a boy you have there."

"Oh, he's stubborn like his father was."

"Was, maim?"

"Yes, I'm afraid my husband passed away last winter."

"I'm sure sorry to hear that, maim."

"Please, call me Beth."

"Well, Beth. Have you heard anything from my brother in awhile? Last we heard he was doing mighty well."

"Yes, I received a letter from Dottie awhile back," she said as they walked into the house, "They are both doing fine, still full spark as usual. Do you like blueberry pie?"

"Oh, yes, maim. It's my favorite."

- - - - - - - - - - - - - - -

When Matt pulled the wagon up in front of the Braymyer home, Kizzie was on the front porch sweeping and after her first day of no whiskey, she wasn't looking so good. Callie jumped off the wagon and ran into the house to find her mother.

Will walked up from around the house and was met by Matt and Travis who filled him in on everything that had happened. Everyone gathered in the dining room to discuss a solution to their problem.

"Poppa," Callie said, "Just let them take me to jail. I don't want to cause you and Momma any trouble out here."

"Callie, you're not going to cause us any trouble," he answered looking across the table in her direction, "You did the right thing getting them out of there."

"Will," Dottie said, "What about Beth? Couldn't they go stay with her?"

"Well, I don't think we have any other option. Callie, go fetch a few things from your room and pack some clothes for Ann Marie as well. Hurry now, we don't have much time."

Callie and Ann Marie went upstairs and quickly packed while the men went outside and prepared the wagon for the trip. Kizzie and Dottie ran through the kitchen, packing every little bit of food they could find.

They Braymyer home was gleaming with chaos as everyone hurried to complete their task. It would only be a matter of time before Mayor Styles sent some men out to look for them so they needed to put as much distance between them and Lebanon as possible.

After everything was completed, Callie took a seat next to Matt on the wagon while Travis and Ann Marie rode separate mares at their side. Will and Dottie said their good byes to Travis and Ann Marie before coming over to the wagon.

Callie leaned down and allowed herself to be wrapped up in her mother's arms. "Oh, Momma, I'm so scared for you and Poppa."

"Hush child, everything will be fine. Your Poppa and I can handle anyone they send our way. Now dry those tears, you hear?"

Callie wiped away her tears and shook her head. "Matt," Will said taking his hand, "You take care of my daughter, you hear me?"

"Yes, sir. I promise I won't let anything happen to her as God as my judge."

"I know you won't son. Any luck with that topic we discussed yesterday?"

Matt grinned, "Slowly making progress, sir."

"Good boy." Will turned to Callie, "Don't be stubborn, Callie. Matt's a good man and you let him take care of you, okay?"

"Yes, Poppa," she said leaning over Matt's lap into her father's comforting hug.

"All right, now get going and don't stop till you can't go no farther."

The four of them rode off as Dottie stood next to Will with his arm around her. They stood in front of their home and waved goodbye to their small family. Callie turned in her seat and returned the gesture as she waved back at them, letting the tears fall across her face.

She threw her head against Matt, hoping for some comfort, which he gladly gave to her by putting his arm around her. This was Callie's first time away from home and she only hoped that home would still be there when she arrived back, whenever that might be.

Three hours after the group of four left, seven riders rode up to the Braymyer house, all armed and ready. Will and Dottie stepped out onto the front porch armed only with their California charm and watched as the group of men approached them.

The leader of the pack was the sheriff that had been horsewhipped earlier that day and it was obvious that he wanted nothing more than to kill the person responsible for damaging his face.

"Where's your daughter, Mr. Braymyer," he asked reining up his horse just short of the front porch steps.

"I don't know. She went on a buggy ride earlier today. Why do you ask?"

"Don't you lie to me, mister, or I'll shoot you both right here."

"Shoot us? What are you talking about, sheriff?"

"Don't play stupid. You know darn well what I'm talking about. Now where is she! The mayor wants to have a special meeting with her as do I."

Dottie cut in between the two of them, "We haven't seen our daughter since this morning, honest. What business do you have with our Callie?"

Just before the sheriff was able to answer there was a loud crash coming from the kitchen. Everyone stopped and stared toward the front door. In a sudden instance, Kizzie came flying through the front door shouting and screaming, "Hiya! The devil's come! The devil's come!"

Kizzie had a kitchen knife in her hand and darted towards the group of riders. Just before she stepped off of the front porch, the sheriff fired a bullet into her head, dropping her right beside Dottie's feet."

"Kizzie!" She shouted. "What have you done!"

The group of men began laughing among themselves as they stared down at Kizzie's lifeless body. The sheriff ignored Dottie's question and turned his pistol in their direction, "Who's next?"

"Mister," Will said stepping closer, "You get out of here, you've caused enough trouble as it is."

The sheriff cocked his gun and aimed it towards Will, "I won't ask you again you fool. Where's your daughter?"

"I told you…"

The sound of a gunshot erupted into the otherwise peaceful California sky. Will fell to the ground with a bullet lodged somewhere behind the hole between his ever so blue eyes. Dottie screamed as she knelt down beside her dead husband and placed his head in her lap.

She was ecstatic as she begged God not to take her husband, but it was too late, Will had already left his body and ventured into the land of unknown. Dottie looked up at the men with her face soaked in tears and her yellow dress stained in her husband's blood.

"Why would you do this!" She sobbingly screamed, "Why?"

All the men could do was laugh as if they had just shot a wolf. The sheriff looked down at her and smiled, "Tie her up boys. We'll make her talk yet!"

Two of the men dismounted their horses, one carrying a rope and walked towards her. She clutched onto her husband's body tighter than she had ever grasped for anything in her life. She kicked and screamed in protest as they drug her away and into the front yard.

"Let me go!" She shouted.

They tied her hands and feet together and threw up the slack to the sheriff who was still amount his horse. He looked back behind his horse at Dottie Braymyer, "Wanna' go for a ride, or would you like to tell me where your daughter is?"

Dottie lie on her stomach with her hands stretched out in front of her. She wiped her face on her sleeve and looked up at the sheriff with a look that showed no fear. "I've dealt with worse criminals than you. You don't scare me and you're the farthest thing from a sheriff I have ever seen. Now drag me across this land, this land that has more value than your life ever will because you sir, will never get to my daughter."

The sheriff looked at her in disbelief and shook his head in disappointment. He turned back and looked in front of him towards the fields and gave his horse a strong kick. The horse shot off across the Braymyer land, dragging Dottie across the ground behind it.

Dottie made no sound as the life was drug out of her and just before she became lifeless, that wind she had been caught up in so long ago wrapped itself around her and carried her soul up into the sky. When the horse returned to the house, the battered body of the former Miss Dorothy Travis was thrown onto the porch next to her husband and the riders rode off towards Lebanon.

Chapter Eighteen

Much to Aj's displeasure, Johnny Braymyer had been at the Douglas home for nearly a week and without knowing it, had grown remarkable feelings for Beth. It helped that they shared family members as it gave them a special connection and something to talk about that brought them both pleasure.

Johnny had arrived too late to join the cattle drive in Los Angeles as it had left just two days before his arrival. Rather than travel on, he stayed and helped Aj with the farm and was slowly gaining his trust.

Johnny had spent the most part of his life driving cattle across the country, mostly working as a body guard to the cattle and their herders and had killed more outlaws along the way than many cared to discuss. He had traveled the Chisolm Trail many times, but it was growing dry and there wasn't the same sense of adventure in it that there used to be.

He was forty-eight years old and like all the Braymyers before him, he still looked as handsome as he did when he was younger. He had been married once to Ellen Burns who had died eight years earlier down in Fort Worth. They had one son, Abram Braymyer, who was now in his early twenties and was in the United States Army trying to keep peace between whites and Indians alike.

Beth missed her late husband more than anything in the world, but she felt an instant connection with Johnny. She watched from the kitchen window as he showed Aj different ways to do things and was glad her son had someone to look up to whether he wanted it or not.

Johnny walked through the wheat fields, one row over from Aj and observed the ankle high crop as it slowly sprouted up toward the clear sky. It had taken everything Aj had to allow Johnny to teach him new ways about farming, but it looked as if God had intended for the Douglas' to incorporate into the Braymyer home and all the qualities of life Johnny had learned throughout his life, he was now teaching to them.

"Aj, you've done a real fine job out here," Johnny said as they continued walking, "Why if you hadn't of worked so hard to get these fields ready there's no way the crop would have made it this year."

"My Pa taught me everything. It all just sort of came back to me I guess."

"Well, you did good, son. I'm sure your Pa would be mighty proud of you, son."

Aj didn't answer, but instead turned is head and looked up at the hill where his father's body rested. It had been a hard season for Aj, but he knew that his time of being bitter was coming to an end and it was time for him to grow up and be the role model for his younger brothers.

As they neared the house, Beth came out of the door to greet them. "Aj, have you seen your brothers?"

"No, maim. I imagine they went down to the creek though."

"I declare, they stay out later and later every day. Won't you go fetch them and tell them supper is almost ready?"

"Yes, maim." He answered as he walked around the house and headed south towards the creek.

"You know, Johnny," she said putting her arm through his as they walked around the house to watch Aj as he crossed a field, "Some people would say I haven't known you long enough to have the feelings I have for you."

"Well, Beth, I reckon just about everyone has an opinion in one way or another. I'd say that the only one that really matters in your affairs is you though."

"Growing up I would have never thought my life would end up here. Ha, I had always thought I'd end up living a life of luxury in some eastern city somewhere. No, instead I'm a widow with four growing boys and I've hardly got any family members left alive."

"Life can be a funny thing, yes sir. I think the funniest part about the whole thing is how we think we're in charge of it when the truth is, is that the simplest thing like the wind can alter our entire perspective on life and create a strand of events that can forever change us."

"I don't think we're moving too fast, Johnny. My Pa always use to say that love has no time frame. It can happen one day and be gone the next so it's best to grab it by the arms when it does happen and never let go."

Johnny stopped and turned towards Beth and looked into her eyes. "Johnny," she said, "I'm not ever letting you go."

"You won't have to, darling. I don't ever aim on going anywhere, not without you anyway."

He leaned down and kissed her their first kiss and immediately they knew that what they had was more real than either one of them had ever had. There was no guilt over their dead spouses for they knew that they would want them to be happy and move on with their lives. They were, after all, only given one life to live and now that they had managed to find each other they were sure it would be a good one.

As they walked back around to the front of the house they could see a wagon heading in their direction from across the fields. "Who do you suppose that is," Johnny asked her.

"I don't know, is that a woman on the wagon seat?"

"Sure looks that away, but I'll go get my gun just in case."

John went into the small home and got his rifle and then joined Beth back out on the front porch. They sat in rockers as they waited for the wagon to reach them and as it drew nearer they also noticed two riders accompanying the wagon.

Beth stood up as she began to see familiar faces and before John could ask her if she recognized them, Beth was halfway across the yard running towards them. "Callie!" She shouted as the wagon came to a stop beside her. "What are you doing here!"

Callie jumped down and buried her head on Beth's shoulder. Beth looked up and noticed her brother, Travis and Ann Marie riding around the wagon towards them. "Travis! Ann Marie! Oh my! What a pleasant surprise!"

Johnny joined them as he walked up behind Beth. "I take it you know them," Johnny asked.

"Why, Johnny," Beth said, "This is your niece, Callie Braymyer!"

Callie lifted her head up and looked in his direction, seeing her uncle for the first time since she was a toddler. "My uncle?"

Johnny stepped up to her and admired her beauty. He reached out both of his arms, "I'm Johnny Braymyer, your Pa's elder brother."

As Callie hugged him, Travis, Matt and Ann Marie walked up to Beth and exchanged hellos and hugs. Matt joined Callie next to her uncle and shook his hand as he put his other arm around his Callie.

"Travis," Beth said, "What brings everyone out this way?"

"Well, big sister, I think it would be best if we all sit down and have a little talk," he said looking over at Callie.

The small Douglas home was host to a much-needed family reunion that night as they ate the beef stew that Beth had prepared earlier. They brought Beth and John up to date on everything that had happened in Lebanon and no one showed more fear in their eyes than Beth.

She looked around at everyone, but said very few words. She had lost more in this life than anyone else at the table and she had grown an ability to tell when things were not right. She looked in Callie's direction with sympathy and knew something wasn't right.

"Well," Johnny said, "I reckon us men should go back and help my brother with whatever he might be dealing with and let the women stay here and run the farm."

Matt and Travis looked at Callie at almost exactly the same time, knowing she wouldn't stand for it.

"Uncle Johnny," she said, "I am not being left behind anywhere! If Momma and Poppa are in trouble it is because of my own doing and I'll see to it that things are resolved."

"Callie," Johnny said, "There might be trouble, big trouble and that kind of a situation is no place for a girl."

"A girl! I'll have you know," she said standing up, "That this *woman* can take care of herself. I saw no man help when I horsewhipped the sheriff and if need be I won't rely on any man when I go back for my parents!" Callie sat back down.

Johnny was speechless. He had never been talked to in that kind of tone by anyone who had expected to keep their two front teeth. He looked around at the table, pleading for someone to back him up, but they all knew Callie and when she had her mind set on something people got out of the way.

Ann Marie who was sitting next to her put her hand in her lap to try and calm her down, but Callie continued to glare in her uncle's direction. "Call…" Johnny began.

"Good so we're settled then," she interrupted as her face went from an angry stare to the sweetest face Johnny had ever seen.

"Callie, let's just discuss it tomorrow after we have all had some rest."

"Uncle Johnny, I am a Braymyer just like you and I see no point in having the same argument again tomorrow when the issue has been resolved." She turned to Beth, "Cousin Beth this is a fine stew, you must teach me how to make it sometime."

Ann Marie couldn't help but laugh and soon the entire table joined, including Johnny who just shook his head and knew there was no getting out of this one. She was right, he thought, she was most definitely a Braymyer.

After they had finished eating, everyone went outside and sat on the long porch where they continued their visit. "Johnny," Beth said, "Why don't we all go to Lebanon. I am sure there will be a use for us there and besides I want to see Will and Dottie." She looked over in Callie's direction to make sure she had heard her statement, hoping it would restore hope within Callie about her parents.

"What about the farm," Aj interrupted. "Who'll take care of it!"

"Calm down, son," Johnny said. "We've got a week's worth of work left before the fields can take care of themselves for awhile." He looked over at Callie and Matt, "If you think you can stay here for a week, we can all go together."

Callie looked at Matt, "What do you think?"

Matt was halfway shocked that Callie had asked his advice on anything rather than making the decision on her own as she so often did. "Well, we are only a half days ride from Los Angeles. Seems to me that would be a good town to get married in."

Callie blushed at his flirtatious remark he had so boldly made in front of everyone. "Matt Russell! What makes you think I would get married without my parents present!"

"Well, I had a feeling you would say that. So did they." Callie confusingly looked at him as he handed her a letter.

She took it in her hands and read aloud:

Dearest Callie,
Enclosed you will find one hundred dollars. If it is your
heart's desire to marry Mr. Russell it is our wish that you do it
in Los Angeles. With all that is happening in Lebanon it is just
too depressing for a wedding. Use the money to buy you a
store bought dress and know that you have our blessing.
Momma and Poppa

Everyone on the front porch was smiling and anxiously
watched Callie for her decision. Matt stood up from his chair
and knelt down beside her. "Callie, if you decide to marry me
I promise you that I will protect you and I swear that no matter
what I will always do right by you for as long as I live."

Callie looked down at him and searched his eyes for that one
door that would allow her to escape committing herself to
anyone other than herself. She looked desperately, but found
no out and just before she said yes a small teardrop ran down
her cheek.

Chapter Nineteen

May 18, 1892

Lebanon continued to house outlaws and the number grew more and more every day. The few good citizens who had tried to take a stand against the unlawfulness found themselves in jail for various reasons.

The new mayor continued to lead the town down a path of destruction and spent the majority of his days in the local saloon. Lebanon had been taken over by some of the last outlaws of the west and if something wasn't done soon, there was little hope for the small town.

Sheriff Jack Young had a growing scar emerging across his face and he vowed that as soon as he found Callie Braymyer he would see to it that she was killed. He had never been disgraced by a woman and if it was the last thing he did he would get revenge.

He became a joke to everyone in town and none of them understood how he could have let a woman do that to him. With every day that passed he became angrier and as he did, Callie's life became more in danger.

A week before, the Baptist Church that stood at the east end of Main Street was burned to the ground. The mayor and several of his renegade gunmen grew tired of the saloon for a split moment and decided they wanted to burn something down.

Just before sundown they marched to the end of the street with a bottle of whiskey in one hand and a flaming torch in the other. They stopped at all the local business', threatening their owners with the torch until finally arriving at the only church in town.

The preacher, George Rivers stood at the door with his wife and read aloud from the bible as they approached him. The outlaws didn't take too kindly to the word of God being read to them and as Brother Rivers continued to read he soon found that his third generation bible was aflame in his hands.

He quickly dropped the bible and tried desperately to put the fire out, but it was no use. He then put his arm around his wife and began reciting from memory as the crowd grew more violent. The mayor swung his flaming torch at the preacher and hit him on the side of his face, bringing him unconsciously to the church porch.

Afterwards three torches, including the mayor's were thrown into the church building almost immediately sending the building up in flames. Mrs. Rivers tried desperately to drag her husband off of the porch, but was stopped by two of the men dragging her away to a jail cell.

As she was being taken away she watched as the building fell on top of her husband and shot sparks up into the sky. When she tried to break free from the men's grip she was met with the back of hands across her face.

After the church was burnt all the respectable families, but very few, left town and didn't come back. Lebanon had turned into hell on earth and nobody wanted to live there. Of the few remaining families was the widow Betty Reeves and her seventeen year old son, Harold.

 Betty had refused to leave the town that her and her late husband and helped to create and prayed desperately for a miracle to put the town back on track. She knew that if anyone could help get it done that it would be Will and Dottie Braymyer.

The day before she had received a letter from Callie asking her to go and check on her parents. In the letter, Callie explained that she would have sent one directly to her parents, but she feared that the letter would be stolen and her location would be discovered.

As Betty and her son approached the large home outside of town, they knew immediately that something was wrong.

Buzzards swarmed in large circles above the house and made occasional landings near the front of the house.

When they pulled their wagon to a stop near the steps they were horrified at what they saw. Two of the most influential citizens of the area were lying there dead with their house servant. Betty had her son load the bodies up onto the back of the wagon and together they drove the wagon to the Braymyer Cemetery.

The cemetery was in the small clearing that Dottie had first discovered the wind and aside from the three new bodies being interred here were the small children of Will and Dottie.

When they returned home Betty wrote a letter to Callie informing her of the tragedy that had taken place at her home. She sent her son to have the letter mailed and then went back to her praying as the afternoon sun rippled across the sky.

An hour after her son had left she heard him walk up onto the front porch and just before the door opened two shots were fired. She ran out of the house where she found her son with two bullet holes in his back.

"What have you done! Why! Why would you do this!" She screamed.

Sheriff Young dismounted his horse and walked over to Betty who lie crouched over her son's body weeping. He took his pistol and slammed the butt of it down into Betty's head killing her instantly. He looked up at the sky and then at the Reeves home.

"Burn it, boys!" He said to the three men accompanying him. He then reached into his jacket pocket and pulled out the letter Betty had written to Callie, showing the address where he could find her.

The sheriff went back to his office and wrote a letter addressed to Callie, signing it as Betty Reeves.

- - - - - - - - - - - - - - - - - -

Callie and the rest of the Lebanon crew had been at the Douglas home for two days when they all loaded up and rode west towards Los Angeles on a Saturday morning. Travis and Matt had helped John and Aj in the fields, allowing them to make much more progress than they had originally planned on.

There was a constant fear written across their faces about what the latest happenings in Lebanon might be, but they were determined to make this day a day of celebration. Not only were Callie and Matt getting married, but John and Beth would also marry in a double wedding.

Matt and Callie rode in their own wagon and held hands as the eastern sun slowly rose behind them. John, Beth and the boys rode together in a separate wagon, except for Aj who rode a paint horse near Travis and Ann Marie who also sat amount.

The many streets of Los Angeles were packed with people as they went about their business and they paid little attention to the wedding convoy. "Matt, have you ever seen a town so full of people?" Callie asked leaning her head on his shoulder.

"Can't say that I have, darling. I'd say it's quite a site to see wouldn't you?"

"Oh yes. I bet I would fit right in here."

Matt shook his head and laughed, "I bet you would to."

Matt pulled the wagon up to a dress shop that read, 'A Dress for all.' Callie looked in disbelief that a store could sell nothing but dresses. "Matt, look at all the dresses!"

"Why don't you and the girls go on in and see if you can find a dress while the boys and I go on down to the church and talk to the preacher."

Callie didn't even hesitate and before the other two women had time to get down she had already went inside the store. When she entered there was an elderly woman with gray hair in a bun standing behind the counter. She was short and wore

302

a bright purple dress, a shade of purple that Callie had never seen before.

Every wall in the store was lined with dresses of all kinds and they were all kept with other dresses of their own color. As Beth and Ann Marie came into the store, Callie was running her hands across the waves of a row of dresses and turning as she did it.

"Ann Marie! Have you ever seen anything like it?"

She smiled at Callie realizing that the young girl was truly happy, even if it was over a new dress. "No, honey I don't think that I have. In fact, this is more dresses than I have seen in my entire life!"

"You know, Callie," Beth said, "I was there when your Momma and Poppa got married. There were three weddings that day... do you remember Ann Marie?"

"Oh yes, I was pea green with jealously."

"Why were you jealous Ann Marie," Callie said taking her eyes off the dresses only for a split second.

"Because, your Momma was marrying my first crush, that's why."

Callie completely took her attention off the dresses and stared wild eyed at Ann Marie. "You had a crush on Poppa! Oh, do tell!"

Beth and Ann Marie laughed as they told her of the wedding along the trail on their way to California. Beth wiped away a few tears as she remembered that that was also the day she had married Abner. After they had shared stories of their past with Callie they turned their attention back to the many dresses and made their way to the section of white ones.

It didn't take Callie long to find a dress and she was lucky enough that it was just her size and didn't have to be hemmed at all. She put it on and then walked back out into the store where she did a complete turn for Beth and Ann Marie.

"Callie," Beth said, "You remind me so much of your Momma. Up until today she was the prettiest bride I had ever seen."

"Oh isn't that the truth!" Ann Marie added, "Even if she did get married on an old cow trail!"

Callie stopped and thought for a moment, "I sure wish Momma could be here. It doesn't seem right doing this without her."

"Callie," Ann Marie said, "Your Momma is the smartest woman I've ever known. You'll do good to remember that and if your Momma says to get married here, then there is a good reason for it."

"That's right," Beth said, "Besides she's given you enough money that after the wedding you and Matt can go get your picture made."

Callie smiled at the thought because she had always enjoyed when the traveling photographer would come to their home and take their picture. When Dottie would hang the pictures on the wall it made the house seem even more like their home.

Callie looked at them, "What are you two standing there for? Pick you a dress ladies!"

"Oh Callie," Beth said, "We couldn't."

"You can and you will," she demanded, "Besides if you don't pick yourself I'll get you one as ugly as the store keeper's over there."

The two women smiled and searched through the dresses as if they were Callie's age and before long they too wore a new dress. Beth was wearing a deep blue dress that made her look ten years younger than she really was. Ann Marie chose a hunter green dress that made her look as if she were the most important woman in town.

After they had left the dress shop they walked down the boardwalk heading west side by side. Unlike when they had first arrived in town, everyone was stopping to stare at them and all the men tipped their hats.

"Oh, Callie," Beth said, "I haven't felt this young in a long time."

"Me either!" Ann Marie said, "This is such a good day."

"Well," Callie answered them, "Let's get something that we can remember it by forever."

Callie stopped at a glass door that said 'Phillips Photography.' Before even telling the other two what she was up to, she turned and went in as they followed her. "We'll have our picture done before and after the wedding," she said. "And we'll remember this day forever."

Chapter Twenty

It was midafternoon when the women joined the men in the Baptist Church, which sat right in between a store and a blacksmith shop. Ann Marie went in first and soon after an organ began to play.

Beth and Callie joined their arms together and walked through the wooden doors where their future husbands were awaiting. One symbolized a new beginning and the other a young love, but they both symbolized a new life.

Matt stood next to Johnny Braymyer and they watched as the two women made their way towards them. Matt was not made nervous easily, but as he watched Callie approach him there was sudden fear that took over his body.

What if he was not good enough, he thought. What if something terrible happened and he was not able to protect her. His thoughts were interrupted by a whisper from Johnny. "Relax, boy, you're going to do fine."

Johnny had spent little time getting ready for the event, but he still looked presentable enough for a wedding. He was a little rough around the edges, but Beth didn't care one way or the other.

Matt had his hair combed over to one side and had just finished shaving before Callie had arrived. He now wished he had that little bit of facial hair that other twenty year olds had so that his blushing would not be so apparent. He continued to watch Callie as he thought over everything in his head when suddenly his thoughts disappeared and he was wrapped in nothing but Callie's beauty.

When the women arrived in front of them Travis and Aj stood up and gave them both away to their future husbands as Ann Marie watched from the front row pew. The preacher proceeded with Johnny and Beth's vowels first in his scratchy high-pitched voice.

Beth and Johnny's eyes met and they both got lost within each other. The preacher took longer than usual, often times repeating some of the same stuff over again. At the end of their ceremony, Johnny leaned in and kissed Beth and the small audience cheered and clapped.

The preacher then turned to Matt and Callie where Matt was nearly choking on a large lump that had formed in his throat. "Do you Matthew Wilson Russell and… and…" the preacher hesitated for a moment, "California Gold Braymyer?"

Callie slightly nodded her head toward the preacher who then continued. Ann Marie leaned over to Travis and whispered, "I bet Dottie didn't think this one through when it came to Callie's wedding. California Gold… I still can't believe it!"

They both quietly laughed among themselves as the preacher continued on about the meaning of marriage and what it symbolized. "Before I finish up this ceremony, I would like to add one thing," the preacher said. "Here in California there is a rare quality and very few people possess it. In fact, I have only seen one or two in my lifetime. We call that quality California Charm and as I look around I do believe I see it written across the faces of everyone in here.

California Charm is not something a person can acquire, not intentionally anyway. It symbolizes endurance, passion, hope, love for things greater than oneself and above all determination. A person with this charm is sure to make their mark on the world and may the Lord be with this young couple as they embark on their new journey. You may kiss the bride."

 Matt leaned in and kissed her and for the first time in her life, Callie was completely okay with depending on someone else… as long as he promised to kiss her like that forever.

After the weddings everyone went back to Phillips Photography to get their pictures made again. Every couple got their picture taken together and a family portrait was done of Johnny, Beth and the boys. Just before leaving they took one last picture which included everyone in it.

"Well you two," Johnny said to Callie and Matt, "I reckon the rest of us are going to head back to the house and give you some time alone."

They said goodbye to each other and everyone rode out of town except for Callie and Matt who remained on the boardwalk waving them off. "Well, Mrs. Russell," Matt said putting his arm around her and leading her down the walk, "What shall we do?"

"Well, how about pie?"

"Pie?"

"Yes, pie. It sounds really good right now."

Matt shook is head and laughed, "Oh boy, Callie Russell, you're going to be the death of me yet."

The two of them went to the café and ordered pie and tea as they watched people walk along the street from their window seat. When they finished it was almost dark so they went to the hotel and got a room where they would spend their first night together as husband and wife.

The next day the two of them rode back to the Douglas home where they knew their happy moments of husband and wife would come to an end as they prepared their trip back to Lebanon. As they approached the house, Turner Douglas was running towards them waving a piece of paper in his hands.

"Callie! You've gotten a letter from Ms. Reeves!"

Callie jumped down from the wagon and read aloud:

Dear Callie,
I went yesterday to see your Momma and Poppa and they are both well. They tell me to tell you that you should stay there for awhile until things settle down out here. They also said

that within two days of receiving this letter you should travel to Newhall where a package will be waiting for you there.
All the best,
Betty Reeves

By the time Callie had finished reading the letter the rest of the family had joined her outside. She folded the letter and looked up at her husband, "Looks like we will be heading to Newhall, Matt."

"Callie," Travis said, "Let the rest of us go with you, just in case there is any trouble."

"Really it's fine, Travis. Newhall is only a day's ride from here. I'm sure Matt and I will be just fine," she answered him.

Johnny stepped closer to her, "Are you sure?"

"Yes, Uncle Johnny. If we leave now we'll be back by tomorrow night."

Against Travis' better judgement the group agreed to let the newlyweds travel alone, mainly to give them time to themselves. After a few things were packed, Callie and Matt rode north away from the Douglas home…heading right into a trap.

Chapter Twenty One

May 20, 1892

Indian Territory

Two weeks after the two women came upon the cabin, Rachel's fever finally broke one morning. She spent all day eating her weight in soup and fresh bread that Mary Anna had made. Early the next morning, the two women loaded back up into the wagon and continued towards Texas.

"Rachel, dear you really had me scared back there. It's one thing for two old ladies to make this trip, but Lord knows what would have happened if it had only been me traveling."

"Mary Anna, is that why you brought me along? So if something happens whoever it is can get me and then you'll take off running. Why I do declare!"

Both women laughed as hard as a young child thinking the subject over. Mary Anna had started wearing one of her husband's old cowboy hats and Rachel was always giving her a hard time about it.

"Mary Anna, that is not very lady like!"

"I'm too old to be a lady anymore, dear. Besides if people see us coming maybe they'll think I'm a man! I reckon I look rough enough to be one anyhow."

"Yes, Mary Anna. A man driving a wagon across Indian Territory with a colored woman sitting next to him. My! What would people think!"

The next two days were filled with laughter as the wagon rode on until a shot was fired somewhere ahead of them. Mary Anna slowly stood up on the seat to see if she could see anyone ahead and sure enough there were two riders heading their way.

She sat back down and handed a pistol to Rachel as she took one for herself as well. "Rachel, you keep that pistol hidden, but keep it pointed at them, you hear?"

Rachel shook her head. Mary Anna and Rachel both hid their pistols beneath their dresses and had them pointed straight ahead as the two men stopped in front of them, both with guns in hand. Both men looked to be in their mid thirties and both had a cold look about them.

"Well, what do we have here," one of them said.

"Look's like a couple of old maids," the other answered.

Mary Anna smiled and said in her ever so cheerful voice, "Hi there! How do you do?"

The first rider snickered, "Well I'll be doing a whole lot better after I sift through your wagon load and take what I want."

Mary Anna continued to smile, "Oh now come on. I don't think that would be a very good idea."

"Ha! What are you going to do old lady," the second man said pointing his gun at her.

In about as innocent a voice as possible, Mary Anna smiled and said, "Why, I'm gonna' shoot you."

There were two shots fired and both Mary Anna and Rachel had holes in their dresses from where the bullets shot through and whirled towards the two men. Both men were shot in the chest and both of them fell to the ground.

Rachel turned to Mary Anna, "Look's like we've got pretty good aim for a couple of old maids!"

The two women laughed as Mary Anna steered the wagon around their bodies and continued on the trail. She put her husband's hat back on and whistled at the horses, "Hiya!"

Lebanon News

May 21, 1892

Well I think our town is one of the best places to be in the whole state of California! Why look around you, our saloon is open at all hours, Mayor Styles promises us an endless supply of whiskey and above all, there's no taxes! What more could we ask for?

Sheriff Young left yesterday in search of that young girl who horsewhipped him. He informed me that he plans to bring her back alive and make her suffer before he kills her. Sounds like we've got more fun heading our way folks.

On a more sour note, the mayor has still not gotten Ann Marie Turner back in his custody. He has issued a fifty-dollar reward for any man who can bring her to him alive.

Fannie Albright

Chapter Twenty Two

Callie and Matt rode along the dusty trail all day, stopping only once to let the horses water. They were about two miles outside of Newhall when they stopped one last time to give the horses a final break before riding on into town.

Callie unwrapped some slices of ham that Beth had packed for them and gave the majority of it to Matt. He placed his rifle across the wagon seat as the two of them got down to stretch their legs.

"Matt, I wonder what Momma and Poppa are sending to me."

"I don't know, darling. I'm sure it's something pretty important though for them to do it on such short notice."

"I do hope everything is okay at the house. I just have this really bad feeling."

"Well, Callie, you read the letter yourself. Ms. Reeves said they were both doing just fine."

"I know, Matt, but still, something just doesn't seem right about the whole situation."

"I'm sure everything will be just fine. Maybe your Momma and Poppa are trying to settle things up at their home so they can move out this way and get away from Lebanon."

"Oh no, Matt. They would never leave their home. It means too much to them."

As they walked along the bank of a shallow creek two riders approached them from behind. Neither Callie nor Matt even heard them until the butt of Sheriff Young's gun slammed against the back of Matt's head.

Callie screamed and knelt down over Matt's body, hoping, begging for him to be okay. Both riders dismounted their sickly looking mares and grabbed her by the arms.

The man accompanying Sheriff Young was his brother, Jake Young who was three years younger than him. Jake looked almost exactly like the Sheriff only he was taller by about four inches. They both had the same cold darkening eyes and neither one of them showed any sign of sympathy for Callie.

"Let go of me you…"

"Shut up!" The sheriff said slapping her across the face. He threw her to the ground as hard as he could. "Jake, hold her down."

Jake Young squatted down just above her head and held down both of her arms above her. Sheriff Young sat on her stomach with one leg on either side of her. He leaned in to her face and as he did she spit on him.

The sheriff slapped her again and then grabbed her by the chin and forced her to look at him. He turned his head and rubbed his scarring wound with his free hand. "Do you see that you stupid…"

She spit on him again. Once again, she was slapped and the sheriff pulled out a knife. He softly drug the knife across her face sending chills down her spine. "Maybe I'll mark you up like you did me."

He ran the knife down her throat and then across her shoulders smiling the whole time. His stained black teeth nearly made her vomit in her mouth as he continued to sit on top of her. He slowly brought the knife back to her neck and then down to her chest, cutting her dress as he did it.

"Or maybe I'll find better use for you before cutting you."

"Don't you dare…"

He struck her in the face with his fist, knocking her out and sending her into a deep sleep. The sheriff got up and threw her over the back of his horse. Jake looked in Matt's direction, "What do you want to do with him, Jack?"

"Hell, just leave him there, the animals will probably finish him off."

The two of them rode off towards Lebanon carrying their prize with them. Callie Russell drifted in and out of a foggy sleep as the horse galloped northeastward. She knew in her gut that she would have to do something before they got back to Lebanon or there would be no hope for her.

- - - - - - - - - - - - - - - -

Things at the Douglas home remained quiet for only a short time after Callie and Matt had left. On a northern hill five riders watched as the two of them rode off and when they were completely out of sight, the five gunmen rode down to the Douglas home.

John and Travis busied themselves in the barn with Aj while the women and three younger boys sat inside the house. It was Sunday and Beth was very strict when it came to the Lord's day, often times reading from the bible for hours at a time.

The three boys had fallen asleep as Beth continued to read from the book of Revelations and as she neared the last verse of the last chapter she closed the bible and looked over at Ann Marie.

"How about some tea?" She whispered.

"That sounds like a fine idea to me."

The two of them went into the kitchen and sat across from each other at the table sipping on the warm drink. "Beth," she said running her fingers across the flowered pattern on the china cup. "I've been barren since Travis and I first married, nearly seventeen years ago."

"I know Ann Marie, it must be so hard, but the Lord has a plan even if it is not always what we want."

Ann Marie looked up from her cup at Beth as her eyes watered a little bit, "Beth, I think I may be with child."

Beth looked at Ann Marie and was about to rush over and hug her when Ann Marie stopped her, "Don't get excited yet, Beth. I've been pregnant before but have never been able to carry past two months."

Beth looked across the room, searching for the right words to say in order to comfort her sister in law. "Ann Marie, have you told Travis?"

"No, I don't want to get him excited just so he can be disappointed again. Sometimes I think that is all I am…"

"Ann Marie you hush now! You are not the kind of woman to dwell in self pity so don't you start now do you hear me?"

Ann Marie shook her head yes. "I just wish we could have one child. I know how much it would mean to Travis."

"Well, it is the Lord's will. So you just go on with your life and if he intends for you to have this child then so be it. I know it doesn't seem fair, Ann Marie, but sometimes we just have to trust in greater things than our wants."

They went back to sipping their tea as two men snuck into the house by way of the front door. They were both rough looking men and as they tip toed around the sleeping boys the two women instantly smelled their foul odor.

As they stood up from the table and headed to the front room they were both met with a pistol to their head. "Ann Marie Turner," one of the men said, "I've come to take you back to Lebanon to see the mayor."

"The heck you are," Ann Marie said kneeing him in the crotch, "Travis!" She yelled.

The man she had kicked bent over and groaned. Ann Marie reached for his gun, but he threw his entire arm across her face bringing her down to the floor. Beth quickly reached for her as she slowly backed toward the kitchen. The second gunman hit her in the side of the head with his gun, knocking her out.

318

As the three men ran out of the barn, the three remaining gunmen were there waiting for them. Travis drew out his pistol from its holster and fired at them, bringing the man closest to them down to the ground with a bullet in the chest. The second and third man both shot at the same time in his direction. Aj, who was standing behind Travis was struck by a bullet in the head and sent barreling backwards into the barn.

The second bullet that was fired hit Travis in the stomach and brought him hunched over to his knees and then onto his back. Johnny fired just after the two gunmen had shot Aj and Travis and within a swift motion Johnny Braymyer brought the two remaining men down without having a single bullet fired at him.

He ran to the house as Ann Marie was being pushed out of the front door with a gun to her head. "Drop your gun or I'll shoot her!" The man shouted at Johnny.

Johnny slowly lowered his gun to the ground and as he was leaning back up the second gunman shot him just below his right shoulder, knocking him down. Ann Marie screamed in terror as she watched him fall, revealing the body of Travis laying several feet behind him on the ground.

"What have you done to my husband! Travis!"

The man that was holding her had both of her hands behind her back, causing her to lean forward. A few strands of her hair ran down her face, sticking to her growing tears. "What have you done!" She screamed again.

"Shut up, woman! Before we throw a rope around your neck and hang you up somewhere."

When the two men had her back at their horses they used a rope to tie her hands together and placed her in the saddle in front of the smallest of the two gunmen. As they kicked their horses forcing them to jump into a forward run, Ann Marie looked back and screamed one last time, "Travis!"

Chapter Twenty Three

Callie had been traveling with her two kidnappers for almost two days and luckily had not been harmed except for the occasional slap across the face when she smarted off. The sheriff, however, constantly reminded her that when they got back to Lebanon she would get her payback for what she had done to his face.

They made their camps quick and when they slept, they kept Callie's hands tied up with the extra rope extended out and tied to sheriff's hand so she could not escape. Callie endured the crude remarks that the two men made about her and vowed that someday she would get her revenge.

The small group stopped beneath a lone tree where they began to set up camp for the night, it would be their last night on the trail as they would reach Lebanon the next day. Callie worried constantly about Matt and prayed that he was okay and not far behind them.

"My parents will have you killed you ignorant fool," she said as the men tied her up to the tree.

"Ha!" The sheriff said, "Your parents! Should we tell her Jake?'

Jake Young snickered as he lit a cigar and leaned down to blow the smoke in Callie's face. "Why not. I think she has a right to know the truth about her beloved parents."

"Tell me what!" She said frantically, "What is it? What have you done to them?"

They both started laughing, "Well let's just say that after we were finished with them, the old widow was kind enough to go clean up our mess. I believe she had her son bury them in your family cemetery."

"No! You lie! You stupid uneducated baboon! You're lying!"

The sheriff threw the back of his hand across her face, "Listen here little missy, I may be a lot things but I ain't no liar!"

Callie looked up at him and saw the one trait the sheriff did have, at that moment anyway…honesty. She looked back down at the ground and slowly lowered herself to its surface.

As the two men continued to laugh and start a campfire Callie was overcome with sadness and fear. Her world began to spin uncontrollably throwing her into a dark trance she knew she might never escape.

The closest people in her lives were now gone and she felt completely alone, even if her husband had managed to survive she still possessed a great emptiness within her gut. Her world continued to spin around and around for hours that she didn't even notice when the two men tried to give her food.

As the night drug on she overcame the sadness and became angry. Somewhere within her arose a determination to overpower her present situation. The two men were sitting by the fire taking large drinks of whiskey and she knew if she really wanted to she could escape, but where would she go, she thought.

She lifted her head up and glared in their direction, feeling more anger for them than she had ever felt before in her life. Just as she was about to lash out at the two with every ounce of her being the sound of horse hooves could be heard approaching their campsite.

The two men quickly jumped to their feet, guns at hand and watched in the direction of the noise. Callie hoped desperately that it was Matt who had come to rescue her but then feared greatly for his safety.

"Who goes there?" Jake Young shouted.

There was a short moment of silence and then a voice answered, "It's Tom Davidson and Silus Brown. Is that you, Jake?"

"Why hell yeah, it's me and Jack too. Approach the camp."

Callie watched as the two riders approached from the blackness of the night toward the small fire. She blinked twice to clear her eyes of the fog that her many tears had created and immediately noticed the woman sitting on the saddle with one of the men.

The sheriff walked up to the two guests, "Well now, what do we have here." He pulled Ann Marie from the saddle and let her fall to the ground. He then placed his boot at her throat and looked down at her, "The mayor's gonna' be mighty glad to see you."

Silus and Tom dismounted their horses and stepped closer. Silus was the first to speak, "Now, Sheriff, Tom and I did the work so we deserve the fifty dollar reward for bringing her in."

The sheriff looked up at them, "Of course you do boys." He turned around and took one step back toward the fire and then without warning he spun around and shot both the men dead before they knew what had hit them."

Callie continued to watch as the scene unfolded, never taking her eyes off of Ann Marie. Jack stepped up to his brother, "Looks like we're fifty dollars richer brother!"

The sheriff drug Ann Marie over to the tree and tied her up beside Callie. After she had been secured the two men moved the bodies of the dead men out of sight.

"Callie," Ann Marie whispered, "Are you okay? What are you doing here!"

Callie leaned her head over and laid it on Ann Marie's shoulder, "They kidnapped me just outside of Newhall. Matt… oh Ann Marie, I don't know what's happened to Matt!"

Ann Marie turned her head to face Callie, "Callie don't you fret none about that now. We're less than a days ride from Lebanon and if they take us to town there is no hope for us."

"But Ann Marie… Momma and Poppa, they're… they're dead!"

"What! How do you know?"

"The sheriff… he told me and I saw the truth of it in his eyes." She answered her as tears once again whelped up in her eyes.

Ann Marie continued to look at her trying to figure out what words to say, but then she lost it to and began to cry. "Callie, what are we going to do? We're all alone now and no one is here to help us. They shot Travis and John and I don't know if either one of them survived."

"What? How? What happened Ann Marie?"

"They rode up to the house shortly after you left and attacked us. Travis, John and I think Aj were all shot."

"What about Beth?"

"She was knocked out on the kitchen floor when they took off with me."

"Ann Marie we've got to do something. I won't lose another person I care about, as God as my witness I won't! Now I'm sure Travis and John are fine, they are strong men. Did you see where they were shot at?"

"John was shot in the shoulder…Travis…I don't know, Callie," she said crying again.

"Shut up!" The sheriff shouted in their direction as him and his brother took a seat around the fire again.

Callie looked back down at the ground, pretending to obey them. "What happened to Matt," Ann Marie whispered.

"He was hit pretty hard with a gun on the backside of his head. He was bleeding pretty badly, but if the animals don't get to him I think he has a fighting chance."

Ann Marie looked at Callie and admired her courage. She had just found out that her parents might be dead and the last time she had seen her husband he was lying on the ground in a puddle of blood. "Callie, you're so strong. Dottie would be so proud…"

"Don't talk like that, Ann Marie. If I'm strong it's only because you taught me how to be. Now come on, we've got to think of a way to get out of this mess. We'll worry about the others later, we're no good to them if we wind up dead ourselves."

"You're right, Callie," Ann Marie said as the strength and passion to live made its way back into her spirit, "There's got to be something we can do."

"How tight is your rope?" Callie asked.

"It's pretty tight, but I think if I work at it I might be able to get it loose."

"Well, don't do it now. They'll check it before they go to sleep."

The two of them joined hands and faced their heads to the ground as they entered a pretend dreamland where they thought only of revenge and living. Just before the men went to sleep they walked over to the two women to ensure that their ropes were tight enough. When they were satisfied with them, they went back to the fire and went to sleep for the night.

Ann Marie immediately began to mess with her rope and slowly freed one of her hands, and then the other. When she heard both men snoring she untied Callie's hands, careful not to tug on the rope that was connected to the sheriff's wrist.

Once they were both free they moved very quietly toward the two men where Callie picked up the sheriff's gun.

"What are you going to do," Ann Marie whispered.

Callie didn't even look at Ann Marie. She lifted the pistol and pointed it at Jake Young's head who was fast asleep. She pulled the trigger, nearly scaring Ann Marie half to death who didn't think that Callie was capable of such a thing.

The sheriff quickly stumbled out of his sleep and just as he was lifting himself off the ground Callie stopped him. "Don't move Mr. Young," she said pointing the gun towards his head.

"You stupid woman! Why I'm gonna'…"

"You're not gonna' do anything, I'm the one with the gun. No Mr. Young, you're right where you belong in the dirt where filth like you deserves to be."

Ann Marie's mouth dropped open as she watched from behind Callie's shoulder. Deep down she was more proud of Callie than she had been in her entire life. The preacher was right back in Los Angeles, Callie had the true markings of a California woman.

The sheriff continued to watch Callie, "What? You think you're going to kill me? I'm a sheriff you know!"

"You are no sheriff, Mr. Young," she said gripping the pistol even tighter, "Now tell me the truth… Are my parents really dead?"

The sheriff smiled and then began to laugh uncontrollably, making Callie uncomfortable. "Answer my question!" She shouted.

"I told you I weren't no liar. If I said your parents were dead then they are dead."

Ann Marie stepped closer and now stood right beside Callie. Callie blew a strand of her hair away from her face, "Are you the one that killed them?" She asked.

He began laughing again, but not nearly as high pitched this time. "So what if I did."

"I said are you the one who killed them!"

"Well, best I could tell after dragging your mother around the yard behind my horse she was dead so I threw her up on the porch with your father's body…"

Gunshot erupted into the sky.

Callie didn't give him time to finish before pulling the trigger. She had heard all she wanted to hear and at least now she knew that her parents murderer was dead.

She turned back towards Ann Marie who stood there in shock looking down at the dead man's body. "Ann Marie," she said putting both of her hands on Ann Marie's shoulders, "You ride back to Beth's house. See if you can find out anything about Matt along the way."

"Well you're coming to aren't you, Callie?"

"No. I'm going to Lebanon."

"Lebanon! Callie you can't! They'll kill you!"

Callie looked back at the sheriff's body and then at Ann Marie. "Then let them kill me, but that is my town and I am not going to let the likes of people like this take it away from me!"

Ann Marie looked at Callie and saw the truth of it in her eyes. She thought about it for a moment and realized that she couldn't have agreed more. It had been hard enough just making it to California and she wouldn't stand by as the country went to waste

She took a slow look up at the stars and then back at Callie, "You're right, Callie. Something has to be done, but I'm going with you."

"Ann Marie, you don't have to…"

"Are you kidding, I'm not going to let my sister go alone. We'll take back the town together."

"Okay, Ann Marie… but you do realize what this could mean…"

"I know, Callie. So what's the plan?"

"To ride in there and kill as many of them potbelly pigs as possible."

Ann Marie grabbed the gun from Callie and pointed it down at the dead sheriff. "This is for locking me in jail," she said just before pulling the trigger.

Chapter Twenty Four

Buzzards had begun to circle the body of Matt Russell when Johnny and Beth arrived at the scene. He had been laying there over a day in a puddle of his own blood. Johnny had his arm in a sling that Beth had quickly thrown together and the two of them rode separate horses as they headed north.

Johnny slowly got down from his horse, but by the time he made it to Matt's body, Beth was already there checking for a pulse. "Johnny," she said, "He's alive! Hurry!"

Johnny knelt down beside him to observe his wound, "Looks like he got hit with a gun. Help me roll him over."

With Beth doing most of the work, they finally got him rolled over and Johnny began slapping his face. "Matt... wake up! Beth go get me some water from the canteen."

Beth brought the water back to him and he splashed some across Matt's face. He struggled to open his eyes and as he did the blue California sky appeared before him. "Is this heaven?" He mumbled.

"No son, it's California."

"Johnny?" He said attempting to get up, but stopped by the sharp pain in his head, "What happened? Where am I?"

  About an hour after finding him, Matt had gotten up enough strength to sit up on his own and shortly after he was able to stand. "I don't know what happened," he said, "One minute I was standing here and the next I... I, don't know. Callie, where is she?"

"My best guess son is that she was taken to Lebanon."

"We've got to go then! I can't let anything happen to her! I promised her Poppa! Oh what a horrible husband I am! What have I done?"

Beth stepped closer as her face continued to drown in sorrow. She put her arm around Matt and said softly, "You're a fine husband to Callie, don't you worry yourself over that fact. We'll get her back and when we do she'll be just fine… it's Callie we're talking about."

Matt started toward the spare horse John and Beth had brought along with them and then turned back, "Wait, where's Travis and the boys?"

Beth looked away for fear of crying as Johnny stepped over and placed his hand on Matt's shoulder. "Travis and Aj are dead… both shot. The other three boys stayed behind to watch the farm."

Matt looked in Beth's direction who was still looking away at the horizon as if she were searching for her brother and her son, fully expecting to see them walking towards her. After a minute she walked over to the two men, "Well come on now, we don't need to lose any more family members on account of me being mournful."

The three of them mounted their horses and rode north as the afternoon sun shone brightly above them.

- - - - - - - - - - - - - - - -

Callie and Ann Marie took the horses of the two Young brothers and rode into the night towards the Braymyer home outside of Lebanon. Just before the sun came up they dismounted in front of the bloodstained porch.

As Callie stepped up onto the porch she swallowed the lump that had formed in her throat and clenched her fist at her side. She knew now, that there was no denying the fact that her parents had been killed.

She looked around her as Ann Marie approached her from behind and put her arm around her. "Why must we endure so much pain," Callie asked.

"I suppose we are meant to become strong for a bigger purpose, Callie."

Callie turned and looked out over the land as the morning breeze caught her hair, "Well we've got a big task ahead of us, I guess we should rest and get cleaned up, but first I want to go visit Momma and Poppa."

"I'll come with you," Ann Marie said joining Callie's gaze across the horizon.

The two of them looked around to make sure everything was quiet at the farm and that there would be no trouble and after everything had been checked they started walking to the small clearing. The soft California breeze was cool on their cheeks as they walked with their heads lifted high.

Before long they stepped into that small clearing that Dottie had discovered so long ago. There were three fresh mounds, two beside each other and the third a little ways back. Callie stepped closer to them and knelt down beside the small wooden markers that had been placed at the head of the graves.

She ran her fingers across the freshly carved names, "William" and then, "Dorothy." Ann Marie knelt down beside her and placed one of her hands atop the dirt that covered Dottie's body.

"Callie," she said, "Your Momma and Poppa were fine people, don't you ever forget that."

"I don't plan to, which is why I'm going to ride into that town and get even." Callie looked up over at Kizzie's grave and then back to her parents, "Momma, Poppa, you rest easy I'm going to settle things up… I promise."

Before leaving, Callie paid her respects to her five younger siblings, none of which had lived very long and then headed back to the house. When they entered the front doors into the quiet home, Callie's mood completely changed.

Ann Marie, let's boil some water for a bath and pick out some of the finest dresses we can find. If we're going to fight for our town there is no reason we can't do it in class, besides we may die and I'd rather die looking good than a poor farm girl."

They hauled in water by the buckets and boiled it on the stove in the kitchen. After it had heated up enough they poured the water into the porcelain tubs that sat side by side in a room of their own upstairs. When the baths were full they each got in to their own bath water and relaxed.

"So Callie," Ann Marie said, "Do you think we should just go in there and just start shooting or should we come up with another plan?"

"Dynamite."

"Dynamite? What are you talking about?"

"Poppas got some old sticks of dynamite in his bedroom. The first thing I want to do is blow that saloon as far up into the sky as I possibly can."

Ann Marie looked over at her as only their heads were sticking up out of the water and laughed, "Callie that's the best idea I've heard in a long time…a real long time."

When they had finished with their baths they put a little rouge on their faces and slipped into their chosen dresses. Callie found one of her mother's old dresses, it was that same yellow one she had worn the day Will proposed to her. She slipped the yellow ribbon through a portion of her hair in the back and tied a perfect bow.

Standing in front of the body length mirror in her bedroom she observed her looks. She ran her hands down the dress to rid it of any wrinkles and then with her hands on her hips she said to herself, "Why, I look good enough to kill."

Ann Marie wore a red velvet dress that magnified her beauty immensely. She combed out her hair and let her natural waves flow willingly down her back and across both her shoulders.

She joined Callie in front of the mirror and did a small turn, "Callie, I think we are some of the best looking women in California."

Callie laughed, "Ann Marie, why did you choose red?"

"Because silly, I don't want to ruin a dress if there is a chance I will bleed from getting shot."

Both of them laughed and headed down the stairs. Once in the kitchen they scrounged up a few fresh vegetables and ate them with a glass of tea that they had made. It was midafternoon and they both knew very well that it may be the last afternoon they ever saw again.

When they finished they went out the back door to the barn and saddled up their horses. Callie's horse was a palomino with a white streak across his nose. She had had him since she was seven and they had seen many adventures together. Before throwing the saddle atop him she carefully brushed him as she talked softly in his ear.

"It's been a long time since we've been on an adventure ol boy, but I promise you this, if we make it through this alive we'll go out more often."

The horse grunted as if he acknowledged her and shook his head in the yes motion. Ann Marie mounted Dottie's faithful mare who was solid black except all four of her feet which were snow white. The horse was a rare find and when Dottie first laid eyes on the horse she would call, Lady, she insisted on having her.

When everything had finished being prepared the two of them acted like proper ladies for a change and rode their horses side saddled. The two horses marched steadily towards Lebanon as if they were leading an elegant parade.

Chapter Twenty Five

June 01 1892

The Texas Border

"Well lookie' there," Mary Anna said to Rachel as they approached the Red River, "That water is more red than some dresses I've seen!"

"My oh my, it sure is. I don't think I've ever seen anything like it before."

"Well, Rachel just on the other side is Texas. Looks like we've got one more adventure… to cross that river!"

Mary Anna drove the wagon down into the rushing water as Rachel held on for dear life. The water was only deep in certain areas, but the current was moving pretty strong which is why the road on the other side was a little bit down stream than it was on the side they had just entered by.

"Oh, Lord Jesus." Rachel said as the wagon was swept into the river.

"Yipeee!" Mary Anna shouted, "Isn't this so much fun!"

Rachel didn't answer, but rather kept a constant eye on the shore in front of her, hoping and praying they would be there soon. Their wagon was light and the horses had no problem pulling it over safely to the other side and at last, they were in Texas.

Once across it only took them a few hours to reach the small town of Dixie whose sheriff was her son, Nat. When they rode into town, all the streets were busy and full of people who all seemed to be heading over to the churchyard for some sort of gathering.

Mary Anna and Rachel got down from the wagon and headed in the direction of all the people where they found a makeshift stage set up in front of the church. A man stood up and announced as loud as he could, "Put your hands together folks, for the finest fiddle player in Texas…Cotton Braymyer!"

"Rachel!" Mary Anna said, "That's my grandson!"

The two women made their way through the crowd and up to the front of the stage where the Braymyer family was gathered. Mary Anna's journey had come to an end.

Down by Dixie

June 02, 1892

Well friends I don't know if you noticed that wagon that pulled in yesterday carrying two older women with it, well that was my husband's grandmother, Mary Anna Braymyer and Rachel Lloyd. Can you imagine? Two older women traveling all alone across Indian Territory! They are going to live with my father in law over on First Street just as soon as he gets over his heart condition brought on by him finding out his mother traveled all this way with no protection of a man. Just playing Poppa Braymyer.

On a sadder note, I received news this morning that Anna Belle Brown passed away last night. Doc. Ruyle says it was probably a heart attack. She leaves behind her husband, Ben and twelve children…all of whom look like their father.

Our neighbor city, Sandusky has diminished down to only one store and one church. Looks like people are beginning to move on to the railroad towns, I sure hope that never happens to us!

Charlie and Mary Lee Knight were blessed with a daughter two days ago, they named her Rosalee.

Mrs. Abbie Braymyer

Chapter Twenty Six

The two women entered into town on Main Street on the west end and people immediately began to stare and whistle. Their beauty, for a split second, radiated through the hellhole and offered a glimpse of light for the town.

Both women held their heads up high as they marched toward the saloon and luckily no one had noticed their identity, mostly due to the fact that there were so many new comers in town. They rode straight past the saloon, but watched as they went by to observe the crowd behind the swinging doors.

The sun was slowly disappearing behind them, but as they rode by they immediately saw the mayor. Once they had gone three blocks past the drunken hangout they tied their horses to a hitching post in front of the general store.

"Well Callie," Ann Marie said, "Are you ready to do this?"

"As ready as I'll ever be. Come on let's take the back alley back to the saloon."

The two of them walked down the narrow path that ran between the store and the barbershop and emerged on a small alley that ran behind all of the buildings. They looked around them to ensure everything was safe and when they verified that it was they headed back west to their destination.

Almost at once, the light from the sun disappeared and a growing darkness emerged upon the sinful town. The noise from the saloon was so loud that there was not a single place in town that it could not be heard. Just before reaching the rowdy building the two of them ducked into the cover of a porch roof next door.

"Ok, Ann Marie remember the plan. As soon as this dynamite is thrown in there we've got to run as fast as we can away."

"I got it, Callie," she said as she couldn't help but smile, "I'm so nervous!"

The two of them had lost so much over the last week that neither one of them cared if they died or not, they just hoped that before they did a little good could come from their lives.

"Wait," Ann Marie said leaning over, "I think I'm going to be sick."

Callie knelt down beside her but kept her attention on her surroundings. "Hurry Ann Marie, we don't want to draw attention to ourselves."

Ann Marie was as quiet as could be as she got sick, but the noise attracted an unexpected guest. "What are you two doing back here," a woman's voice said as she approached them.

Callie turned sharply to see that it was Fannie Albright, the town whore. She was a short plump woman with a natural mole above her lip and wore enough rouge for the whole town. Her hair was in a bun and it's curly strings stuck out in all directions atop her head.

"Hey, I know you!" She said, "You're Callie Braymyer and that's Mrs. Turner ain't it!"

"Please," Callie said, "Don't say anything."

"Are you kidding, sugar. After the things Mrs. Turner wrote about me in her little paper. Mayor!" She shouted.

Ann Marie lost the urge to be sick and quickly pulled herself back into the upright position. Callie reached her hand out and grabbed Fannie's hair, pulling her closer. "Mayor! Mayor!" She continued to shout.

Ann Marie panicked and as Callie continued to hold her she reached for a shovel that was leaning up against the building. Just before the whore was able to call out for Mayor Styles one more time, Ann Marie swung the shovel into her face knocking her out of Callie's hands and down to the ground.

Both women stood there as if they were frozen in time. "Quick," Callie said, "We've got to hide her body before someone sees it."

Each one of them grabbed hold of one of her feet and drug her into the dark shadow of the porch where they covered her with a few feed sacks. "I hope that was the right thing to do, Callie," Ann Marie said looking down at Fannie's feet which stuck out from beneath the pile of sacks, "I just panicked."

"It was good, Ann Marie, one more shout and we might have been discovered. Are you feeling better?"

"Yes, sorry I don't know what came over me."

The two of them stayed against the building as they slowly made their way next door to the saloon. "Okay," Callie said handing Ann Marie a stick of dynamite, "Get ready."

Callie pulled out a match as they neared a back door and looked all around her one last time to make sure no one was looking. "I'll throw mine up on the roof and you throw yours through that open door, okay?"

"Okay, I'm ready…"

Callie struck the match and as soon as her stick was lit she quickly lit Ann Marie's. "On the count of three," Callie said.

One
Two
Three!

Both women threw the dynamite at their targets and took off running back down the alley. They could hear a man's voice from inside the saloon hollering at the crowd, but before he could warn anyone the building exploded.

Callie and Ann Marie continued to run, not daring to look back until after they heard the explosion. They stopped and leaned forward to try and catch their breaths, Ann Marie holding her stomach as it began to pain her with a pain she knew all too well.

Ann Marie forced the pain out of her mind and stood back up, showing no signs of hurt to Callie. "What now, Callie."

"Hey!" A voice said from behind them.

Callie drew her gun and turned quickly as she saw Matt, Johnny and Beth walking toward them. She dropped the gun and ran as fast as she could into her husband's arms…she finally had a reason for living again.

Ann Marie leaned over again as the pain became unbearable and was caught by Beth's arms just before she hit the ground. "Ann Marie!" Callie shouted. "Beth, what's wrong with her."

"She's with child, honey. Come on let's get her inside the store."

Callie looked up at Matt, "Where's Travis?'

Matt gave her a look that needed no explanation and she knew immediately that her sister's husband was dead. Matt helped Beth carry Ann Marie into the back door of the store as Johnny stood guard outside.

After everyone had entered into the dark room, Johnny joined them. "What in the heck was that explosion?"

Ann Marie who was laying on her back across a table started to laugh through the pain and looked over at Callie, "It was her idea."

Callie looked around the room as everyone looked at her for an answer. "What? I didn't think our town needed a saloon anymore so I… Ann Marie and I blew it up."

"Blew it up!" Matt said in a half-serious, half laughing tone, "Are you crazy! Come here!" He said wrapping her back up in his arms.

Remaining in his arms she turned to everyone who she could barely see in the light of the kerosene lamp that Johnny had lit. "I'm afraid I have some bad news. Momma and Poppa are… they're dead."

It was silent only for a moment when Ann Marie lifted her head off the table, "Travis? Where's Travis?"

Beth leaned in towards her, don't you worry about that right now, you relax before you lose this child ya' hear?"

The streets of Lebanon were becoming crowded as people poured out onto them searching for the bandit who blew up their favorite building. Johnny looked over at his niece in disbelief. He was a Braymyer and he knew that the Braymyer women could do some pretty incredible things, but this one took the cake.

They could hear as men's voices began getting closer to them as they ventured farther down the streets. "Beth," Johnny said, "Turn out that light! Quick!"

When Beth had blown it out the room was filled with complete darkness and the only thing that could be heard was the sound of everyone breathing. "Someone's hit Fannie with a shovel!" A man from outside shouted.

Matt whispered into the darkness, "Darling?"

"Well, technically I just held her while Ann Marie hit her."

Matt had never tried harder not to laugh in his life. "Callie," he said, "Do you have any more dynamite?"

"Yes, I have a few sticks left."

"What are you thinking, Matt?" Johnny interrupted.

"I'm thinking Callie had a pretty good idea. Let's blow them all away with dynamite. There's too many to shoot, we'd all be dead in no time."

"Hand me the dynamite, Callie," Johnny said.

Callie pulled out the dynamite from her dress and struggled to find Johnny's hand in the darkness. Ann Marie's pain had subsided and she was lying very still on the table.

"Matt," Johnny said, let's sneak out the back door and see what we can do."

"Uncle Johnny," Callie interrupted.

"Come on then, Callie," he said already knowing what she was about to say and not wanting to waist time arguing.

Beth kissed Johnny before they went out the back door, leaving her and Ann Marie in the dark building alone. "Beth," Ann Marie said, "I know Travis is dead, please don't let me lose his child too."

Outside, Callie stayed as close to Matt as she possibly could. Occasionally a man or two would walk by them, but paid them no attention. "Callie," Matt said, "You stay beside me."

"Oh no!" Callie said panicky, "It's Mayor Styles!"

Just in front of them the mayor was making his way towards them, staring heavily at Callie as he drew nearer. "Johnny," Matt said, "Break the fuses in half."

Both men snapped the dynamite fuse in half and just as quickly as they appeared onto the back alley they disappeared again, leaving behind them to lit sticks of dynamite. They ran down a side pathway and darted into the tailor shop just as a loud explosion erupted in the back alley.

Men began shouting, some in anger and some in pain. "Mayor!" One of them said, "Are you okay?"

The mayor had been knocked to the ground and slowly stood up, knocking off all the dirt from his clothes. In front of him there were about fifteen bodies who had all tried to stomp out the dynamite before it went off. This combined with the saloon's explosion had taken away most of the town's population.

344

Mayor Styles walked down the same pathway that the three attackers had just went down and went onto Main Street. Seven men surrounded him, which was all that was left in the town as most of them had been in the saloon.

"Get out here!" He shouted, "Or I'll burn every one of these buildings!"

There was no reply.

"I'm the mayor! I'm in charge! I said come out!"

Callie remained hunched down beneath a window next to Matt and her uncle as they watched the mayor with quick glances. He held up a lantern as he continued to threaten them and then turned toward the store where Ann Marie and Beth were as he prepared to throw it in.

"Matt!" She whispered.

Matt had already lifted his rifle up and was taking aim at the mayor. Johnny followed suit and just before the lantern left his hand, a bullet from Matt's gun hit him in the arm. Johnny was able to shoot one of the other men in the head just before bullets began flying their way.

Callie threw herself onto the floor as bullets whizzed through the window into the room. Matt and Johnny continued to return fire and when it was only the mayor and three other men left, the mayor took off toward the store and went inside. Callie had managed to peak out of the side door at the men on the street and watched as the mayor did this.

Leaving Matt and Johnny in the building she darted out onto the pathway and back into the alley. When she came upon the explosion scene she nearly became sick as she looked across all the bodies. She found a gun from some dead man and then ran in the direction of the store through the alley.

As she approached the back door of the store she could hear the mayor threatening the two women inside with his gun.

345

"Get over here and get on your knees!" He said waving the gun at Beth.

Beth looked at him as compassion filled not only her eyes, but also her heart. She wondered how a man such as him could be so vulgar and hateful. Beth stepped forward slightly to shield Ann Marie who still lie on the table with only her head lifted as she watched the mayor.

The mayor continued to hold the gun toward Beth. Beth didn't move, but rather stood there looking him in the eye hoping her kindness would somehow find its way into his soul and save her from what was sure to be an execution.

"I said get over here woman!"

Callie slowly cracked open the door and peered into the room, which was now lit by the light of Mayor Style's lantern. Her yellow dress that had belonged to her mother was stained with dirt and other things from all the action in town. She watched as Beth slowly walked towards the mayor who had vengeance written all across his face.

Callie crept slowly into the room until the mayor was in full view. She lifted the small pistol she had picked up and prayed that her aim would not fail her. Breathing slowly she cocked the gun as quietly as she could and as soon as it was ready to fire she pulled the trigger.

Beth screamed as loud as she could, not knowing what had just happened. Callie jumped up and ran over to her as the mayor held his forearm of the hand that had held his gun. Blood was seeping out of his grip and his gun lie on the floor next to him.

Callie stepped forward and kicked the gun away from him as she pointed her pistol at him. "Don't move, Styles."

The mayor's true colors showed as he feared for his life and did everything Callie had told him to. Callie instructed him to turn around and led him out onto Main Street which had grown quiet again.

As the mayor walked down back toward the tailor shop with Callie right behind him, they discovered that the remaining men on the street were dead. Matt and Johnny were walking towards the two of them side by side. As Callie and the mayor passed the bodies of the dead men, the mayor swiftly ducked down and reached for a gun that lie on the street.

He spun around on his rear and with gun in hand faced Callie. Callie pulled the trigger sending a bullet into the mayor's head and dropping him to the ground. Matt ran toward her and took her in his arms. The town of Lebanon was quiet and there in the middle of the street stood the yellow light of California Charm.

Matt looked down into her eyes and smiled, "Looks like we got your town back, darling."

"Yes," she said staring up at him realizing that now their life together could truly begin. "Now we just need to find a new mayor."

Matt kissed her the same way he had kissed her on their wedding day and she was completely swept away in his love for her. The two of them headed toward the west end of town knowing that they hadn't anything to fear any longer.

Land of Lebanon

January 15, 1893

My son Travis Junior is now a month old… it is hard to believe how fast time flies. Parents, cherish your children and enjoy their younger days for they won't last long.

A new hotel has been erected where the old saloon used to stand, the hotel keeper Ben Berry says that it has a total of fifteen rooms! This Friday the city board and I will meet in the hotel ballroom where we will hold our monthly meetings henceforth. A lot of things have changed in our town over the past year, but due to the joint efforts of other city members and myself I am proud to say that things are looking bright for our little town.

The former Styles farm sold at auction last week for two dollars. Auctioneers said they were not able to get a penny more for it due to the reputation of the former owner.

Matt and Callie Russell have postponed their newly created Gold Rush Barbecue that was to be held this Saturday. The couple are expecting their first child any day now and Mr. Russell says that as much as he loves his wife, she is driving him plum crazy as they prepare for the birth. They said they will plan a date after the baby is born and everyone is welcome to come.

Turner Douglas is here visiting with me all this week and I have to say that he has been a great help with my son. If there are any young ladies out there, I would love to have you over for supper and introduce you to him.

Ann Marie Turner

Dusty Williams

Chapter Twenty Seven

July 14, 2011

Johnny and Beth Braymyer raised all three boys to adulthood and added one more family member, Phebe Ann Braymyer, the daughter Beth had always wanted. She was born three years after the couple married in Los Angeles and was spoiled not only by her parents, but also by all three of her older brothers.

Beth never really got over Aj's death, but having Phebe sure helped the mourning process and at the age of one hundred and three Beth was buried up on the hill overlooking her house. When she died she had a total of sixty-three descendants and every one of them attended her funeral.

Ann Marie never remarried but instead devoted her time to her only child, Travis Junior. She continued to write the paper for Lebanon until the town finally closed down in 1914. She was one of the first women to cast a vote when women were finally able to cast a ballot due to the nineteenth amendment. After she had voted she looked up at the sky and said, "See Travis, I didn't need you to vote for me anyhow."

A year after she voted cancer got the better of her and she was laid to rest next to her husband whose body had been moved to the Braymyer Cemetery in the small clearing. It was one of the saddest days of Callie's life when Ann Marie passed away and nearly every day she visited her sister at the cemetery.

Callie was the first woman on her mother's side of the family to have more than one child that lived to adulthood. Her and Matt had eight children and every one of them married and had children of their own. Her first children were the twins, William and Dorothy and then, Henry Travis, Matt Junior, Mary Beth, Abner Douglas, Ann Marie and Nathaniel John Russell.

Callie and Matt continued grape farming until they were not able to do it anymore, which is when their children took over the business. Braymyer wines has been a successful business for almost a hundred years and I doubt if the family has even had to touch that golden rock beneath the dining room floor.

Callie and Matt both died in 1955 just a day apart. Matt was the first to go and the next day Callie went to bed and had told her youngest daughter she didn't know how she would go on if her husband wasn't there to kiss her like he always had. When her daughter went to wake her mother she found her with the most peaceful look written across her face. The two of them were also buried in the Braymyer Cemetery and to this day a strange wind seems to blow through that area guiding people to a place of past times.

The last time I was at the old Braymyer home near the lost town of Lebanon there were several family portraits hanging up in the entry. Among the many, I remember seeing the pictures that Callie had taken in Los Angeles on her wedding day. They looked so happy and I suppose that if a stranger were to look at them they would have no idea what the family was going through at the time the pictures were taken.

I was nine years old when my Pappy, Nathan Sanders told me the story about his Grandfather's cousin, California Gold Braymyer and it is one I will never forget. I would visit him at his old plantation home on Braymyer Hill in northern Texas and he would tell me all kinds of stories about the Braymyer family. Each one holds a special place in not only my heart, but in my entire being.

It's amazing how a person can go through their life and have no idea how they truly got to be where they are. It is not by the efforts of themselves alone, but it is a joint accomplishment of all the family members of the past. What a shame it would be to disappoint them and their hard work if we choose to waste away through the world.

I hope that somewhere out there, whether it be in the form of a wind or beneath the shade of a cottonwood tree that the Braymyers of long ago are looking down upon us as they are remembered. This was just one of the stories my Pappy told me and is only a portion of the many more yet to come.

One of my favorite of Pappy's stories is how our family inherited the Indian blood running through our veins by way of Mary Anna Walker…but then, that is a story for another day.

The End

Part III

The Road to Braymyer Ridge

"The amount of hatred that can exist between two bodies of people can be greater than the strongest storms known to man. We as a body must push past this devilish habit and seek the love and compassion that patiently awaits to take charge of our actions"

Mary Anna Braymyer

June 03, 1827
Tennessee

Anna Walker had once been one of Georgia's finest southern bells and had lived a life of luxury on her father's plantation near Crawfish Springs, which would later become Chickamauga. Now, the thirty one year old woman was sitting on a wagon seat next to her Cherokee husband, Walks Tonight, with their one year old daughter, Mary Anna in the back beneath the canopy.

Anna was pregnant with their second child and was due at any time. Given the roughness of the wagon ride she knew it wouldn't be long. She had given up her entire life in Georgia to marry her husband and the marriage of a white woman to an Indian was unacceptable.

A month after meeting him, Anna ran away into Tennessee and had not been back to Georgia since, but now after three years she was heading home. They had been living in the Cherokee Nation in northeastern Tennessee, but for a white woman and a Cherokee husband they found it hard to live up to society's expectations.

She didn't know how her parents would react upon the arrival of their only child and the truth was, is that in the three years' time she had only exchanged maybe five letters between them. Her father, George Walker, was a respectable man and the last thing she wanted to do was to bring him disgrace, which is why she left in the first place.

She couldn't help it that she had fallen in love with an Indian and that her passionate desire had gotten the better of her, so she married him. Her parents might have discouraged the thought, but she knew people would talk and she didn't want her parents to be victims in her choices.

Anna was a short thin woman with blonde hair atop her head and even now that she was nine months pregnant there was only a slight bulge above her hips. All the southern boys had been after her for her hand in marriage, but she always found a reason to tell them no.

She had been on a walk alone near the creek on a summer day when she first met her husband. When she saw him for the first time emerge from a thicket, she had almost fainted with fright.

His first words to her were, "Hello Madam," as if he had just arrived from London. She was astonished at how well his English was, contrary to what she had heard about these so-called savages.

Every day she would sneak down to the creek and have long conversations with him until one night she left to meet him and didn't come back. It had been the best summer of her life and had taken her no time at all to fall in love with him.

Walks was a tall, handsome man and wore nothing but white man's clothing. He had the same appearance most Indians did, jet-black hair, brown eyes and high cheekbones. He loved his wife and daughter with all that he had, but he often felt like he would never be able to provide for them the way he should, given their different backgrounds.

They had traveled longer than normal that day and had they had a clock they would have realized that it was past eleven o'clock when they stopped for camp. They were in the Sequatchie Valley of eastern Tennessee, buried within the many trees of the forest and the rock cliffs with rivers winding through the scenic landscape.

Walks pulled the wagon into a small clearing that had obviously been used as a campsite before. Once he had climbed down he went around and helped Anna down from the seat. They both stretched for a moment and then walked to the back of the wagon and peered into the opening.

"Looks like she is still sleeping," Anna said, "Might as well let her sleep through the night."

"Our daughter is beautiful like her mother," Walks said reaching his arm in and rubbing his hand over her brown hair.

Anna placed her hand on her stomach and looked into her husband's eyes, "And maybe this child will be as handsome as his father."

Walks kissed his wife and held her in his arms before tending to the two paint horses that pulled their wagon. After things had been situated the two of them joined their daughter in the wagon and went to sleep.

The next morning, Anna awoke to find her husband coughing and he had a slight fever. Noticing that Mary Anna was awake, she took her out and fed her to let her husband sleep a little longer. After Mary Anna was satisfied, Anna put her down and let her crawl around while she made some bacon before they headed back to the trail.

She had to force her husband to eat and it was obvious that he was in no shape to drive the wagon beneath the hot sun. Determined to get to Georgia, she cracked the whips at the horses mid-morning and drove the wagon herself.

After three days of traveling her husband's condition had only gotten worse as she approached the long driveway to her father's home. As the wagon drove down between the large magnolia trees lining the path on both sides, the noises of rattling pans, a coughing Indian and a whining baby erupted into the air.

A strand of her hair had fallen out of her bun and hung loosely across the front of her face as sweat trickled down in all directions. She felt horrible arriving under these conditions and she feared what her parents would think of her and who she had become.

After what seemed like forever, the path took a small left turn and left the shade of the trees as it approached the house. It was white stone and had large columns stretching from the base all the way up to the second story roof. The trim around all the windows was green along with the two double doors out front.

The wagon came to a halt in front of the stairs and Anna took in a deep breath and prayed that things would go well. Before she could get down from the wagon, the front doors opened and both her mother and father appeared in the entry. George and Ann Walker cautiously stepped out onto the front porch, unaware of whom their visitor might be.

Ann Walker was carrying a black baby in her arms whose name was Rachel Lloyd. She had been born just four days earlier and her mother, Telitha had died during the process. Rachel was very small and very light complected and only George and a few of his slaves knew why her color was so different from that of her dark mother.

George was tall and stout and had a silver moustache above his lip, which matched his thinning hair. He had naturally red skin from being out in the fields so much and hands that were nearly as big as his wife's head. He was a confident man and more honest than anyone around, but George Walker had his fair share of secrets.

He was the type of man that knew what he wanted and he almost always got it, no matter what the price. Last fall he had made his usual rounds into the slave's quarters to check up on them and he found Telitha alone. There was something about the way she looked at him that had made him desire her.

He knew it had been a mistake to sleep with her and he now had a black child as his punishment that his wife had no idea was actually his. His actions had not changed his feelings for his wife and he would always cherish her more than anything in the world.

Telitha Lloyd had only consented to the adulterous act in hopes that she might have a child that would have a chance to amount to something in this world. After two days in labor she didn't even get to hear the baby cry, let alone see her face, but it was a small price to pay to ensure a bright future for her child.

Ann Walker was a small frail woman, light skinned and green eyed, but had the largest heart in the state of Georgia. It had been a joke to some local families to say that Ann Walker was the heart of Georgia and if ever anyone needed anything to go see her.

She couldn't turn a living soul away from her front door and she knew neither anger nor any type of hatred. Most people would have given a black baby to one of the other slaves, but not Ann. She cared for that child like it was her own, not realizing that it was in some strange way actually her step child.

Ann shielded her face with her hand to prevent the sun from shining down onto her face as she neared the wagon that had now diminished its noise to only coughing and a crying baby. "Who's there?"

"Mother?" Anna said.

Ann screamed and ran toward her daughter that she had thought she would never see again. "Anna!" She said wrapping her arms around her as she tried to get down from the wagon. Once on the ground she let herself be taken into her mother's arms while her father wrapped his around the both of them, almost squishing Rachel in the middle.

Ann left the group hug and went around to the back of the wagon with George and Anna close behind. "Is this my granddaughter?" Ann said reaching in after Mary Anna.

"Yes, Mother. That's Mary Anna."

Ann handed Rachel to her daughter and scooped up her granddaughter into her arms, kissing her all over the face. George peered into the wagon. "Is he sick? What's wrong with him?"

"Yes, Father. Three days ago he took ill with fever."

"Well," Ann said, "George let's get him inside!"

George looked pleased that his daughter and grandchild were home, but he wasn't so sure about the man in the back of the wagon. He had, after all, been the reason he had lost his daughter in the first place and as he brought the sick man into the house he made a silent promise to himself, "As God as my witness, my daughter will never leave again."

September 14, 1994
Baptist Church, Dixie Texas

I sat still and minded my manners as best as a seven-year-old boy could in a straight back wooden chair in the kitchen at the back of the church. Grandma Rose and my great grandpa, Nathan Sanders whom I called Pappy and I were the first ones there at nine am.

I scratched at an itch on my left shoulder and as with any itch, when you think about it they soon multiply. I wiggled in the chair, moving my back side to side to relieve some of the annoyance but it was to no avail.

Pappy and Grandma Rose were unloading food dishes into the church stoves to keep them warm until everyone else arrived for lunch. That year had been one of the hardest times of my life as I had lost both my parents in a car accident the spring before.

It was the Braymyer family reunion and it would be the first year I had gone without my parents. As bad as it may sound, I desperately wished they were there, not because I had missed them, but because had I came with them we would not have arrived until much later.

I was an only child living with my Pappy just outside of town on what was known as Braymyer Hill. Grandma Rose thought it better I lived with him since he was all alone in a big house and the two of us could take care of each other. And besides, she didn't need anyone interfering with her bingo schedule. I had a lot of fun with Pappy out on the farm and had it been up to him I truly believe he would have let me skip school to swim in the creek all day.

Pappy looked in my direction and then turned to his daughter and whispered something into her ear. He soon came over in my direction and stopped directly in front of me as I continued to combat the invisible chiggers.

"John, what do you say we go for a walk around the church yard?"

I didn't hesitate to answer as I jumped to my feet, miraculously ridding myself of the itches. "Yes sir!"

My small body arose to just barely his hips and we walked side by side out of the front church door. I wore a pair of overalls and had crammed my feet into a pair of shoes that I hated. For most kids, growing up in the 90's was wearing the latest trend and having the most up to date technology or toys. But for me, I was a country boy that looked to have walked right out of a picture show from the 1930's.

I rarely wore shoes and if I was not wearing overalls I was wearing a vintage pair of trousers with no shirt. I didn't mind swimming in the snake infested creeks and often times I would catch one or two of them and bring them home to Pappy.

Since I was so different, I had very few friends. Even my cousins gave me dirty looks and shunned their noses up at me. They had dreams of being doctors and lawyers and on more than one occasion they had reassured me that I would never amount to anything.

Living with my 75-year-old great grandfather didn't help my popularity status any, but things such as that never did bother me. Living with him, I had learned more things about the true meaning of life than most other people ever would. The most important thing to Pappy was family and I saw the hurt in his eyes when more and more of his descendants showed little interest.

The family reunion that we had every September acted as a way for people to come together and share the latest gossip on certain family members, but not for Pappy. Every year he observed everyone and embedded in his mind the changes that had occurred since the previous year. These family gatherings served for him a way to remember the family of past times and every year, one less person showed up.

As soon as I was outside I kicked off my shoes as Pappy laughed at me and waited for me to catch up. We walked across the browning grass and I could feel the crunch of rusty colored leaves as I stepped on them with my bare feet.

"You know, John. You remind me a lot of myself when I was your age."

"I do sir?" I said surprised.

"Sure do. In fact, when I was your age I came to this very spot, let's see that would have been about 1925 or so."

"Really? What did you come here for?"

"It was our first reunion here, son. We had family of all sorts show up. In fact, my great-great grandmother came. She was 100 years old that year!"

"Wow, that's a long time," I said astonished.

"It sure is, son."

"What was her name, Pappy?"

"Well, her name was Mary Anna, but we all called her Granny Braymyer. You know, now that I think about it she was one of the spunkiest women I knew. But then again most Braymyer women were."

"Really? How come?"

"They had to be. Times were hard back then, especially for a woman. You know, Mary Anna was half Cherokee Indian."

"No way! So that means I am Indian too?"

Pappy laughed a little at my remark, "That's right, son, I reckon you are."

"So what happened to her?"

"Oh she lived a great life, full of adventure and courageous battles. Why, her and her younger brother had to run away in the middle of the night one time when they were children."

"How come?"

"Well, let's see if I can remember correctly…

March 31, 1838
Walker Plantation

Twelve year old Mary Anna Walker sat on the front porch of her grandparent's large plantation home with her best friend, Rachel Lloyd right next to her. She watched as her ten-year-old brother, George Walks Walker or, "Walkie" as she called him, ran about the front yard chasing the chickens.

Their mother had died on a cold December night the year they had arrived from Tennessee. Her grandmother had said it was from a broken heart because she had lost her husband only days after arriving. Anna did her best to survive for her two children, but the passion to live was just not there anymore and she finally gave up on life.

Ann Walker was saddened over her daughter's death, but she was so thankful that she had two grandchildren to care for, whether they were part Indian or not. George Walker on the other hand was filled with anger over his daughter's demise. He blamed no one but Walks Tonight for his daughter's death.

He loved his grandchildren very much, but there were times his temper got the better of him and when he looked at Walkie he was reminded of his daughter and the man he held responsible. Had it not been for Ann, the children would have probably been sent away somewhere, far away, but she was the type of person that saw past the color of one's skin.

Mary Anna did not look completely Indian, but after close observation a person could definitely tell that she had it in her. She had tan skin, but not as dark as an Indian, brown hair and brown eyes. She looked a lot like her mother only darker features which she had inherited from her father.

Walkie was the spitting image of his father, which is why he took the brunt of his grandfather's anger. Even with short hair, there was no doubting that he was Indian.

365

What made George the maddest was that Rachel was staying in the house and being treated like one of the family. He had never told his wife the true story about the girl, but if one were to look close enough they would see that she looked just like him.

It was a school day, but the children stayed home and played because there had been talk about Indian Removal in the area. Ann had said it was too dangerous for them because there was a chance the army would take them away.

It didn't matter that they were half-white, or civilized for that matter. The government wanted all Indians out of the territory and moved west and that is exactly what officials were out to do.

Mary Anna continued to sit on a rocker next to Rachel and watched the day go by. She wore a pink dress and her hair was brought back into a braided ponytail where it ended into a pink ribbon.

Rachel wore a lovely green dress and since she had inherited her real father's hair type she was able to wear it just as Mary Anna did. Rachel was probably the finest dressed Negro in the whole south and she wasn't ashamed to say it either.

"Rachel," Mary Anna said, "Do you think the Army will really take Walkie and I away?"

"Well Mr. Walker says that you stand a better chance than Walkie on account of your looks. He says the government thinks that if there is Indian blood in a person then there is always a chance they will start wars and such."

"But that's ridiculous, Rachel. I mean do you really think Walkie and I could start a war?"

"No, Mary Anna I sure don't, but I'm not the one in charge."

"I know you're not, Rachel. But what is the point in having a president if they are not going to do anything to help the people?"

"Well, I reckon Mr. Jackson and Mr. Van Buren are only trying to protect certain ones."

"That just doesn't seem right, Rachel. And if they took me away, I would never see you again!"

"Yes you would, cause I'd go with you. No point in staying around here if you're not here. Besides that would mean I would have to get all the repercussions of Mr. Walker's temper and I really don't mind sharing."

The two of them lightened the mood with a little bit of laughter as Walkie approached them with something hidden behind his back.

Mary Anna stood up, "Walkie! Whatever it is, put it away!"

Rachel noticed that the boy had that special grin on his face and she too stood up to offer Mary Anna some support. "Now, Walkie! You do as your big sister tells you to now."

He kept stepping closer and closer as the grin continued to grow across his face. "Catch!" He said throwing a handful of baby frogs up at them.

The two girls screamed as loud as they could and jumped up and down all around the porch. Walkie knelt over as he drown himself in laughter, clutching his abdomen as hard as he could.

The noise came to a quick a halt when the front door opened and George Walker stormed out onto the front porch. "What's going on here! What's all the screaming about?"

He noticed the dead frogs on the porch and then turned his attention to Walkie. "Boy, did you do this."

Walkie was terrified. George had already begun to storm toward him where he was sure to get a beating. Mary Anna threw herself in front of Mr. Walker just before he started down the stairs.

"No, Grandfather, don't!"

"Get out of my way, girl!"

"Grandfather! It was me! I made the mess."

"Don't you lie to me girl!"

"No, really sir. The frogs they jumped up here and I started squishing as many as I could, honest."

Mr. Walker reached his hand out and grabbed her by the shoulder. He pushed her back into the house, leaving Rachel and Walkie all alone. Rachel looked down at Walkie, "Now look what you've done!"

"I didn't mean to, honest I didn't."

Their conversation was interrupted by the cries of Mary Anna, followed shortly after by Ann Walker scolding her husband. Mary Anna returned to the front porch and took back her seat in the rocker, letting the screen door slam behind her.

She let her head bow down and looked sobbingly at the ground in front of her. Walkie stepped a little closer, "I'm sorry Mary Anna, honest I didn't mean to cause no trouble."

Mary Anna leaned forward a little more and let her hand rest atop the front porch. She then lifted her self back up and looked at her brother. "You promise?"

"Yes, Mary Anna, I swear it."

Mary Anna stood up and walked until she was an arms length from him. "Come here!" She shouted, grabbing him in both her arms. As he struggled to get away she dropped one of the dead frogs down the back of his shirt and sent him away running like a little girl.

The two girls sat back down and laughed as they watched him run across the yard. "Mary Anna," Rachel said, "You're going to get in even more trouble if Mr. Walker hears all this commotion."

"Don't worry, Rachel, Grandmother is handling him right now."

"Yes, but Lord knows she can't handle him forever... no one can."

After Mr. Walker had been calmed down and the redness from his temper had left his face, Ann came out and joined the girls on the porch. She took a seat next to Mary Anna and placed her hand on her granddaughter's lap.

"Don't you pay no mind to your grandfather, do you hear? He's just a grouchy old man that has seen better days."

"I know, Grandmother. Do you think he hates me cause I'm part Indian?"

"Why Mary Anna! Don't you fret over no such thing! Being part Indian makes you special and special people are hard to come by."

Mary Anna smiled at her grandmother and then turned her attention back to her brother who was now exploring beneath the shade of one of the magnolia trees. A faint sound could be heard in the distance and as it drew nearer they realized it was the gallop of a horse.

Just as the lone rider approached, Mr. Walker stepped out onto the porch to join the women who were now all standing up. Mary Anna looked at the rider and immediately recognized him as Doug Hawley, a friend of the Walkers from a couple plantations over.

"Doug," Mr. Walker said scratching his stomach, "What are you doing out this far?"

Doug was in his forties and had not had the luxury of owning as many slaves as Mr. Walker had. He looked much older than he really was, mostly because of all the hard work he had had to endure himself.

He was somewhat out of breath, but managed to speak rather calmly to the group on the front porch. "They're coming. They're forcing all the Indian's out of the area. I overheard Doc. Bartlett at the store tell one of them about your grandchildren and they plan on being here tomorrow morning."

"Oh, George!" Ann said as Mary Anna wrapped her arms around her. "What are we going to do."

"Thank you, Doug," he said to the man who had never dismounted his horse. Doug turned his horse and headed back down the long driveway to warn the others. He was a good man.

"We need to send them away," Mr. Walker said. "Send them north."

"I don't think so," Ann said, "You'll go away from this home before these children do!"

Mr. Walker looked somewhat shocked at his wife's remark. "Ann," he said in a stern voice, "It is not safe for them here!"

370

"And you think it would be any safer for three children to travel alone! Especially when two are part Indian and one is *part* black! No George! If they must go I will go with them!"

"Ann you can't go."

"And why not?"

"Because I said so, that's why. Now I am sure the three of them will be just fine. They can take to the woods and hide."

"No, George," she said, her voice carrying an angry tune for the first time in her life, which she must have enjoyed because it continued. "My mind is made up, I am going with them! Come along children, let's get some things together."

All three children followed her into the house, half-scared and half-shocked at their grandmother's tone. George stood there dumbfounded as they marched past him into the house. "Ann! If you leave I'll shoot myself!"

Just before the sun went down, the three children and Ann Walker were loaded up onto the covered wagon, which was to be pulled by two expensive black mares. They carried little luggage so they could travel faster and longer and did not plan to stop until they had reached their destination.

It was agreed that Ann would travel north into Tennessee and stay with her sister until things had calmed down. George approached the wagon and looked up at Ann who sat on the wagon seat.

"George," she said, "You can kiss me if you like, but I am still not letting these children travel alone."

Mr. Walker stepped up as close as he could to her and kissed her on the forehead before stepping back down. "Travel safe, Ann and write to me when you can."

The wagon roared down the long drive into the dark shadows of the trees as the sun finally disappeared behind the western horizon. Just as they reached the end of the driveway a shot was heard from the plantation home. Ann's heart sank for a moment, but then she was reminded of the children's safety.

She had loved her husband dearly, but he had caused her more grief than anyone else ever could. A small portion of her finally felt free from the burden of trying to make a man happy and she rode on as she lost only one tear. There was just too much to think about right then.

Mr. Walker had a good life, but he never got over losing his daughter and the circumstances surrounding it. He knew that if Ann were to leave with those children, she would probably wind up dead. Surely the army would discover them and knowing Ann she would march right along the Trail of Tears with them.

But if he truly believed that Ann would let someone take those children in the first place, well he was mistaken.

September 14, 1994
Baptist Church, Dixie Texas

Pappy's blue eyes shimmered in the Texas sunlight as he thought back on the story of Mary Anna. A slight wind blew, causing a few more of the leaves to fall to the ground.

"Pappy, why was Mr. Walker so mean, especially to his own granddaughter?"

"I don't know, son. Some people are funny like that I suppose. Back then it was not right for an Indian and a woman to marry, but even then those children shouldn't have had to suffer. I guess Mr. Walker was just an angry man."

"Was Ann really not sad when her husband died?"

"Oh sure she was sad. It was after all her husband, but she had more important things to worry about than that. You know, if Ann Walker hadn't of drove that wagon into the night, you and I might not be standing here."

"Well, I suppose your right. Did they make it to her sister's house?"

"Let's go get us a bite to eat, John. Look's like everybody is just about here."

I turned around to see the once empty parking lot now full of cars. Looking up at the sun I judged it was just about eleven o'clock so I followed Pappy back into the building. Once inside I stayed near his legs as people began rushing up to me and squeezing my cheeks.

"Oh, John I was so sorry to hear… Is there anything you need… How is your Pappy treating you… Why your feet are just filthy…"

After Pappy and I made it through the crowd and he had said his hello's to a few of his closest cousins we were in line to get our food. There was a long row of wooden tables, probably three or four six-foot tables total. They were covered in white tablecloths and on top was food of every kind.

The main course was barbecue and after passing all the vegetables I loaded my plate down full of the juicy meat. Pappy tossed a small dill pickle right on top of my plate and by the time we had made it to our seats I had already eaten it.

Grandma Rose sat across the table from me so I had to mind my manners, but every time she turned away I would stick some barbecue in the pockets of my overalls. It would make a good treat for my dog, Yancy, who Grandma Rose had insisted stay at the house.

The room was full of people talking and sharing stories and every little section of the room had its own little group. You had the older people who tended to migrate to the tables that held family photos and such. Then you had the middle aged adults who proudly showed off their new grandchildren with their young adult children not far behind. The teenagers slipped in and out of the room, constantly ensuring that their appearance was above average. And finally you had the children like myself.

Aside from me, all the other children were in a room adjoining that one, where there was television and movies to watch, along with some board games. Amongst all the chattering I would occasionally hear someone over my shoulder say to someone else how sorry they were for me.

After the majority of the people had finished eating, my Pappy did something I will never forget. Right there in the middle of all that chaos he stood up and hollered for everyone to get quiet.

I continued to sit there beside him, cautiously looking up at him wondering what his plans were. After the room fell completely silent he cleared his throat and began to talk.

"In 1925 we started this reunion for our family to get together and share stories of past times and for us to update one another on the family. I would like to continue a story about our family that I was just telling to my grandson, John outside."

I noticed that several of the teenagers were sneaking out the back door and I could feel my cheeks turning red as Pappy announced my name in front of the crowd. There were looks around the room from people who truly felt this was going to be a waste of time.

My embarrassment soon passed and I turned my attention back to Pappy who had moved his chair up onto the table. So there it was, a 75-year-old man sitting in a chair atop a table, fixing to tell a story I was anxious to hear.

Dusty Williams

April 01, 1838
Tennessee-Georgia border

Ann drove the wagon as hard as she could and by sunup they were crossing into Tennessee. Her plaid dress had once been full of form, but now it sat rather flat across her lap and her graying hair was such a mess that she hardly felt like a woman.

The children rode in the back underneath the canopy and had slept through most of the night. They slowly began to awake from their deep sleep and poked their heads out of the back to see what new adventure might lie ahead.

She pulled the wagon into a small clearing to let the horses rest a bit and to try and calm her nerves. Ann and the three children dismounted and plopped themselves onto a small grassy patch near the wagon.

"Grandmother," Walkie said, "Are we almost to Aunt Liza's house?"

"It won't be long, darling. Here eat a biscuit, you'll need all the strength you can get."

The four of them sat there and ate their biscuits while the horses watered in a nearby creek. Rachel seemed to be the one that was the most frightened. Her large brown eyes remained opened wide as though she were taking in every detail of her surroundings.

She was the first to spot the older Indian woman approaching them from the south. She had long pigtails across her shoulders with streaks of silver intertwined with the black. She wore buckskin clothing and carried a small blanket over one of her arms with an acorn necklace around her neck.

Ann got up and smiled a loving smile at her as she approached.

377

"Are… you… hungry?" She asked the Indian.

The Indian woman's eyes grew heavy and she soon began to cry. Ann wrapped her in her arms and comforted her with a kind hug. The Indian had managed to somehow escape all of the roundups that were being held to capture the Indians and she now wandered across the valley alone.

Ann convinced her to sit down and handed her a biscuit to eat. The woman enjoyed every bit of its flakiness and savored the softness of its texture. She watched Mary Anna and Walkie as if she knew them and the two of them gazed back in her direction with a sense of confusion.

She knew very little English, but managed to spit out a few words. "Who… they… father?"

Ann smiled in the children's direction and replied, "Their father was Walks Tonight."

The woman immediately began to cry again and continued to do so until she stood up to leave. She walked over to Mary Anna and her brother, who promptly stood up in front of her where they were engulfed into a hug from the stranger.

After hugging them she wandered back into the protection of the trees heading north. The children watched her as she disappeared into the woods, wondering who had just given them a hug.

They didn't know it, but the woman who had just stood in front of them was their grandmother on their father's side. A few days after leaving them, she was captured somewhere outside of Chattanooga and forced onto The Trail of Tears, where she died.

The Army buried her alongside the trail in an unmarked grave that is now covered in a beautiful acorn tree. Mary Anna and

Walkie were the only descendants of the woman and although she knew who they were, they never did find out who the woman was eating biscuits with them that day.

Shortly after the Indian woman left, the four of them loaded back up onto the wagon and continued up the trail. The children had to stay in the back just in case they came across any soldiers who would recognize them as part Indians.

Tennessee was warm and for a strange reason, Mary Anna felt somewhat at home. She felt as if for the first time in her short life, she was exactly where she belonged although she didn't know why.

Rachel continued to be nervous as they traveled along the trail to what would become their new home. They kept mostly to the less traveled roads, which tended to keep them hidden deep within the woods.

Occasionally they would come to a small town, but no one ever stopped them to check their wagon which was very fortunate for them. They rarely stopped on their desperate journey to safety and had the horses been able to do it, Ann would not have let them stop.

For two days they traveled north and east until they were in the Smokey Mountains where Walks Tonight had became sick so many years before. Deep within the woods near a place called Keedy Cove the wagon came to a stop in front of a wooden two-story home.

Just before they dismounted the wagon a lady who was older than Ann stepped out onto the front porch with a broom in her hand. Her hair was completely silver and wrinkles had taken over the majority of her face. She was short like Ann, but to Mary Anna she seemed a lot stronger.

"Ann?" She called out to them in her query but steady old voice.

"Liza!" she said getting down from the wagon and meeting her sister halfway across the yard. When the two met they embraced each other in a long overdue hug as the children waited patiently behind them. "Did you get my letter, sister?"

"Yes, Ann, but my goodness I wasn't expecting you for three or four days yet."

"We couldn't wait any longer. The army was removing Indians and we got word they were heading for our house so we left as quickly as we could," Ann said turning to the children. "These are my grandchildren, Mary Anna and Walkie and this is Rachel."

"How do you do, children?"

The children politely answered their great aunt and waited for further instruction. "Girls," Ann said, "You two come with me. Walkie take the horses to the barn and then you may join us inside."

The women stepped into the shack and shut the thick door behind them. The floorboards creaked as they stepped across it and although it wasn't in horrible shape it was not near as fancy as what the children had grown accustom to. Mary Anna and Rachel stayed close to each other as they looked around the dusty room.

Directly in front of the door was a narrow staircase that Mary Anna prayed she would never have to climb. The stairs were built of what look liked rotting wood and she feared that she might fall through if forced to ascend them.

The women went into the dining room, which was to the right of the front door and Mary Anna was immediately drawn to the north wall. There was a magnificent drawing of a woman that was done so greatly that she thought she was looking at a real live person.

"That's your great grandmother," Liza said.

"She's beautiful," Mary Anna answered, "What happened to her?"

"Childbirth, dear. It's not as great a miracle as people think."

"Come children," Ann interrupted, "Let's sit down at the table."

There was just enough chairs for them at the oval shaped table with one extra left over for Walkie. Rachel, Ann and Mary Anna sat down while Liza stepped into the kitchen and then re-entered the room.

She was carrying a jar with a clear liquid inside of it and four small tin cups. She placed a cup in front of everyone and then began to pour a drink for her company. As soon as it was poured into Mary Anna's cup she immediately got a whiff of something she had never smelled before.

Liza poured her cup last and then took a seat at the head of the table. "Drink up, girls, it will do you all some good."

At the same time they lifted their cups cautiously and downed the small drink. Mary Ann let out a loud cough and spit out her entire drink across the table where her grandmother was sitting. Ann was covered in the foul smelling drink and nearly fainted when she was soaked.

"Mary Anna!" She shouted.

"I'm sorry, grandmother, really I am. What is that drink?"

"Why that's moonshine," Liza said, "Don't you like it?"

"Um… yes maim," she said lying to be polite.

"Here, have some more." She poured more into Mary Anna's cup and then proceeded to hand Ann a small wash cloth.

"I think I'll go upstairs and freshen up," Ann said excusing herself from the table.

Rachel's face had somehow managed to remain calm even though she herself almost vomited up her drink as well. Luckily, she had only taken a small sip, but her throat still felt as if it were on fire.

Liza sipped on her moonshine and watched Mary Anna like a hawk. "Well drink up, darling."
Mary Anna steadied herself as she lifted the cup to her mouth and took a sip of the stout drink. Liza smiled as if she were pleased that Mary Anna was drinking her concoction.

She continued to slowly drink and just when she thought it was almost over, Liza refilled her and Rachel's cups and then continued to stare at them. Just before they began drinking on their second cup, Walkie walked into the room and Mary Anna prayed silently for him like she had never prayed for anyone before.

"Come in, Walkie, have a seat," Liza said.

He sat down in the empty chair across from Rachel as Liza handed him Ann's cup. "Here you go darling, drink up."

Walkie smelled the drink and then looked over at Liza, "What is it?"

"It's moonshine, now drink up, it will make you feel all good inside."

Just before Walkie put the cup to his mouth, Rachel ducked down beneath the table and just as her head disappeared her empty chair was soaked in moonshine.

"What in the tarnation is that stuff, Aunt Liza!" Walkie half shouted toward her, continuing to spit in protest.

Liza looked over at Mary Anna and Rachel who was now emerging from beneath the table. All three of them turned their stare to Walkie who looked at them as if they were crazy and then they all began to laugh uncontrollably with the exception of Walkie.

"I mean it!" Walkie said, "What is that stuff."

He received no answer, only more laughter as the three women continued to sip their moonshine. Walkie pushed his cup away and crossed his arms as he continued to look at the three of them in disbelief.

The next day, Mary Anna and Rachel found themselves in the small vegetable garden beside the house pulling weeds. They had never done this kind of work before and as the sun beat down upon them they felt as if they were going to get sick. They did know exactly how, but they held the moonshine they had drank the day and night before responsible for the way they were feeling now and swore never to touch it again.

Walkie was busy in the barn cleaning out stalls and feeding the animals while Liza and Ann sat beneath the shade of the front porch and watched the girls. The two old sisters talked amongst themselves as they rocked steadily in the chairs enjoying each other's company.

Liza had been married once to William Davis who many had thought was a scoundrel and an outlaw. No matter what he was, Liza loved him and she ran off with him much to her father's disappointment. The two of them never had any children and after leaving Virginia they settled in the Smokey Mountains where they farmed and made moonshine.

383

William had died ten years before, but Liza refused to leave her home and insisted on taking care of herself. She would hire local boys to help her with her cornfields and if she couldn't pay them in money, she would pay them in moonshine. Many people in the area referred to her as Grandma Davis and although she was a tough old woman, she had a heart of gold.

Mary Anna thought she was a nice enough person, but she didn't think she would ever forgive her for serving her moonshine the day before. She had been up all night getting sick and now she was working in the hot sun, something she had never done before. Rachel was right beside her and she agreed with Mary Anna in all her feelings.

"This don't make no sense," Rachel whispered, "Don't she got slaves to do this kind of work."

"Maybe she can't afford them," Mary Anna said, "You've seen her house."

"Isn't that a sight! I swear I seen three ghost last night whilst I was laying in bed."

"Ghost?"

"Sure did and I don't think they was friendly either. Their faces looked a might messed up if you ask me."

"Well did you recognize who they were?"

"Well, they wasn't anyone I had ever seen before, but I figure one of them was ol' Mr. Davis."

"Really? Why do you say that?"

"Cause he said to me in a real queer voice, 'Rachel I'm Mr. Davis.'"

"Did you answer him back?"

"No, I turned my head and then went back to sleep. I told myself I have no business talking to the dead so they shouldn't talk to me either."

"Oh my, Rachel, that's a real fright if you ask me."

"Sure was. I wonder what's been done here to cause such a thing."

"Do you think Aunt Liza's killed people, Rachel?"

"Well, I don't rightly know, but if you ask me, too much of that moonshine could very well kill a person."

"Oh, Rachel, have you ever tasted anything so horrid!"

"Can't say that I have. Did you see the look on your poor grandmother's face when you spit it all over her."

"Oh I know, I felt so horrible. It was not lady like at all. If Grandfather were here I would have been whipped for sure."

"Well, I guess it's a good thing Mr. Walker isn't here."

When the sun was almost directly above the two girls, they dusted off their dresses and joined the women on the front porch. They sat down in the two vacant chairs and watched as a rider drove up to the house.

"Hello Grandma Davis!" He shouted pulling the wagon to a halt.

"Howdy, John! Come on over here and let me look at you."

The man jumped down and stepped onto the front porch where he leaned down and gave Liza a hug. "John," she said, "This is my sister, Ann Walker."

"How do you do, maim." He said taking off his hat.

"Just fine thank you, this is my granddaughter, Mary Anna and that there's Rachel."

John turned toward them, but never took his eyes away from Mary Anna, he was engulfed in her young beauty. "Ladies," he said, "My name's John Braymyer, I live a few miles from here over on a farm."
"How do you do," they both answered at the same time.

John Braymyer was remarkably handsome and Mary Anna returned his quick glances. He had just turned 19 and stood tall with his six-foot body over looking the women. When he had taken off his hat, it revealed the blondest hair any of them had ever seen and eyes bluer than any shade they had known.

"Grandma Davis," he said interrupting their lustful thoughts, "I came out to see if you needed any help today."

"Well, John. Mary Anna's brother, Walkie is out in the barn so I figure I don't have much today, but I thank you for coming out."

"Oh you know it's always a pleasure to help you. I think I'll go for a buggy ride anyhow, it has turned out to be a nice day."

"It sure has. Here," she said pulling something out from underneath her chair, "take this bottle of moonshine with you. I don't feel right you coming out all this way for nothing."

"Thank you, Grandma Davis. Pa will sure appreciate this."

"Say," she said, "If you're going on a buggy ride would you mind taking Mary Anna and her little friend along with you."

Mary Anna was shocked at the boldness of her great aunt. She had been raised in the southern ways that one must never invite themselves somewhere, they must always be asked. Ann also acted a little shocked as she looked in her sister's direction.

Before any of them could protest, John spoke up "It would be an honor to have someone as beautiful as her join me, but only if she would like to."

Mary Anna had to search for her voice and after what seemed like minutes for her she spoke, "I would love to, Mr. Braymyer."

"Well then," he said, "This day has just gotten even better. Grandma," he said putting his hat back on and tipping it, "Ms. Walker. Ladies are you ready?"

John helped Rachel into the back of the wagon and then lifted Mary Anna into the front seat where he joined her. He lifted the reins and smacked them back down onto the brown mares as they left Liza's yard.

The wagon rolled through the narrow trails within the woods and as they did birds could be heard chirping high above in the trees. John looked over at Mary Anna no more than five minutes after they had left and said, "You know what I think?"

"What's that, Mr. Braymyer?"

"I think I'm going to marry you someday."

Rachel had to place a hand over her mouth to keep from laughing. Mary Anna looked at him shocked, "Marry me? Mr. Braymyer, how much of that moonshine have you had to drink today?"

John started laughing, "Oh I never touch the stuff, little missy, especially Grandma Davis' brew. It'll kill a man if he drinks too much of it."

Mary Anna's eyes grew big and she turned to see that Rachel's had done the same. John realized they were a little frightened and then spoke again, "Not to worry though, I don't believe your aunt's ever let a man die from it."

The girls were a little relieved and then turned their attention back to the trail ahead and let the silence take over again. John continued to glance over at Mary Anna who would occasionally let a small smile slip in the corners of her mouth.

"You sure are a beauty," he said.

"Mr. Braymyer, you mustn't flatter me so. It is improper."

"Improper? You're saying it's improper for a man to compliment his future wife?"

"Mr…"

"John, call me, John."

"Jo… Mr. Braymyer, you mustn't say such things!"

"Well, little missy, I only speak the truth. Honest to God, I aim to marry you, you just wait and see."

"And what if I refuse?"

"Well now, I don't know that I could bare that. Why I might just go find me a cliff and jump off of it. You wouldn't want my death on your hands now would you?"

"I think I would probably push you, Mr. Braymyer, seems like it would only benefit us both."

John started laughing and Rachel could be heard in the back trying to contain her laughter as well. "Little missy, you are something else. I bet I will be in love with you before the summer is over. And please, call me John."

"John, do you normally fall in love with girls who threaten to push you off a cliff?"

"Well, you're the first one to threaten that, so I suppose that makes you different."

"Humph," she said crossing her arms and turning her head, then turning sharply back, "Besides you can't marry me, your family wouldn't approve."

"Wouldn't approve? Are you fooling around with me or something?"

"No sir I am most certainly not. Your family wouldn't allow you to marry me on account that I am part Indian."

"Indian! Why I thought you were Chinese!"

"Really, sir! That is quite enough of that!"

"Awe, come on little missy, I'm just kidding around with you. Besides, what's wrong with you being part Indian?"

"Because it isn't proper, your family would not approve of me."

"Well now, I think you being part Indian makes you special and I've always fancied special things. Besides you haven't even met my family yet so you can't say that they'll like you or not."

Mary Anna looked at him dumbfounded. Nothing she could say or do would change his mind, he was out to marry her and all she could do was make it the hardest chase he had ever been on in his life.

As the wagon continued onward she would occasionally look back in his direction and he would immediately turn to her and smile every time, which would result in her quickly turning her stare back in front of her. Never in her life had she met a man so bold and so sure of himself.

Although she fought his every remark with witty comebacks, she secretly wanted desperately to laugh along with him, but that wouldn't be proper and a lady must always mind her manners.

April 05, 1838
Smokey Mountains

The Braymyer home sat atop a small hill that overlooked a beautiful valley to the west. The two story rectangular home was made from freshly cut wood from the mill and had a stone fireplace at each of its ends.

There was a small wooden fence that enclosed the front yard with a gate directly even with the front door. The front porch was made from the same stone as the fireplaces and it had four large tree logs serving as pillars stretching to the top of the roof.

To the right of the house and just a short ways off was a large barn that provided adequate shelter for the large number of livestock that resided on the Braymyer land. Just beyond the barn and almost completely hidden within the trees was the Braymyer Cemetery, which had grown tremendously over the years.

Alice Braymyer was forty-seven years old and was still just as full of life as she was when she was a young teenager. She was taller than most women, standing just under six feet tall, but was one of the prettiest women in all of Tennessee. She had red hair that she always wore in a bun atop her head and several freckles scattered across her face.

She had been born Alice Morgan and like her husband, David, she had lost most of her family members due to Indian attacks in earlier days. She had been born into a wealthy Virginian family, but when she was four years old her family made the move into Tennessee for new opportunity.

David Braymyer was fifty-one and although his age was apparent he still had a sense of youthfulness about him. His blonde hair had started to thin and was turning into a snow white blanket on top of his head, but his blue eyes still carried the special spark that Alice had fallen in love with so many years before.

He was taller than his wife, standing near six and a half feet tall and was thought to be one of the tallest men in all of Bledsoe County. He had been born in North Carolina to a whale hunter and his Irish wife and when his father didn't return home from sea on one of his journeys, he came with his mother and grandparents to Tennessee.

David and Alice had been blessed with eight children with a ninth one on the way, which they vowed would be their last. Their oldest son was David Jeremiah, whom they called Jerry and he was the spitting image of his father. All of the older people in town swore that they were looking at his father when they saw him.

John Nathaniel Braymyer was the next born and although he wasn't his father's exact image he still carried on many of the same traits and habits. Somehow the next two children, Ralph Morgan, 15 and Mary Alice, 12 had neither their father's nor mother's height. They both struggled to stand five and a half feet, thus making them the shorter of the family members.

Cynthia Ann Braymyer was nine and like her mother had red hair. She was the favorite to her older brother John who gave her whatever she wanted whenever she wanted it. Growing up, he had often been scolded by his mother for spoiling her so bad, but it never stopped him from doing it anyway.

The last three children were Wilson James, 7, Thomas Douglas, 5 and Missouri Texana who was one. They all carried traits of their mother and father having blonde hair with light streaks of red throughout it and a combination of their father's dark blue eyes and their mother's lighter ones.

 The Braymyers were happy people, perfectly content in just being satisfied that they were alive. When David and Alice were both young a band of Indians had come through and killed half the population in the area, including their parents. Their lives had started out rough, but in time everything worked out and David was able to profit greatly by working in the logging business.

Often times he would dam up the nearby river and allow more logs that would float down river to become jammed in his dam. After he was satisfied that there was enough wood there he would fish them out one by one and take them into town to sell to the mills.

The sun was slowly fading away to the west as Alice brought the rest of dinner into the dining room where her hungry family was waiting. Jerry had butchered a hog the day before and tonight they would feast on it along with a fresh loaf of bread and apple pie.

She took her seat at one end of the table with her husband opposite of her and looked around the full table at her family. They joined hands in preparation to bless the food when suddenly she noticed her right had was left free. She quickly opened her eyes and looked over to see that one of her children was missing.

"Where's John?" She insisted.

Ralph looked over at the empty chair, "He went over to Grandma Davis' this morning to see if she needed any help, but I figured he'd be back by now."
"That's not like John to miss his dinner," Alice said.

"He'll be fine, Alice" David said bowing his head again, "Now let's bless the food and eat. He'll be along shortly I'm sure."

Alice took one last look at the empty chair before bowing her head again as her husband said the prayer. Just after they had said amen and just before digging into the food the front door flew open and John burst into the dining room behind where his father was sitting.

"Sorry I'm late," he said walking alongside the table, rubbing his hand across the heads of his younger siblings. Once at the end he knelt down and kissed his mother on the cheek before taking his seat.

"John," Alice said, "What took you so long?"

"Sorry, Ma. I didn't mean to stay out so long, but I went on a buggy ride and lost track of time."

"A buggy ride?"

"Yes, maim. And then afterwards I had to take Mary Anna back to her aunt's house before heading home."

"Who's Mary Anna?"

"Why that's the girl I'm going to marry."

"Marry? John, what are you talking about? Have you had some of Grandma Davis' moonshine?"

John laughed a little as did his brothers and then said, "No Ma, but she did give me a jar to bring home to Pa."

"So, John," David interrupted, "Who is this Mary Anna?"

"Oh she's Grandma Davis' niece. Well, actually Grandma's sister, Ann is her grandmother."

"Are they visiting Grandma Davis?" Alice said taking back over the conversation as everyone began to eat.

"No, Ma. They are living with her. They are from Georgia. Walker is their last name."

"As in Walker Plantation Walkers?"

"I don't know, I think so."

"Well why on earth would they move up here to the Mountains?"

"On account that they had to, Ma." John said taking a big bite of ham.

"Had to?"

"Yes, you see Mary Anna and her brother, Walkie…"

"Walkie?"

"Yes, Ma, that's her brother's name." There was more laughter in the room from some of his siblings. "Anyway, they had to move because their father was a Cherokee and since the Indian removal they figured it would be safer to hide out up here."

Alice coughed, "They're Indians?"

"No, Ma only half Indian."

"Half Indian?"

"Yes, Ma like I said their father was a Cherokee and their mother was Grandma Davis' niece. Oh, and Rachel came to."

"Rachel?"

"Yes, that's Mary Anna's colored friend."

"Colored friend?"

"That's right, only I don't think she is all colored, she's pretty light if you ask me and her hair looks just like a white woman's, only dark."

"John, honey are you sure you're feeling alright?"

"Yes, maim. Anyhow Mary Anna and I are going to get married."

David Braymyer interrupted, "What do you mean you're going to get married?"

"Well just what I said, Pa. We're going to get married."

"And what does, Miss Walker think about this?"

"Well she's not so agreeable right now, but she will be soon enough."

There was a small second of silence and then the table erupted in laughter, that is everyone except John who just took a bite of his ham and looked around the table as if he didn't have a care in the world. "Y'all can laugh now, but mark my words me and Mary Anna will be wed soon enough."

"Well, son" Alice said in between laughter, "When will we get to meet this future wife of yours?"

"Soon enough I hope. She's a might scared you won't like her on account that she's part Indian."

"Well I hope you assured her that we won't hold it against her?"

"Oh yes, maim. I told her that and I think I just about have her convinced."

There was more laughter and the only words Alice was able to get out was, "Okay son, you be sure and bring her on over."

The family continued eating on their large dinner and soon David and all the boys, except John, were sipping on Grandma Davis' moonshine and laughing into the night. After all the children had gone up to bed, David continued to sit at the table and smoke his pipe.

"Alice," he said looking over at his wife who was clearing the table. "You don't suppose John was serious in what he said earlier do you?"

"Are you kidding, David. That boy means every word of what he says. There is no doubt in my mind that we'll have a wedding within the year!"

"Lord have mercy," he said, "I feel for this poor girl. I hope she's able to keep up with John and all his crazy ways."

"Well, if John has his cap set for her there's not much any of us can do, but go along for the ride and try and not laugh too hard at the things John says."

"You know, Alice, he gets that from you."

"Oh believe me, I know, David… I know."

September 14, 1994
Baptist Church, Dixie Texas

There were a few people who looked as if they were enjoying Pappy's story, but when he excused himself to the restroom I could see the relief written across their faces. Everyone moved around to other parts of the room, leaving me sitting alone at the table with a chair still sitting on top of it.

I figured they thought if they got far enough away then they wouldn't have to listen to his stories anymore. Even Grandma Rose was nowhere to be found, she had managed to sneak out the back door and light up a cigarette with several others who were craving their daily nicotine.

I hadn't seen the teenagers since Pappy began telling the story about our family and the few older people that remained were half awake as they sat in chairs trying to keep their heads from falling forward.

When Pappy returned he looked eager to pick back up the story he was telling, but when he realized everyone had scattered off there was a great look of depression about him. He took a seat beside me and looked around the room at everyone.

"Looks like I can't even get up and go to the bathroom without people running off."

"I'm still here, Pappy. I'll listen to the story."

"John, don't you want to go play video games with the rest of the kids?"

"No, sir! I want to stay right here with you. So did John and Mary Anna really get married?"

"Ha," Pappy said a bit of relief overcoming him. "Well I don't want to ruin the story, son. We'll get to that in a little while. You know that the Walker plantation was burned down?"

"It was?"

"Sure was. After Ann and the children left the Army found it empty with Mr. Walker on the front porch dead. They didn't have time to dig a grave so they just set it aflame. Even the barn ended up burning when it was all said and done.

Shortly after the Second World War was over I went down to Georgia to see the old place for myself and all that is there now is two tombstones."

"Only two? Whose are they?"

"One is Anna Walker and the other is her husband, Walks Tonight."

"And that's all that is there?"

"Sure is. It was kind of sad to see it, because it didn't look anything like it did in the stories my mother use to tell me about it."

"So how come Anna Walker died after she got home to Georgia?"

"Some say she was ashamed to be back in her father's house, but I think it was from a broken heart."

"Like a heart attack?"

"Ha, no son. Sometimes a person can love someone so much that when they die they don't see how they can go on with their life and before long they just die too."

"So how come you didn't die of a broken heart when Great Nanny died?"

"Well I almost did, but then you came to live with me and gave my life meaning again. I guess you're like the glue that holds my heart together in a way. I remember the day I met your Great Nanny. It was the summer of 37 and I was down at Sandusky fishing with some of my buddies.

Well a few of them had went out and got some beer somehow and had invited a bunch of girls to come out there. So we were all sitting there having a good ol' time when suddenly an Angel came walking up to us."

"An Angel?"

"Yes, sir. She was wearing a white dress, long brown hair and she looked completely peaceful. Well, almost peaceful. She had an awful mean look on her face when she walked up to us. Turns out we were fishing on her daddy's land and she didn't take to the fact that we were out there drinking and all.

Why your Great Nanny took one of them beer bottles and beat my good buddy upside the head with it. Boy everybody took off running, everyone except me that is. I stuck around because as soon as I saw her I knew I wanted to marry her."

"You did? So did she talk to you when you stayed behind?"

Pappy began laughing, "No son. She took another beer bottle and smashed me upside the head! It took me six months to get her to go out on a date with me and another six after that to marry me. But now that I look back on it, getting hit upside the head with a beer bottle that year was one of the best things that has ever happened to me.

It is unbelievable the things we will do for love, John. We can be ourselves one day and the next we will be a complete stranger to who we used to be. Sometimes I wonder if real love even exists anymore, of course I'd like to think it does.

But always remember this, John. If it's real love, it never comes easy…never. Sometimes you have to fight harder than you've ever fought before and at times it can seem silly to spend so much time and effort over one person. But believe you me it is worth it in the end."

"What if you fight for something as hard as you can, but you still don't win?"

"Son, most of the time we have it deep within ourselves to fight for whatever we want, so before searching for an alternate source of strength we need to make sure we have first searched ourselves. If the love is true and real, it will find a way to blossom and no amount of fighting will prevent it from happening. Do you understand?"

"I think so. So, did Mary Anna and John have to fight?"

"Well, let's see now…"

April 26, 1838
Aunt Liza's house

Ann Walker sat on the front porch thinking over everything that had happened in her life over the past several years. She knew she would never make it back to Georgia and even if she did there wasn't anything left for her there.

She was sixty-eight years old and if there was one thing she knew more than anything else it was the knowledge of endurance. She prayed every night to be forgiven for leaving her husband in the state he was in, but deep down she knew it was something that had to be done.

Her husband's name was not mentioned by anyone at the house, not even the children. Everyone somehow sensed that things would not be the same in that concern and there was no need to discuss it.

Although Ann was sorrowful over the past events, she found a strange comfort in sitting on the front porch with her sister day after day. The children seemed more alive than ever and truly looked to be enjoying themselves. Even though Ann didn't completely agree with her sister's boldness and love for moonshine, her ego and outlook on life was exactly what her and her family needed.

She was also especially concerned with her granddaughter's future and what prospects it might hold. She differed from her late husband in the fact that she never really believed in marrying well, but rather she ventured to hope that people would marry for love no matter what their position in society was.

Although Mary Anna was dead set in her ways and fully opposed every attempt Mr. Braymyer made towards her, Ann watched and knew there was something special there. Sure Mary Anna boldly refused his offers time and time again, but secretly within herself she rather enjoyed his endless chase and found herself looking forward to it each day.

Even though the fact that she was part Indian and Indians were the ones who had killed off most of his family, he remained constant in his pursuit after her. Every day he would come to Liza's house pretending to want to help her with work, but as soon as she told him there was none, his attention was turned and directed towards Mary Anna until the day was almost over.

The two sisters sat in their usual spots on the front porch while the children talked among themselves near the barn. Walkie had become quite fit after all the work he had been doing on his Aunt's farm. He tended all the animals and often found himself in the cornfields checking up on the crop.
The three children walked along the edge of the woods, which surrounded Liza's house and watched as the afternoon slowly drug across Tennessee. Walkie was always a few steps ahead of the girls and every chance he got he would pick up a rock and throw it off into the trees.

"Mary Anna?" Rachel said looking up at the sky. "Do you think Mr. Braymyer really intends on marrying you?"

"It sure seems that way, Rachel. Honestly I don't know how any man can be so persistent after being told no so many times."

"Well, maybe you should tell him yes."

"Rachel! How could you say such a thing!"

"Well, why not? He's very handsome and he's got one of the best personalities that I have ever seen, course Mr. Walker was about the only man I had been around."

"But still, it doesn't seem right. I mean, I don't know if I am ready to marry."

"You know, Mary Anna. You just have to let yourself see the answer."

"Mary Anna's in love! She's gonna' kiss Mr. Braymyer!" Walkie shouted back at them as he skipped along.

"Walkie!" She said chasing after him. "You stop saying those things this instant!"

He continued to taunt his sister as she chased after him and once she had caught up with him, she threw herself on top of him bringing them both to the ground. They rolled around in the dirt as he laughed and sang made up love songs with his sister punching him in the shoulders as he did.

"Walkie! Stop it I said! That isn't funny!"

"Mary Anna Braymyer... kissed her husband, held his hand and ran to Tennessee!"

"Walkie!"

Rachel stood behind and just laughed at the absurd scene until she noticed a man standing over Mary Anna and Walkie. At this point, Mary Anna was on top of Walkie and had him pinned down as he shouted, "Mary Anna's in love! Mary Anna's in love!"

Mary Anna saw the man's feet just in front of her brother's head and slowly moved her gaze up his legs until settling on his face which sat beneath the shade of his cowboy hat.

"Well now, I sure hope she's in love with me or else I just might have to go fight this other fellow on account that it's the only way I think I could mend my broken heart."

Mary Anna had never been so embarrassed in her life and she quickly threw herself up to her feet and began brushing off her dress. Walkie remained lying on his back laughing as hard as he could up at the blue sky as Mary Anna struggled to push her hair out of her face.

"Mr. Braymyer," she said. "You shouldn't sneak up on people like that… it's not polite."

"My apologies, maim, but it looked like you were having a good time. I had only hoped to join in on the excitement." He kneeled down and lifted Walkie up to his feet by the pits of his arms and then helped him by brushing his back off. "So, Walkie, who's this fellow that your sister's in love with? I may need your help to go teach him a lesson or two."

Walkie's face had still not rid itself of a smile and as seriously as he could he answered him. "Why, she's in love with you!"

"Walkie!" Mary Anna tried to interrupt, but it was no use as John's voice over powered hers.

"Really now? Why do you say that?"

"Oh I heard them talking. She thinks you're handsome and witty and manly and that you have a good personality."

Mary Anna's embarrassment continued to climb to its max as her face began to turn red. She thought she would burst out into tears at any moment and run far away into the woods.

Rachel kept both of her hands over her face to try and contain her laughter, but a small portion of it would slip through on occasion.

"She thinks I'm handsome and manly, huh?"

"Yes, sir she sure does," Walkie answered smiling over at his sister who had the blankest look on her face he had ever seen.

"Well I suppose that's a relief, I sure didn't want to get into a fight today. Say, Walkie, you think you and Rachel could give me and your sister a moment alone?"

Mary Anna shot a pleading look in her brother's direction, but he paid no attention to it. "Sure."

John slapped his hand across Walkie's backside as he ran off toward the house with Rachel close behind whom once far enough away let out all the laughter she had been holding in. It was so loud that it sounded as if a wolf was howling out at the moon.

John watched as they walked away and then turned back to face Mary Anna. "Well, looks like you've got some explaining to do, little missy."

"Mr. Braymyer, they were…"

"John, how many times do I have to tell you to call me John?"

"John, Walkie was just fooling around. He doesn't know what he's saying, honest."

"That sure is a shame then, I got my hopes up for nothing."

"Well, I am sorry, sir. Now I've got to go."

Mary Anna turned quickly and just before she had taken her second step away from him, John reached out and grabbed her and pulled her back.

"Now wait a minute, I came all this way to see you and you're just going to walk away?"

"I'm sorry, I just don't feel very well."

"Awe, we was all just joking with you. No need to get yourself upset."

"I would very much appreciate it if I am not the source of your jokes in the future."

"Okay, deal. So have you decided when we're getting married yet?"

"Ugh!" She said and halfway turned, but was again stopped by his hand and this time was pulled into his arms.

She looked up at him and suddenly the feeling of embarrassment had completely left her and she couldn't help but smile as she looked into his eyes. "You want to kiss me, don't you?" He said looking down at her.

"John! What a thing to say! And besides I think you're the one who wants to kiss me!"

"Well, little missy, I can't deny that. Whenever you give me permission I'd be happy to do it."

Mary Anna was so overcome with shock that she didn't know what to say or do, so she just closed her eyes not knowing what to expect. John leaned down and kissed her startled lips where she returned the favor.

She quickly pulled away and stood firm directly in front of him. "I'm sorry, I don't know what came over me."

"Mary Anna, there's nothing to be sorry about, really there isn't. Now I've been after you for almost a month and you still tell me you don't want to marry me. I come from good people, got lots of farm land and like you said I'm mighty handsome."

"John!"

"Sorry, little missy, didn't mean to joke again."

"Why me? Why do you insist on marrying me?"

"There's something about you, Mary Anna. Even saying your name gives me chills. I want you more than anything in the world and I want to spend my life taking care of you if you'll let me."

"But, John we've barely known each other very long."

"Look me in the eyes and tell me you don't feel something special between us."

She looked up at his soothing look and then turned her head, "I can't do that."

"See there, so marry me. I promise to be a good husband to you, honest I do."

"But, John, I haven't even met your family yet."

"Well that's why I came calling on you today, I want you to come have dinner with us tonight."

"Tonight?"

"That's right, you will come won't you?"

"I suppose, but Rachel will have to come too. It's not proper for a lady to travel alone in the company of a man."

"Absolutely, little missy, she can come to."

"And, John," she said.

"Yes, Mary Anna."

"I shall think about your proposal, but if I do decide that I will accept I want to wait until the fall when I turn thirteen."

"Take all the time you need, little missy. I'm not going anywhere."

- - - - - - - - - - - - - - - -

It was late when John and his company pulled up to his parent's house, but the sun had still managed to hang around long enough for them to reach their destination. When the wagon came to a complete stop, nervousness had taken up residence in Mary Anna's body.

She wanted desperately to turn around and go back home, but she knew that would be impolite. She waited patiently for John to walk around the wagon to her side where he gently helped her down. He wrapped his arm around her as Rachel walked up behind them, "Are you ready to go in?" He asked.

"I suppose, John. I do hope that they like me."

"Don't worry, they're going to love you."

John opened the front door and the three of them stepped inside where the entire Braymyer family was waiting for them. The room remained silent as John hung his hat up on the hat rack and then turned to face his awaiting family with Mary Anna at his side.

"Everyone, this is Mary Anna Walker. She's Grandma Davis' niece I have been telling you all about."

The family was taken aback by her beauty, they had not expected someone with such remarkable looks as hers. One by one everyone introduced themselves to her where she responded with, "How do you do."

After the greetings they were ushered into the dining room, which was jammed packed with people and chairs. Mary Anna sat next to John in between him and his mother and surprisingly, they had set a place for Rachel. Most people would not allow colored people to eat at the table with them, but the Braymyers were a different kind of breed.

Mary Anna held Alice's gentle hand as David blessed the food. After everyone had said amen, a platter of salt pork was being passed around the table. There were also biscuits, bacon, fresh green beans and carrots and somewhere in the kitchen was a blueberry cobbler that could be smelled clear into the other room.

"So Mary Anna," Alice said handing the plate over to her, "How do you like Tennessee?"

"Oh, it's just fine maim. It's different than Georgia of course, but it is beautiful within itself no doubt."

"Yes, it does grow on you after awhile. Are you getting along good with all the folks in these parts?"

"Oh yes, maim. Everyone has been most kind to me."

"Especially, John," Jerry interrupted as the other boys joined in with small laughter.

"Don't mind them," Alice said, "They are just jealous that John found someone like you. I think I shall come to like you as if you were my own daughter."

John looked over and winked at her. "Thank you, maim" she answered, "I only hope I can live up to your expectations."

"Oh don't you worry yourself over that, honey. You're going to fit right in with us."

"That's what I told her, Ma," John said, "I told her you would like her."

"Well of course I will. I shall like to go on a walk with you sometime, Mary Anna. Of course I will have to wait until after the baby is born. I'm getting so close to the day now that I can barely get in and out of bed!"

"That sounds lovely, maim. I should look forward to it."

The Braymyer children continued to stare at Mary Anna and her beauty and wondered how their brother had found someone such as her. The girls watched in hopes that they might act like her while the boys watched in hopes that there might be another one out there just like her.

"So, Miss Walker," Ralph said, "When are you and my big brother to be wed?"

Mary Anna tried not to choke on the piece of pork she was eating at the remark. "Well, I haven't told him yes yet."

"So I guess maybe I have a chance with you, then." He said.

John interrupted, "Oh she'll be saying yes soon enough and besides you don't have what it takes to catch a girl like her." He winked at Mary Anna again as the table began to laugh.

"We'll see about that," Ralph said smiling over at her.

"Well," Mary Anna said, "I cannot accept John's proposal until I know that his family approves of me."

There was more laughter and Mary Anna began to wonder what she had said to cause such a stir. "You'll do just fine for John," David said, "Just be ready for an adventure!"

"David," Alice said to him and then turned to Mary Anna. "Honey, if he makes you happy and you are good to each other then you have our blessing."

"See there," John said, "They like you already."

"I do appreciate your kindness," she said looking around the table at everyone.

"So Miss Walker," John said getting up from his chair and kneeling down before her, "Will you marry me?"

Mary Anna was shocked, but not surprised at his boldness. What if she were to refuse him in front of his family, how sure of himself he must be.

"You got to talk sweet to her," Jerry interrupted.

"Little Missy," he said in a sarcastic voice, "You and I can have some good times together. All you have to do is say the word and I'll make you the happiest woman alive."

"John," she said, "Are you sure you haven't been sipping on Aunt Liza's moonshine?"

The table was full of laughter yet again and John's brothers began making faces in his direction as if they were drinking the moonshine. John smiled as he looked around the room at them and then turned back to Mary Anna.

"I mean it, Mary Anna. I'll provide for you better than any man alive and anything you want or desire I'll do my best by you to get it. Why, we'll be the happiest couple in all of Tennessee."

"Just Tennessee?" She said.

"Ha, no maim. We'll be the happiest couple in the whole world."

She looked over at Alice who was smiling in a pleasing way and then back down at John. Her head was spinning on what she should do and she couldn't find the words to tell him. She knew she loved him, but a decision like this had much fear that accompanied it.

She always knew she would one day get married, but she had never planned on it being this soon and let alone this sudden. She continued looking down at him as he took her hand in hers and she was immediately calmed by his warm touch.

She thought about her life and everything that had happened thus far and decided to act on her gut feeling, which luckily for John was the answer, yes.

"I'll marry you, John."

"Yippee!" He shouted as he lunged into the air and danced around. "I'm gonna' have me the finest wife out there!"

He leaned down and kissed her on the forehead as she blushed and swallowed a lump that had formed in her throat. The boys, especially Ralph, looked disappointed that she had said yes and had a sort of depressed look about them.

"Congratulations to you both," Alice said reaching over and taking Mary Anna's hand in hers. "Now let's celebrate with some blueberry cobbler."

"Forget the cobbler, Ma" Jerry said, "Let's get the moonshine."

Ralph went to the kitchen and came back with another jar of Grandma Davis' moonshine and began passing it around the table. He walked around the table to Mary Anna and held the jar up to her mouth, "Here you go, sister, have a swig."

"Heavens no!" She said.

"Awe come on, Mary Anna. Here John, you take a drink."

"Ha, none for me, Ralph boy, none for me."

September 14, 1994
Baptist Church, Dixie Texas

The church had begun to clear out as Pappy stood up for a long overdue stretch. I got up and followed him out the door to find that only Grandma Rose and one of her cousins were left.

She walked over to us as her cousin entered her car and drove off. "Are you two ready to go home?"

Pappy looked around the churchyard and then over at his daughter, "I think we'll walk home, Rose."

"Walk? But daddy, it's three miles away!"

"We'll be fine, Rose. I've walked a lot longer than that in my day."

Grandma Rose looked dissatisfied, but when Pappy made up his mind there wasn't much anyone could do. "Okay, you call me if you need anything, ya' hear?"

"Yes, maim," I said as she kissed me on top of the head and then hugged her father. She turned away from us and got into her Buick and was soon out of sight.

"Come on, John. Let's head on home."

I walked beside Pappy down the dirt road that led away from the small community of Dixie and we headed west toward Braymyer Hill. The sky was colored in a weird shade of orange and blue, which Pappy said meant rain for the next day.

We passed no houses, only empty fields patiently waiting to be harvested before the winter. There was an occasional roadrunner that would dart across the road in front of us and every time I tried unsuccessfully to catch it.

"Pappy," I said looking up over at him. "How come Mary Anna waited so long to tell John yes?"

"Ha, well it was only a couple of weeks and I suppose she was going through so much in her life at the moment that she truly didn't know what she wanted."

"So did Alice have her baby?"

"Sure did, it was a girl and they named her Dolly Ann after David's grandmother."

"Was Mary Anna's grandmother glad that she was getting married?"

"Oh yes. She liked John very much and was very happy at their marriage. It's a shame what had to happen though."

"What do you mean? What happened?"

Pappy looked down at me and smiled as we continued down the road. "Let's get home and I'll tell you about it when you're tucked into bed."

July 20, 1838
Aunt Liza's house

"Mary Anna! Mary Anna! Hurry up! John will be here any minute!" Rachel shouted up the stairs after her.

"I'm coming, Rachel," she said running down toward her. "Here, tie this bow in my hair for me."

Mary Anna stood in front of a full-length mirror near the foot of the stairs and admired herself. She wore a green dress from her mother's plantation days and a matching bow on top of her head.

After Rachel had finished tying it, the two of them went outside where Walkie and the sisters were sitting on the front porch.

"Mary Anna, you look beautiful!" Ann said standing up and hugging her.

"Thank you, grandmother."

"She reminds me a lot of our mother, Ann." Liza said looking Mary Anna up and down.

"I think she looks like a girl!" Walkie laughed.

"That's because she is one," Ann said cutting him off. "You look beautiful, darling."

John and his wagon pulled up in front of the porch just as Mary Anna was about to throw a comeback at Walkie. "Afternoon!" John shouted.

"Hiya', John. How are you today?"

"Just fine Grandma Davis, just fine. You two ladies ready?"

Mary Anna hugged her grandmother and aunt and then walked over to John, pushing her hand into Walkie's head as she passed him. John helped her up onto the wagon seat and then walked around to the front of the wagon.

"Can't I come this time?" Walkie begged.

"No, Walkie," Mary Anna said.

"Awe, come on Walkie don't get upset," John said reaching into his pocket. "Here have a peppermint stick."

"Gee thanks, John."

The sisters stood up and joined Walkie in waving them goodbye from the front porch as the wagon rolled out of sight. Mary Anna allowed John to hold her hand as they rode down the winding path throughout the woods.

"You two ready for some good food?" He said whipping the reins.

"I can hardly wait," Mary Anna said, "Seems like your mother makes some of the best cobbler around."

"That she does, little missy, that she does."

"So where is the picnic at?" Mary Anna asked.

"Just a few miles from our house at the Widow Douglas' home."

They drove on until the morning turned into early afternoon until finally they had arrived at the small picnic that several of the local families had created. The wagon pulled up to a few small trees that sat atop a hill where several people were sitting on quilts and blankets.

Once they had gotten down from the wagon they walked over to where the Braymyer family had gathered, which was underneath a tree of their own to the south of the group. "Mary Anna!" Alice said getting up with Dolly in her arms. "So good to see you!"

The two of them hugged one another and then sat down on the blanket with the other girls while the men stood and talked amongst themselves. A fiddle was being played a few blankets over and the melody rang out into the sky.

"How's your grandmother and your aunt?" Alice asked as she rocked her newest baby.

"Oh they are both doing well. How are you holding up?"

"Oh I'm fine. Number nine was no different than the eight before it!"

They laughed and continued to make small talk until they were interrupted by John. "Come on, Mary Anna let's dance."

"Oh, John I don't know about that. I mean really..."

"Come on, Little Missy," he said taking her by the hand and bringing her up to her feet.

"You two have fun!" Alice shouted after them.

John led her over to where other couples had gathered and formed a dance floor in the short grass. John swung her around and moved in and out of the growing number of dancers.

"John, where did you learn to dance like this?"

"Ma taught me, a long time ago. Here, follow my lead."

They continued to dance with the other couples and at one point had a small circle of onlookers form around them and cheer them on. A slower beat began to ring out around them and just like the beat, they slowed their steps as well.

"So, little missy. When do you figure on having our wedding?"

"Well, I turn thirteen in September."

"So September it is!"

After they had had all the dancing they could handle, they went back over to the blanket and joined everyone else as they ate. There were a few hams floating around, but the meal mostly consisted of sweets and deserts.

After hours of visiting and catching up on local news it was finally time to go. It had been a fun day for the three of them, but they had no intention of sitting out in the hot sun on a blanket all day anytime soon.

When they pulled up to Aunt Liza's house, the sun was just about gone, but there was a glow about the place as they drew nearer. They looked hard in the direction of the house, but they couldn't find it anywhere.

"No!" Mary Anna said leaping out of the wagon and running toward the charred remains of the house.

Smoke still floated up into the sky in small spurts. John and Rachel were right behind her as she ran frantically around the farm looking for her family. The barn was still standing and written in red was the word "I N D I A N."

"Mary Anna!" John said chasing after her as she headed back to the front of the house. Just before she reached where the front porch had been she looked over at a tree where she heard a small creaking sound.

"Walkie!"

John wrapped his arms around her to prevent her from going any closer and turned her head away from the sight she had just witnessed.

Walkie had his hands tied behind his back and was hanging from the tree by way of a rope around his neck. His body still slightly moved back and forth a little bit, hinting that he had not been there long.

His small body had marks all across it, likely caused from a horsewhip and in small letters across his forehead the word Indian was written. Mary Anna fought as hard as she could to get away from the grip of John, but he was not letting her out of his arms.

Rachel had her back turned to the scene and was sobbing into her hands. Who would do this to little Walkie, she thought.

"John," Mary Anna said, "Let me go! That's my brother! I should be up there to!"

"Calm down, little missy." He said rubbing his hand across the back of her head. "I'm going to let you go, but I want you to go wait by the wagon while I cut him down, okay?"

She nodded and John slowly let her go as he looked up at Walkie's body. Since Walkie was just a child, he wasn't hanging very high so John was able to just reach up and cut the rope loose. His fragile body fell into the arms of John and he slowly let it rest onto the ground as Mary Anna emerged from behind the wagon with Rachel.

They walked over and knelt down beside his body, both sobbing in tears. Mary Anna ran her hand through his hair wondering how this could have happened to her little brother.

"I should have let him come with us," she said. "It's all my fault."

Rachel put her arm around her and John wrapped his on her other side and spoke softly into her ear. "It's not your fault. You had no way of knowing this would happen."

"Grandmother," she said softly at first, then louder as she stood up and ran toward the house, "Grandmother!"
The house was completely destroyed except for one wall of the dining room, the one that had the drawing of the sister's mother on it. John caught Mary Anna just before she threw herself onto the rubble.

"Hold on, let me help you."

John held her arm as they walked across the charred remains of Grandma Davis' house. They stepped over where the staircase had been and made their way back toward the kitchen, or to what used to be the kitchen.

Mary Anna turned her head sharply and buried it into John's chest when she saw the bodies of her grandmother and her sister covered in ash. They were hardly recognizable and had been burned to such a degree that large portions of their flesh were missing.

"John, no. This can't be. Why would someone do this! It's not fair."

"Let it out, little missy," he said, "Let it all out."

John held her amongst the smothering ash and vowed that if anyone tried to hunt down his wife for being part Indian that he would let nothing stand in his way and would protect her with everything he had. For the first time since he had become a man, the happy John Braymyer had to wipe away a few tears from his face as he held his future wife.

In a single night, Mary Anna had lost her entire family with the exception of her faithful friend, Rachel and her future husband. She couldn't process everything that had just happened, but the one thing she was sure of is that she was glad John was there to hold her.

September 14, 1994
Braymyer Hill, Dixie, Texas

As I lie in bed beneath quilts that had been in the family forever, Pappy held up a large a picture frame as he sat on the edge of the bed. Inside the frame was an old piece of paper that looked to have been charred around the edges.

"This is Ann Walker's mother," he said running his wrinkled hand atop the glass.

It was a beautiful colored painting of a woman with light hair that was flowing freely across both her shoulders. She looked to be a teenager and was not at all what I had expected it to be. She wore a blue dress and had a blue ribbon around her neck, she was one of the prettiest girls I had ever seen.

"How did the picture survive the fire?"

"Not sure, son, but it was the only thing that survived the fire."

"So they killed Walkie and the women just because they were Indian"

"No, they killed Walkie because he was part Indian. They killed the sisters likely because they were allowing him to live there. A lot of people back then were killed for being kind to those that society saw unfit."

"How come?"

"I don't know, son. That was just the way they thought back then. Had Mary Anna and Rachel been there that day, they too would have likely died and you and I would not be here today."

"So what did Mary Anna do after her brother died?"

425

"Well, she was never the same, that's for sure. Seeing her brother hanging up in that tree caused her to grow up real quick, but she always had a sense of passion about her that very few have. When something like this happens, most people drown themselves in sorrow and want others to feel sorry for them, but not her.

Sure she was sad for awhile and after the fire she locked herself up in an upstairs bedroom of the Braymyer house and didn't come out for nearly a week."

"Really? What did she do up there all alone?"

"Nobody really knows, but when she came out she was changed and for the better. Why, she barged out of that room ready to start her life. She figured if she was the only family member left then she ought to honor the deceased and live her life to the fullest."

"Did she rebuild Grandma Davis' house?"

"No, in fact I don't think she ever went back there, not that I can blame her. The day after her brother died, John and his brothers went and retrieved the bodies of the dead and brought them over to their family cemetery and buried them there. Rachel didn't appear to be sad in front of everyone else, but she was often caught looking in the direction of the cemetery with a sad face. Ann Walker was the closest thing she had ever had to a mother and when she died it was just like losing one."

"So when did Mary Anna and John get married already!"

"Ha, you better get some sleep son. We'll finish the story another day."

"Okay, goodnight, Pappy."

"Goodnight, son."

July 26, 1838
The Braymyer Home

Mary Anna emerged from an upstairs bedroom and into the quiet hallway for the first time in six days. She didn't even come out for the funeral of her family members, she felt closer to them when she was alone anyhow.

She had had a lot of time to think and most things she thought about more than once, but alas it was time for her to live her life. John had checked on her several times a day and he was the only one she permitted into the bedroom with her, not even Alice or Rachel were allowed in there.

Her long dark hair was freshly brushed and sat on top of a yellow dress that Alice had given her by way of John. She wore a yellow paper flower on the back of her head where two strands of her bangs met.

She looked around at the empty house and then peered over the rail into the downstairs portion of the house…everything was quiet. She walked around the railing until she came to the stairs and slowly descended them until she was facing the front door.

This would be the first time she had even looked outside since she had locked herself away in solitude. She placed a hand on the doorknob and pushed the door outward, allowing sunlight to at last meet her face. Just as she stepped out onto the front porch, Alice was walking up the stairs and met her head on.

Alice looked up startled and was pleased to see the appearance of Mary Anna and looking so well at that. She wrapped her hands around her and hugged her without saying a word. After a long hug she pulled away, but kept both hands on her shoulders and looked her up and down.

"It's good to see you, Mary Anna. Real good."

"Thank you, Mrs. Braymyer. Where's John?"

"Please, call me Ma and he's over yonder at the cemetery. I can go fetch him for you if you'd like."

"No, it's okay. I suppose it is time for me to make a visit there anyhow."

Alice smiled as Mary Anna left the comfort of the porch and ventured across the yard. A slight wind from the west caught her hair and dress and sent it flowing towards the east. In the distance she could see Rachel and the other children playing atop a hill and she smiled at the joyous sight in the midst of so much tragedy.

After she had passed the barn she wandered down an old foot trail until coming upon a cast iron fence. She rested her hands on its pointy top and looked over at John who had his back to her.

He was knelt in front of Grandma Davis' freshly carved tombstone and placing a jar of moonshine in front of it. His hat was lying on the ground beside him and she watched as he opened the jar and held it up to the stone.

"Grandma Davis', you know I don't fancy this here moonshine, but I'll make an exception for you. Here's to you."

He took a small swig and liked to have knocked the tombstone clear off its foundation as he staggered around trying to catch his breath. Mary Anna couldn't help but let out a laugh at his heartfelt clumsiness.

"Mary Anna!" He said standing quickly and heading in her direction.

She opened the gate and gracefully walked toward him, meeting him just inside the small cemetery. "You know, you look a lot like Aunt Liza when you drink that stuff."

He put his arms around her waist, "Now that would be a shameful sight to see. It's good to see you out of the bedroom, are you feeling okay?"

"Yes," she said walking away from him and towards her brother's grave. "I figured it was time for me to embrace life and play with the hand I'm dealt."

She knelt down and ran her hand over the letters in Walkie's tombstone, 'Walks Walker. Loving Brother.'

"This is real nice, John. Did you put this on here."

"Yes, I figured he earned the title by and by."

"He would have liked it. Walkie was always getting into something or causing some kind of a fuss. I don't know how many times I had to save his hind end down in Georgia when it came to Grandfather."

"He was a good boy, Mary Anna. You must have been proud to have him as a brother."

"Oh I was," she said fighting back tears. "We may not be very old, but we have been through our share of things believe you me."

John knelt down and put his arm around her as she continued to talk. "My favorite memories are of him always sneaking in some kind of animal into the house down on the plantation. He liked to have given everyone a heart attack on more than one occasion, but he was always out for a good laugh.

Of course, I'm the one who got the beatings from Grandfather. I'd always take the blame, I just didn't have the heart to see him hurt and in the end it was hurt that took him away anyway. Well, I suppose he's in a better place now."

She stood up and looked around as she wiped away the tears. After she had contained herself she looked into John's eyes who stared back at her with a sense of understanding and compassion. His kind look nearly sent her into tears all over again.

"How's Rachel holding up to all this?" She asked trying to change the subject.

"She's doing okay. Cynthia Ann is keeping her busy. They play day and night and hardly catch a wink of sleep."

There was a little laughter between them. Mary Anna put her arm through John's and headed back toward the cemetery entrance. "Has that moonshine messed with your head yet, John?"

"No, I reckon I spit most of it out back on top of Grandma Davis."

"Ha, John you shouldn't say such things, but Lord knows she's up there laughing right now and if there's moonshine in Heaven she's sure to have her fill of it."

"I suppose you're right, little missy."

"John, I was thinking."

"Oh?"

"Yes, about our marriage and all."

"Mary Anna if you want to wait longer we can, it doesn't bother me. I completely understand."

"Actually, John it's just the opposite. I'm ready to start not only my life, but also our life together. We don't have to wait until the fall, I'm ready to marry you now."

"Are you sure, Mary Anna? I don't want to pressure you into anything."

"I'm sure, John. I'm in love with you and everything there is about you. I'm in love with your charm, your kindness to others and even your arrogant boldness."

John started laughing softly, "Well it's about time. I've been in love with you since the day I saw you and it's taken you this long to fall in love with me. Hmm, what if I change my mind about this whole mess?"

"John Braymyer, if you make one more joke towards me I swear I'll run away and never come back!"

"Easy, little missy. You know I couldn't ever let that happen, I love you too much. So when do you want to marry?"

"Next Saturday is fine with me, John if it suits you."

"Well shoot, Mary Anna, today would suit me just fine. What do you say?"

"John B…"

"I know, I know… no more jokes."

She smiled at him as they stopped walking and got lost somewhere in his gaze. "John you are a joke. That's what you are, a handsomē, smart mouthed, arrogant manly joke. But I love you none the less."

John leaned down and kissed her and as he did, all her troubles seemed to be somehow washed away.

- - - - - - - - - - - - - - - - - - - -

The next Saturday the family gathered in the meadow behind the barn and prepared for the first wedding in the Braymyer family since David and Alice. Cynthia Ann was in charge of watching the children because Alice had become so excited that she engulfed her time in preparation for this big day.

She had been up every night for the past three nights cooking every kind of pie imaginable. She had Jerry slaughter three hogs, way more than was needed for this event, but she insisted just to be sure. Other than the family, the guest list included seven other families, bringing the total number of people to thirty-three.

Alice dug out her old wedding dress and other than it being too long for Mary Anna, it fit her perfectly. Alice and Rachel trimmed the dress and made the train longer and on the Friday before the wedding it was finished.

The Braymyer home was filled with joy and excitement and everyone was anxious for the wedding. Mary Anna and John had very little time alone and were both looking forward to getting this over with. They had managed to sneak away twice during the previous week and had went for a midnight stroll.

As everyone began arriving, Mary Anna looked out the upstairs window down onto the growing crowd as Alice tied her ribbon in the back. Rachel combed her hair for her and between her and Alice adjusting every little thing on her she imagined that she looked just near perfect.

After everyone had arrived, the only people who remained in the house were the three of them. They went downstairs and waited patiently behind the front door for the fiddle to begin playing.

At exactly noon, a high pitched melody arose throughout the crowd from the fiddle and the front door was opened by Ralph who was on the other side. The three women stepped out onto the porch and made their way through the guest to where John and his father were waiting beside the preacher.

They walked slowly, trying to stay in tune with the music and it seemed like hours for Mary Anna until she had finally made it to John's side. Her white dress stretched nearly the entire length of the crowd when she stopped beside him and she dreaded the fact that someone at any moment could give it a tug and she would end up on her back.

The preacher began saying something and there was a prayer, but Mary Anna completely tuned him out. She was once again lost in those rare eyes of John Braymyer and it seemed that every time she ventured into their depth, she had an even harder time finding her way out.

She managed to catch the part where he asked her to say 'I do,' and luckily she said it without any trouble. The next thing she heard was you may kiss the bride and she closed her eyes as her husband leaned in to seal the deal.

She was truly happy and nothing in the world could bring her down off this mountain she was now standing atop. Then the preacher shouted out, "Alright! Now let's have us some moonshine!"

"Great," she whispered to John, "Half the people here will be bent over getting sick before the day is over."

John started laughing, "You're something else, Mary Anna and I've got a good feeling that we're going to have the best marriage ever."

"I sure hope so, John, I'd hate to think I got this dressed up for nothing."

"Well, Mrs. Braymyer, shall we dance?"

"We shall, Mr. Braymyer."

November 17, 1994
Braymyer Hill, Dixie, Texas

It had gotten a lot colder since the family reunion and Pappy said that it had been a long time since it was cold this early. He rarely ran the heating and air conditioner unit and this year was no exception as he instead had the six fireplaces in the large plantation like home full of warm flames.

Unlike most young children, I did not like the cold weather. I would much rather the sun be beating down upon me than to set one foot in the smallest amount of snow. Even given my unnatural hate for the cold, the abundance of fireplaces in place of a heater still provided adequate warmth for me.

It was mid afternoon and the two of us were sitting in rocking chairs in the front room when he told me what our plans would be for that winter. He looked up from his newspaper and then over at me.

"John, what do you think about taking a trip over the Christmas break this year?"

"Well sure, Pappy that sounds nice to me, but where would we be going?"

"Missouri."

"Missouri? What's up there?"

"Braymyer Ridge. I haven't been there in years, I think it would be kind of nice to go up there again."

"Okay, what family do we have that settled up there?"

"Well, why don't I wait and tell you on the way. But first, I want to walk over to the cemetery out back. Why don't you go get your coat and meet me on the back porch."

I hurried upstairs and threw on my old coat on top of my overalls and then met Pappy out back. It wasn't snowing yet, but it sure felt cold enough that it could start at any moment. We walked past the old barns and onto a trail that ran throughout the empty fields.

I could see little pieces of ice in the black Texas dirt as we made our way across the vacant land. Soon, we came to the old cemetery that sat atop a tree-covered hill overlooking the land. The two of us made our way up the slick slope and stepped into the cemetery.

"What did you want to come out here for Pappy?"

"Oh, just thought I would pay my respects. There's someone buried here that died on this day many years ago."

"Really?"

"Sure is, but first let's go see your great nanny."

We made our way across the cemetery to the resting place of my Pappy's wife. He brushed off some grass and dirt that had collected onto the double monument and then put his hand on my shoulder.

"She was a good woman, John… a good one."

I looked down at the stone and read aloud, "Blanche Dement Braymyer. Was her family from around here, Pappy?"

"No son, they were from east Texas, but her parents and her settled over at Sandusky shortly before I met her."

"Oh, I see. So who is it that died on this day?"

"Come on and I'll show you."

We walked past his grandparents and great grandparents and then he stopped at a fairly large stone. "Right there, son."

I knelt down and traced my fingers through the letters:
Mary Anna Walker Braymyer
September 30, 1825
November 17, 1928

"Is this *the* Mary Anna?"

"Ha, sure is. There was only one of them."

"So she came to Texas?"

"Sure did, but not until her later years. She had a lot of adventures in her life in between."

"Where's her husband, John?"

"Oh, he's not buried here."

"But why not?"

"Well, we've got a lot to cover in the story before I get to that part, but I'll get to it eventually, I promise."

"Is that the same Rachel buried there next to her that is in your story."

"Uh huh. They were like sisters until the day they died."

Dusty Williams

September 3, 1838
The Braymyer House

Mary Anna and Rachel were in the kitchen preparing a dinner of beef stew while Alice sat in the dining room and nursed the baby. The Braymyer children were out doing the required farm chores and getting ready to settle down for a nice quiet evening when John announced the news to everyone.

He came into the kitchen where David and Alice joined them and frantically searched for the words he knew he must speak. He walked closer to Mary Anna and took her hand in his as he cleared his throat.

"Darling, we can't stay here any longer. We've got to head west."

"West? John what are you talking about."

Alice and David stared at their son as if he had lost his mind as he continued the struggle to speak. "There's been three more homes burned by Indian haters, it is not safe for us here any more."

"But John," Mary Anna said, "We can't just leave. I can go hide somewhere."

"No, little missy, I don't want you to hide your beautiful face ever. We've got to go somewhere where we are free to live in peace."

"John," Alice interrupted, "Surely there is something else we can do."

"I don't want to risk it, Ma. It's too dangerous."

"Where will you go, son?" David asked a bit concerned.

"I hear Missouri is settling up pretty nice. I figured on heading there and getting a nice piece of land."

"What will you do out in Missouri?" His father continued to question him.

"Farm. Last week Frank Sutherland said his cousin wrote to him from out that way and said that the land was the best he had ever seen."

"But, John," Mary Anna said fighting back tears. "We can't just leave, it's not right for us to have to run."

"I know, darling, but I would rather run than risk something happening to you. You mean the world to me."

Alice had tears streaming down her face as she rocked the baby. She knew as well as anyone that when John had made up his mind about something there was very little anyone could say or do to change his mind. It was a trait she had personally handed down to him.

"John," Mary Anna said, "There's something I have to tell you."

"What is it, little missy?"

"I… I'm with child."

The room fell silent. This was the first time Mary Anna had mentioned this to anyone and everyone in the room seemed taken aback at the news. John took her in his arms and embraced her with a hug as she let out tears of both joy and fear for what was up ahead.

"Well, darling that's all the more reason we need to leave. It's just not safe here."

Alice talked as she fought back tears, causing her voice to sound a little deeper than normal. "When will you leave, John?"

"Tomorrow morning."

"Tomorrow!" Mary Anna said hysterically. "Can't we wait a few weeks?"

"I'm afraid not. It's too dangerous here and winter will be upon us soon."

"John," David said, "How bout we go on a walk?"

John and David left the room, leaving the three women alone in the kitchen. Alice handed Dolly Ann to Rachel who held her across her shoulder and patted her back.

Alice wrapped her arms around her and gave her a rocking hug. "There there," she said as Mary Anna began to cry.

"What am I going to do? I don't know anything about having babies, what if something happens and you're not there to help me."

"There will be other women around, child. Someone will be there for you, John won't let you be alone when it is time."

"But I don't want to go, Ma Braymyer. It just isn't fair."

"I know, honey. But no one ever said life is fair. You should just look at this as an adventure."

They continued to hug each other and exchange tears and heartfelt disappointments that they would have to part ways.

Meanwhile, outside John and his father walked along the edge of the family property and didn't speak a word to each other until they had been walking for a good ten minutes. Neither of them knew what to say to the other, but both of them knew that it was an action that had to be made. Truth be known, David couldn't have been more proud of his son for stepping up and doing what was best for his new family.

"You can take the extra wagon and three of the mares." David said looking out over the horizon as the sun began to set. "Also, take one of the milking cows and a pig."

"Thanks, Pa. I'll pay you back as soon as I can."

"Never mind that. I was going to give it all to you anyway when you started up a farm out here. I'll also give you two hundred dollars that was to be left to you in my estate."

"Gee, Pa. Really you don't…"

"It's yours, John. It was all going to be left to you in my will anyhow."

John didn't reply, he was speechless.

"Be sure and stick to the less traveled roads, you'll have less a chance for trouble there. You also probably have to stop somewhere for winter. I doubt if you can make it to Missouri before the first snow fall and you don't want everyone getting sick on account of the cold."

"I had kind of figured I would have to. Hopefully the snow will hold off for a little bit though."

"And, John. You take care of Mary Anna. She's young and this is her first child. There will probably be complications."

"Yes, sir."

"I'm proud of you, son. I think you're doing the right thing, just be sure and write to your Ma to keep her heart at ease."

"I will, sir."

"Well come on then. Let's get you ready for the trip."

The two men worked well into the night to prepare for the journey to Missouri, while the women busied themselves inside packing things for them to take along with them. Alice had given Mary Anna a golden plate that said 'Braymyer' on it. It had been handed down three generations on David's side of the family and now it was about to embark on yet another journey.

Everyone went to bed late that night, but hardly anyone slept a wink. There was too much on everyone's mind to even think about sleep. Early the next morning and well before the sun had come up, everyone was wide awake and sat in the dining room eating their last breakfast together as a family.

It was a solemn meal and hardly anyone spoke a word. The hearts in the home were weighed heavily by not only regret, but fear as well. There were no savvy Braymyer jokes from the boys and the women rarely took their eyes off their bacon and ham.

When finished, John, Mary Anna and Rachel headed out of the front door where their wagon patiently awaited their arrival. So this is it, Mary Anna thought, this is what will take us on our long journey west. All the family was standing beside them except for Ralph who had not been seen since the night before.

"Here," Alice said to Mary Anna as she handed her a small package that was wrapped in a cloth.

"What is it?"

"Well, open it up, silly."

Mary Anna unwrapped the weathered cloth and when she did it revealed two books. One was a family bible and the other was a small blue book full of empty pages. "They're lovely, Ma." She said hugging Alice.

"I'm glad you like them, honey. You can write down all the adventures you have on your trip in that little book there so they'll never be forgotten."

John shook his father's hand and those of his brothers, while giving his sisters kisses on their cheeks. "Ma," he said saving his goodbye to Alice for the last, "We'll see each other again soon, I promise."

"I hope so, John. You be careful and take good care of the girls."

"Yes, maim." He said hugging her.

John helped Mary Anna up onto the seat and Rachel into the back of the wagon before taking his seat next to his wife. Just before pushing the wagon away from the only home he had ever know he turned back to his family and said, "Be sure and tell Ralph I said goodbye and that I'm sure sorry I missed him."

The wagon disappeared as the winding trail lead them deeper into the woods of the Smokey Mountains. For a moment, Mary Anna thought she could smell Aunt Liza's moonshine and said a silent goodbye to her three family members who lie in the ground somewhere behind her.

Three hours after they had been traveling they could see a lone rider in the road up ahead of them. They were on one of the few straight ways of the trail and just after the mysterious rider, they could see that the road began to twist and curve again.

As they drew nearer, John stared hard at the rider. "What the hell?" He said as if he had just uncovered something unexpected.

"John!" Mary Anna said at his use of words.

"Sorry, darling. But that's Ralph up there, I know the way he sits atop a horse and that's him, I'm sure of it."

When they approached the horseback rider, John was proven to be right. There, in the middle of the road sat Ralph Braymyer with his saddlebags full of things as if he were planning a long trip.

"Ralph, what are you doing?" John said un-approvingly.

"I'm coming with you, John."

"What? No you're not. You best get back home to Ma and Pa before they discover you're gone."

"I left them a note in the barn. Besides, you might need my help, one man and two women is easy prey for people out there who are looking to do harm."

"Ralph, you're only sixteen. You're needed back at the farm, not here."

"Needed? You know as well as I do that Pa's got more help than he needs and besides I don't aim to be a logger anymore anyhow."

John looked at his brother and saw that the Braymyer stubbornness had taken over him. He knew, just as if he had been in the other position that there was nothing that could be said to change his mind. "Are you sure you want to do this, Ralph? It's going to be dangerous and there is no turning back."

"I'm sure, John. I'm ready to make a life for myself and be somebody."

"Well, let's go then. But first town we come to I want you to send word to Ma and Pa and let them know you met up with me okay."

"Will do, John."

September 04, 1838

Dear Journal,

We left the Braymyer home early this morning and after only a short time traveling we got a great surprise. John's younger brother, Ralph has joined us on this adventure we are now embarking on. I was sad to leave the faces of the ones I love behind, but John says that we must leave for my safety. I am half Cherokee Indian and the army has been sent out to remove all Indians from their homeland and force them west into designated areas.

We are on our own adventure west… Missouri bound. My devoted friend, Rachel sits quietly in the back of the wagon. I fear this journey has affected her the most, although she says very little about it. She has always had a tendency to hold her feelings back, but by and by she will eventually let them all out.

I am almost thirteen and am with child. I am told that the women in my family have a history of becoming women at a very early age and I suppose I am proof of that. I never knew that someone could feel as close to something as I do my unborn child. Often times at night, I dream about who the life inside of me will become and I get so excited that I cannot sleep.

We didn't travel as far today as John wanted to, in fact we are not even out of the Smokey Mountains yet. We have set up camp for this first night underneath the large canopy of trees and as I am writing this I can hear the strange callings of the bugs that are hidden well beyond my sight.

I have written everything I know how to tonight and I must now rejoice in prayer. My eyes grow heavy and the darkness shows no sign of light in its presence.

Yours truly,

Mary Anna Braymyer
P.S. This is the first time I have signed my married name to
any paper.

September 10, 1838
On the trail in Tennessee

The small group of travelers had been on the trail for six days and already they were becoming drained by the journey west. The fall breeze offered a hint of colder weather somewhere out there and they feared they would not be able to travel much longer before they had to settle down for winter.

The sun had not been up long and Mary Anna and Rachel had just finished preparing the usual breakfast; bacon and biscuits. Ralph fed the livestock while John drank a cup of coffee and looked out over the horizon.

"John," Mary Anna said approaching his side, "Breakfast is ready."

"Okay, darling." He said putting an arm around her waist. "Isn't the land beautiful?"

Mary Anna looked, but only saw the usual… trees and hills. "Yes, John. But is it any different than our usual scenery?"

John laughed, "No, but I've noticed it slowly start to change. Not only the number and type of trees, but there is a smell in the air that seems to be getting stronger and stronger the farther west we go."

Mary Anna didn't even pretend to understand, she just stood at his side and watched the sky as the sun started to light it up from somewhere behind her. When the two of them made it back to their small campfire, Ralph and Rachel were already eating.

Ralph looked up at them as they approached. "Where have you two lovebirds been?"

"Just enjoying the view, Ralph boy, enjoying the view." John answered him slapping his hand across the back of his head in a playful mood.

"You always were a bit on the sensitive side, John. I guess not much has changed."

"Sensitive huh?" John said tackling his younger brother.

The two of them rolled around the ground while Mary Anna and Rachel laughed from the sidelines. At one point, John had his brother in a headlock, but within a matter of seconds the role was reversed. Mary Anna scooped up a small handful of the loose dirt in her hand and when John had turned just right she tossed it onto his head.

"Hey what is this, little missy! You're supposed to be on my side."

"What can I say, John," Ralph interrupted. "She's betting for the better team!"

Just as Ralph had finished talking, a pile of dirt found its way into his open mouth from the hand of Rachel. Both the men looked up at the girls who both recognized the familiar look on their faces.

Rachel and Mary Anna flew to their feet and started running as fast as they could. The men were right behind them with their longer legs and as they got closer the girls screams became louder.

Rachel was the first to get caught by Ralph who grabbed her in his arms and began tickling her. Shortly after, Mary Anna was swept off her feet by her husband and spun around in circles. When the spinning had stopped she found herself still off the ground in the safety of her husband's arms who began to kiss her.

She looked over his shoulder and saw that Ralph was looking over Rachel's shoulders into her face. Both Rachel and Ralph were lost in each other's eyes and just stood there…not making a single move. Mary Anna quickly looked away back at her husband who was waiting with another kiss.

It was late morning when the wagon left their campsite and continued westward along a trail that looked to have been traveled frequently. The sun shone brightly above them, but the September wind almost made the heat completely disappear. Mary Anna was glad that she was pregnant in the fall, for she had heard many stories of how unbearable it was to give birth in the summer time when the heat was at its climax.

There was still another hour or two of daylight left when they rode into the small town of McMinville. John parked the wagon in front of a hotel and jumped down from the seat. "Ladies," he said. "I know you two love sleeping in campsites, but how would you feel about sleeping in a nice hotel tonight?"

"Oh, John. Must you joke all the time."

"I agree," Rachel said from the back of the wagon. "You know good and well what the answer is to that question."

John just laughed as he headed for the two double doors of the hotel. Just before he stepped up to them, they both flew open and a short man with thinning hair stepped out in front of him.

"Can I help you?" He said looking up at John.

"Sure can. I need to get a couple of rooms tonight."

The man looked at John and then over towards the wagon. "Not with them two you aren't." He said loudly.

"What do you mean?"

"Exactly what I said, son. We don't allow no Negroes or Indians. And from the looks of it you got yourself one of each."

Just before John could say anything Mary Anna's voice rang out from behind him. "Don't waist your breath, John. I wouldn't rest my head on a pillow in any establishment that this man is running."

"Now you watch your tone, young lady." The man started to say.

"I sir, will speak exactly how I see fit. Tell me sir, which one of these rooms are yours." She said looking up at the windows on the second floor.

John was completely taken aback by his wife's sudden outburst and for some reason he didn't dare interrupt.

The hotelkeeper looked at Mary Anna strangely as he responded. "I don't see why it makes any difference, but the one there" he pointed, "right above the door."

"And I see you are wearing a ring. So you're married I take it?"

"Yes... where exactly are you going with this?"

"I find it funny, that's all."

"What, that I'm married?

"No. I find it funny, sir that you would refuse us a room simply because of our ancestry but you have no problem sleeping with a whore even though you are married."

Mary Anna's voice had steadily begun to rise and after her last comment a few onlookers had gathered around the scene.

"Now wait just a…" the man tried to spit out, but was overpowered by Mary Anna.

"Oh please, sir. Don't try and make excuses. I saw the whore up in your room just now. She peeked out your window down at you. Tell me, is this a respectable hotel or a whore house you're running here?"

The man's face was turning red. "Lady, this is one of the most respectable hotels in Tennessee. Now I would appreciate it if…"

"Well, hopefully after today's little incident your hotel will be the next saloon on Main Street. Good day, sir."

Mary Anna turned her head in the opposite direction, but the man was not finished talking. He looked at John and in an angry voice demanded, "Are you going to do something about your *Indian*?"

John reached back and then brought his fist smashing down into the man's face, bringing him down to the ground. "If you are referring to my wife, then no. She is standing exactly where she should be. And her name is Mary Anna."

John got back up onto the wagon and drove it out of town as fast as he could as several townspeople stood around the hotelkeeper and laughed. Once they were out of town, John stopped the wagon and looked over at Mary Anna.

Half-laughing he said, "Are you out of your mind?"

"What's that suppose to mean, John."

He shook his head as the wagon started rolling again and said, "Looks like I've been a bad influence on you yet."

"Well, just remember, John. If I can put an old hotelkeeper in his place I have no problem putting you in yours."

"Oh, Lord," he said. "Looks like we're going to have an interesting life together, Mary Anna. Interesting life."

"Mary Anna." Rachel said, "I think John's right. You've lost your desire to be proper."

"Hell, Rachel" Mary Anna said, "We're going to be living in the west now. Things like being proper and such don't seem to matter anymore." She looked around at John and then Rachel. "Besides, I won't have anyone talk to me the way that man did or to any minority for that matter."

Rachel was too shocked to say anything and John was laughing so hard that Mary Anna thought he might fall off the wagon. "I declare," he said, "I do believe you are acting more and more like Ma everyday."

"Why thank you," she said and turned her stare toward the western sky.

A week after they left McMinville they came upon another small town called Lebanon. They had no trouble in this town and were able to lodge with a small family in their log cabin for the night.

September 18, 1838

Dear Journal,

We spent last night in a small cozy log cabin with the pleasant company of the Lemon family. They all had red hair just like Ma Braymyer and each one of them showed us kindness in their own way. We are now back on the trail and John says that in little over a week we will be in Kentucky.

I fear again for my dear friend, Rachel. I notice a small interest between her and my brother in law, Ralph. This would be good news because it would mean that her and I could become sisters in reality. But the fact remains that she is half Negro and the two of them would have all kinds of trouble trying to live out a peaceful life together.

My dear friend told me recently that she fears she will never find love as long as she lives. She said that she feels as though she is too black to be white and too white to be black. How hard it must be for her to carry this heavy burden on her mind. I keep her in my constant prayers and I know that wherever life may lead her it will be toward a good place.

We got word while we were in Lebanon that the hotel in McMinville was burned down shortly after we left. I suppose I should feel somewhat bad for the fiery outcome, but I honestly feel nothing. The hatred that can exist between two bodies of people can be greater than the strongest storms known to men and sometimes I feel as though it is my duty to rid the world of such people.

Ralph killed a deer early this morning so we are all anxious to set up camp tonight and feast. John says that he thinks I am getting fatter on account of the baby, but every time I look down at myself I see nothing different. Perhaps he is just excited about becoming a father. I secretly hope that it is a daughter, just so I can see the look on his face when he realizes it is not the son he has been wishing for. I know it sounds cruel, but I think a daughter first would be good for him, perhaps soften him up a bit.

Ralph says that I am having a boy for sure, because all the Braymyers produce a boy child as their first born. I told him that girls are more dominant on my side, but he said it didn't matter because the Braymyer seed was stronger. I had never heard of a child being referred to as a seed before, but I suppose it makes enough sense.

Each day that passes I grow more anxious to get to our new home, wherever that might be. Unfortunately, John says we will most likely have to stay in Kentucky for the winter and that we might be there for six months. I have never been to Kentucky and just to think that my child might be born there. It gives me a sense of excitement.

Rachel and John both say that I am changing. They say that I am becoming tougher and much less proper. This is much to John's approval, but Rachel worries I will lose my southern roots. The only change that I see is that my chest slowly grows outward.

I will be thirteen next week and when we were in Lebanon, John bought me something. It is sitting in the back of the wagon with Rachel still neatly wrapped up. He said I could not have it until the day of my birthday. Oh how I hate to wait for such things. It is a lot like waiting for the birth of this child.

We got a letter from Ma Braymyer a few days ago. She wrote and told us that someone bought Aunt Liza's old home place. It doesn't make any difference to me, I shall never visit that place again. Especially so long as that tree still stands that I found my brother hanging from that dreadful day… But alas, life goes on and the best thing I can do for my family is to live not only for myself but for them.
A heavy heart,
Mary Anna Braymyer

September 20, 1838
Smokey Mountains

David Braymyer and two of his sons, Jerry and Wilson were headed down to the river to check for some driftwood that they might make some money off of. The autumn leaves had begun to fall heavily to the wooded ground and they were hoping to get one more good run of wood before winter settled in.

When they approached the riverbank they were excited to see that three logs had jammed themselves together side by side right in the middle of the water. David stepped out towards them with a rope in his hand and by the time he was mid way toward them he had to swim due to the depth of the water.

 When he reached the large log closest to him he tried to pull it away from the other so that he could get the rope around it and stretch it back ashore. He desperately tried to separate the log, but it was too heavy for him.

"Boys!" He shouted, "Come help me get this log loose. I'm not strong enough."

The two boys swam out to their father and began to try and help him with the task at hand. The water was flowing rapidly and it had been cooled drastically from the changing of the seasons.

David was in the middle of the log with one of his sons on each of his sides. He would count to three and all at once they would try and pull it away together. It slowly started to move away against the current in their direction.

Just as it had almost been pulled back enough to wrap the rope around it and unseen enemy was making its way down river behind them. None of them saw it until it was right upon them and there was nothing they could do.

Another log, larger than any of the three they were now after slammed against them, pinning them between itself and the log they had been trying to free. The three of them were knocked unconscious and as the log bobbed back and forth they slowly sank to the bottom and were carried down river.

Three hours later, another logger found the bodies and fished them out of the cold water. He loaded them up onto his wagon that had been meant to carry his logs and headed toward the Braymyer home.

The next day, Alice walked away from their family cemetery a widow with five small children. She wasted no time after she had buried her sons and husband and within an hour she was aboard a wagon with her surviving children headed to Missouri. There just wasn't anything left for her in the Smokey Mountains.

December 12, 1994
Oklahoma

Pappy's old Chevy truck, or Old Blue as we called it, rolled down an Oklahoma highway heading north as I sat in the passenger seat with my feet on the dash board chewing on a piece of straw. It had been a light winter so far and we hadn't had any snow or ice yet.

A country station played quietly on the radio and I enjoyed every bit of this adventure we were now on. Our windows were cracked and occasionally I would get a scent of someone burning firewood somewhere nearby as we drove past.

The truck suddenly pulled over into the shoulder and Pappy looked over at me. "Son, why don't you drive for awhile? I need to rest my eyes."

"Me? But I'm not old enough."

"Shoot, you'd probably do a whole lot better than some of these Oklahoma drivers. Come on now, you can handle it."

He got out of the truck and walked around the back end of it until re entering the now empty passenger side as I had crawled over the console. "Are you sure about this, Pappy? I mean I don't know where to go. What if I get lost?"

"You just stay on this highway here and it will take us all the way to the border. Now come on, put it in drive and let's go. And don't tell your grandma about this. She'll skin both our heads."

I cautiously shifted into drive and put my foot on the pedal, nearly sending Pappy through the front windshield. "Easy son! Not so hard!"

"Sorry, sir."

I pulled back out onto the highway and for my first time to ever drive a vehicle I thought I was doing a pretty good job. Within minutes, Pappy had already fallen asleep and was snoring, just as most old people do.

Since I had been blessed with the luck God had given a fly, it began to snow shortly after I had taken control of the wheel. After turning on every other light the truck had to offer I finally managed to get the windshield wipers on as Pappy continued to sleep the day away.

It suddenly hit me as I sat behind the wheel that it was a truck very similar to this one that had killed my parents. My daddy was a bull rider and he and my mama were on their way back from a rodeo when the accident happened.

Normally I would have gone with them, but they wanted some time to themselves so they left me behind with Pappy. I was sitting in the front room of the house when Grandma Rose came through the front door with the news. It's sad to say, but I don't even really remember how the news affected me.

I think I felt more badly for Grandma Rose. There is something about seeing your grandmother, or your mother for that matter cry. And when I saw the tears stream uncontrollably down her face it was like someone turned the water on to my eyes. Like I said though, my daddy was a bull rider so I was raised to be tough and crying was not an option, but he wasn't there that day so I cried.

Driving the truck made me feel as though my parents were with me somehow, which up until this point had never happened. I would occasionally pass other drivers and wave at them just as Pappy always did, but most of them had to take a second look at me and then they slowed down dramatically.

Sitting behind the wheel I felt like a new person, more grown up. I wish the cousins could see me now and say that I would never amount to anything. I was driving a truck, while most of

460

them were still probably playing with toys and such. From this point forward I felt like an adult and I have never been happier in my life.

As I drove down the road to Braymyer Ridge I found myself wondering more about the journey of John and Mary Anna and how hard it must have been to do it by wagon. I was glad Pappy and I had the truck or I'm not sure how I would have managed the snow falling from the sky.

Dusty Williams

September 25, 1838
Near the border

The wagon continued to roll and bump along the muddy trail as it neared the Kentucky border. A steady drizzle of rain blanketed the travelers and their surroundings, making the air thick and hard to draw breath from.

Mary Anna was now thirteen and already more a woman than most girls her age. She waited patiently for John to give her whatever he had hidden for her in the back of the wagon, but the day continued to dwindle away and he showed no sign of handing it to her yet.

It was late afternoon when they crossed the border and entered into Kentucky. It was the first time the Braymyer brothers had ever left the state of Tennessee and they truly felt as if they had now embarked on the journey that would lead them throughout the rest of their lives.

Almost as soon as they crossed over the rain ceased to fall and the warm sun attempted to shine down on them. It seemed as though Tennessee was crying for their departure, but Kentucky was glad to have them.

John pulled the wagon off of the trail and forced the horses to a stop by pulling back on the reins. Mary Anna was the first one out of the wagon and as soon as she hit the ground she knelt down and grabbed a handful of dirt. She let it slowly fall from between her fingers and rather than hitting the ground immediately, a light wind carried it away a little ways.

"So this is Kentucky." She said.

"That it is, my darling," John said walking up behind her. He put his arms around her and when they appeared in front of her she saw that he was holding the mysterious package in his right hand. "Here you go, little missy. Happy birthday."

Mary Anna took the package and then turned around to face him. She never took her eyes off of the present as she ripped the brown paper away from it. Within seconds she was holding up a beautiful blue dress, the likes of which she had never seen before even in her southern plantation days.

"Oh, John. It's beautiful. Rachel look!" She said turning toward her friend who had just exited the wagon with Ralph's help.

"That's beautiful, Mary Anna," she answered her.

"So you like it?" John said looking down into her eyes.

"Like it? John I love it! And look, it's got a blue ribbon for my hair as well."

"I know you lost most of your nice clothing in the fire, darling so I thought we should start building your wardrobe back up. Go on, go put it on."

Mary Anna ran around to the back of the wagon where no one was and quickly changed into her new dress. It fit her perfectly and the satin material felt like heaven against her skin. Once she had it the way she wanted it, she tied the matching bow in her dark hair and smoothed the wrinkles in the dress out one last time before emerging in front of everyone again.

When she stepped out from behind the comfort of the wagon, John had to catch his mouth from dropping so low that it near hit his chest. He had always thought his wife was the most beautiful woman on earth, but never had he thought that she could look as good as she did at that moment. It was as if she were an angel that had just descended down from the sky above and was now blessing everyone with her presence.

"Well," she said walking up to John, "What do you think?"

"Never in my life have I seen a woman as beautiful as you are now, darling," he answered her as he leaned down to kiss her.

While they were in the midst of engaging in one of the most romantic kisses either of them had ever experienced, Mary Anna felt something nudging against the back of her legs. She pulled away from John's touch and turned to see what it was.

"Shoo!" Rachel yelled, "Go on and get out of here."

Behind Mary Anna was a small puppy that was trying to wrap itself up in the bottom of her dress. It was black and white and had longer hair than most dogs she had seen.

"Oh, John," she said leaning down and picking him up. "He's nothing but skin and bones. Can we keep him?"

John looked at his wife and ran his hand over the dog's head and started laughing. "If I were to tell you no, would it matter anyway?"

"No, I don't suppose it would. Come on, he can't eat that much anyhow."

"Alright then, I guess you had better come up with a name for him."

"Where do you suppose he came from, John."

"Who knows, he probably ran off from a nearby farm and as young as he is I imagine there's more out there somewhere."

She looked down into the puppy's face and thought long and hard about what she should call this small animal that had immediately been drawn to her. The dog began to lick the tan skin on her arm, "I think I shall call him, Cherokee."

"Hey," Ralph said, "That's not a bad name at all."

Shortly after discovering their new friend, they set up camp beneath a large tree that had already lost most of its leaves. Ralph had killed another deer earlier that day and they feasted on it well into the night in celebration of not only Mary Anna's birthday, but of their arrival in Kentucky.

The moon was barely a quarter and had they not had a large fire there would have been little light as they sat around the warming flames. Mary Anna rested her head on John's shoulder with Cherokee in her other arm, while Ralph and Rachel sat on opposite sides of the fire at their sides.

"John," Rachel said, "How about telling us a story?"

"Yes, John," Mary Anna said looking up at him, "That's a good idea."

"A story? Hmm, I think Ralph should tell us one, he's a lot better at that sort of stuff. What do you say, Ralph?"

"Well, let's see if I can think of one. Did you ever hear about the witch in Kentucky?"

"Witch?" Mary Anna said tightening her grip around John's leg.

"In Kentucky?" Rachel said.

"Oh, yes… it's a famous story in the Smokey Mountains. You see, a long time ago not very far from where we are now there was an old lady that lived all alone in a little old log cabin. Only, she wasn't a normal old lady, she was a witch and she had bears for pets.

"Bears?" Rachel interrupted.

"That's right. And you see, every night she would send these bears out to catch young women and bring them back to her."

"Why only young women?" Mary Anna asked.

"Because, she was real ugly and when the bears brought her back a young woman she would suck the beauty out of them for herself, leaving the women deformed and so ugly that they couldn't even look at their own reflection.

I would guess that about seventeen women were taken and only two of them were found. When the law found them, they didn't even recognize who they were. Well a posse was formed to try and catch this witch and take her to the gallows to be hung.

All eight men that were in that posse rode out to her house and none of them were ever seen again. The witch's house was empty when the second posse rode up onto it and the witch has never been seen again."

"What happened to her?" Rachel asked as her eyes continued to widen.

"Nobody knows exactly. Some say that she's still around with her bears, looking for young girls to snatch away into the woods and suck their beauty away. Me, I think she still wonders Kentucky and since she gained so much beauty from her victims, why I wouldn't be surprised if it's someone we know... you just never know."

Just as Ralph finished the story the two girls swore they heard a bear growl from somewhere in the woods. They both screamed as loud as they could, Mary Anna jumping into John's lap and Rachel into Ralph's. They didn't get hardly any sleep that night for fear that they would be taken away and lose all their beauty, but the next day as the wagon rolled away from camp the two of them found themselves lost in sleep beneath the Kentucky sun.

Dusty Williams

October 01, 1838
Dear Journal,

We received the most dreadful news today. When we stopped in a small settlement of no more than fifty people, John had a letter waiting for him from his mother. It pains me to write this down, but I know I shall feel better if I put it to paper. John's Pa and two of John's brothers, Jerry and Wilson were killed in a logging accident.

I feel so terrible for John and Ralph and I can tell that they wish they would have stayed behind in Tennessee so that they could have been there to help. I can see the face of regret as it takes over them and fills their bodies. Ma Braymyer also said in her letter that she and her children will be joining us in Missouri.

I suppose in the face of so much tragedy that this is a small bit of good news, for we will all be together again…those of us remaining anyway. John says that she is already on the trail and that we will stop soon and set up our winter camp to allow them to catch up to us.

John puts on a strong face every morning, but I know he is hurting inside. We have decided that if we have a son we will name him David Walker Braymyer, after his father and my family, but we shall call him Walkie after my brother. So much has happened this past year that I can hardly believe any of it to be true.

I started the year in my southern plantation home where we were forced away from it because of the hatred man has for my father's people. We then found ourselves in the Smokey Mountains where moonshine is a necessity and now we are on the trail to Missouri. I am lucky to have a husband that loves me so and I try as hard as I can to show him as much love as he does me every day.

John is my life long companion and if anything should ever
happen to him I do not know how I will proceed with my life.
Love, I think, is a strange little thing. No more than six
months ago I had no idea what the word even meant, but now
I cannot imagine my life without it...without John.

Confused and emotional,
Mary Anna Braymyer

December 12, 1994
Oklahoma

The road continued to stretch out before me as Pappy continued to sleep. The snow came and went, but the trees and grass around us held tightly to their white blanket. The highway showed very little signs of much traffic other than ourselves and only occasionally would I see a car coming from the other direction as we passed each other.

The road began to twist and curve throughout large hills that I had convinced myself were ancient Indian burial grounds. Up and down went the road and I felt completely in control of not only the truck, but of the world. As I ventured around a turn in the road, the snow began to pour down with greater force than I had seen at all that day.

I could barely read the sign as I sped past it that read, 'Arkansas.' Had I taken a wrong turn, I questioned myself. Pappy never said anything about driving through Arkansas. Oh boy, I've really done it now. Who knows where I'm driving us to.

"Pappy? Wake up."

There was no sign that he had heard or acknowledged my attempt to wake him from his deep sleep. I stretched over as far as I could and began to shake him to try and stir him from his sleep. As I continued to shake his body, I soon noticed that the whole truck was rocking back and forth.

When I looked back at the road in front of me, it was no where to be found. There was only the side of a snow-covered hill as we quickly descended down it toward the bottom. I began screaming as loud as I could and had the tightest grip on the steering wheel I have ever had in my life.

October 12, 1838
Kentucky

John had just lost his father and he was not there. Had he been there, perhaps it could have been him that would have been killed, rather than his younger brother, Wilson. If only he had been there, then maybe he could have stopped the rolling log from slamming into his beloved family.

Surely he could have protected them. They were not supposed to die. He never dreamed that the day he left his home was going to be the last time he was to ever see them again. And now, his mother with small children was making the journey alone. What if something happened to them? How could he live with himself?

The only thing in the world that brought him hope and peace was his wife, Mary Anna. She had a way of lifting his spirits so high that he felt as though he were flying and she didn't even have to try. She had a special way about her that made her different from all other women out there.

She could be polite and the most proper woman any man could ever know, but if crossed she could turn into the wild west woman she had just gotten to know herself. John loved her for all of this and couldn't imagine his life without her.

He was glad Ralph had come along. That was one decision he didn't regret, because had he told him no, Ralph would have probably ended up dead with the rest of his family. Ralph was hurt by the news of his father and brothers just like John, but Ralph was able to push past most anything with greater ease than most people.

He spent very little time dwelling on things no matter how severe a problem might be. Rather than wilt away, he saw things how they were, accepted them and moved on with no regret. John envied his brother for this passion of life he seemed to have about him and although he had much of the same quality within himself he had a harder time of noticing it.

John was now the head of his father's family since he was the oldest surviving son. He had spent very little time debating this new fact that had blessed itself upon him, but vowed that he would not let his father down. He would tend to his wife and their unborn child, while ensuring that his mother and siblings were afforded the same opportunity in life.

Since crossing into Kentucky they had traveled seventeen days across the new land as they headed west. John had decided that he wanted to get as close to the Mississippi River as possible so that when spring came all they had to do was cross it and they would be in Missouri.

Mary Anna was greatly saddened over the death of her new father in law, but she had a secret perk in her step over the fact that Alice would soon be joining them. From the moment she first saw her mother in law, they became instant friends and she became to Mary Anna the mother she had never had.

"There it is," John said pointing ahead of them.

"My goodness," Mary Anna replied, "That has to be the biggest river I have ever seen."

"That there is the great Mississippi," Ralph interrupted as he rode up beside them.

The water rushed before them as it headed down toward the great unknown with its whitecaps and terrific speed. The other side was Missouri and as they looked out across it they felt a sense of relief even though they knew they must first cross the raging river in front of them.

But for now they could rest easy because they wouldn't be crossing the river until sometime next year. John's mother would be meeting them sometime within the next month and he didn't want her to try and cross the river alone.

"John," Mary Anna said as she looked upon the river. "Have you ever seen a river like this one?"

"No, can't say that I have, but I have heard plenty of stories about this one. They say that once you cross the river you are officially in the west. Look out there at Missouri, darling. Isn't it beautiful?"

"It is, John. I can't wait to make our home here."

"Well, we've got to find a place to settle down for winter. The store clerk a few miles back said there was a cabin nearby that we could hold up in. I reckon we ought to see if we can find it. Ralph, you want to ride with me to scout for the cabin?"

"Will do, John."

"Darling," John said to his wife, "You and Rachel stay here while we go search for it. Don't wander too far from the wagon, okay?"

"I won't, John. Just promise me you'll be careful."

"I will, darling," he said kissing her.

John and Ralph rode north east from where the wagon was in search of their temporary home. Mary Anna and Rachel watched them in the morning sun as they headed out of sight.

"Come on, Rachel. Let's go down to the water."

"But, Mary Anna. Isn't that a little dangerous."

"Oh, who cares. Come on. Just think, in minutes we'll be touching the great Mississippi River and have its water running smoothly across our feet. Now come on."

Mary Anna led Rachel by the hand down to the eastern shore of the river. It was mostly rocks as they approached the water, but there was also some driftwood and sand scattered across the riverbank.

Once down, Mary Anna was the first to put her bare feet into the cool water. Cherokee anxiously drank from the river at her side as she ventured a little farther into its midst. Rachel eventually got up the courage to join her and before long the two of them were ankle deep in the Mississippi River.

"Doesn't the water feel wonderful, Rachel."

"Yes, it's a little cold. Not warm like the water in Georgia."

"Well, we're not in Georgia anymore, Rachel so I guess we best get used to it."

"I suppose you're right. Mary Anna, don't you get scared about this whole ordeal?"

"The river? No, water has never really frightened me."

"No, not the water. The trip to Missouri. I mean, what if things don't work out, suppose something goes wrong and we're helpless."

"Rachel, you've got to learn not to worry so much about things. Besides, I've never been helpless a day in my life and I doubt if God will lay that upon me now. It's an adventure, Rachel so we should just make the best of it and hope things turn out in our favor."

"What about the baby, Mary Anna?"

"The baby? What do you mean?"

"I mean aren't you scared? Doesn't it frighten you that you will soon give birth to a child? What if something was to go wrong there. I don't know anything about birthing children and you know as well as I do that neither does John and Ralph."

Mary Anna hadn't thought about the danger in childbirth and the thought had just struck her. Several of her grandfather's slaves had died during childbirth and she remembered well the nights that their screams of agony had kept her awake.

She quickly pushed away the fear that had somehow managed to sneak up on her. "No, Rachel I am not scared. And besides, Ma Braymyer will be here by then and she'll know exactly what to do."

"I suppose you're right, but I still worry for you. How are you able to remain so strong and fearless?"

"I don't know, Rachel. A year ago I would have been just as frightened as you, but I feel as though something has changed within me. Perhaps burying the last of my family has sparked something inside of me that has taken control of my outlook on life. Or maybe, having a child inside of me has caused me to think more like a mother than a schoolgirl. Whatever the reason is, Rachel, I am certain it is all a part of life and I'm going to enjoy every bit of it."

"You're brave, Mary Anna, I wish I could be more like you. Besides, you haven't buried all your family yet, I'm still here."

"I know you are, Rachel. But you'll always be there no matter what, if something were to happen to you I am quite certain that the exact same thing would happen to me. We're best friends and we do everything together, which is why I think we'll go out at the same time."

"You know, Mary Anna. I overheard a story from one of Mr. Walker's field hands that I have never told another soul before."

"Really," Mary Anna said swishing the water around with her feet. "Do tell."

"Well, I do not know it to be truthful or not, but I don't see why they would lie about it. Last year I was sent to the barn to fetch some milk for Mr. Walker and when I stepped into the barn there were two field hands standing there talking.

I was curious, so I didn't make my presence known and I listened in on their conversation. Mary Anna, they were talking about my Ma."

"No! Really? What did they say?"

"Well the part I heard was that her and Mr. Walker was sweet on each other and often times he would come and find her in the middle of the night. I know this sounds horrible and I'll stop if you like."

"Are you kidding, keep telling…please."

"So the field hand, he said to the other that Mr. Walker was my Pa."

"What? Oh my goodness, Rachel! That makes us blood related!"

"Yes, I know, but I never wanted to say anything on account that it might hurt your grandmother's feelings. But I guess since she's dead now, there's no hurt in telling the story."

"Did they say anything else?"

"Not really. Only that they thought I resembled Mr. Walker a whole lot, even more so than your Ma is what they said."

"Oh, Rachel. That means you are my aunt."

"I suppose, but Mary Anna, don't tell anyone. It would only bring trouble to you and John and I don't want that at all."

"Trouble? Don't be ridiculous, Rachel. I should be proud to call you my aunt, even if you are younger than me."

"Please, Mary Anna. You must promise not to tell our secret, I only ask this for your protection."

"Well, if you insist. But if you change your mind, let me know and I shall tell the whole world about our relationship."

Cherokee refused to venture very far out into the water and after awhile he simply laid down and took a nap on the bank. Mary Anna and Rachel continued to wade across the shallow portion of the cool water. They soon joined the happy puppy on the bank and sat down on either side of him.

"Rachel," Mary Anna whispered.

"What? Why are we whispering?"

"Shh. There is a rider just to the south of us."

Rachel started to turn her head to look, but Mary Anna snapped out at her. "Don't look! We don't want them to know we see them. Now, we need to very slowly head up to the wagon, okay?"

"Okay. But what are we going to do? What if it's the witch?"

"Just come on, Rachel. Follow me."

Mary Anna casually stood up and headed up toward the wagon with Rachel and Cherokee following close behind. By the time they reached the wagon, the rider was even closer than before.

Mary Anna took small quick glances in the rider's direction and pretended as if she were carrying out her daily duties around the wagon. "It looks like an Indian," she whispered to Rachel.

"But you are part Indian, Mary Anna. So he will be friendly to us."

"That's not how it works, Rachel. Some Indians hate each other. It's kind of like the English and the French."

"The what?"

"Never mind. Wait here, I am going to go get John's gun."

Mary Anna stepped into the back of the wagon and pulled out John's shotgun. She had only loaded a gun once before in her life when her grandfather had insisted on her doing so. She carefully poured the powder down into it just as she had been showed and when everything was situated she cocked it back.

She leaned the gun up against the wagon and stepped around to the other side where Rachel was waiting. When she emerged next to her, the Indian rider was standing directly in front of the two of them. Something about his face scared Mary Anna and caused her to fear for their lives.

He had red and black paint under his eyes that gleamed with anger and hatred. He looked down on the two of them from his white horse which had also been painted up by the same stuff underneath his eyes.

He didn't speak a word, his only sign of communication was his fierce stare upon the two girls. "Can we help you?" Mary Anna asked.

The Indian began screaming in a foreign tongue as he waved his left hand throughout the air.

Mary Anna looked at him as silence conquered the scene. "Look, if you want something you're going to have to tell us in English or there's nothing we can do."

The Indian appeared to become even angrier with her although he couldn't understand a word she was saying. He reached behind his back and pulled out a bow and arrow. He lifted it up and pointed it toward the girls, holding the feather end of the arrow between two of his fingers.

Mary Anna who was right next to the wagon slowly reached behind her and stretched her arm around to the back of the wagon where she had left the loaded gun. She struggled to find it as if she were looking for something in the pitch darkness of the night. Finally she felt the barrel and she slowly pulled it towards her, keeping it hid behind her back.

The Indian began to shout again and was now waving his weapon back and forth between the two of them. Just when Rachel feared that an arrow was about to strike her chest, the air was taken over by the loud crash of a gunshot.

The Indian fell to the ground and Mary Anna looked down at her gun in disbelief. She had not fired and it was still loaded, how had this happened. The girls turned sharply behind them to see John and Ralph standing there with guns in their hands. John's gun had smoke fusing out of the barrel as they looked upon them.

He ran up to his wife and wrapped her in his arms. "Are you okay, darling?"

"Yes, John, I'm fine. I was about to shoot him myself you know."

John laughed, "Gee thanks, little missy. I'll see to it that I don't interfere next time."

Rachel was still in too much shock, but Ralph could be heard behind his brother laughing right along with him.

"Well, did you find the cabin?" Mary Anna asked.

"Sure did, you ready to go?"

She looked over at the dead Indian. "Yes, I think I'm ready now."

- - - - - - - - - - - - - - -

The cabin was about a half a mile from where the Indian had just been shot and it didn't take them no time to get there. When they rode up to it, they could tell that it had been sitting empty for quite some time.

It was made out of large logs, about seven or eight, stacked on top of each other with an old roof made of a combination of wood, mud and grass. At the west end, which was the end facing the river that could not be seen from this point, was a rock fireplace that barely stretched above the peak of the roof.

Around the base of the home the wild grass had grown up and had turned brown due to the fall weather. It was in a clearing that looked to have been farmland at one time, with trees to the north and east of it. The front door as they approached it was on the south end and only had a small square shaped porch.

Mary Anna looked beyond the house and on a small hill just before the tree line she could see three tombstones. She was reminded of the family cemeteries back home and how scattered her family had become.

John helped her in and she slowly made her way inside, being the first one of the group to do so. She brushed away spider webs from her face and hair as the floor beneath her creaked the farther in she went. To her left there was a small mantel above the fireplace and three rocking chairs. There were also two beds, a kitchen table and another long table that could be used to prepare food on.

In all, the four of them had lucked out in getting so lucky as to find a place like this one. It would keep them warm during the winter and protected from the outside storms that would normally threaten to freeze them to death.

"What happened to the people who used to live here, John?"

"Man's wife and children got sick and died so he headed farther out west. Just left it sitting here, or at least that's what the store clerk told me."

"That's a shame. Well, after a little cleaning up I think it'll make a fine home."

"Well don't get too comfortable, little missy. We've still got some journeying to do once spring gets here."

"I know that, silly. But it will make us a fine winter home. That's what this place will be to us, our very own winter home."

John leaned down and kissed her on the forehead, "Make it up however you want, darling. Ralph and I are going to go check out the barn out back and see if it's suitable for the animals.

The men left the girls alone in the small, but cozy house and headed to the barn that sat just to the east of it. Mary Anna and Rachel continued to explore their winter home and everything it had to offer.

"Isn't it wonderful?" Mary Anna said.

"Yes, I suppose it will do the job. I don't understand you, Mary Anna. You grow up in a big plantation home in Georgia and you think this log cabin is wonderful?"

"Well, it's John and mine's first home together as husband and wife. Oh, Rachel can you see it. We'll get it all cleaned up and by the time Ma Braymyer gets here, she'll be so thrilled."

"Well," Rachel said looking around at the dust filled house, "We had better get started now."

The two of them moved all the furniture outside into the front yard and when the house was completely empty they began scrubbing the floors. There was a small well to the west, barely large enough to fit the bucket down into, but it managed to reach water just the same.

They hauled in eight buckets full of water and threw them onto the floor, drowning it in water. After the floor was completely soaked they took some small cloths and a broom that they had found in the cabin and began to clean the floors. Mary Anna brought in one last bucketful of water and dipped her broom into it.

She lifted the wet broom up and began sweeping the walls and ceiling, ridding them of their ancient cobwebs. There was a window on the east side of the one room house which is where the kitchen was and the autumn wind pushed through it giving the house a scent of freshness.

When the floors, walls and ceiling were done, they began cleaning the fireplace. They threw in two buckets of water and scrubbed away all the old ash that had been left to rot in the fireplace. Mary Anna took one of the cloths and wetted it down, using it to dust off the mantel above the rock fire pit.

Alas the inside of the house was finished and it looked like a completely new home than that of what they saw when they first arrived. The two of them went outside and began cleaning all the furniture.

Slowly, one by one they brought the furniture back into the house and placed it where they wanted it. They put the long table beneath the open window in the kitchen and the eating table in an open area right near it. They pushed in the four chairs around it and were satisfied that the kitchen was complete.

Next, they brought in the two large beds, which could sleep two people easily. They placed one on either side of the fireplace and then scattered the rockers out in between them. Mary Anna brought in the quilts from the wagon and she made one bed while Rachel made the other.

There was a nail hanging on the north wall directly in front of the front door and Mary Anna hung her elegant blue dress from it so that it would be the first thing someone saw when they entered. She then dug around the wagon and pulled out the painting of her great grandmother that had hung on Aunt Liza's wall.

She hung it up on the same wall as the front door near the dining room table, just as Aunt Liza had had it. She carefully placed the golden plate that read 'Braymyer' on top of the mantel and on one side of it she put their family bible, which would soon hold the name of their unborn child.

On the other side of the large plate, she placed the journal that Alice had given to her and the ink pen next to it. After everything was situated, Mary Anna and Rachel began to unload the wagon of everything else. They placed the smaller blankets on the back of the rocking chairs and sat the sewing material in the seats for it would soon be time to begin making the baby's clothing.

They hauled in all the food that they had with them, including the cornmeal sacks, flour, sugar, bacon and salt pork and placed it all on the long table beneath the window. Mary Anna hung John's shotgun above the front door and had to stand on a chair to do so, although John could reach it with ease.

Mary Anna removed the two kerosene lamps from the wagon and placed one in the kitchen and one on the mantel. The house was finally looking like a home and she couldn't wait until John and Ralph saw what her and Rachel had done. The two girls placed their hands on their hips and looked around the room in satisfaction.

"Come on, Rachel. Let's go see what the boys are doing in the barn. We should probably take them a glass of water anyhow."

They stepped out onto the freshly swept porch and walked towards the barn whose double doors were wide open. John and Ralph had thrown a bunch of the molding hay out of the doors and it smelled of horse manure as Mary Anna and Rachel walked across it to get inside.

When they stepped inside the door, which faced the house it revealed four separate stalls, two on each side of the main walkway. John and Ralph were finishing up the last two stalls when they approached them.

"Will the barn be good enough for the animals, John?" Mary Anna asked stepping into the stall her husband was in.

John turned around relieved to see his wife with a cup of water. He ran the top of his arm across his forehead to rid it of the small amount of sweat that had accumulated there. "I reckon it will do just fine. It's in a lot better shape that I had thought."

He took the water from her and drank from the tin cup, just as Ralph did to the cup that Rachel had brought him. "How's the house looking?" John asked.

"It's all done."

"You work fast, Mary Anna and lookie there," he said looking down at her stomach. "I think your stomach is a little bigger today."

Mary Anna laughed as John knelt down and kissed her belly and then arose to kiss her. "John, I think you may be going blind."

"It's growing, Mary Anna I swear it is. Tell her, Rachel."

"Well… wait a minute, don't get me involved in this."

The echo of laughter filled the barn and their winter home for the first time in probably a very long time. "Come on, John. I want you to come see the house."

Mary Anna took him by the hand and led him inside while Rachel and Ralph waited in the barn. "What's the hurry, little missy?" He said as her short feminine body pulled his tall masculine one.

"I just want you to see, that's all."

Mary Anna pulled him inside through the front door and she could tell by the look on his face that he was satisfied with her work. "Wow, Mary Anna. It looks amazing. How did you learn to keep a house so well?"

"I don't know. I suppose it is my Georgia roots."

"Well, it looks like I lucked out. I done got me a wife that can keep a house better than any woman I know."

"Ha, I think you lucked out in more than one area, John. I can do a lot of things better than any woman you know."

"Oh, well aren't you just a little smart thing. Come here you."
He took her in his arms and kissed her in their first home
together.

"John, do you think Ma Braymyer will be pleased with the
house?"

"Are you kidding? I mean sure I had my doubts when I first
saw the place, but now. I mean look at it."

"Good, I hope she likes it."

He kissed her again.

"So which bed is ours?"

"This one over here." She pointed to the bed that was along
the same wall as the door.

"Well let's try it out and see if it's comfortable enough."

He threw himself down onto the feather mattress and looked
up at the shining ceiling. Mary Anna lay down beside him,
resting her head in the pit of his arm with her hand on top of
his chest. She looked down and noticed that there was no
space between them due to her stomach, which was sticking
out more than she had ever noticed.

"John," she said joining his gaze at the ceiling. "I think you're
right."

"Well I'm always right, darling, but what am I right about this
time."

She lifted her hand and slapped him playfully on the chest,
"About my stomach. I think it's growing."

"Told you so."

"John, do you ever worry that something might happen? I mean with the baby and all."

"Well sure I do, you're the most important person in the world to me and I'd die if something ever happened to you."

"John, I'm real sorry about your Pa. I know we haven't really talked about it."

"I know you're sorry, darling. But dwelling on the past doesn't get us anywhere in life so it's best to just look and live for the good things, like you and I."

"When do you think Ma Braymyer will be here?"

"Depends on the trail and the weather. Two months or so I'd say."

"Oh good, maybe she can help me keep you in line."

"Keep me in line, huh?" He said tickling her and then rolling over on top of her where he met her with a kiss. Though they both knew they wouldn't be here long, they were proud to make their first home together in Kentucky, right near the Mississippi River.

December 12, 1994
The bottom of a snowy hill

The truck continued to slide and bump its way down to the bottom of a snowy hill. As I look back now, I can't help but to laugh at the reaction on Pappy's face as he was awakened from his deep sleep.

He must have hit his head three or four times on the roof of the truck before he finally started to speak. My Pappy never cursed, but in all my life I have never heard the S or the D word as many times as I did in that bumpy truck. The two words seemed to go hand in hand with each other as he continued to spit them out on our descent.

I think I feared more that I had disappointed Pappy than I did for my own life. Given my unnatural bad luck, when we finally hit the bottom of the hill we found ourselves on another road, being spit out right in front of a car that was heading west. Luckily, the car laid on its horn and swerved around us as it continued down the road.

The truck sat there in the middle of the road as I caught my breath and Pappy viewed our surroundings. "Pappy, I think you should drive now."

He looked over at me and in a laughing voice said, "No, John. You're doing fine. Just keep on driving."

"But Pappy…"

"It's okay, son. We needed a little bit of adventure anyhow. Now come on, give it some gas and let's get back on down the road."

"But, Pappy, we're in Arkansas."

"Arkansas! What do you mean?"

491

"Well, I passed a sign that said, Arkansas. I did what you said, I never turned off the highway. Not once."

Pappy began laughing uncontrollably, "Well I guess that was my mistake then. It doesn't matter anyhow, just head west and we'll cut up north towards Missouri here in a little bit."

"Pappy, are you sure I should be driving?"

"Of course. No one is perfect, we all make some sort of mistakes. Shoot, I've been in wrecks before, but that didn't keep me from getting back behind the wheel."

"But what if we die like Mama and Daddy?"

Pappy looked at me with a sense of understanding. "I know you're scared, son. But what happened to your parents shouldn't make you afraid of driving, just because it happened to them doesn't mean it will happen to you."

"But why did it happen to them, sir?"

"It was God's will, son. He needed your Daddy up in Heaven to ride bulls for him and Lord knows anywhere your Daddy went your Mama was right there beside him. Now, if you don't want to drive, I can take back over."

I sat there behind the wheel and gripped it between the palms of my small hands as I looked out across the land. Something within me told me that I needed to do this, that I needed to overcome this and push forward.

"I'll drive, Pappy."

"Good boy. Now head that way," he pointed to our right, "And I'll look over this map and see where we need to turn."

"Okay, sir."

"And, John?"

"Yes, sir."

"Try and stay on the road."

"Yes, sir," I said laughing.

November 19, 1838
The Winter House

Mary Anna was outside pulling the tall grass up from around the house while John added more wood to the fire in the fireplace. It was getting colder, a lot earlier than normal and the sky looked as if it would drop a blanket of snow upon them at any moment.

Mary Anna was almost four months pregnant and her stomach had already began to stick farther than normal. She had heard that sometimes it took several months for a woman to grow, but this was not the case for her. She noticed that she had a harder time standing up and moving around than she normally did and she found herself often times getting frustrated with herself.

Ralph was in the barn cleaning out the stalls with Rachel near his side helping him do whatever he needed her to. It was obvious that the two of them had feelings beyond friendship between them and it was a subject that no one spoke of. If they decided to act upon their feelings for one another then everyone would support them, but there were a lot of risks to take into thought.

John and Ralph had cut down several trees from the woods to the north and had created enough firewood to last them through the winter. It was in a large, but neat pile on the side of the house that faced the barn and it was Cherokee's favorite place to nap.

A thin line of smoke arose from the chimney into the grayish white afternoon sky as Mary Anna finished pulling up the grass. She slowly lifted herself to her feet, but halfway up she found herself being lifted up by John's strong arms.

"Take it easy there, little missy. Maybe you should go rest."

"John I'm not even four months along yet. I still have a long ways to go, I can't very well just sit around the whole time."

John picked her up in his arms and carried her through the front door. "Oh yes you can."

"John," she demanded, "Put me down. Really, I can manage just fine."

"Darling, please just put my mind at ease and rest in the rocker for awhile. This is your first child and you are more at risk for things to go wrong. I don't want to lose you, that's all."

Mary Anna saw the sincerity on his face and consented to sit in the chair. "Okay, but why don't you sit next to me and read."

"Okay, I can do that." He said pulling down the bible from the mantel and sitting in the rocker next to her. Before opening the book, he lifted up her feet and let them rest across his lap. Mary Anna took out her sewing and began to work on her child's first outfit as John began to read from the book of Esther.

His voice somehow managed to soothe her entire body and any kind of fear or discomfort she had somehow managed to waste away into nothingness. She listened intently to the story of how a common Jew arose to be the queen.

"John," she interrupted. "I think Rachel might be a lot like Esther."

"Really. Why is that?"

"I don't know. I can see her as Esther and your brother as the King."

"Oh, I see where this is going."

"Should I not talk about it?"

"You're my wife, Mary Anna. We can talk about anything, even if other people say we shouldn't, it's our business. So, what's on your mind?"

"I don't know, John. I mean, I know people wouldn't approve, but then people approve of very little these days. I guess it's like my Ma marrying an Indian and it turned out that they had a hard time surviving. I guess I'm just worried that something will happen to them."

"I know what you mean, darling. But in the end, nothing we can say or do can make up their mind for them. Would you disagree at their companionship?"

"No, I love them both dearly, I just worry is all. Would you disapprove if your brother married someone who was half Negro?"

"He's my brother and I'll always love him no matter what. We can't help who we fall in love with, I just hope he understands the consequences that will come with it. The two of them will never have an easy life together and as wrong as it may be, they will always be on the outside of society's inner circle."

"Sometimes it feels like things like society and expectations don't matter much. John, do I meet your expectations?"

"You exceed my expectations more than I thought possible, darling."

"Okay, keep reading then."

"You don't want to talk about this anymore?"

"No, if the two of them decide to be together than that is their choice and I will always be there for the both of them."

John smiled and went back to his readings as Mary Anna resumed her sewing. The fire crackled in between the many logs that John had stacked up in the fireplace and allowed the room to fill with the glow of warmness as the first snow flakes started to fall outside.

In the barn Ralph and Rachel continued to clean out the stalls and make small talk to avoid talking about what was really on their mind. Even the horses disagreed with the choice to overlook the more important topic and would occasionally stomp their feet in protest.

"Rachel," Ralph finally said leaning himself up on one of the partitions separating the stalls. "What do you think about us?"

"What do you mean?"

"You know good and well what I mean, Rachel."

"Ralph, we both know that we can never be more than friends. It's just unheard of, even though I'm only half colored."

"But maybe we could change the rules."

Rachel laughed, "Well, when I am able to call you Mr. President I will believe that, but until then there is nothing we can do. If we were to act on our feelings, I would only feel as if I were ruining your life. Somewhere out there you will find you a white girl to have your children, you don't want me."

"Rachel, how can you say those things. Not only do I want you, I need you. I don't care what people will say…let them talk. Your half white yourself so there is proof that we will not be the first black and white couple."

"Oh yes we would. A white man sneaking into a colored woman's bedroom does not make a couple, Ralph."

"But still, surely we can find a happy life together somewhere."

"Ralph, I do have feelings for you, just as I know you have them for me, but can you imagine how hard our life would be together? By law I am a slave to Mary Anna, not that she would ever ever consider me as such, but she doesn't write the law."

"Let's go to Mexico, Rachel. Surely we can be happy there. No one can judge us and we can be completely free from the hatred that surrounds us in this country."

"Ralph, you're talking out of desperation, you must stop this talk."

"Let me kiss you then. If you don't feel nothing I will never speak of it again, I promise."

"Ralph…"

He leaned in and cut her words short. She submitted her lips to his and became lost within the kiss from the love of her life. She quickly pulled away and ran toward the barn door in embarrassment.

"Did you feel anything?" Ralph shouted after her, but she didn't turn back, she ran straight inside and joined Mary Anna and John as he continued to read from the bible.

Shortly after she entered, Ralph made his way inside. He hung his hat next to John's beside the door and sat on the bed where he too joined in on listening to the bible story. He stared intently at Rachel, hoping for some sign of acknowledgment, but every time she noticed him looking at her she quickly focused herself back to her sewing.

They had a light supper that night, no one seemed to be in the mood to eat much except Mary Anna who had three helpings of food. The silence between Rachel and Ralph continued through supper and before long everyone was fast asleep in their beds.

Rachel slept in the second bed while Ralph slept on a feather mattress he had made shortly after arriving at the winter home. During the day it was kept beneath Rachel's bed and when it was time to sleep it slid out with ease.

When Mary Anna awoke the next morning, John had already gone out to the barn to tend to the animals. She wrapped herself in a small blanket and threw some extra logs onto the fire. When she was satisfied that it would produce enough heat for Ralph and Rachel who were still sleeping she made her way into the kitchen to prepare breakfast.

She looked out the window and could see her husband in the midst of all the snow as he shut the barn doors and headed back to the house. Overnight the snow had fallen so much that the ground was completely covered in it as was the roof of the barn.

John stepped into the house and banged his boots onto the wooden floor to rid them of the snow. He walked into the kitchen and wrapped his arms around Mary Anna's waist and then kissed her on the cheek. "Good morning, darling."

"Good morning. Do you want some coffee?"

"Of course, little missy."

Mary Anna handed him a cup and then poured herself one. The two of them sat at the table and watched the snow continue to fall from the warm side of the window.

"Ralph," John shouted, "Coffee's ready!"

"It's strange they are still asleep, John. I've never known either one of them to sleep this late."

John got up and walked over to the two of them who were still sleeping. He noticed that both Ralph and Rachel were covered in sweat. He knelt down and felt his brother's head, which was hot to the touch.

"Mary Anna! Quickly, bring me some water!"

Mary Anna poured water into a large cup and hurriedly took it to her husband. "Go back over there, Mary Anna. You don't need to be over here."

"John, what's wrong?"

"They've got fever."

Mary Anna stayed back toward the window and watched as her husband forced water down both of their throats. Neither one of them were very responsive and when they did try to talk it was mostly unrecognizable words.

The rest of the day John tended to his brother and Rachel while Mary Anna frantically watched from the kitchen area. She desperately wished that there was something she could do, but she knew she must not risk the health of her child.

As nightfall fell upon them, John brought her some blankets to her side of the room and told her she must sleep on the floor tonight. She made a small pallet near the kitchen table and fell asleep as she watched her husband do his best to nurse the two of them back to health.

The next morning she awoke to find that John was sleeping in their bed and that Ralph and Rachel were still covered in sweat. She slowly crept over to her husband's side and placed a hand on his chest to try and wake him from his sleep.

When she touched his bare chest she quickly removed her hand to find that it was soaked in her husband's sweat. "John," she said. "John wake up. Please don't be sick too, John. I don't know what to do."

She ran her hand through his hair, but there was no response to her action. She brought some water to him, but had little luck getting him drink it. Next she attempted to get Ralph to drink, but he seemed to have the fever the worst.

When she got to Rachel, her hand was stopped as she proceeded to move the cup to Rachel's mouth. Rachel clasped her hand around Mary Anna's wrist and tried to speak.

"Rachel?" She said, "What is it?"

"Tell…"

"Tell what?"

"Tell him."

"Who? What?'

"Tell him I felt something." Rachel said as she drifted back into sleep.

Mary Anna sat in a rocking chair and trying to figure out what to do. She was all alone with a unborn child in her stomach and she feared everyone around her was dying.

For three days she tended to the people who were closest to her in the world and none of them seemed to be getting any better. Somehow she had managed not to become sick, although she spent night and day trying to get the three of them to eat and drink, most of the time unsuccessfully.

When she wasn't at her husband's side, she was in the barn tending to the animals and making sure that they had enough to eat. It was a chore for her to march through the accumulating snow and often times she found herself having to stop and rest halfway to the barn.

"John," she said holding a spoonful of soup up to her husband's mouth, "Please eat, John."

There was no response from him. She laid her head on his shoulder and began to let out all the tears that she had been holding in over the past three days. She knew the outcome of this was not going to be good and if the three of them were going to die, than she only wished that she would soon join them.

After she had released all her tears onto John's chest, she proceeded to try and force Ralph to eat. When she knelt down beside his body, her hopes were suddenly lifted when she realized his body was much cooler than it had been. "Ralph," she said shaking him, "Ralph wake up. Eat some soup."

There was no response from him. Something about him looked different than anything Mary Anna had ever seen. But then she soon realized that he had the same look about him that her brother had had when she found him hanging from a tree.

"Ralph!" She said refusing to believe that he had died, "Ralph you wake up right now!"

Mary Anna was crying even harder than she had been before. She felt his chest for a heart beat, but could find none. She found courage somewhere within her and brought herself back to her feet. She pulled the blanket back and covered his head.

"This is it," she thought. "One by one we are all going to die. By some stupid fever."

Suddenly there was a knock on the door. Her heart skipped a few beats at the surprise and she quickly moved the chair next to the door. She reached up and grabbed the gun and then moved back down to the floor. There was another knock.

She slowly opened the door, letting in a few flurries of snow. "Mary Anna?" A woman's voice said from the other side.

"Who is it? And how do you know my name?"

"Mary Anna! It's Alice!"

Alice Braymyer wrapped her up in a hug as she forced her way inside with her children following close behind. Mary Anna collapsed and would have landed on the floor had Alice not kept her in her arms.

When she awoke, Alice was throwing buckets of snow onto John and Rachel, nearly covering their bodies completely. Alice had sat her in a rocker near the kitchen table and covered her with a blanket.

"Ma?" She said rubbing her eyes.

Alice ran over to her and knelt down in front of her. "Take it easy, child. Don't move too quickly.

"Am I dead?"

"No, darling. You're going to be just fine."

"What happened? Do I have the fever?"

Alice ran her hand over the top of Mary Anna's head. "No, you were just tired is all."
"John, where is he. I need John."

Alice was fighting back tears. "You'll see him soon enough, dear. Now you rest here awhile."

"Ralph, where's Ralph. He's not really… is he?"

Alice looked down at her. "We moved him to the barn, darling. I'm afraid so."

Alice was being strong, stronger than Mary Anna could ever imagine to be. She had just lost another son and she showed no sign of hurt or sorrow. But Mary Anna was sure that it was there somewhere within Alice, a hurt so great that if ever released the whole world would hear about it.

But Alice had other children to tend to and Mary Anna knew all about pushing forward and living for other people. The time for mourning could always be put off for another day, but when life demanded for you to live, you must always obey.

Alice moved around the snow across John and Rachel's bodies to try and break their fevers and it was the last sight Mary Anna saw as she drifted into another spell of sleeping. She could feel that something wasn't right with her body, but she had no idea what it might be. It didn't matter, right now she needed sleep and as hard as she tried to fight it so that she could be by her husband, she found herself in Georgia on a summer day with her little brother.

- - - - - - - - - - - - - - - - - - - -

When Mary Anna awoke she was in the comfort of her own bed and when she looked up and saw John's face she knew she must be in Heaven for certain now. "Where's Walkie?" She said, "He should be here too."

"Darling?"

"John? What's going on? You're sick."

"No, darling. I'm all better."

"You can't be. We must be in Heaven. Where's Walkie and Esther? Where's grandmother?"

"Ma," John called out to his mother, "Come over here."

Alice joined her son beside Mary Anna and looked down at her. "Mary Anna, you take it easy and don't move too fast."

"Where am I? Why is John out of bed?"

"Darling, you've been sleeping for two days."

"Two days? But why? I was sitting in the chair and… and I…"

"You're pregnancy is making you sick, darling. You lost some blood and were too weak to stay awake."

"My baby. Is it okay?"

John took Mary Anna's hand. "The baby's fine. Please rest, Mary Anna. I don't want to lose you."

"What about Rachel?"

"She's fine. She is out in the barn helping with…"

"With what?"

"Ralph, darling."

"What about him?"

"Darling, do you not remember?"

"Remember what? Ralph? Of course I remember him."

John looked at his wife and fought to hold the tears inside him. "Darling, Ralph is dead. The fever took him from us."

Mary Anna suddenly remembered. "Do I have the fever?"

"No, you don't have the fever. Do you want something to eat?"

"Yes, I'm hungry."

Mary Anna tried to prop herself up on the bed, but was too weak to do so. John put his arm behind her and slowly lifted her to the sitting position. He put the pillows behind her back, never letting go of her hand.

Alice brought over some salt pork and a slice of bread for her to eat, which John had to hand feed to her. She tried to stay awake for as long as she could, but soon found herself falling asleep in her husband's arms.

December 25, 1838
Dear Journal,

It is Christmas Day and I am confined to my rocking chair near the fireplace. John is worried that if I am not careful that either me or the baby could have a fatal outcome. I am thankful that Ma Braymyer is here, her company is what gets me through the day most of the time.

Since Ralph's death, Rachel seems somewhat depressed and finds it hard to carry on a very lengthy conversation. I do not think the death has fully settled in with John yet, but I am sure one day soon the reality of it all will hit him hard. He is good to me as always and if ever I need anything he is always right there at my side.

With John's younger brother and his sisters here, our house is now full of people and I think it is exactly what we all need. Ma Braymyer says that she likes how I have done up the house, which is to my pleasure since I was so afraid that she would not.

I remain hopeful that once my child is born I will be able to get back to my normal life. It is hard to think that we still have to travel further in order to get to Missouri. I will be sad that Ralph will not be with us when we cross the Mississippi. He will stay east of the river along with all the other precious family members we have lost this year.

The snow continues to fall, but we have had a few breaks from it and it has allowed the snow on the ground to become less thick. The other day, John surprised me with a gift, which is unlike him since he rarely gives gifts early. He made a small crib for our unborn child and it is now sitting beside my bed.

John says that we will not leave our Winter Home until after the baby is born. He says it is too dangerous for us to travel in my condition. I am having such a time with it that perhaps I am not meant for childbirth or perhaps my body was not fully ready for the burden.

Ma Braymyer has been cooking all sorts of things today and tonight we will have a large Christmas dinner. Of course, I am sure I will be made to eat the meal from my rocker, but I do so hope to see smiles on everyone's faces. It has been a hard year for everyone and I only hope that the upcoming one blesses us with little death.

Wasting away in a rocker,
Mary Anna Braymyer

December 13, 1994
Arkansas

Pappy decided that we should stop and get some rest rather drive all the way to Missouri in one day. So shortly after we plummeted to the bottom of an Arkansas hill, we found a Days Inn and I cautiously parked the truck between two smaller cars.

We ate pizza and watched colored tv, which Pappy never had in his house. The next morning, after a Denny's breakfast we were on the highway somewhere north of Benton heading toward Missouri with me behind the wheel again.

We had had such a time on our road to Braymyer Ridge that I could only imagine how hard it must have been for John and Mary Anna. As we continued to drive I found myself in one of my frequent questioning moods as most young boys do.

"Pappy," I said. "Did Ralph really die?"

"Sure did. They had to wait a week before they could bury him. The ground was too cold to dig a hole and John was recovering from being sick himself."

"So what happened with Rachel?"

"Well, of course she took it the hardest, but no one truly knew how the two of them felt about each other at that time. She mostly stayed to herself and kept quiet. You see she had just lost the love of her life and very few people out there find that more than once."

"Did she ever find love again?"

"Well, that's jumping ahead in the story a little bit, but I can tell you this. She didn't find love for a long long time."

I felt sad for Rachel as I listened to Pappy talk about her. She must have lived a hard life and after the things she went through, she must have turned out to be a strong woman.

"Well, did Mary Anna have the baby?"

"You're getting a little anxious there ain't you, son?"

"Yes, sir."

"Well, between Christmas and March of that year nothing much happened. John had Mary Anna stay in her rocker and most of the time he was in the one right next to her. Day after day he showed her more love and affection than any man had ever shown a woman before.

He would also spend hours on his knees talking to her stomach and listening to make sure he could still hear a heart beat. His younger sisters and his one surviving brother helped with the chores around the house, so he found himself able to spend a great deal of time with Mary Anna.

The winter had gotten off to an early start and it also seemed as though it would have an early end. By late February the snow was almost completely melted, although it was still very much cold.

March 16, 1839
The Winter Home

"John, take your brother and go wait for us in the barn."

"But, Ma. I want to be here. What if something happens?"

"If we have any problems I will send for you. Now go on, childbirth is no place for a man."

John leaned down and kissed Mary Anna on the forehead. "I love you, darling. You listen to Ma and she'll take good care of you."

Mary Anna was in the middle of a contraction and couldn't respond to him at the moment.

"Come on, Tom," John said putting his hand on his little six year old brother's shoulder as they headed out of the door.

They made their way across the muddy ground with the morning sun in front of them and stepped inside of the barn with Cherokee at their side. It was still cool outside, but something about all the hay and warmness of the animals made the barn seem a lot warmer than it really was.

"Is Mary Anna going to be okay, John?"

"I'm sure she'll be fine. Ma is in there and she will take good care of her."

"Oh, I guess you're right."

"I know I'm right, Tom. I've got to be."

"Yeah, yeah you're *always* right, John."

"So, you and I are the only Braymyer boys left."

"I know. I miss the other brothers, but I'm glad I still have you."

"Well, I'm glad I still have you too, little man. You know, us being the only men left we have a big responsibility."

"We do?"

"Absolutely. You see, it's our job to make sure our Ma and sister are taken care of. And if anyone, and I mean anyone, ever tries to mess with them, well then, you and I will handle them won't we?"

"Sure will. I'd like to see them try and get through these fists of mine." Tom said holding up his small hands at the air pretending to be fighting an unknown enemy.

Meanwhile, back in the house Mary Anna thought for sure that she had lived to see her last day. The pain, she thought, was too unbearable and she didn't see how anyone had ever done it before.

Alice and Rachel stayed by her side as the other girls brought Alice things that she requested. She had several cloths and two buckets full of cold water from the well. Rachel placed a wet cloth on her forehead and tried to soothe her as best she could.

"You're going to be okay," Rachel said forgetting about her depression, "It will all be over soon."

Rachel tried to be brave, but she was probably more scared than Mary Anna. She didn't know how they would have managed if Alice had not been there to help.

After everything had been gathered all the girls gathered near Mary Anna and watched with anticipation. She felt as if she were a caged dog being observed by anxious onlookers.

John's sister, Mary Alice sat in the rocker and began reading from the bible. She opened it up to the last page John had read earlier that winter from the book of Esther. In no time, she had finished the book and then looked over at Mary Anna.

"What book would you like to hear next?"

"I... don't... care..."

Mary Alice quickly flipped the bible shut and then reopened it, allowing it to land on whichever book it pleased. It was the book of Ruth and she began reading loudly to try and drown out Mary Anna's screams.

About an hour after John and Tom had left for the barn, Alice looked up from the foot of the bed and screamed, "Okay, Mary Anna. Start pushing, it's time, honey."

"Start pushing! I've been pushing! Where have you been!"

Alice couldn't help but laugh and shake her head as she proceeded to help with the delivery. She felt very blessed that she was able to deliver her first grandchild and knew she would never forget this moment as long as she lived.

Rachel continued to hold Mary Anna's hand, looking away from the terrifying scene as often as she could. As she continued to listen to Mary Anna rant and rave she made a promise to herself to never have children.

"Ok," Alice said, "You're almost there."

"Almost there? Shouldn't this be over by now!" Mary Anna shouted back.

Mary Anna suddenly felt a relief within herself and it was followed shortly after by the crying of a baby. Alice stood up and walked around the bed toward Mary Anna.

"Here," she said, "You have a baby girl."

Mary Anna looked up at her and was about to reach for the child when pain struck her again. She began to scream and yell all over again.

"What is it, darling?" Alice asked looking at her as if she were crazy.

"I… don't know. Something… hurt…"

"Here," she said handing the baby to Rachel.

Alice ran back down to the foot of the bed and couldn't believe her eyes. She looked up toward Mary Anna, "Come on, darling. It looks like you've got another one coming."

"Another one! This wasn't part of the deal!"

A few of the Braymyer girls could be heard laughing from somewhere behind Rachel. Screams and shouts continued to fill the house and carried out far enough that John and Tom could hear them from the barn.

John paced back and forth as he patiently awaited to be called upon. He feared he would never see his wife again and he didn't know what he would do if something were to happen to her.

Shortly after Alice went back to the foot of the bed, a second child was born from Mary Anna. She again felt a relief and once more another baby's crying could be heard.

"Another girl!" Alice shouted.

She started back around the bed, but was stopped by Mary Anna's voice. "Wait! Are you sure there's not anymore!"

"No, darling" she said resuming her steps toward her and laughing, "I think you are all finished. Cynthia, go fetch John."

Alice placed the baby beside Mary Anna on the bed and then took the second child from Rachel and did the same. "Honey," she said to Mary Anna, "It's no wonder you had so many problems during your pregnancy. You're too small to be having twins!"

"Well," Mary Anna said, "Had someone given me the choice I might have chose otherwise."

John ran through the front door and was by Mary Anna's side before anyone had even realized that he had came through the door. He knelt down beside her, nearly knocking his mother to the floor.

"Are you okay? You didn't suffer any did you?"

"No, John" she said rather calmly, "It was as pleasant as that buggy ride you took me on back in Tennessee."

"John," his mother interrupted, "You have two beautiful daughters."

John looked down at his children that he had not noticed before, as he was more concerned with his wife. He slowly picked them both up, cradling one in each arm. "Oh, darling," he said looking down at his wife, "They're beautiful."

"So does this mean I can get out of that damn rocker now?"

Alice nearly fell over laughing at her daughter in law's comment. "Sorry, John," she said, "Sometimes childbirth makes a woman a bit moody."

John, who was laughing too, simply looked down at her and said, "Of course, darling. You can even help me clean out the horses' stalls if you'd like."

"Don't you joke with me, John Braymyer!"

"Sorry, little missy. So what should we name them?" He asked kneeling down beside her once more with the babies still in his arms.

Mary Anna's temper that had been brought on by childbirth suddenly disappeared and she pondered her husband's question. "What do you think, John?"

"I don't know, darling. I had my hat set on a boy."

"Well, what about Esther Alice and Ruth Ann?"

"Hey," he said, "Those aren't half bad. Ma, what do you think about one of these pretty young ladies carrying your name?"

"I would be honored," she said leaning over Mary Anna and kissing her on the forehead. "Now, Mary Anna, I know you don't like the stuff, but it got me through seven of my deliveries."

"What are you talking about?" Mary Anna asked confused.

Alice pulled out a jar and handed it to her, "It's some of Grandma's Davis' moonshine."

Mary Anna didn't care a bit about the promise she had made to herself, swearing she would never touch it again after her previous episode with it. She graciously took the bottle and took a big gulp, letting out a loud burp after she had downed it.

Everyone in the room started to laugh. "Mary Anna," John said, "You are something else."

John crawled into bed beside Mary Anna and held his daughters and his wife tightly. Not only did he have four sisters, a mother and a wife to care for, but now he had two daughters as well. He couldn't help but feel as if his life and his family were being taken over by the women.

As he lay there, all his sisters and his little brother made their way over to the new family to see Esther and Ruth. The moonshine had taken away Mary Anna's pain and she was soon talking up a storm with everyone. She was truly glad that she had a husband like John and looked forward to their future together wherever it might take them.

December 13, 1994
Arkansas

The farther we drove across Arkansas, the less the snow made its presence upon the landscape. I could tell that Pappy was growing tired from the driving, but he didn't dare fall asleep in the truck again.

Any time we passed an old antique shop or any kind of southern café he insisted that we stop and check the place out. In Arkansas alone I would guess that we stopped at nearly twenty different places to eat and the floor of the truck was full of to go boxes.

In the back of the truck was an old plow of some sort that Pappy had bought off a antique shop somewhere around Benton. The man who sold it to him said that it had belonged to a Williams family of the area and that they were very prominent farmers in those parts.

When Pappy saw the old rusted piece of metal there was no telling him no and we soon loaded it up into the back of the pickup truck. He also bought us both a pair of straw hats from the same store and we wore them proudly atop our heads with our trademark overalls covering the rest of our bodies.

I really enjoyed the scenery of Arkansas, or the Ozarks as Pappy called it. He assured me that as we drew nearer to Missouri that the land would only get more beautiful. I had to admit that the land took my breath away, but after awhile I grew homesick for the flatlands of Texas.

I could tell Pappy was happy as we drove along the winding roads, bound to the home place of our family from long ago. He looked out across the vastly wooden land as we went up and down throughout the hill like mountains. At times, I thought we would for sure die when the road followed along the edge of a cliff that had at least a four hundred foot drop below us.

521

But I managed to stay on the road somehow and soon we were on better roads that were not so high up in the sky. Pappy never tired himself of talking and along the way we covered more subjects than I suspect most people cover in their entire lifetimes. I suppose it is the same with most older people, they fear that if they do not share their stories with a younger generation than they will be forgotten and their lives would have been pointless.

"Pappy," I said, "Was the story about the witch in Kentucky real?"

"Of course it was," he said, "But she was not nearly as bad as the one from Arkansas."

As gullible a young boy I was, I slammed on the brakes of the truck. When Pappy realized that he had been lucky not to have been thrown through the windshield he began laughing.

"What is it, son?"

"What do you mean, the one from *Arkansas*?"

"Well, the witch from Arkansas."

"Pappy are you pulling my leg?"

"Now why would I pull your leg? I'm serious, John. She lived up in the hills long ago and she was just like the one from Kentucky, only she didn't have bears, she had mountain lions."

"Mountain lions?"

"That's right. And you see, this witch didn't just go after young girls, she also went after boys too."

"Well what happened to her?"

"No one knows. She just disappeared one day, but I think it's strange that people still occasionally disappear around these parts from time to time."

"They do?"

"Yep. Especially people who are from out of town and just driving through."

I turned my head back to the road and slammed on the gas pedal, sending us down the country highway as fast as I could.

April 01, 1839
The Winter Home

John had moved two of the rocking chairs out into the front yard just beside the small porch. Mary Anna and her husband each sat in one rocking the babies as the morning sun stretched out to their left.

Mary Anna was feeding Ruth Ann while John held Esther as she patiently awaited her turn to eat. They watched as John's younger sisters ran across the yard and played child games and it reminded Mary Anna of her Georgia youth.

Alice stepped out onto the porch with her hands on her hips and watched as her children enjoyed their childhood. "Those girls are rotten to the core," she said laughing, "But at least they are able to grow up in a time of peace."

"What do you mean, Ma?" Mary Anna said, "Did you not grow up in peace?"

"Me? No. I was too busy trying to stay alive. When I was seven we were held up in the woods for ten days hiding from the Indians, the same ones that had killed my parents the week before."

"How terrible. What did you do?"

"We just survived. There were about three families with us and it was late November, but we didn't dare start a fire. The Indians would have seen our smoke and then it would only be a matter of time before we lost our scalps.

So we just wrapped up in as many blankets as possible with the little bit of food we had. By the time it was all over I was just skin and bones, I figure that's the reason it took me nine years after I was married to have my first child and then I just couldn't stop. I had been convinced that I was barren and wouldn't ever have any children, but look where I am now.

Not only have I been blessed to have had so many children, but I have also had to endure the suffering of losing some of them.

You know," she said looking down at John, "I met your father for the first time when we were hiding out in the woods. He was one of the families there, which was back when his Ma and Pa were alive. They were killed a few months after we were able to return to our homes and he was left an orphan. I guess I was lucky I still had my grandparents, but most of my Morgan family was completely killed off.

I've got a brother somewhere down in Arkansas, but I haven't seen him in years." Alice looked out over her children and fought away the melancholy mood that was trying to take her over.

"Ma," John said, "I think we should head out tomorrow. The weather has warmed up enough that we should be able to get there in no time."

She looked over at her son, "John, I've traveled a lot in my life and I have no problem doing it again, but I don't want to leave Ralph here alone, not yet anyway. I think the children and I will stay here for awhile."

"But, Ma," John said standing up with Esther. "You can't stay here. Pa wouldn't approve if I just left you and the children here. You've got to come, besides how would you support yourself."

"John, we're right by the Mississippi, which means there will always be travelers and they'll always be hungry."

"But what if something were to happen?" Mary Anna interrupted.

"Honey, I've been through a lot in my life and there isn't anything Kentucky can throw at me that I can't handle. Now, John, you prepare for the trip, we'll be just fine here."

"But Ma, I can't just leave you here with the children. You're in a strange land and who knows what kind of people it is home to."

"John every land is strange unless we civilize it and to be honest, I'm tired of running. Trust me, we'll be fine, I'll send word to you if something happens and who knows we may end up in Missouri eventually anyhow. Now, go on. You've got a lot to do before you leave."

John started to speak back, but he was cut off by his mother again, "I've made my decision, John and that's final. Now go on, get ready for the trip."

Mary Anna watched them, but didn't say a word. Just before Alice turned to go back inside, Rachel appeared from around the side of the house. She had her hands folded across her chest as if she were cold in the warm weather that the day was graciously offering them.

"Mary Anna," she said, "I think I'd like to stay behind too."

"But, Rachel! You're my best friend, I can't leave you here. You must come with us."

"It's not that I don't want to go, but I had a real chance at love and although it has disappeared, I'm just not ready to leave it behind."

Alice took a step closer, but remained on the porch. "Rachel, you're welcome to stay here, but are you sure that's what you really want to do?"

She looked over at Alice, "Yes, maim. I've made up my mind about it."

Mary Anna was in shock and was fighting back tears. John handed Esther to Rachel and headed to the barn to be alone. Alice went inside and Rachel sat in the now empty seat beside Mary Anna.

"I'm sorry, Mary Anna, I just can't leave, it is too soon still."

"But Rachel…"

"You'll be fine without me, I promise. And besides, I'll see you soon enough, just wait and see."

"Time has a way of stealing things from us, Rachel and I just don't want to see it take our friendship."

"I know, but you and I don't have to worry about such things. We'll always be friends, no matter what is thrown our way."

The two of them sat there in the rockers as the morning turned to afternoon and then as the afternoon turned to early evening. John didn't come out of the barn all day, except to grab a few things to load onto the wagon that he was preparing.

The two girls stood up from their chairs and their conversations about past memories and people and headed indoors to eat supper with the family. John stayed outside with Tom and busied himself at whatever task he could find for himself to do.

"Tom," he said throwing a rolled up blanket onto the back of the wagon, "You're in charge. I don't care if Ma tells you not to, you write to me if there are any problems, you hear me?"

"I will, John. Can't I come with you, though?"

"I'm afraid not. Ma's going to need a man around here and besides I wouldn't be surprised if she changes her mind and heads across the river before the year is up."

After everyone was fast asleep, John and his mother remained outside in the two rocking chairs and talked the night away. John knew that there was no changing his mother's mind and even though she was a woman, he also knew that she could take care of herself better than anyone he knew. She was as stubborn as he was, so there was no point in trying to change either of their minds.

The next morning Mary Anna sat on the wagon seat holding Esther and Ruth Ann, who had turned out to look just alike. They both had olive skin and thin light brown hair on top of their heads. Their eyes were the same color blue as John's and when a person looked upon them they couldn't help but to be carried away into a dreamland.

John climbed up onto the wagon that had been loaded up with all their stuff and headed it toward the Mississippi River. Alice and everyone else who was staying behind followed them afoot and would see them off as far as the river.

Shortly after leaving they arrived at the waters of the great river. It had been said that the Mississippi River was the most dangerous one to cross, but John said that since there had been little rain so far it should be manageable.

The two of them got down from the wagon and walked over to where their family was waiting for them. It had been the second time within the year that they had been forced to say goodbye to those they loved, but it had never been as hard as it was on the banks of the Mississippi River. That winter had brought them closer than ever before and the group of Braymyers felt a special connection that neither time nor space could take away.

Mary Anna exchanged hugs with everyone, saving Rachel for last. She wrapped her hands around her and spoke softly in her ear, "You're my very best friend, Rachel. Don't forget me."

"I'll never forget you, Mary Anna. How could I? Now, don't you let the west make a scoundrel out of you."

The two of them laughed as John brought the twins over for Rachel to kiss goodbye. When everyone had said their goodbyes, John forded the rushing river as Mary Anna held tightly to her daughters.

Alice, Tom and all the girls stood side by side waving them off as the wagon began to float across one of the river's shorter gaps between banks. Water rushed up all around them and at times Mary Anna had to shut her eyes for fear that she would be sucked down into the river.

The wagon began to rock back and forth and was then carried down river a short distance. The horses were having a terrible time trying to keep their heads above the water and looked as if they would go under at any moment.

The wagon canvas rattled and swayed back and forth as small amounts of water began making their way to the floor beneath it. Just when Mary Anna thought for sure they were never going to make it across the river the horses stumbled onto ground somewhere beneath the water and began trudging along to the western bank.

John turned the wagon sideways once they were on shore and stood up in the seat as tall as he could. He lifted up his hat with his right hand and shouted into the sky, "YEE-HAW!"

Mary Anna sent one last goodbye wave across the river to everyone on the other side. They were in the west now and everyone else they cared most about in this world stayed behind on the eastern side of the river. They were in Missouri at last and were on the road to their new home somewhere just beyond the horizon in front of them.

December 13, 1994
Arkansas

"I thought you said Rachel and Mary Anna stayed together forever and ended up in Texas together?"

"Well, don't get too far ahead, son. Hey look up there." Pappy said pointing ahead.

I looked out ahead toward the side of the road where he was pointing and there was a sign that read, 'Missouri.' I slowed down as we passed it, watching it as it disappeared beside us.

"So we're in Missouri now?"

"That's right, it won't be long now."

I couldn't tell much of a difference in the area of Arkansas we had just left and that of Missouri we were now driving through. There was a little snow here in there in small patches across the fields alongside the road that were lined with some of the tallest trees I had ever seen.

"How far into Missouri do we have to go?"

"Not too much further, but we've still a little ways yet. Hey, look there it looks like another café. Let's pull in there."

I pulled the truck into the rock parking lot of what looked like a shack on the side of the road. Once the truck had been turned off we both stepped out and went through the rotting doors of what a sign said was the 'Happy Trails Café.'

Once inside we saw that there was only one other table in the entire rather large room that had a customer at its side. I followed Pappy to the right and we walked toward the back of the room where we sat at one of the wooden tables that had four chairs pushed up against it.

Shortly after sitting down an elderly lady who wore too much makeup and perfume was standing next to us with a small notepad and an ink pen. "How are you boys doing today?"

"Just fine," Pappy said, "And yourself?"

"I'm doing well, thank you. What would you two like to drink?"

Pappy ordered a water and I a Dr. Pepper. The waitress exited our side and went back into a kitchen at the very back of the building next to a sign that read 'Bathrooms.'

I picked up the weathered menu that mostly consisted of things such as old-fashioned burgers, root beer floats and chicken fried steak and scanned through what I might want to eat. Pappy only took a minute to look at his and then placed it back in the center of the table and looked around the room.

"Pappy, are you sure this place is okay to eat at?"

"Of course it is, son. These hole in the wall places like this often times give home to the best food around."

Although I didn't completely agree with what he said I ordered the same thing as him, Chicken fried steak, a root beer float and two orders of french fries. As we waited for our food, Pappy began telling me a story about a café he had once been to in east Texas that was a lot like this one.

I tried to listen, but my mind was focused in more on John and Mary Anna and what became of them. "Pappy," I interrupted, "What did John and Mary Anna do when they got to Missouri?"

"Oh, well let's see now."

May 03, 1839
Missouri

John, Mary Anna, the twins and Cherokee had traveled across Missouri for a month and the farther they went the more anxious they became to start their new home. They passed only a few small settlements along their way and most were so new that they offered very little for the travelers.

Mary Anna enjoyed the smell that Missouri had bestowed upon them, it was a combination of cedar and wild flowers and she knew she would never tire of its sweet scent. The trails they followed were like the towns they had passed, fairly new and less traveled than the ones they had previously been on.

John pulled the wagon off of the trail and said it was time to make camp for the night. He freed the horses from the wagon and led them over to a large apple tree where they gladly feasted on the fallen fruit.

Mary Anna spread out a blanket beneath another tree and laid the twins down to take a nap beneath its shade. John made a small campfire in a clearing near the trail and unloaded their necessary items for Mary Anna to unpack. Just before nightfall, she handed John his supper, which was bacon, two slices of bread and beef jerky.

The twins were fast asleep on their blanket about four feet away from the couple as they ate their food. The stars began appearing one by one and before long the entire sky was illuminated with their presence. A few bats flew across the sky in front of the moon as they left the comfort of their caves in search for food.

"John," Mary Anna said leaning against him as they sat beside the fire, "How much longer are we going to travel?"

"There's a new town called Springfield, probably about a week away. Once we get there we'll start looking for a place to settle."

"Do you think everyone is managing okay back in Kentucky?"

"I'm sure they're fine, darling. Ma will take good care of everyone."

"I hope so, it worries me to think of them back there all alone."

There was a slight crack from the woods behind them as if something had stepped onto a stick. John turned quickly to observe the situation as he ran his hand along the butt of his gun that lay at his side.

"John, what was it."

"I don't know, probably a wild animal."

"You don't suppose there are witches in Missouri too, do you?"

"No," John said half laughing but never taking his stare off of the trees. "You'll be scared of witches till the day you die, won't you?"

"Well, yes. Aren't you afraid of them, John?"

"Oh, darling… yes, I suppose I am."

"Well you sure don't act like it."

John just started laughing, "Come on, let's go lie down with the girls."

Mary Anna kept her eyes wide open most of the night for fear that a witch would get her and take her away. She had only just fallen asleep when the sun arose and they were soon on the trail again.

Seven days after leaving their camp and whatever noise they had heard that night, they arrived in Springfield, where new buildings were rising on Main Street. The echo of a hammer could be heard all across town and the smell of freshly cut pinewood filled every street.

 Mary Anna and John rode down the dirty street and observed the many people that walked along the front boardwalks of the false front buildings. It was the most people they had seen since they had crossed the Mississippi River and it was welcomed with great relief.

Women in bonnets watched the newcomers as they were dragging along their small children behind them in a hurry to get to an unknown destination. Other wagons passed them going the opposite direction, most of them carrying wood from the sawmill at the other end of town.

John pulled up to a bank building that also had a sign in the window that offered land grants. John pulled the wagon to a stop and then looked over at his wife. "You wait here, little missy… I'm going to go find us some land."

He kissed her on the forehead and then jumped down and went inside the building. Mary Anna watched as life in the tree surrounded town continued to thrive. It would be, she thought, a good place for a family to live.

About thirty minutes after entering into the bank building, John came back out with a piece of paper that had been folded in three ways. "Well, darling. Are you ready to go see your new home?"

"Really, John? It was that easy?"

"Sure was. Seems like there's a whole lot of land just sitting here waiting for people to take it. You and I are going to be among the first people to settle up this land, just you wait and see."

"Well, where is the land at?"

"It's about twenty miles north of here outside a small little settlement called Walnut Grove."

As the wagon drove out of town, Mary Anna said a silent goodbye to the town she had hoped to call home, not only for herself, but for her family as well. Even after they had left Springfield, she could still hear the ringing of hammers somewhere behind them as they headed north.

Late the next day, John stopped the wagon on top of a grassy ridge that faced west. Below was farmland that had been cleared out by someone before them and left to sit empty in the Missouri sun. It wasn't a large area of cleared land, but it could easily be added to since John had just acquired 500 acres of land.

"What do you think, Mary Anna?" He said putting his arm around her.

"It's one of the most beautiful sights I have ever seen, John. Is it all ours?"

"Sure is. Every bit of it. Come on," he said jumping down and then helping her down as well. "Look here, we can put a big house right here on top of the ridge. We'll make it just like the one you grew up in, in Georgia. What do you say?"

"It's wonderful, John. I can't wait. It's going to be the best house ever."

"That's right, darling and I'll buy you all the fancy dresses you want, just you wait and see."

"But how are you going to afford all this, John?"

"Easy, I'm going to plant corn and wheat and invest in cattle. I bet cattle will do just fine out here."

John leaned in and kissed her as they stood atop what would become known as Braymyer Ridge. They would have to wait until tomorrow to start building their dreams because the sun had already started to disappear in front them and the twins were getting hungry.

June 24, 1840
Dear Journal,

We have been in Missouri just over a year now and how blessed our lives have become. The corn crop last fall did so well that John has been able to buy nearly a hundred head of cattle and has almost finished building our new home.

It looks so beautiful sitting atop the ridge overlooking all of our hard work and I cannot wait until it is finished. I have grown so tired of living in a tent and to think we had to stay in the barn over the winter. Oh well, this coming winter we will be nice and warm in our new home without the company of the horses.

Esther and Ruth Ann are trying so hard to walk, but they often times find themselves falling to the ground. They are so much like their father and yet so much like myself as well. John says that maybe next year we can try for a boy and he will become known as the first Braymyer born in Missouri. My husband's sense of humor has a tendency of breaking down even the most stubborn walls of seriousness and it is a trait I truly love and admire about him.

We have not heard from our family in Kentucky in some time now, but the last letter we received from them revealed that they would stay on there for a while longer. It's strange to think that that winter home in Kentucky served as John and mine's first house as a married couple. But now, we shall have the grandest home in all of Missouri and our sweet girls shall grow to become the most eligible women in the state.

We finally have some neighbors that are not more than a day away from us. The Hunter's moved less than a mile away and they too plan to engage in farming. They only just arrived last week, but I think that we shall become great friends. They are a young couple like John and myself and have but one small son who is near the twin's age.

A happy Missouri wife,
Mary Anna Braymyer

December 13, 1994
The Road to Braymyer Ridge

I turned the truck left down a rock road that had a sign pointing down it that read 'Braymyer Ridge Bed and Breakfast.' Pappy cracked his window and let the cool December air flow through the truck as it brought with it a scent of past times.

Pappy sat up a little taller as we followed the road that was lined with tall trees as it made several small curves toward our destination. About a mile after turning down the road it ended in a small clearing where a large two-story building sat welcoming us.

It was a perfect rectangle with windows all across it and large columns stretching to its second story roof. The porch ran the entire length of the house and had four stairs in the middle of it leading it down to the ground. The front door was actually two smaller doors that were painted green and when both opened at the same time it created a rather large entry.

When we stepped in there was a short lady that looked to be in her forties standing behind a podium like desk that was nearly taller than she was. "Hello, Mr. Sanders. We've been expecting you."

"Hello, Georgette," he answered her. "How have you been?"

"I've been doing just fine, thank you for asking. Would you like me to show you to your room?"

"Oh that's okay. I think we can manage alright, cant we, son?" He said looking over at me.

"Yes, sir."

I followed him up the stairs, which were right beside the desk and were the widest set of stairs I have ever been on. Once we climbed about ten stairs we found ourselves on a square shaped platform and directly in front of us was a giant picture of a man and woman.

"Who is that, Pappy?"

"Why, that's Mary Anna and John, son."

"Really?"

"Sure is."

In the picture they looked to be quite a bit older, but even for their age they were still very good looking. To both our right and our left were more stairs, which had about five or so steps on them

"This way, son." Pappy said heading up the stairs to our left. Once up the stairs the only option we had was to turn down the partial hallway to our left. The reason I call it a partial hallway is because on our left hand side was railing and everything was open below so that we could see all the way down to the entry.

The right hand side, however was lined with several different doors all leading into different rooms. Had we followed the hallway all the way down, it would have turned left and forced us over to the other side where the other set of small stairs emerged. This made the open space below in the shape of a large rectangle.

The hallway was covered in antique carpet that had little blue diamonds across its red surface. I followed Pappy all the way down the walkway until we came to the very end. Instead of turning left and continuing down the hall in front of a large window, we went right and went through a large wooden door.

Once inside we found a large bed the likes of which I have never seen and this room too was covered in the same type of carpet. There was a large vanity and matching mirror on the left between two windows with a bed to our right on the west wall.

"This room is giant, Pappy!"

"I'd say it is, son. You know whose room it used to be?"

"Whose?"

"John and Mary Anna's."

"Really?"

"Sure was. They lived here a long time."

"Well, what happened to them?"

"What do you mean, son?"

"I mean, where did they end up?"

"Ah, well before we talk about where they ended up, perhaps we should start back in their younger days, eh?"

"Yeah, I guess you're right. So they got here from Tennessee after staying in Kentucky and built this house. Then what?"

Pappy began to laugh. "Let's take a walk around the house and I'll tell you all about it."

April 15, 1848
Braymyer Ridge

Twenty two year old Mary Anna Braymyer had just given birth to her sixth child ten days before, a son that they named Nat. Other than the nine year old twins there was four year old John Junior, or Johnny as they called him and two year old Will. The other child, a daughter named Molly was born in 1842, but only lived a few months.

Although the twins had light brown hair, all their sons had blonde hair just like their father, carrying only their mother's tan skin. John had finally gotten his sons that he had always wanted and spoiled them, along with the twins as much as he could.

Mary Anna had grown into an even more beautiful woman than John had imagined she would. She had grown to be tough, but calm and loving at the same time, which made for an interesting combination.

Their family that had stayed back in Kentucky remained there still and they had not seen them since they left them on the Mississippi nine years before. They exchanged letters as much as they could and always made promises to visit each other, but none of them had the time for the long journey.

John was now twenty-nine and had made a successful rancher out of himself. He grew a little corn and wheat, but the ground proved to be too rocky to produce good crops. He had, however been successful in raising cattle and selling them to people down in Springfield who were trying to populate the west with cattle.

After being in Missouri for over a year and half, their house that sat atop Braymyer Ridge was completed and it truly was one of the finest houses in all of Missouri. Mary Anna took care of the entire mansion all by herself, while raising her children and still managed to have supper ready every night.

The barn sat to the north of the house and was big enough that it could hold twelve horses with ease. It had double doors on both ends of it so that it would create a nice breezeway during the summer.

John had four ranch hands working for him throughout the year and they were all local men who had homes nearby, which allowed John not to have to worry about building a bunk house. Every morning during the summer, except for Sunday they would be at Braymyer Ridge where Mary Anna would feed them a large breakfast before they headed to the cattle. Everyone became very good friends and the Braymyers became the center of the community around them.

Mary Anna moved all the furniture in the front room to the outside walls and then began to sweep the wooden floor with the broom that John had made her the year before with some of his wheat crop. She then dusted the mantel that was mounted above the large stone fireplace, carefully lifting the Braymyer plate.

She was preparing for the party that was to take place there that night and wanted everything to be perfect. When she was satisfied with the front room she made her way down the hall into the large kitchen where Ruth Ann and Esther were monitoring their mother's pies that were sitting on top of the cast iron stove.

"Go upstairs and change girls, it's almost time for the guest to start arriving. I left a surprise for you both on your beds."

Esther and Ruth Ann hurried upstairs and flew into their shared bedroom. There, on each of their beds was a new dress for them to wear that night. Esther's was white, with small pink flowers scattered across it and when she put it on it fluffed out so much that she could barely fit through the door.

Ruth Ann's looked almost exactly like her sister's except hers was yellow with blue flowers. They also had bonnets that matched their dresses perfectly and a new umbrella to complete their outfits.

While they were changing, Mary Anna carried Nat up to her bedroom and began to search for the dress that she would wear that night. John had meant what he said when telling Mary Anna that she would have as many dresses as she wanted and her only dilemma with it was that there was so many to choose from.

She placed Nat on her large bed who quickly fell asleep while his mother searched through her clothes. She tried on three dresses before deciding on the blue one that John had given her for her birthday when they crossed into Kentucky. She had since acquired a blue bonnet that matched it in every way possible except for the fact that it had white feathers coming out of the back of it, but it would do.

She stood in front of the body size mirror and examined her figure, making small turns to ensure that everything looked correct. She then picked Nat back up and headed downstairs as John came in through the front doors.

"John," she said, "Hurry up and change, it's almost time for the guest to start arriving."

"Well lookie there. Girls," he said looking over at the twins who had just joined them from the sitting room, "Have you ever seen something of such beauty?"

Mary Anna smiled as the girls laughed and went back into the sitting room. "And who's that handsome thing you have there in your arms?" He continued.

"Oh, just some child I found out back. It appears that a buzzard laid a rotten egg and the sun hatched it, or so that's what the buzzard told me anyhow."

547

"Is that so? Well, let me see this little fellow."

John took Nat from her arms and held him up where he returned the favor by spitting up on his father's face. "Yep," he said squinting his face up, "I'd say he came from a buzzard alright."

Mary Anna took Nat back into her arms and wiped him off with a cloth she was carrying. After Nat had been cleaned she then proceeded to wipe off her husband's face.

"So, is this beautiful wife of mine going to bless me with a kiss?" He asked wrapping his arms around her waist.

She pulled away at the smell of his face and the few traces of Nat's throw up that remained behind, "Not until my husband goes upstairs and cleans himself up."

John laughed and headed up the stairs as Mary Anna watched him and he hollered back at her, "Okay, but when I get back I'll expect my kiss."

"I'm sure you will, honey. I'll try and not give it away to anyone else."

Mary Anna took Nat into the dining room where she had his crib and laid him in it while she busied herself bringing the food to the table. She had made every kind of pie and cobbler imaginable and several batches of apple cider.

Just as she finished getting everything in order, Will and Johnny ran through the dining room running their fingers through one of the apple pies and then promptly running away into the kitchen.

"Johnny! Will! You get back here!"

It was no use, they were long gone. She used her own hand to try and fix the mess that they had made of the pie and when she realized there was no hope for it, she simply threw a cloth on that portion of it.

Nat had fallen asleep so she left him to his dreams and went to join her daughters in the front room. Esther and Ruth Ann twirled around the floor and pretended to be dancing with their future lovers whoever they might be.

"Girls, do you like your dresses?"

"Oh yes, Ma," they said at the same time as they had a habit of doing, "They're lovely."

Mary Anna smiled and headed to the front door where she heard a knock. She opened the door only to find that Cherokee was scratching on the opposite side and when he had the chance he darted inside the home.

"Cherokee! Get over here!"

She ran after the playful dog, even though he was ten years old and chased him up the stairs and then back down where they ended up in the place she feared the most...the dining room. Cherokee had propped himself up onto the table and was graciously eating the apple pie that the boys had already made a dent in.

"Cherokee!" She screamed, "Get down."

The normally loyal and obedient dog paid her no mind and did not move away from his treat until forced to do so by Mary Anna who pulled him down from the table. She drug him out the back door by his front two paws and then threw what was left of the apple pie outside after him.

"I guess you deserve a good treat just as much as the rest of us," she said closing the door behind her.

549

When she re-entered the house she was surprised to find that Polly Hunter was standing there in a beautiful green dress that brought out her matching eyes. She looked at Mary Anna and fought back laughter as she saw the distress her dear friend was in.

"Mary Anna, do you need some help?"

"Polly. You startled me. I didn't hear you come in."

"The girls let me in. Really though, would you like me to help."

"I think everything is ready, let's go sit in the sitting room."

The two women walked down the hall and joined the twins and Polly's son, Ben who was a year older than them. She noticed that Polly's husband was not there and immediately began to fret. "Where's Frank, Polly?"

"Oh he's here. The minute we came in John called him upstairs to show him his new rifle."

"I swear, men and their guns. Did he bring his fiddle?"

"Sure did, he sat it over by the front door."

"Oh, good. A party wouldn't be very eventful without music now would it?"

"No, I don't suspect it would. Mary Anna are you sure you have everything under control here? I mean it is a big house and I'm sure if you were to get a slave to help you…"

"I don't believe in buying people, Polly, you know that. And yes, I've got everything under control, I rather enjoy staying busy."

"Okay, but you let me know if you change your mind."

"I'm quite certain I won't, but if lightning strikes me twice and I survive I will be sure to send word to you."

"Oh, Mary Anna I do love your southern charm. It reminds me of the old days back in Virginia."

"Old days? Polly you're only twenty six."

"I know, but the way things are changing here lately it seems as though I am a might older."

"Believe me I know, it seems like ages ago that we spent that winter in Kentucky before the girls were born, but like my Grandmother always used to say, you've got to keep on marching."

"Isn't that the truth. Oh, did I tell you what I heard about Bonnie Kaiser?"

"Oh dear, what has she done now?"

"Well, I went over to Morrisville with Frank last week and there she was walking down the street screaming and shouting at the sky."

"Why ever for?"

"Well, evidently she found her husband in the bed of Henrietta Cox."

"No!"

"Oh, yes. Poor woman, I don't know what she is going to do. Their neighbor, Mrs. Lane said that she paid them a visit and that Bonnie told her that her husband refused to quit seeing Miss Cox."

"Oh my, the poor soul."

"I know, but what can you do about it. I suppose we will just have to sit back and wait for more gossip to roll in."

"Well, you do love your gossip, Polly."

"It makes life in the Ozarks interesting I must say."

"That it does, Polly, that it does."

The two women continued to chat and make small talk as more guests continued to arrive until the last ones had arrived just after nightfall. Frank Hunter pulled out his fiddle and struck the first note so hard that Mary Anna was sure she felt the walls shake.

Esther and Ruth Ann were the first two out on the dance floor, Esther dancing with Ben Hunter and Ruth Ann with Wyatt Harrison who was eleven and already smitten with Ruth Ann, even though her and her sister looked almost exactly alike.

They may have shared their looks with one another, but where their opinions and actions were concerned they were most definitely two different individuals. Esther preferred the lavish lifestyle of a young rich girl that her father had so willingly provided for them while Ruth Ann was much happier getting her hands dirty as she explored the Ozarks around their home.

Mary Anna and John stepped out onto the dance floor after a few more couples closer to their age had gotten up the courage to join the younger ones and soon everyone in the room was dancing. There were about fifteen people in all and their laughter and high spirits filled the home with happiness.

When Mary Anna's legs refused to allow her to dance any longer, her and John made their way out to the front porch and sat down in two of the many rockers that were sitting there. Mary Anna hunched back and let her neck bend in such a way that it allowed her face to stare straight up at the ceiling of the porch.

"I haven't been this tired in a long time, John."

"You're not getting old are you?" He said putting a hand on her knee.

"Well, if I'm old then you're just about dead I suppose."

"Ha, I'm not dead yet, darling."

There was a small moment of silence and then John continued. "Darling, are you happy here? I mean are you truly happy here?"

"Of course I am, John. We've made a good life for ourselves here and we have some fine children to prove it. Occasionally I do find myself thinking back to those times in Tennessee," she said laughing a little bit, "Aunt Liza and Grandmother on the front porch and my sweet brother, Walkie running through the yard.

I can see their faces still so clearly that it's as if I was with them only yesterday. And Rachel and Ralph too, how I do miss them and Ma Braymyer. But someday I suppose we'll all be together again."

They looked out into their dark front yard and thought back over past times. "Well come on," Mary Anna said jumping up and taking John's hand, "Let's go dance some more."

"But I'm dead remember?"

"Not yet you're not, now come on."

The Braymyers and their guests danced well into the night and it was early the next morning before the last of them drove off into the darkness. After all the children were in bed, Mary

Anna and John went into their bedroom and slept in their large bed with baby Nat in the crib beside them.

The next morning word was sent to the home by one of the eight Taylor boys that there was a Cholera outbreak in Walnut Grove and that none of John's hired men would be there for work that day. The two of them didn't worry about the news too bad, so long as they stayed near home and away from anyone that was sick they should be fine.

John ate a large breakfast and drank his coffee as the children slept into the early morning. After finishing he kissed his wife and headed out to check on the cattle and move them into another field that offered more food for them.

Not long after he had walked out the front door, Mary Anna heard him holler from somewhere out back. She rushed out to what was the matter and shouted back. "John! Where are you?"

She heard another shout and her heart sank when she realized where it was coming from. She ran over to the ridge and looked down into it and there at the bottom was her husband surrounded in a pool of blood.

"Esther, Ruth Ann!" She shouted back at the house, hoping that they were already half awake.

The back window opened and Ruth Ann stuck her head out, "What is it, Ma?"

"Listen to me, child. I need you to go get on a horse and ride into town."

"But…"

"Listen to me. Your Pa has fallen and it looks like he's broken his leg. Go fetch the doctor, but don't talk to anyone, there's been a cholera outbreak."

"Cholera!"

"Ruth Ann, do as I say. Send Esther down here, I'm going to need her help."

Mary Anna slid down the ridge and landed just beside her husband who was groaning in pain. She looked him over and the only sign of injury she could find was his leg, which she could tell had most definitely been broken.

"Ma," Esther said from the top of the ridge, "What's going on? What's happened to Pa?"

"Come on, Esther. I need you to help me get your Pa up to the house, he's broken his leg." She turned down to John, "Come on, John. You're going to have to help us as best you can."

He groaned as he pulled himself off the ground, allowing one arm to rest around his wife and the other around Esther. It took them thirty minutes to get him up the ridge and into the house through the back door. They slowly ascended the stairs, leaving a trail of blood all the way to their bedroom.

Just after they had gotten him into bed, Ruth Ann and Doc George could be heard running up the stairs and following the trail of blood into the bedroom. As soon as he entered the room the doctor took control of the situation.

"Esther, go fetch me some water, Ruth Ann go get as many cloths as you can find."

The doctor pulled back his trouser leg to reveal the tip of a bone sticking out through his skin. He quickly covered it back and started digging around for something in his little black bag.

Ruth Ann and Esther came back into the room with the supplies the doctor had requested. Mary Anna took Nat from

555

his crib and handed him to Esther, "You girls go keep an eye on your brothers and wait outside."

The girls left, but after getting Johnny and Will they returned to the bedroom door and waited outside as the screams of their father took over the house. Esther covered her ears and refused to hear her father's pain while Ruth Ann tried to calm the boys.

Inside the bedroom, Mary Anna held tightly to John's hand as the doctor tried to fix his leg. In between her husband's shouts, she could hear the crackling of bones as the doctor tried to put everything back in its place.

 The doctor worked for three hours on his leg and at times had just considered sawing it off, but Mary Anna wouldn't allow him to do that. "Doctor," she said, "Either you fix his leg or I'll make yours to where it needs to be fixed."

After the three hours he finally stood up and Mary Anna desperately wished she had some of her aunt's moonshine to give to her husband. "I've got it fixed as best I can," Doc George said. "He's lost a lot of blood so make sure he gets plenty of food and rest."

"Thank you, doctor," Mary Anna said looking down at the face of her husband that was soaked in sweat.

"That's not all, Mary Anna," he said. "A wound like this, there is a high chance he'll contract gangrene and there won't be much I can do except remove the leg."

"Well, we just won't let that happen."

He looked at the two of them with a sad face as if he were telling them that John only had a day to live. "Mary Anna, can I talk to you out in the hallway before I go?"

Mary Anna followed the doctor out of the room and as they entered the hall, the children scattered in different directions. "What is it, doctor?"

"Mary Anna, I think you should know that every one of John's hired men has cholera in their household. They won't be out here for quite some time and I know there is work to be done around here."

"I'm rather good at working, Doc. I reckon I'll manage just fine."

"I just thought you should know is all. Now you keep an eye on his leg, keep those bandages changed daily. With the cholera going around I doubt if I will be able to make it out here, but if there are any problems you send for me."

"Thank you, doctor."

Mary Anna stepped back into the bedroom and knelt down beside her husband. She ran her hand through his hair as he opened his eyes from a short nap. "Hello, darling," he said looking up at her, "Am I dead yet?"

Mary Anna let the tears flow down her cheeks and in a laughing cry said, "No, you're not dead and not for a long while yet."

April 23, 1848
Braymyer Ridge

John had been in bed for a week and only once did the doctor come back by. He said that there was still no gangrene, but he doubted that John would ever walk the same again. John regained most of his strength the first couple of days after his accident, but was unable to get out of bed without the help of Mary Anna.

He spent most of the day sitting there in bed looking out the window with Nat lying near his side. He hated the feeling of helplessness that had taken up residence in his body and wanted nothing more than to be able to get up and take care of the necessary chores.

The cholera epidemic continued to sweep through the Ozarks, but no one in the Braymyer home took ill with the disease. Unfortunately though, all four of John's employees were killed over the first week of the outbreak.

Mary Anna tended to the cattle as best she knew how, often times having to come back inside and ask John what to do in a certain situation. On one occasion, a cow became stuck in the mud and since Mary Anna wasn't strong enough to free him, he eventually starved to death.

Night after night, Mary Anna would come in from the cattle covered in mud and manure and go straight to the kitchen to begin preparing supper for them. Ruth Ann tried to help, but Mary Anna remembered how her mother had once said that it was important for children to grow up in a time of peace and she refused to put her children through anything but that.

She stopped five times a day to come back to the house and feed Nat and then shortly after his stomach was full she returned to the chores and didn't stop until the rest of her family became hungry. They received no visitors due to the cholera and thus had no help with what needed to be done.

During all of this, not once did Mary Anna complain. Even if John would never be able to walk again she would be just fine taking care of everything that needed to be done, she was born to be a survivor and that's exactly what she was going to do.

Mary Anna pulled herself out of bed as if she could smell that the sun would soon be arriving and made her way downstairs to the kitchen. She made eggs, bacon, ham and a large pot of coffee. She had rarely drank the stuff in the past, but now that she was doing her husband's work she realized it was a necessity.

Ruth Ann, Esther and the two boys came into the dining room where she was serving the food and they quickly dug in. Mary Anna joined them and sat at her usual place at the end of the table.

"Ma," Ruth Ann said, "Please let me help you out there today. You're doing too much work for one person."

"I'll manage it, darling. Now you eat your food. You need to stay here and take care of your Pa anyhow."

"But can't Esther take care of him. Please let me help you."

Mary Anna looked at her daughter and saw the same determination she had once seen in herself long ago. "I'll think about it, honey."

There was a slight tap at the door. "I'll get it," Esther said standing up."

"Sit down, Esther. Eat your food and I'll get the door." Mary Anna said leaving the dining room.

She walked through the front room and into the entry where the green double doors were, she took in a deep breath hoping that it was no one with more bad news about the cholera.

When she opened the door she was shocked and half-frightened to find herself being pulled into the arms of an unknown person.

When she was able to get a good look at the person who had snagged her, she realized she was wrapped into the arms of her friend from long ago, Rachel Lloyd. She looked over her shoulders and saw Ma Braymyer and her two children that were still under age, Tom and Dolly… John and Mary Anna's family had finally made it down the long road to Braymyer Ridge and they couldn't have come at a better time.

Mary Anna returned her long lost friend's hug and shortly after was wrapped into Alice's arms. She had dreamed so long for this day and now that it was here she could hardly believe it was real.

"What are you doing here?" She said as tears of joy ran down her face. "I had no idea you were coming."

"Well," Alice said, "We got tired of Kentucky and if you'll have us we'd like to live here."

"Of course! You are all welcome here!"

"My goodness, Mary Anna," Rachel said looking up at the front of the house, "I don't know that I've ever seen a house this big in my life."

"Well come in," Mary Anna said. "We were just sitting down for breakfast."

Alice was still just as tall as Mary Anna had remembered her and had the same red hair she did when she had last seen her, only it seemed a little lighter now. Dolly was about to be ten and she had more of her mother in her appearance than any of the other Braymyer children.

Tom was now fifteen and had turned out to look almost exactly like Ralph did at that age. While they were in Kentucky, Alice had to bury one more child, Missouri who had taken ill with the fever the autumn after Mary Anna and John had come to Braymyer Ridge.

Rachel was quite obviously a Walker and there was no denying it. It was apparent that she was colored, but her dark hair flowed down her back just as gracefully as the whitest woman in the south. She had grown to be tall, making Mary Anna the shortest person in the house other than her children.

They followed Mary Anna into the house and down the hall to the dining room where the children were anxiously waiting to see who their guests were. Alice was the first one in the room and when she looked upon her grandchildren her breath was taken away.

"Children," Mary Anna said, "This is your grandmother and your aunts and uncle."

The children stood up as Alice looked them over, followed shortly after by Rachel. Mary Anna introduced them and Alice seemed pleased with their names. Ruth Ann had gone upstairs and had just re-entered the room carrying Nat.

"Now," Alice said, "This baby looks just like John did when he was born. And Will looks so much like my David. Where's that son of mine anyhow?'"

"Alice," Mary Anna said, "Maybe you should come upstairs with me."

Alice's face went blank as she knew immediately that something was wrong. Tom and Dolly stayed in the dining room with the children while Alice and Rachel followed Mary Anna up the stairs as she told them the story about John's accident.

Mary Anna opened the door to their bedroom and the three of them stepped inside where John was just waking up. "My Goodness, John. What have you done to yourself!" Alice said rushing over to her son's bed.

"Ma? What are you doing here?"

"I'm just passing through. What do you think I'm doing here? I'm here to see you."

"It's nothing much, just a hurt leg."

"Nothing much! John, you've broken your leg. I swear honey, you don't have the balance God gave a goat."

"Thanks, Ma," John said rubbing the sleep out of his eyes like a small child. "Darling?" He said searching the room for his wife.

"I'm here, John," Mary Anna said stepping closer.

"Come give me a kiss and I want you to stay around the house today. You've been working too hard as it is."

"But John…"

Alice interrupted her, "So you're telling me Mary Anna has been doing all her work and yours?" She said looking at John.

"That's right, Ma. She's about working herself to death."

"I always knew you were strong, honey," she said to Mary Anna, "Something about marrying a Braymyer man tends to make a woman damn near invincible. But don't you worry yourself none, you'll have plenty of help now."

"But, Ma. There's been a cholera outbreak it's sure to make its way here soon enough."

563

"Mary Anna," Rachel said, "When we went through Walnut Grove there was word that the epidemic is almost gone from these parts. I don't think you have anything to worry about."

"Well that's the first bit of good news I've had in a long time," Mary Anna said, "Well other than finding you all at my front door. Let's go eat. John I'll send Esther up with your plate."

"Thank you, darling," he said as the women left the room and then said to himself, "Boy I'm really in for it now. Ma and Mary Anna in the same house... I don't stand a chance."

Tom was able to handle most of John's work by himself, allowing Mary Anna to focus more on her children and the housework. Another week after their family members from the east had arrived, John started to show signs that his health was improving.

Mary Anna brought his supper up to him and found her husband sitting in a rocker on the other side of the room. "John, how did you get over there?"

"I walked, darling."

"But you're not suppose to be out of bed. You're leg shouldn't even be working."

"Well, not perfect, no, but it'll do."

Mary Anna gave him a displeasing look as she took him his food. "John, if you're not careful it won't heal correctly and then..."

"I know, I know. I may not be able to walk at all. But hell, honey, lying in bed all the time can't be good for a man either."

"Okay, John, but don't say I didn't warn you."

"Will you send Tom up when you go downstairs? I need to talk to him about some things that need to be done on the farm."

"Why don't you walk down there yourself, John?"

"Very funny, Mary Anna," he said as she kissed him on the forehead.

The first time John made it down the stairs was a month after he had had his accident. He moved slowly at first, but eventually he was able to get back on his feet as normally as he could. He walked down the wide stairs just in time to overhear his wife snap at Polly Hunter.

Mary Anna, Polly, Alice and Rachel were sitting in the front room having a cup of tea and discussing the latest happenings of the area when Polly suddenly turned to Mary Anna and said, "I see you've taken my advice on getting a slave."

"I most certainly have not! Why would you say such a thing, Polly?"

"Well, you have a Negro sitting here, I only assumed she belonged to you." Polly turned to Alice, "Is she yours then?"

Alice didn't have time to answer as Mary Anna took control of the conversation. "She is no slave, Polly. She's my…"

"Housemaid," Rachel interrupted. "Mrs. Braymyer has always been sensitive about word choices when it comes to us Negroes."

Polly looked at her and then over at Mary Anna. "I see. Well, nonetheless I am glad to see that you have some help around here. I had best be going, Frank's going to want a large supper tonight after spending all day fishing. Lord knows he isn't bringing any fish home to cook."

Rachel and Mary Anna followed her to the door and watched her as her wagon rolled out of sight. "Mary Anna," Rachel said, "I told you that you must never tell our secret."

"But that secret was made so long ago, Rachel. Aren't secrets supposed to be told after a certain amount of time?"

"Not ours, Mary Anna. Ours shall be a lifelong secret."

"Oh, Rachel," Mary Anna said putting her arm around her, "Old Polly will be all over the countryside by this time tomorrow telling everyone how I now have a slave and treat her as if she were one of my friends."

"You better be careful, Mary Anna. Before long you'll have trouble knocking at your door."

"Trouble? I've built my life around trouble, Rachel. If trouble is what they send, then troubles what I'll give them in return."

"My, my… you are one crazy woman."

"Eh, it makes for an interesting life."

February 13, 1853
Braymyer Ridge

"Housemaid, servant, whatever you are. Bring me some more tea."

Rachel looked at Polly Hunter as if she had lost her mind before she headed to the kitchen to get her the drink. "My, my," she whispered, "I wish I had some of that moonshine to pour in here."

"Here," Alice said stepping into the kitchen from behind her. She walked over to the cabinet and pulled down a jar.

"Oh, Alice. We're so bad, but I would like to see the way she reacts to this stuff."

"You and I both, darling. Now here, pour it in."

She returned to find Polly ranting and raving about how service and Negroes in general were just not what they used to be. Rachel handed her the glass of tea and took a seat beside Alice where they kept a sly eye on her. When she had grown tired of talking about that subject she then moved on to discussing how horrid Indians were.

"But, Mary Anna," she said coughing a little bit from the tea, "You're secret is safe with me, I shall not ever tell a soul."

Alice looked up at her and half choked on her tea, this promise coming from a woman who couldn't go five seconds without keeping her mouth shut, she thought.

"I'm sure you will, Polly. I'm sure you will." Mary Anna said.

"Now let's talk about your Esther, Mary Anna."

"What about her?"

"Well, she'll be fourteen next month and my Ben has it in his head that he's going to marry her. I never have been able to tell him no and I can't start now. We've got lots of money, so your Esther will never want for anything."

"Well, Polly that's not my decision."

"Right, where's John then?"

"Polly, it's not his decision either, it's up to Esther."

"Well very well then, we'll just have to have a talk with Esther."

Esther came down into the room after Polly had shouted several times throughout the house after her. "Yes, Mrs. Hunter?" She said as she walked in.

"Esther, how would you like to marry my son?"

"Now, Polly!" Mary Anna said, "wait just one second. Esther, darling, why don't you sit down."

Polly began speaking again, "Esther, my Ben is in love with you child. You two could make a real fine couple and have a nice, long life together."

"Well," Esther said. "He is somewhat handsome and I know he'll always have the funds to take care of me."

"That's right, dear," Polly said.

"Now, Esther," Mary Anna interrupted. "This should be a decision made on love, not money!"

"Oh, mother I know, but it's my choice just the same so I should be the only one who gets to decide!"

Ruth Ann had been standing near the door and when her sister got hateful with their mother she stormed out the front door.

"What's wrong with her?" Polly asked burping.

"Oh," Esther said, "I am quite sure she is just jealous that I might marry well. Mrs. Hunter, please inform your son that if he wishes to have my hand he shall have to ask for it himself. And between you and I, I will think about the proposal until that time."

Polly stood up satisfied and nearly fell sideways onto the floor. "My, I believe that tea has made me light headed. Negro, what did you put in my tea?"

Rachel looked at her and as she tried to hide her laughter she simply said, "Nothing, Miz Hunter, iz juzt a old Smokey Mountain recipe."

Alice nearly fell over with laughter as Mary Anna looked upon them with suspecting eyes.

"Well," Polly said. "I suppose I should be going anyhow." She headed for the door, nearly tripping on everything she came in contact with, including her own two feet. Mary Anna, Rachel and Alice watched from the doorway as it took Polly ten minutes to climb aboard her wagon.

"What did you two do?" Mary Anna asked as she watched Polly drive away, barely able to remain on the wagon seat.

"Oh, nothing," Alice answered, "Like Rachel said, just a Smokey Mountain recipe, which may or may not have included Grandma Davis' moonshine."

Mary Anna shook her head and couldn't help but laugh. "I don't suppose she'll ever have tea with us again."

Rachel laughed, "Is that such a bad thing, Mary Anna?"

"Ha, I guess it's not…I guess it's not."

May 12, 1858
Walnut Grove, Missouri

Twenty year old Ruth Ann Braymyer walked along Hickory Street with Washington Michaels at her side. He was the dashing son of the owner of Michaels Mercantile, which had found its success during Missouri's earlier days.

Esther had already been married to Ben Hunter, in fact she wasted no time in snagging the richest bachelor in the county. She made a quick wedding and was soon out of the house making her home over on the Hunter land, where she nearly forgot all about her family.

Ruth Ann on the other hand had spent time enjoying her youth and getting everything out of it that she could. If there was ever a case of good twin, bad twin, the two of them could have been the perfect candidates. It wasn't that Esther was bad, she was just greedy and tended to become jealous over the smallest things.

But Ruth Ann had found her love in Mr. Michaels and they were soon to be wed. Her father very much approved of this union and had become rather fond of his future son-in-law. They were the perfect example of a young couple that would grow to do good things and help all those in need along the way.

They stepped into his father's store in the early afternoon where they were greeted by his parents who acted as if they had been waiting for them. His father was tall and elderly looking, while his mother looked to be some years younger with a kind look always about her.

"Wash? Ruth Ann? How are you?"

"Hi, Mrs. Michaels," Ruth Ann said, "I'm doing well, thank you. How are you?"

"Enjoying this fine weather is what I'm doing! Wash, are you being good to Miss Ruth Ann?"

"Of course, Ma. You taught me better than that. I brought her over to look at dresses."

"It's about time! I declare with a wedding a week away you couldn't have waited any longer! Now come on, child," she said taking Ruth Ann's hand. "Let's get you a dress fit for a queen."

Mrs. Michaels led her to the back where she handed her a beautiful white satin dress that she had obviously already picked out. "It's lovely, Mrs. Michaels! Just lovely!"

"Well, I can't have the wife of my only son settle for anything less. Now come on, let's see it on you."

Ruth Ann slipped the dress on and made a full turn in front of her future mother-in-law. "How does it look?"

"Are you kidding, child? It's perfect!"

It was midafternoon when the two of them left the store and headed for their wagon that was parked just a few buildings down. Ruth Ann put her arm through Washington's and they walked side by side down the boardwalk. His six and a half foot body towered over her and the muscle of his arms nearly completely hid her thin arm.

The sky was growing dark like that of Washington's hair and it looked as if they would be having a spring storm at any moment. As the two of them continued down the walk, Ruth Ann immediately heard a familiar voice coming from the group of wealthy women up ahead. Ruth Ann smiled as they got nearer, determined not to let them ruin her lovely day.

"Well what do we have here?" Esther said when the couple was right up on them.

"Hello, Esther," Ruth Ann said in a pleasant voice. "You remember, Washington."

He tipped his cowboy hat.

"Ah, yes. The son of the local shopkeeper. Well I guess it's a good thing one of us married well. But don't expect to get a cent from me."

"Esther," Ruth Ann said somewhat calmly. "I won't allow you to talk about my future husband in that manner and you needn't worry. I'd sell my last piece of bread before asking a cent of you."

"I don't see how you can walk so close to a man like you are. You aren't married yet and the way you have your arm through his, why it just isn't proper."

"Esther, not all of us marry for money. Some of us are perfectly content on just having love. Good day, ladies."

Washington and Ruth Ann walked past the flabbergasted group of women and headed for their wagon. Washington helped her up onto the seat, "I reckon we'd better get you home. Looks like it's going to storm."

As Washington joined her on the wagon seat she once again put her arm through his and leaned her head against his shoulder. "Washington, don't pay no mind to the horrible things that my sister says."

"Don't worry, darling. I've never held much stock in the opinions of rich folk. Besides, I've got the most beautiful woman in the whole world sitting right here next to me, I'd say I'm a might lucky."

Ruth Ann smiled as they headed east down the road to Braymyer Ridge with lightning and thunder shaking the skies behind them. It didn't take long for the storm to catch up to them as the wagon rolled along the dirt road. It soon began to hail and as it landed upon Washington and Ruth Ann it felt like they were being shot with bullets made of ice.

"Come on," Washington shouted through the loudness of the storm. "Let's get under the canopy so we're not hit anymore."

The two of them crawled into the back of the wagon as the hail pounded the canopy above their heads. They looked out of the opening at the back of the wagon and saw that the clouds were moving with great speed and seemed to be going in all directions. Washington put his arm around her as they watched the approaching storm slowly head in their direction.

"Washington, are we going to be okay in here?"

"We should be fine, so long as the wind doesn't pick up."

Just as he said that and as if someone had put a curse on him, the wagon began to rock back and forth with the pressure of the oncoming wind. The massive gusts frightened the two mares that had been pulling the wagon and they soon took off running down the road. The speed at which they were traveling sent the wagon airborne at times as it hit every hill and hole in the road.

Ruth Ann screamed with terror as she held tightly to Washington who was bracing himself against the frame of the wagon. As the wagon topped a small hill and once again flew through the air, the two of them happened to look out of the opening at the back. Just down the road and heading straight for them as if it were chasing them was a tornado.

"What are we going to do!" Ruth Ann screamed.

Washington looked out at the storm again as a thick rain covered the entire area. Even the two of them were soaked although they had been under the limited protection of the canopy. He looked back at Ruth Ann as water dripped down from his hat, "We're going to have to jump and head for the trees."

"Jump! But, Washington the wagon is moving too fast!"

"Not fast enough. That twister will be here in no time. Now come on, darling, we've got to."

The two of them crawled to the back of the wagon as it continued to speed uncontrollably down the road. "We'll count to three." Washington shouted, "As soon as we hit the ground, we've got to run for the trees. Understand?"

"Yes, I understand."

He took her hand in his as they balanced themselves on their feet, knees bent and peering out of the wagon.

"One...two..."

Just before he said three, the wagon hit another bump, sending the two of them hurdling out into the storm. When they hit the ground they did several flips and tumbles before coming to a stop.

Adrenaline rushed through Washington's veins like a sea of wildfire, causing him to ignore his cuts and scrapes and quickly jump to his feet where he helped a dizzy Ruth Ann to hers. The two of them continued to hold hands as they ran through a small field headed towards the woods. The storm rumbled and growled behind them, threatening at any moment to take them away.

Dirt and other debris filled the air, making it hard for them to breathe. At last they made it into the woods where the rain seemed to be just as heavy regardless of the tree cover. Once they were in the protection of the trees, they didn't stop, but rather they just pushed forward trying to get as deep into them as they could.

When they finally thought they were safe the unthinkable happened. Just as they had slowed from a dead run to a steady walk, trees began snapping and falling down all around them. Washington pulled Ruth Ann back into a run toward a giant tree. It was an old oak and judging from the size of its overly large trunk, it looked to be well over one hundred years old.

They knelt down at its base on the north side, which was the opposite direction that the storm was coming from. Washington covered Ruth Ann with his body as the disastrous storm continued to conquer the woods. Just before the brunt of the super cell was overhead them and in the midst of the pouring rain and crackling trees, Washington kissed Ruth Ann.

"I love you, Ruth Ann. No matter what happens, I'll love you forever."

"I love you too, Washington…"

He once again shielded her with his body as the tornado ripped through right beside them. Limbs began falling all around them as the storm pushed through. Ruth Ann shut her eyes as tightly as she could, hoping that this would all go away and she would wake up in her bed.

Just before Ruth Ann had given up all hope for their survival they were suddenly on the back side of the storm as it marched northeast. Ruth Ann peaked over Washington's arms, which were still wrapped around her and watched as the tornado headed away. Almost immediately the heavy rain turned into a much lighter and softer drizzle.

They stood up with cuts, scrapes, bruises and the occasional tree limb stuck to them and emerged into what looked like a battlefield. All around them the trees lie broken and crumbled and the only thing that stood up in that entire disaster area was the large oak tree that they had taken shelter near. They felt incredibly fortunate and knew that God had spared and protected them.

"Well, darling," Washington said putting his arm around her waist as they continued to watch the tornado spin away. "Looks like we were meant to get married after all."

"Oh, Washington. I don't ever want to lose you as long as I live."

"Don't worry, darling. I'm not going anywhere and I'll always be by your side."

Washington leaned down and kissed her as the last of the rain drifted off with the fleeing tornado. There was no sign of the wagon, so they began walking in search of what used to be the road to Braymyer ridge.

The next week everyone gathered at the Braymyer home for Ruth Ann's wedding. Almost all of Walnut Grove turned out for the event, which made Esther pea green with envy since only half the population had shown up for hers.

Washington waited at the foot of the stairs as Frank Hunter played a light tune on his fiddle. Ruth Ann emerged and slowly descended down the stairs where she took everyone's breath away, even with the few scratches she had across her forehead and cheeks.

The home was filled with complete happiness and everyone had high hopes for the couple. When she walked away that day to her new home, she walked away as Ruth Ann Michaels.

December 13, 1994
Braymyer Ridge

Pappy and I walked around the house and then made our way outside and found ourselves at the barn. It was just as big as Pappy had described it in his story and it had been kept in good condition all these years.

We then walked over to the ridge where John Braymyer had fallen and broken his leg. I looked out down into the small clearing that was now nothing but wild grass and small rocks and then noticed something in the distance atop a very small hill.

It looked to be fenced in and there were some cement blocks of some sort sitting inside of it. "What's that?" I said pointing to my discovery.

"Well, son let's go check it out."

We made our way carefully down the slick ridge and proceeded to walk across the small clearing. As we went through it I looked all around me at the same scenery that my family had once looked upon.

"Pappy, did my daddy ever come here with you?"

"Once, when he was about your age."

"Really? Did you tell him the same story you're telling me?"

"Sure did. He would have told you someday, son, but well, he's not able to now."

"Well, I'm glad you're telling me, Pappy. Does Grandma Rose know the story?"

"Shoot, I've told her a hundred times, but she listens about as well as a cat."

579

"So that means, you, me and my daddy are the only ones who know this story?"

"I suppose it does, son."

I suddenly felt a great responsibility not only to John and Mary Anna, but also to my dad and Pappy. I swore I would never forget this story and someday I would pass it down to my children whom I were certain would listen.

When we walked up to the area that I had seen from above, it revealed itself to be a small cemetery of only four or five tombstones. All the stones were well kept and there were iris' growing around their bases.

"Whose cemetery is this, Pappy?"

"It's the Braymyer Cemetery, son."

"But I thought the Braymyer Cemetery was at our house."

"There's two, one here and one down in Texas where Nat settled. There's also one in California which is where Will moved to."

"Oh, I see."

I stepped inside the small gate and began looking over all the stones. I was ecstatic at the first stone I came to. "Is that, *the* Alice Braymyer?"

"Uh, huh."

I knelt down and read what the stone said:

Alice Elizabeth Morgan Braymyer
May 31, 1790
October 18, 1859

The heart of the family has gone away and now another must try and take her place.

"What happened to her, Pappy?"

"Well, everyone must die, son."

"I know that, but she was so strong. What happened to her?"

October 16, 1859
Braymyer Ridge

The twins were both married now and Tom and Dolly had moved down south toward Texas somewhere. This only left, John, Mary Anna, Rachel, Alice, the three boys and five year old Georgia Tennessee Braymyer at the home.

Mary Anna had insisted on naming her last child after the states that both her husband and herself were born in and just like always, she got her way. Luckily with this birth, just like with the birth of the twins she was able to ease the pain with some of Aunt Liza's moonshine that Alice still carried with her.

Just as Alice had predicted, ten year old Nat had turned out to be the spitting image of his father and he acted just like him as well. Between Mary Anna and Alice's suaveness and the boy's sense of humor, things were never dull in the Braymyer home.

Alice was always the first one awake in the morning and by the time John and Mary Anna had come down the coffee and half the bacon had already been made. One morning when Mary Anna awoke and went downstairs she noticed that Alice was no where to be found.

She went upstairs to her bedroom to check on her and found her in bed holding tightly to her right side and clenching her teeth together. "Alice," she said, "What's the matter?"

"I don't know, honey, but something ain't right."

"Let me go fetch John, I'll be right back."

When she returned she had John at her side whom quickly began to examine his mother. "When did you start hurting, Ma?"

583

"Sometime during the night."

"Mary Anna," he said, "Send Johnny into town to fetch the doctor and then bring up some water."

Mary Anna did as she was asked to and when she returned she found that Alice had not improved any. She began throwing up in a pan that sat near her bed and had a hard time moving around at all.

It took almost two hours for Johnny to return with the doctor and as soon as he stepped into the room he had that same look on his face that he had had when John had broken his leg. He knelt down beside Alice and began to look her over.

He poked around on her stomach, occasionally asking if it hurt and checked all her reflexes. When he had finished looking at her and taking note of all her symptoms he asked to see John in the hallway.

"What is it, Doc?"

"John, I'm afraid there is nothing I can do for her. I've only seen a few cases like this and it is in God's hands. She'll either overcome it, or she won't. Something is wrong with one of her internal organs and it's basically up to her body with whether or not it can fix itself or not."

"Come on, Doc. Surely there's something we can do."

"I'm afraid not, John. I would suggest making her as comfortable as possible and contacting all your family."

John watched as the doctor walked away and as soon as he left John turned and slammed his fist into the wall. His mother wasn't suppose to die yet and not like this. People lived to be much older than she was now, surely God wasn't going to take her, not yet.

After he had contained himself he walked back into the room to where Rachel had joined the two women. "Well," Alice said who seemed to be overpowering the pain at the moment, "What did the doctor say?"

John looked at them, but couldn't say a word. Mary Anna stood up and started toward him. "John... what did the doctor say?"

She went to put her arms around him, but he moved away. "John Braymyer," Alice said, "Don't you move away from her. Now it's obvious the doctor didn't have good news, so if I'm going to die then just spit it out."

"How can you be okay with dying, Ma!" John said as tears ran down his face.

Mary Anna looked at him and then back at Alice who showed no sign of fear. Mary Anna ran to her side and threw her head on top of her chest. "Ma, you can't die. You just can't."

Alice struggled to sit up in bed and once she got situated she looked out across the bed toward her son. "John, come here. Rachel you too."

The two of them joined Mary Anna at her bedside, John putting his arm around Mary Anna. "Now you three listen to me. I don't want a big fuss made over my death, just go on with your lives like you normally would."

"But..." Mary Anna began to say.

"Hush, child and let a dying woman talk. John, I'm proud of you, son and I know your Pa would be proud... you done good. Mary Anna, you're going to be the new heart of this family and I know you'll beat strong enough for the both of us. Don't you ever let life drag you down, you hear?"

Mary Anna nodded her head.

585

"And anytime John gets out of line, you just grab him by the ear and take him where you please."

She turned to Rachel who was on the opposite side of Mary Anna and John. "Rachel dear, you've been a true blessing to me. Now I know I've never said this before and for what it's worth I want you to know, that I would have been one of the few people who would have supported you and Ralph had you had the chance to move forward. I'll be sure and tell him hi when I get to Heaven."

Rachel began crying harder than she had ever done before as memories of both the past and the present flooded through her mind.

"Now," Alice said, "I've said my words of wisdom, let's enjoy the next couple of days or however long it is I have. John?"

"Yes, Ma?"

"Over there in that cabinet is the last of Grandma Davis' moonshine. Would you bring it to me, please?"

John walked over to the other side of the room and opened the large cabinet. He removed the old bottle of shine and brought it back to his mother.

"Good boy," she said. "If this stuff can take the edge off of childbirth I imagine it'll help with this pain too."

"Ma," Mary Anna said, "Do you want something to eat?"

"No, honey, I don't think I could hold it down. Now ya'll go do your chores and send those grandsons of mine in here so I can have a few words with them."

The three of them stood up and kissed her on the forehead one at a time. "We'll be right outside Ma," John said, "If you need anything."

Johnny, Will and Nat stepped into the room as the adults left. Mary Anna leaned her body against John's as he wrapped her in his arms and held her tight. "I'm sorry for pulling away from you, darling."

"Oh, John it's okay. I probably would have done the same thing. Rachel come over here."

Rachel joined in on the group hug as the clock in the hallway slowly ticked away.

Inside the room the three Braymyer boys gathered around their grandmother's bed, a little confused at what was happening so suddenly. "Boy's, before I get started I want you all to know that what I'm going to tell you is not the moonshine talking, okay?"

"Yes, maim," they all said at once.

"Now I guess you all know I'm dying."

"But why grandma?" Nat asked worriedly.

"Well, I guess the Lord is finally ready for Alice Braymyer to come home. Don't worry any, child, I'll see you again someday, but hopefully for your sake not in a long while. Now you boys listen to me. You are Braymyer men and there is nothing better in the world than to be a Braymyer man.

When you see something you want then by, God you had better go after it. Nat, I know you're only eleven but I see how you look at little Rosalee Burns. If that's what you have your cap set for then go after it, besides I think she reminds me of myself many years ago.

That's another thing, you boys be good to your wives and don't you ever treat them wrong. You treat them just like your Pa treats your Ma, do you hear me?"

"Yes, maim."

"And you mind your Ma and Pa and do what they say, okay?"

"We will."

"Alright then, you boys go out and get some fresh air while I rest awhile."

The boys started to leave the room, but before they were able to Alice stopped them. "Now wait just a minute. Don't you think you owe your grandma a kiss? Get over here."

They came back and each one of them tried to only kiss her on the cheek, but every time she turned and kissed them right smack on the lips. They left the room and gave their crying mother a hug before going out to play.

Mary Anna never left Alice's side as her health continued to decline. John had found the strength within himself to be strong for his family and overcome the shock he had first felt at the news. He stayed outside with his sons and would occasionally make visits to his mother to see that she was comfortable.

Rachel busied herself taking care of Georgia and making sure that everything in the house was in order. She brought Mary Anna food at every meal and would relieve her when she needed to go out back to the outhouse.

Other than that, Mary Anna ate, slept, prayed and cried right there beside Alice Braymyer as she slowly dwindled away. Even on the last day that she was alive, she was still just as much full of life as she had been the day she first met her back in Tennessee.

"Mary Anna," she said through a weak voice. "I don't suppose any of us know where life is going to take us, but I sure am glad it brought you and I together."

"Oh, Ma. I'm the one who is thankful. You have taught me so much not only about how to do things, but things about life itself. I just know that I shall never meet another person like you so long as I live."

"Darling, what you just said is what every person wants to hear before they die. Life isn't about trying to meet the richest and greatest people, it's about trying to be great yourself. Mary Anna, darling, I think you are great and you are a fine daughter in law."

"Thank you, Ma. But any amount of greatness I have about me is only because it was a gift from you."

"You're sweet, but you had greatness within you when I first saw you, you just needed someone to show you how to find it. Well, looks like there is one swig of moonshine left. Won't you be a darling and hand it to me?"

Mary Anna stood up and brought her the jar that truly only had one swallow left. She held it up to Alice's lips and watched as the jar slowly became empty, taking with it the last piece of Grandma Davis that was left in this world. Alice puckered her lips as if she were satisfied at the taste and then as she stared up at Mary Anna her eyes became cloudy as the life disappeared.

The next day the family gathered around a small hole down below the ridge and took one last look at Alice before her casket was lowered into the ground. Mary Anna had taken her blue dress that John had bought for her and put it on Alice to be buried in.

Alice had smiled so much in life that even in death her soft lips were naturally moved upward. She looked at peace in that little blue dress and everything around her was covered in flowers. Slowly, her body was lowered into the rocky ground and Mary Anna now carried the heart of the family within her chest.

Later that night after everyone was inside by the warmth of the fire it began to rain uncontrollably. It seemed as though even Missouri was able to cry and the great state showered the countryside with its tears of sadness over the truly remarkable, Alice Braymyer.

December 13, 1994
Braymyer Ridge

Pappy and I walked up the stairs and onto the large platform in front of the picture of Mary Anna and John. I looked over to my right and on the wall just above where the smaller staircase came to an end there was a hole in the wall.

I walked the short distance up and stopped in front of my discovery. "Pappy," I said as he joined me at my side. "Is this the hole that John punched when his mother died?"

"Sure is, or at least that's what I've been told."

I looked over the hole and concluded that John Braymyer must have been a strong man to make such a mark. About three feet below the hole that he had created I took my fist and slammed it into the wall, causing a much smaller hole to form.

"John!" Pappy said, "What are you doing?"

I clutched my hurt fist with my good hand, "Well, I was making a hole for my Mama and Daddy."

"Son, you don't just go around punching holes in walls when someone dies."

"But John did it."

"I know son, but… well never mind, I guess you had a right to do that."

Pappy looked at the two holes in the wall and shook his head. "I guess this wall has more than one story to tell now, doesn't it?"

"I guess so," I answered him still holding my fist.

591

We headed around to the front windows upstairs and looked out as the Braymyer land stretched out in front of us. Georgette was leaving and since we were the only guests we were all alone in the big house.

After her car had driven off we made our way back downstairs and sat in the front room as the fireplace glowed from the flames within it. Pappy picked up a small blue book and began to read.

March 14, 1861
Dear Journal,

I fear that we are on the brink of war. It seems that it is the only gossip of the area here lately and I think it is only a matter of time. I support John in his decision to declare our household one of Confederate support and we shall do whatever it takes to support the cause. We do not agree with owning slaves, or any person for that matter, but we firmly hold true to the belief in state's rights.

All across the state neighbors are being separated and families are being turned against one another. Even my own daughter, poor Esther is now against our household. Her husband, Ben Hunter has chosen to support the union and like a good wife she supports him. The last time they were over here, Ben and my husband got into a fistfight over the matter and they have not been back since.

Ruth Ann and her husband Washington Michaels are with us in supporting the confederate, but like us they neither see nor speak to my darling Esther. Johnny swears that if there is a war he will be the first boy to sign up on the confederate side and will serve the cause proudly. It pains me to think that he might go off and get killed, but he is like his father and there is no changing his mind.

John says that there are enough confederate supporters around here that we should be ok, but he has built a new cellar beneath the house that can be accessed by a trap door beneath the dining room table. If the Union forces happen to cause us any trouble, we are to go down there and hide until it is safe to come out.

I do hope that somehow this war will be avoided, but it doesn't look like there is going to be any way around it. How I wish the hatred for one another would just disappear, but so long as there is envy between our great nation war is truly inevitable.

Ready for battle,
Mary Anna Braymyer

March 23, 1862
Braymyer Ridge

It had been almost a year since the start of the Civil War and like the Braymyer family, many other families found themselves being split right down the middle. Johnny who was now 18 had joined as soon as word had reached Missouri that the war had started and his parents knew very little about his whereabouts.

John's cattle operation had nearly completely plummeted, there was too much of a risk that his cattle would be stolen by hungry troops so he sold out and hid the money in the basement so that he could restart his business after the war. He knew that when the war was over either the confederate money or that of the union would have no value so he split his earnings holding half his cash in confederate and the other half in union.

Neighbors were fighting against neighbors and there had been talk that several of the union supporters were planning a march through the area to remove all the confederate supporters. Esther Hunter was right at the head of this movement and cared very little that her older brother was off fighting somewhere.

Even Polly Hunter, her mother in law who had been so supportive of owning slaves had taken sides with the union. The war seemed to bring out the true reality of who people really were and often caused them to do the horrible things that they had so desired to do, lie, cheat and steal.

But for the Braymyers, they remained the same people that they had always been, valuing their family and striving to survive whatever the world threw their way. Every Sunday, the local confederate supporters would come to the Braymyer home and share their stories and news that they had heard about their loved ones who were somewhere far away.

Will, Nat and Georgia continued to live out their childhood on the ridge in the midst of the war as Mary Anna tried to keep them as far away from it as possible, even though their older brother was fighting in it somewhere. She read them stories from the Bible and took them swimming in the nearby creek, she did just about anything she could to allow them to enjoy their childhood.

As much as she tried to protect them, the day that Esther rode up with three other union wives, including Polly, she knew that it was only a matter of time before the war ended up in her home. Mary Anna and Ruth Ann were clearing out some flower gardens in front of the house when she rode up, wearing one of her fancy store bought dresses and carrying a union flag across her lap.

She was driving the wagon and on the seat beside her was Polly Hunter, who was still just as full of gossip as she had been before. In the back were two other women who looked to be around Esther's age and they too held union flags in their laps.

"Mrs. Braymyer," Esther said to her mother as she pulled the wagon to a stop in front of her house.

"Esther, since when do you call me, Mrs. Braymyer?"

"Since you abandoned the union cause and devoted yourself to the confederates."

The other women shunned their chins up at Mary Anna who couldn't help but laugh a little bit and shake her head. Ruth Ann leaned her tall thin body up against the hoe and looked at the group of women with a displeasing look as she began to talk.

"Esther you always were one to strut your stuff around like you were the town whore, now what is it that brings you out here?"

Esther looked shocked at her sister's compelling remark. "I only came to see if you had come to your senses and would like to join our cause. But I can see now that you are still the same sassy person you have always been."

Ruth Ann turned to her mother and smiled, "You hear that, Ma. She called me sassy, I think that's the closest thing to a compliment she has ever given anyone."

"You know Ruth Ann," Mary Anna said, "I do believe you're right."

"This is your last chance to join us," Esther said, "If you refuse now I can't promise that your fate will be a good one."

"Esther," Mary Anna said, "I had had such high hopes for you and had thought that maybe you would be like the Esther in the bible and lead the people. But, hell, you can't even lead yourself."

"Do you understand that I could have union supporters out here as early as this afternoon to take over your house and turn it into a headquarters?" Esther said.

"And do you understand," Mary Anna said, "That I could take you out back with a switch like I had to do when you were a little girl? Besides, as long as there is breath in my chest I'll keep my house. Now go on."

Esther looked at the two of them as Georgia stepped out onto the front porch. "Well at least let me take Georgia with me. She'll be safer at my house anyhow."

Mary Anna looked at Esther as if she had just offered to spread wings and fly away like a bird. "I don't think so. Besides, the last time I checked Georgia was a part of the confederacy. Now get out of here!"

The wagon rolled off in the same direction it had come from, leaving the three of them standing in front of the house. "Come on, Ma," Ruth Ann said, "Let's go have ourselves some tea."

They went inside and sat at the dining room table with their tea as the boys headed in from the wheat fields. They spent the rest of the day taking supplies down into the cellar for fear that it would only be a matter of time before they had to make it their new home.

"Ma," Ruth Ann said as they carried things down to the basement. "Do you think Johnny and Washington are okay?"

"I'm sure they're fine, dear. They are in the same regiment so I am sure they are taking good care of each other."

"I know, but I can't help but worry about them."

"It's hard, darling, but we've got to push on. Now, come on let's get the last of this stuff down here before it's too late."

Sure enough, just before the sun went down they heard several horses heading up the drive toward their house. One by one they stepped down into the cellar and made themselves comfortable as people came into their home.

Above them they could hear the footsteps of about seven or eight people walk around above them. They heard the familiar voice of Esther as she stepped from the kitchen into the dining room, "I've always wanted to own this house and now it's mine."

"Pa," Ruth Ann said, "What are we going to do?"

"Don't worry, darling. It will be over soon."

"But how?"

"Let's just say that help is on the way."

They remained quietly tucked away inside the newly built basement as more and more Yankees came into their home. Most of the time it was the sick and injured who were brought there and the house turned into a hospital of such.

The enemy forces above them had no idea that they were hidden beneath the floor where they could hear everything that was going on above them. Mary Anna patiently paced back and forth across the dirt floor as men that she did not know slowly took control of her house.

Help did finally arrive, but not until seven days after they had been held up in the basement. "Look!" They heard one of the men say from above them, "Heading this way, it looks like confederate supporters."

They heard the men run toward the front door and as they did, John and his two sons headed up the stairs. "Mary Anna, you and the girls stay here, no matter what happens."

John, Nat and Will emerged into the dining room to see that it was completely empty and they headed toward the front of the house. Standing on the porch were six union men that had been staying in their home and out in the front yard there was a battle going on between the north and the south.

John and his sons slowly crept up behind them and when they were sure enough of themselves they started firing. Three fell to the ground, followed by two more leaving only one left standing on the porch. Ben Hunter who was here on leave turned around to face John.

"So this is how it's going to be, John," he said. "You going to kill your own son in law?"

"That depends, are you or anymore of your union obsessed friends going to be back at my house?"

"Pa, No!" Esther said running in front of her husband.

"Esther, get out of the way." John demanded her.

"No, Pa. I won't let you shoot my husband."

Ben was lifting up his rifle, allowing it to point at Nat's head. Ben had the look on his face that showed no sympathy and revealed the fact that he had no problem killing him.

"Esther!" John said, "Get out of the way!"

"I won't do it, Pa!"

"What's the matter, John?" Ben said, "You don't want to hurt your daughter?"

"Ben get out from behind her, a man should never hide behind a woman."

Ben half laughed at him as he readied himself to pull the trigger. John clenched his teeth together as he knew he must pick only one of his children to save. He quickly pulled the trigger, sending a bullet into Esther's chest and entering into Ben's head.

The couple fell to the ground, halfway on the front porch and halfway inside the house. John rubbed his hand through Nat's hair as the girls emerged into the room and observed the scene.

The shots were still being fired out in the front yard and the Braymyer men quickly ran outside to join in on the effort to rid their land of the union forces. Mary Anna was right behind them with a musket in her hands and she immediately began firing shots at the Yankees.

There had been just about as many confederates there as there had been Yankees, but since the confederates were more familiar with the land they soon outnumbered their enemy. Within thirty minutes of stepping outside, the Yankees ran for the hills being chased closely by the confederates who John had sent word to the day that Esther had first come to the house.

John and Mary Anna walked back to the door where their daughter lay dead in a pool of hers and her husband's blood. Mary Anna knelt down and placed her head in her lap as she slowly ran her hand across her daughter's head. John joined her as his tears began to flow.

"What have I done, Mary Anna?"

"You did what you had to, John. You did what you had to."

John and the boys went right away to the cemetery and dug a hole for their sister and daughter. The family marched down the ridge and buried her before the sun went down, Esther Braymyer had been but one of many casualties of this dreadful war.

After she had been buried, John went upstairs and didn't hardly come down at all. The war had not only separated a nation, but it had torn through his family and forced him to kill his first born child, his once sweet Esther.

The war continued to plague the small settlement that was neatly tucked away in the Ozarks. It seemed that everyday news was received that some local boy had been killed and would never return home, the soldier was rather buried in an unmarked grave near his death place.

Most of the battles around the Braymyer home were disagreements between neighbors and even family members. Missouri was so split that nearly every other farm was on the opposite side where the war was concerned.

Dusty Williams

September 23, 1863
Braymyer Ridge

Nat and his little sister, Georgia walked through the small clearing at the bottom of the ridge and headed into the trees. Nat carried a rifle across his right shoulder and was on the lookout for anything that he could shoot to provide some food for his family.

Georgia walked along in a southern plantation style dress and eagerly followed her older brother. She could be the most feminine of all girls or she could wrestle with the toughest boys around, it made no difference to her. The friends that she had had, like her brother's friends as well, were mostly union supporters and they were now not able to be sociable with them.

For a child growing up in the Civil War it was especially hard, not knowing why they were no longer allowed to see certain people and even family members. Overall, families just stuck together and persevered in hopes that the dreadful war might soon be over.

At the house, Will sat at the table with his parents as Ruth Ann read aloud a letter from her husband. The war had been extremely stressful for Ruth Ann as she continued to worry for her husband's safety. Just before he had left to go to war their two month old child, a son died. So not only had she lost a child, but she had now lost her husband and feared that she may have lost him for good.

Mary Anna and John tried to comfort her as best they could, while also dealing with a son in the same war. John received a letter from his sister, Dolly down in Texas that informed him that their brother, Tom was killed in a battle. Tom had three daughters and no sons, meaning the only male Braymyers that were left to carry on the family name were John and his sons.

For months it seemed that a dark cloud hung above the country and threatened at anytime to start spinning like a tornado and destroy everything in its path. Food became scarce and what little there was, was at a high risk to be stolen by runaways and union officials who showed a sort of revenge on southerners.

The family held close to one another during this time of depression and the only thing that kept them afoot was knowing that they had each other. Luckily, no Yankee troops had been to the large Braymyer home, for if they had it would have surely been taken over and used for their cause.

Nat and Georgia continued into the woods looking for wild game to bring back home to their mother. A cool breeze somehow made its way into the thick trees and felt good to their bodies. In the midst of all the war and fighting, they somehow felt at peace as they explored the area in no particular hurry.

The tops of the trees rustled and as they did, more rustic leaves fell to the tree covered ground. Nat and Georgia tried to step lightly across them so they wouldn't scare off their prey.

Nat steadied his gun in front of him, taking aim at a fairly large rabbit that had stopped in front of them. He looked down the barrel and ran his finger up and down the trigger until slowly, he pulled it back towards him as the area echoed with the crack of a gunshot.

The rabbit fell over and the two of them began walking toward their next meal. The leaves crunched beneath their feet as they excitedly walked toward the dead animal.

When they were about ten feet from it, a tall lanky man stepped out just behind the rabbit. He was dressed in a Yankee uniform and looked to have not had a decent shave in about a year.

His skin had been dyed red from the sun and his shaggy
brown hair stuck out from beneath his military hat. He let his
musket rest over his shoulder as he looked toward the two of
them.

"Children," he said, "Thank you for the rabbit. I'm so hungry
that I couldn't get a steady aim at him."

"Hey," Georgia said, "That's our rabbit!"

"And this is our land!" Nat insisted.

The Yankee stepped over the dead rabbit and walked closer to
them. He looked at them as if they were adults rather than the
children they were.

"What do we have here? Little Rebel children?"

"That's right, mister!" Georgia said, "Now leave us be or
we'll go fetch our Pa."

The man started laughing and continued in their direction.
"You're Pa? Ha, is that suppose to scare me?"

"That's far enough," Georgia said, "I swear I'll scream!"

The man rushed up to them, pushing Nat down to the ground
and grabbing Georgia, putting his hand over her mouth. He
pointed the gun at Nat who lie on his back.

"Aren't you a pretty little thing," he said running his tongue
behind Georgia's ear. "Now what should I do with you?"

He began running his hands down her body, holding her
mouth tightly all the while. He was breathing heavily down
her neck, forcing her body against his.

"Stop it!" Nat shouted.

"Shut up, boy!" He said taking the gun away from him. "Or I'll shoot you both!"

He kicked Nat in his rib cage, causing him to roll over onto his stomach and then turned his attention back to Georgia. He began to unzip his blue pants and ran his hand over her stomach. He removed his hand from her mouth and used both of his hands to explore her.

"If you scream," he said, "I'll snap your neck."

The surroundings continued to offer all the signs of a peaceful day, a mask to cover the devilish act that was taking place just beneath the shade of the trees. Georgia stood there strong, never letting a single tear fall from her face.

Just before he started to undress her, a shot was fired and Georgia's body was covered in blood as it poured out of the Yankee's head. The man slowly fell to the ground, nearly bringing Georgia down with her. When the smoke cleared, it revealed Rachel standing there with a gun in her arms.

Rachel dropped the gun and ran toward Georgia where she took her in her arms. Nat rolled over, finding that his hand was resting on his rifle.

"Negro!" A voice said from behind Rachel. "Did you shoot this soldier?"

Rachel and Georgia turned to see that another Yankee was standing there pointing a gun at them.

"I… I…"

"Answer the question, Negro!"

"Yes, sir. I was protecting this child."

The Yankee looked toward Georgia. "Well, I think I'll shoot you and then take care of this beautiful girl myself."

The Yankee had not noticed Nat lying on the ground who was clutching his broken ribs on his right side with his left hand. He used his right hand to slowly lift his rifle in the direction of the soldier.

He took aim just as he had done with the rabbit and squeezed the trigger. A bullet struck the Yankee in the chest, causing blood to spill out of his mouth like tea being poured into an empty glass. For a dead man, he remained on his feet longer than he should have.

Georgia stepped over to him and kicked him in the stomach, sending him to fall backwards onto the ground. Rachel picked up her gun as Georgia grabbed the dead Yankee's weapon and then the two of them joined Nat on the ground and watched as they were sure more soldiers would be there shortly.

Rachel wrapped one arm around each of the children, just as Mary Anna would have done, allowing the gun to rest in her lap. Birds began chirping somewhere up above them as if they were telling the world what had just happened.

"Georgia," Rachel said. "You run back to the house and fetch your Ma and Pa. Run as fast as you can child and don't stop until you get there."

Georgia immediately ran toward the clearing leaving Rachel and Nat alone in the woods. From beneath the tops of the trees, the two of them looked up at what little sky they could see and determined that it looked like it was going to rain.

"Rachel, do you think Georgia will be okay?"

"I'm sure she'll be fine. If there was anymore Yankee soldiers out there, I imagine they would have already stumbled upon us by now. Now, you just rest while we wait for your Ma and Pa, they'll know what to do."

About twenty minutes after she left, Georgia returned with her parents, Will and Ruth Ann to find Rachel and Nat standing near the dead bodies. Nat was leaning down and to the right a little, still holding his right side as little drops of rain made their way through the trees down on top of them.

Given her motherly instinct, Mary Anna looked right over the bodies and ran to Nat to make sure he was okay. She put her arm around him and examined him from head to toe.

"Nat, son. Are you okay?"

"Yeah, I'm fine, Ma. Just some hurt ribs is all."

"Should I send for the doctor?" Rachel asked.

"We can't," Mary Anna said. "Doc George is a union supporter and he won't help us."

"Really," Nat insisted, "I'm fine."

"Ruth Ann," Mary Anna said. "Help Nat to the house while we get this mess cleaned up. Georgia you go with them and put your dress in the fire place. We don't need a blood covered dress at our house in case someone comes sneaking around. Now go on."

Nat's sisters took his arms and put them around their necks as they headed out of the woods. When they were completely out of sight and the rain had began to come down more steadily, Mary Anna turned to her husband.

"John, what are we going to do?"

"We've got to get rid of the bodies. If Yankee soldiers find them, they'll kill us all."

"What are we going to do with them, Pa?" Will asked.

"We need to burn them, but the rain is coming down too hard. Will, run back to the barn and get some shovels. Rachel go with him and help him carry them back."

After they were gone, John and Mary Anna drug the bodies to some softer ground as the rain continued to pour down and thunder ripped through the sky. They used their feet to clean up some of the blood by stirring the dirt around as it became muddy.

In no time, the two of them were soaked in water, but the water nor the cool September weather stopped them from completing their task. The trees started to shake roughly as wind caught them and ripped through their branches down to their trunks.

"John, how could this happen to our children?"

"I don't know, darling, but it's over now."

When Will and Rachel returned, the four of them immediately began digging two holes into the muddy ground. They jabbed and stabbed the ground as the muddy mess continued to grow, it was as if they were in a mini flood. Once the holes were deep enough they threw them down into the ground where they hit a growing puddle of water inside them.

Afterwards, they gathered up all the blood stained leaves that they could find and threw them into the holes as well, leaving nothing behind as evidence. When everything was done and looked to their satisfaction they covered the graves with the mud and then threw leaves all around them so that the sinkholes would not be as visible.

September 26, 1863
Braymyer Ridge

Three days after the Yankees had been buried, Nat continued to lie in his bed as his mother learned how to be a doctor. She took care of him just as she had done for his father in the past while everyone else busied themselves downstairs.

It had not stopped raining since the day the graves were dug and it showed no signs of stopping anytime soon. There was constant lightening and thunder across the gray sky as the area was consumed by water.

Ruth Ann sat in the front room near a window with her sewing and a book as she listened to the slow tick of the clock on the mantel. She kept a constant eye out of the front window, patiently watching for someone who might be carrying mail from her dear Washington.

She desperately longed for her husband's touch and hoped that someday soon they could try once again to start their family. He had been the best thing that had ever happened to her and now he was away fighting in the war. Ruth Ann hated the war and what it was doing to families and neighbors all across the states, but she was proud to say that her husband was a soldier, even if he had promised never to leave her side.

Georgia wandered the house trying to find something to occupy her time and most of the time she found herself in the basement pretending to be hiding from Yankees. She showed very little signs that the attack on her in the woods had affected her and her only regret about the whole situation was that Nat was not able to play with her.

Rachel busied herself doing all the house chores since Mary Anna spent most of her time up in Nat's room. Rachel would occasionally join Ruth Ann in the front room and try to keep the young girl's lonely heart company.

John and Will sat at the dining room table and smoked on a pipe as they talked about things that most father and sons talk about. What the plans were for the farm after the war; making preparations for the upcoming winter and lastly, what to do if Yankees were to attack.

Time seemed to drag on for days inside the house and there was no outside communication whatsoever, which made for long rain filled afternoons. Even the animals that were in the barn made noises in protest of the boredom that had taken over the Braymyer home.

Ruth Ann sat in a rocker with her head down as she slowly drifted into an afternoon nap. The rain continued to pour down and it wasn't until the second knock on the front door that Rachel heard it.

She hurried down the hallway toward the door and opened it. As the door was opened she found herself nearly being knocked over as four Yankee soldiers barged into the house.

Rachel, who was terrified, shut the door behind them as they began walking through the house. Ruth Ann stood up, wide eyed and watched as they went down the hall and into the dining room.

John and Will immediately stood up.

"Sit down," the lead Yankee said. "I'm Major Turner and this is, Johnson, Cato and Merriman." He continued as he pointed to the two men on his right and one on his left.

John and Will slowly sat back down. "What can we do for you?" John asked.

"We're looking for two missing soldiers and need a place to stay until the rain clears up. We'll be taking over all the rooms upstairs, you and your family may remain downstairs. We'll expect every meal just the same as you and your family."

"Sir," John said thinking of Nat. "There's more than enough bedrooms for everyone."

"Would you rather us move you and your family to the barn?"

"No," John said seeing the seriousness on his face.

"Good then. You have ten minutes to go upstairs and get what you need. After that, no one is allowed up there except the four of us. Understand?"

"Yes," John said not able to come up with anything else to say.

"And I want our meals to be brought up by the good looking lady in the front room. Do you have livestock in the barn?"

"Not very much. Two pigs, three cows and six horses."

"Very well. We'll be taking them when we leave."

The major looked cautiously at John and Will. "Say you two haven't seen the two missing soldiers have you?"

"Sure haven't," John replied.

"What about you, boy?"

"Um… No, sir. I haven't seen anyone."

"Alright then, go upstairs and get what you need. Make sure all the weapons are left up there."

John and Will headed for the stairs where Ruth Ann and Rachel were waiting for them. They had been listening in on the conversation that had been taking place in the dining room and had fright written across their faces.

Will, Ruth Ann and Rachel scattered once they reached the top of the stairs, collecting small things they might need and hiding all the family heirlooms. John went into Nat's room where he found Mary Anna sitting beside his bed and reading from the book of Esther.

"Yes!" Nat said, "Thank you, Pa. I don't think I can take anymore bible stories today."

"Sorry, son. I'm not here with good news."

"John," Mary Anna said, "What is it?"

"Come on, darling. We've got to get Nat downstairs. Yankees are taking over the upstairs of our house and have ordered all of us to remain downstairs."

"Yankees! Here! Oh, John what are we going to do?"

"We're going to do whatever they ask. Now, come on."

Nat put his arms around his parents and they slowly began making their way down the stairs. When they reached the bottom, the major was waiting with his three men near his side.

"What happened to him?" He asked.

"He fell down the ridge," Mary Anna said right away.

"Boy, is this true?"

"Yes, sir." Nat said.

The major stepped closer and lifted up Nat's shirt to examine his right side. He pushed his hand against the large bruise across his rib cage, nearly causing Nat to fall to the ground.

"You sure that's what happened boy? Looks to me like it's a boot print."

"No, sir. And yes, sir I'm sure," Nat nervously said. "I hit some rocks on the way down and that's what done it to me."

Rachel, Ruth Ann and Will were heading down the stairs with blankets and clothing in their arms.

"Very well," the major said. "Take him to the front room."

Everyone headed in that direction where Georgia was already waiting for them. Ruth Ann was bringing up the rear and as she stepped off of the last step, the major stopped her by putting his hand around her wrist.

"I'll be expecting you to be bringing up my supper here shortly, little lady."

Ruth Ann gave him a disgusted look and then calmly said, "Would you prefer coffee or horse piss with that?"

"Young lady, you had better watch that southern mouth of yours or me and the boys here might have to teach you a lesson."

She rolled her eyes and pushed passed the four soldiers as she mumbled, "And you had better watch your Yankee arrogance."

The soldiers went upstairs to enjoy their new home while the family gathered together in the front room.

"Ma," Ruth Ann said, "What are we going to do? Do you think they know the Yankees are buried in the woods."

"Ruth Ann," John interrupted. "There will be no more talk about that. We will cross that bridge if and when we get to it. Do you hear me?"

"Yes, Pa. But I don't like these Yankees here. These same Yankees that Johnny and Washington are off fighting somewhere are staying in our home!"

"Hush, child," Mary Anna said. "We just have to get through this. The war will be over soon enough."

That night Ruth Ann walked up the stairs with the soldier's food and with each step she took she added one more drop of spit onto their plates. By the time she reached their doors her mouth was so dry that she could hardly speak, which was probably a good thing for her sake.

After the lustful looks of the soldiers over her body had became too much for her, she hurriedly collected their empty plates and ran back downstairs to join her family. The family slept in the front sitting room that night by the warmth of the fireplace as their enemy slept upstairs in their beds.

September 27, 1863
Yankee Ridge

The next day and after little sleep, Mary Anna went into the kitchen before anyone else was awake. She proceeded with making coffee and preparing breakfast as she listened to the rain while it continued to fall from the sky.

She heard a loud thud upstairs and assumed that one of the soldiers was awake. Her thoughts were proven right when the soldier named Merriman shouted down the stairs. "Someone bring me some firewood!"

Mary Anna stepped into the back room just off the kitchen and where the hallway ended and loaded her arms with firewood. She then went down the hallway and up the stairs and once on the platform took a right up the small set of stairs and into Ruth Ann's bedroom.

She knocked on the door. "Come in!" The grouchy man replied.

Merriman was a tall man unlike the major and had reddish blonde hair with a well trimmed beard. It was obvious that this group of soldiers were better taken care of than the two they had buried a few days before.

When she stepped into the room, Merriman was hunched over the fireplace poking the smoldering ash with a metal rod. She was shocked to see that the immodest man was wearing absolutely no clothing. He stood up and turned to face her, hiding nothing from her sight. She dropped the logs quickly and turned back towards the door.

"Wait!" He said.

She remained facing the door. "What do you need?"

"Well first of all you can show me a little more respect," he said. "I'm a member of the United States Army you know."

"Sir you're just another heartless Yankee and if you want respect I would suggest that you start showing it first. How dare you invite a married woman, or any woman for that matter into your room when you are not properly clothed."

"Oh come on, now. Why don't you lie in bed with me for awhile? Us Yankees are nothing like the confederate men you're so accustomed to."

"Sir!" She said, "What is it with you, Yankees! You are all like wild animals, especially towards us women."

She could hear him getting closer to her as he approached from behind, but she didn't realize how close he was until he put his hands around her waist.

"Come on," he said, "Let's have us some fun."

Mary Anna clenched her fist together and sent it flying back over her shoulder where it met his nose. He turned and leaned forward, holding his nose as it began to bleed.

Mary Anna stepped out of the door. "Hey," he shouted. "Where are you going?"

"I'm going to get a gun and I'm going to shoot you, that's where."

Merriman started laughing in disbelief as Mary Anna marched down the stairs. When she reached the kitchen, Ruth Ann was pouring her a cup of coffee.

"Ma? What is it?"

"I'm going to kill me some senseless pathetic Yankee pigs!"

Ruth Ann had never seen her mother this angry before in her life. It somewhat scared her, but more so it excited her and gave her an adrenaline rush. "Ma, let me come help you."

Mary Anna knelt down and opened a cabinet where four revolvers were hidden. She took them all out and handed two of them to Ruth Ann. "Come on then," she said.

The two of them walked side by side up the wide stairs and then right, up the smaller set. Once they got to the top, Mary Anna was looking straight at the door she intended to go in.

"Ma," Ruth Ann said. "I think I'm going to go pay the major a visit."

Mary Anna kissed her on the forehead, "Be careful, darling."

Ruth Ann passed two doors after leaving her mother at Merriman's door until she was at the last door, which was the major's room. Ruth Ann knocked, "Breakfast, sir."

"Come in!" He snapped.

As Ruth Ann went into the major's room, Mary Anna went into Merriman's, where she found him lying in bed.

"Ah. I see you changed your mind and want to have a little fun after all."

"I told you I was going to get a gun. Here they are," she said pulling the revolvers out from behind her back.

"Now wait a minute," he said jumping out of bed still unclothed with his hands halfway in the air. "You can't do this."

"Oh yes I can. Now move away from Ruth Ann's bed, I'm not in the mood to clean blankets today."

"Now, missy," he said moving towards her, "You don't know what you're doing."

"I know exactly what I am doing," she said as she pulled the trigger, striking him between the eyes. He fell forward and she exited the room back into the hallway.

When Ruth Ann entered the major's room he was still in bed, but unfortunately for her, he had his gun in bed with him as well. She kept her hands behind her back keeping the guns hidden as she approached him.

"What is this? Where's my breakfast? You said…"

"I'm sorry, sir. I just couldn't resist. There's just something about you that draws me nearer. I feel as though I should want to always be in your presence."

The major smiled, "I suppose it's not your fault. Most of the girls back north felt the same way. Come closer and sit with me.

Ruth Ann slowly stepped closer to him as she tried with everything she had to hide her disgust. Just as she got within reaching distance of the major, the shot from Merriman's room filled the house. The major looked at Ruth Ann with a hint of anger and a bigger hint of confusion written across his face.

She pulled the gun out quickly before he had time to grab his, which was still beside him and pulled the trigger. The first shot clumsily missed and landed just over his left shoulder, but the second one struck him in the neck creating a rather bloody mess.

She ran back out the door only a few seconds after her mother had emerged back into the hallway. Mary Anna was at one end and Ruth Ann the other and they both looked at each other as the two doors in between them opened.

The remaining two soldiers stepped out into the hallway, one looking directly at Ruth Ann and the other at Mary Anna. Mary Anna didn't hesitate to fire and when she did she brought the man in front of her to the floor. Ruth Ann shot once, but again the bullet missed her target and whizzed over his head toward where her mother was standing.

It struck her mother in the shoulder, causing Ruth Ann to nearly faint with terror. Mary Anna just looked in her daughter's direction dumbfounded and shouted at her. "Ruth Ann! I'm not the Yankee here! Shoot him!"

The last remaining Yankee was so confused that he nearly forgot to raise his weapon, but just as Ruth Ann pointed her gun in his direction, he too pointed a gun at her. The two of them looked at each other as if they were testing to see which one of them was the stronger of the two.

Ruth Ann pulled the trigger, but all she got was a click…she was out of bullets. The Yankee smiled and began walking towards her, but just before reaching her he was brought to the ground as a bullet hit him from behind. Mary Anna had shot him and the bullet went straight through his neck and hit Ruth Ann in the same shoulder that her mother had been hit in.

Ruth Ann remained standing and looked over at her shoulder, still half unaware of what had happened. When the man fell to the ground she saw her mother standing against the opposite wall.

The two of them couldn't help but laugh at each other as John, Will and Rachel ran up the stairs to see what was going on. Ruth Ann made her way over the two dead soldiers to where her family was gathering.

"Mary Anna! Ruth Ann!" John said, "You're shot! Are you okay? Sit down."

"Ma," Ruth Ann said sitting down next to her mother, "You just had to shoot me back didn't you."

"Ruth Ann, darling. You really need to work on your aim."

As they joked among themselves, John checked all the rooms to ensure that all the Yankees were dead. As he stepped back out into the hallway the morning thunder shook the house. Rachel held a lantern over Mary Anna and Ruth Ann to examine their wounds.

"Now," John said leaning down to them, "How in the world did you both get shot in the same exact place."

Ruth Ann started laughing and Mary Anna said in a calm voice, "Ask her, she shot me first."

"Geez, you two! Come on, let's get you to the bedroom so we can have a look at them."

They helped them back across the stairs and up the other set of small ones on the left. As they crossed over the platform, Mary Anna looked down and saw Georgia standing at the foot of the stairs.

"Ma," she said, "Are you shot?"

"Yes, honey. Your sister shot me!"

"Well, Ma shot me too!" Ruth Ann protested.

They went down the hall and into John and Mary Anna's room where the two of them laid side by side while Rachel picked the bullets out of them. Luckily the wounds weren't very deep so it didn't take her long to get them out.

"Boy, you two really made a mess of things this morning," John said.

"They sure did," Rachel added, "And then they went and shot each other so they wouldn't have to clean up the mess!"

"That's right," Mary Anna said. "We did the dirty work now you two can clean up, isn't that right, Ruth Ann."

"Sure is, Ma. I guess getting shot wasn't such a bad thing after all."

John shook his head and half laughed as he left the room, "Women and guns," he mumbled, "Women and guns."

John and Will drug the bodies out back and just as they got the last one outside, the rain suddenly stopped and the sun began to shine. They drug them down just below the ridge and buried them there while Rachel cleaned up the mess inside.

It had been a lucky thing that it rained so much, for if it had been good weather those soldiers would have more than likely stumbled upon the graves of the first two that had been buried and the Braymyer family would have been hung. After John and Will buried them, they vowed never to let another Yankee soldier near Mary Anna and Ruth Ann again for fear that they might shoot each other.

The rest of the year was fairly good weather with a mild winter and not a single Yankee soldier came looking for any of the missing ones that were buried on the Braymyer farm. Life of the farm went back to normal, or as normal as could be expected with the war going on, but they were all glad to be rid of the Yankees that had occupied their home, even if it was for one night only.

Dusty Williams

July 24, 1864
Braymyer Ridge

It was early afternoon and Ruth Ann had resumed sitting in her usual spot near the front window. Nat and Georgia were playing in the barn while Will and John surveyed their cornfields.

Everyday, usually by the light of the moon, deserters would come through the fields and take from the dwindling crop that was to see the family through the rest of the year. By the end of July, there was very little of anything left in the form of food at Braymyer Ridge. All the livestock had almost withered down to skin and bones and on more than one occasion, John had to chase off thieves who were trying to steal the sickly animals for food.

Rachel and Mary Anna were in the back yard beating all the dust out of the many rugs that occupied the home beneath the hot July sun as a few birds scattered across the blue sky on occasion. It would have made for a rather peaceful Missouri day if one were to keep their stare away from below the ridge in front of them where it looked like wasteland with the thinning corn crop in the valley. If they were lucky, there were maybe four rows that had not been picked through, not nearly enough for them yet alone the starving animals.

Ruth Ann closed her book, sat it in her lap and watched as a wagon rolled toward the house. She stepped out onto the porch with Uncle Tom's Cabin still in her hands and watched as the mule drawn wagon drew nearer. The large round wooden wheels rattled and made small cracking noises as it continued up the long drive.

At last it stopped in front of the steps and Ruth Ann was relieved to see that it was a family friend and fellow confederate, Caroline Williams. She was also a cousin to Ruth Ann's husband, her mother being a sister to Mr. Michaels.

She was in her mid thirties and the war had transformed her looks drastically. Before the southern boys had left to fight, she was considered one of the prettier women in the area, but now malnutrition and an abundance of stress had taken her over. Her face contained very little shape and her skin held tightly to her bone structure, almost making her look as if she were nearly a skeleton. But even with all this, she still had the kindest smile and the most loving eyes that she gave most willingly to anyone she met.

Her husband, Henry had been like Johnny and Washington and were among the first to leave for battle. This left her home alone to raise their nine-year-old son, Seth. Mary Anna and Caroline had become good friends over the years and she had in fact been the one who had introduced Ruth Ann to Washington. But Caroline made her home in Morrisville and with the growing number of bushwhackers in the area, it was too dangerous to try and visit one another.

Caroline stepped down from the wagon with her son close behind and headed in Ruth Ann's direction. She was one of the nicest women that Ruth Ann knew and it was always a pleasure seeing her. She stepped up onto the porch where the two of them embraced each other in a long overdue hug. "Ruth Ann, how are you?"

"Caroline, it's so good to see you. What brings you out here? You know it's dangerous to travel alone like this."

"I know, dear," she said pulling away from the hug and revealing an envelope in her hand, "But I've got a letter for you from Washington and I have some other news as well."

Ruth Ann smiled as she took the letter and held it to her chest looking up at the sky, silently thanking God for protecting her husband. She suddenly looked back at Caroline, realizing she had nearly forgotten her. "Oh come in. Seth, Nat and Georgia are out playing in the barn."

"Can I go, Ma?" He asked looking up at his mother.

"Of course you can, but don't wander off too far."

The two women stepped into the house where Caroline took off her bonnet and hung it near the door. She followed Ruth Ann down the hallway toward the kitchen. "Ma and Rachel are out back. I'll put some tea on and go fetch them and then you can tell us what news you have."

"Oh tea. It seems like ages."

"Caroline, you really do need to take better care of yourself. There's apple pie over on the table. Help yourself."

Ruth Ann stepped out back and returned shortly after with Mary Ann and Rachel. After more hellos and hugs were exchanged, the women went into the sitting room with their tea. Ruth Ann opened her letter and read it aloud to them.

'My darling wife,
We are in eastern Arkansas and I am happy to say that I still have all my limbs that God gave to me. We continue to fight battles and occasionally lose a few men, but over all our regiment is lucky.
Your brother, Johnny sends his love to you and all your family. He is unable to write at present because he was wounded at Fitzhugh's Woods. Not to worry though, he is expected to be well soon enough and will send word to everyone. I hope life is treating you fairly dear Ruth Ann, and someday soon I hope to be by your side once again.
Your loving husband,
Washington

Ruth Ann once again held the letter against her chest as a small amount of relief came over her. Mary Anna wiped away a tear from her face, "I do hope Johnny will heal up well."

"I'm sure he will, Ma," Ruth Ann said in an understanding way. "Besides, Washington would tell us if there was anything to worry about."

Mary Anna pushed away the frightful thoughts that had taken her over and turned to Caroline. "So what news do you have to tell us, Caroline?"

"Well," she said, "I'm afraid it's not good news, not for us confederates anyhow. We've received word that Atlanta has fallen into Union hands under General Sherman and nearly the entire town was burned."

"Atlanta!" Mary Anna said. "My word! How could this happen?"

"They broke through the Confederate forces and marched into town."

"How awful."

"I know. Listen, Mary Anna, a few of the other Confederate women and I are thinking about hosting a party to try and improve the moral among the Confederate supporters. It seems times are just getting harder and we feel that if we don't do something soon that things will get completely unbearable."

"That's a wonderful idea, Caroline."

"I was hoping you would think that. I wanted to ask you on behalf of our group if it would be okay if it was held here at the ridge. You have more room than anyone else and with your home being out here away from everything we wouldn't have to worry about the Yankees interfering."

"I'd be delighted, Caroline. Of course I'll have to talk to John about it first, but I don't see why he wouldn't support the idea."

"Bless you, Mary Anna. This will mean so much to the Confederate families. It will be to them just like before this dreadful war started. Now, I know food is scarce so we'll have each family bring a dish."

"That sounds like a great thought," Ruth Ann answered. "When should we plan to have it?"

"In three days if it would be alright with you."

Mary Anna stood up, "I'll go talk to John now."

Three days after Caroline's visit the women were busy making preparations well into the late afternoon. Mary Anna insisted that everything be just right and she wanted all her guests to forget about the impending war that continued to knock so fiercely on their door just outside. This would be a time of celebration and a place where good friends could come together and rejoice simply because they were still alive.

She often found herself wondering how things would be if Alice were there in the midst of so much war. Alice had been so passionate about ensuring that her children knew nothing but peaceful times, but how could she manage such a thing with everything that was happening. No matter how hard Mary Anna tried, the war still managed to find itself inside her home through the smallest of cracks. But even so, she knew that if Alice were there that she would come up with a way somehow to keep it as far away from the children as possible.

Even though she had been fighting so hard, Mary Anna could not have prevented those two Yankee soldiers from attacking her children in the woods. Was she supposed to lock them in the house and never let them out? No, she couldn't do that. What kind of peace would that be for them?

So over the past three days she had not only convinced herself that this party would be good for all the local families, but that it would benefit her children as well. It would allow them to get dressed up and be a part of the small social community that was left. Even if it was just for one night, she was sure that they would remember it forever and then at least they would have one fond memory of their childhood.

Mary Anna and Georgia cleared out the sitting room, moving all the furniture across the large entry and into the guest bedroom. When it was completely empty of everything except the mantel décor and the elegant red velvet curtains, they began sweeping the wooden floor. Georgia was enjoying herself and made a game of it as she ran the broom back and forth across the already clean floor.

Ruth Ann and Rachel cleaned the kitchen and dining room until everything was sparkling. Even the dark stained table that had seen so many family meals glowed with cleanness and looked to have never been used before.

After the boys had returned from a small hunting trip, which proved pointless other than sharing their manly talk and escaping the cleaning duties, everyone headed upstairs to change. For the girls, this was the most exciting part, but for the boys it was the part they dreaded the most. It wasn't enough that they had to get cleaned up for the event, but now they had to put on tight fitting clothing as well and prance around like aristocrats.

John slipped out of his shirt and sat on his bed as Mary Anna dug through the wardrobe looking for an outfit for her husband to wear. He watched her and thought back to that very first day he had seen her in Tennessee. Sure she had grown and changed, but she was still the same girl he had fallen in love with and just as beautiful as ever. No matter how the war affected everyone, he knew nothing would ever change the way he felt about her.

She walked toward him with his chosen clothes neatly sitting across her hands. As she approached, he stood up and looked at her, causing her to get lost in those blue eyes just as she had done so many times before. He stepped closer, smiling down upon her as chills overcame her body before he had even touched her.

Once close enough he put his hands on her waist and pulled her against his body. He leaned down and began kissing her as she dropped the clothes and wrapped her arms around his neck. Their love and passion for one another had only grown stronger over the years and they both had high hopes that it would continue to do so.

"John," she said. "We really need to get ready."

"It can wait," he said between kissing her. "A beauty like yourself needs all the love and affection it can get and I aim to give it to you."

An hour after going upstairs to change, John and Mary Anna left the bedroom arm in arm. John was wearing the light brown suit that Mary Anna had picked out for him and had his blonde hair neatly combed to the right side. His blue eyes shimmered the way that they only did after leaving the bedroom with his wife.

Mary Anna had her soft brown hair swirled up on top of her head with a few white feathers mixed in with it. Even after seven children, she still managed to keep up her slim figure and it shone brightly behind a white lace pattern dress that ruffled as they walked down the hall.

Remaining arm in arm as if they had just gotten married, they descended the stairs where the children were patiently waiting for them. Ruth Ann was wearing a lavender dress and like Georgia, had her hair in curls. She stood taller next to her other siblings with the exception of Will who was not much shorter than she was.

Georgia was in a small blue dress that stuck out about ten inches all the way around her petite body. Will stood in a suit that was just a little lighter than that of his father's and smiled in their direction. All the children stood there neatly with arms folded behind their backs and it would have made for a lovely painting, but then there was Nat.

He was sixteen now and just as Alice had foreseen he looked just like John. It was bad enough that he looked just like him, but he had the same joking habits and manly tendencies as him as well. It was obvious that he was not comfortable in his very fashionable suit and he had no problem showing it. His fingers were stuck between the collar of his shirt and the front of his neck as he tried to let air make its way to the covered portions of his body.

His blonde hair, though clean as it was, was sticking up in several places across his head as he used his free hand to scratch his waistline, which felt the pressure of his tucked in shirt. He was slouched over to the right a little bit, which made him look completely out of place next to his straight-backed siblings.

"Look, darling," John said as they continued down the stairs, "It's a miniature me."

"Oh my," she replied trying not to laugh. "What am I going to do with two of you?"

"Ma," Nat protested. "I don't like this thing one bit! And these shoes hurt my feet. Can't I go barefoot and shirtless?"

John rubbed his hand over Nat's head as they walked up beside him while Mary Anna put her arms around him and tried to remove his hands from his suit.

"Nat, it's a party. We're supposed to look decent for these types of things."

"But Ma…"

"No buts. And besides, Rosalee Burns will be here tonight. Don't you want to look nice for her?"

Will started laughing, "Ooh, Nat likes little Rosalee. She's going to kiss him and hold his hand…"

Will was cut short as Nat jumped on top of him. "I'll show you, Will!"

Just before Will had overtaken the small brawl, Nat was lifted into the air off of his brother by John. "That's enough you two. Your Ma has worked hard for this party, now let's not disappoint her."

Nat walked away into the empty sitting room as his siblings quietly laughed, but he was relieved that his suit was not quite as tight as it had been due to the scuffle with his older brother. The rest of the family soon joined him after they were able to contain their laughter except Mary Anna who went to help Rachel serve the food onto the dining room table.

Shortly after everything was finished around the house the guests began arriving, the first being Caroline Williams and her son. It wasn't long until the entire house was filled with happy people, which included Ruth Ann's in-laws.

Peter Rivers from Springfield had heard about the party and brought two of his buddies with him. Together the three of them each played separate fiddles, which almost immediately lifted the moral of everyone. The table was covered in food and there had in fact been so much that some of it had to be taken to the kitchen.

John and Mary Anna stood near the doorway of the sitting room and watched as their children laughed and danced. Will had managed to convince one of the Talley sisters to dance and they were soon all over the dance floor. Nat had found his sweet little Rosalee and with his shirt hanging freely from his body he spun her around to the beat of the music.

Even Georgia had managed to make it out there, finding herself dancing with Seth Williams among all the other happy couples. Ruth Ann stood near her in-laws and watched joyously as everyone enjoyed themselves inside the large home. She silently wished that Washington Michaels would have been there to dance with her as he loved to do, but knew they would be together soon and there would always be other dances.

People came and went all through the house and talked about everything except the war. One of Mary Anna's conditions to hosting the party was for everyone to leave the war talk at the door when they came in. But even Mary Anna couldn't prevent the inevitable from happening and just four hours after the party had begun, war came knocking on the door once again.

John and Mary Anna were still standing in the entry watching all the talkative people when they heard a shot fired from outside. John darted toward the door where he grabbed his gun belt that hung on the wall. After strapping it around his waist he then snatched his hat off the nearby nail in the wall and placed it atop his head before stepping out onto the porch.

When he emerged outside, the porch and half the front yard was glowing with lanterns that the party guests had brought. There were however, no guests outside at the moment as they were all inside dancing.

Mary Anna stepped out onto the porch behind her husband as the music came to a stop. There in the yard, directly in front of the front steps was Frank Hunter who was on leave, with Polly off to his right.

John stepped off the steps and stopped as the two men looked at each other. "I see you found a fiddler to replace me," Frank said.

"Didn't have much choice, Frank. I don't reckon this is your kind of crowd anyway."

"Even so, don't seem right. Is it true you killed my boy?"

"Tell that Indian to go inside!" Polly interrupted.

Mary Anna stepped up to the porch railing. "Polly, you'll hold your tongue when you're at my house or I'll hold it for you."

"I'm not scared of you, Mary Anna. You're nothing but a domesticated Injun!"

Mary Anna half laughed as the windows of the house filled with onlookers. She wrapped her hand around one of the wooden railing bars and yanked it free from the porch. She stepped down the stairs and walked past her husband keeping a sharp but calm look on Polly as she twirled the small wooden post in her right hand.

As she neared her, Polly had a terrified look over her face and even the overly talkative woman could not find the courage to speak. Mary Anna continued toward her as Polly only took small half steps back. It wasn't long until Mary Anna was right up on her and when she got close enough she raised up the post fully intending to whack her upside the head.

"Who said I was domesticated, Polly?"

"Ahh!" Polly shouted running into the darkness. "Indian! Indian! The Indian's going to kill me!"

Mary Anna just stood there laughing and watching her until she had completely disappeared.

"John," Frank said turning his attention back to him, not caring that his wife had almost been attacked and knowing full well that she deserved it. "Did you kill my boy?"

John had always had that youthful calm look about him and it didn't disappear now. He looked at Frank, observing his two revolvers at his side and knew once he gave him the answer there would be only one solution and one survivor. "It was either your boy or mine, Frank. And seeing as how yours was the one pointing the gun I saw only one way to fix the problem."

Frank quickly reached for his guns as did John and shots rang out on both ends. There was so much smoke surrounding them that for a moment neither of them could be seen.

"John!" Mary Anna shouted. "John, where are you?"

She began walking toward the cloud of smoke desperately searching for her husband. Just as she approached the thick cloud she could see a figure walking towards her. It was the right height… the right build…

"John! Is it you?"

John emerged out of the haze unharmed, still in his suit, cowboy hat and gun belt loosely hanging around his waist. "Yes, darling. It's me."

Mary Anna ran into his arms where he kissed her as the house erupted in applause. When the smoke had cleared they went back inside to join the rest of the party.

"Where do you think Polly ran off to?" John asked her after they were in the house.

"Hell, John. She's probably in Arkansas by now."

That night everyone danced their hearts out and went back to living in the times before the war. The Peter Rivers band made up a song about Mary Anna, which everyone enjoyed dancing to.

'Well Mrs. Mary Anna she's one tough breed,
She's rare and fair and a might might pretty.
You can cross her once, you can cross her twice,
But cross her thrice and she'll hunt you down.

Now swing yer partner to and fro,
Now round and round and back and forth.

Well Polly Hunter headed for the hills and ain't been back,
But with the biggest mouth in all of Polk it won't be long and she'll be calling.
Oh thank heavens for Mary Anna,
She'll put that Yankee in her rightful place.

Now swing yer partner to and fro,
Now round and round and back and forth."

June 31, 1865
Braymyer Ridge

Ruth Ann and Mary Anna sat on the front porch as someone afoot was heading their way from down the long driveway. He looked to be staggering and swaying side to side as continued in their direction. Mary Anna let her hand rest on the rifle that sat at her side whom she had named Cherokee after the dog she had once had.

She liked her little Cherokee rifle and it had served her a good many uses since she had had it. The man slowly came nearer to them until he was right at the edge of the porch and staring the two women in the eyes.

He wore an old tattered confederate uniform that had more holes in it than it did clean spots and his face was covered in dirt and mud from the long trail he had obviously just endured. He was nothing but skin and bones and didn't look like any man either one of the women had ever seen before.

"Can I help you?" Mary Anna said to the man as she gave Cherokee a good rubbing with her right hand.

"Ma? Don't you recognize me?"

"Johnny," she said standing up, "Is it really you?"

"Yes, Ma. It's me."

Mary Anna ran over to him and gave her oldest son the longest hug he had ever gotten in his entire life. Tears of joy ran down her face as she felt around to make sure her son still had all his limbs.

She pushed him back, keeping her hands on his shoulders and taking one last look over him to ensure that it really was him and after looking into his eyes a second time, she knew there was no mistaking it. "Ruth Ann, your brothers home!"

Ruth Ann stepped closer and looked at her younger brother before giving him a hug. "Johnny, where's my Washington?" She said pulling away from the hug.

Johnny just looked at his sister in a sympathetic way, as he couldn't find the words to speak to her.

"No, Johnny. Don't say it. Not my Washington! Not him! It's not possible! Please say it isn't so!"

"I'm awful sorry, Ruth Ann," he said looking down at what was left of his boots. "A Yankee came at us from behind and well I tried…but by the time we knew what had happened he was… he was already…"

"There now," Mary Anna said taking Ruth Ann into her free arm, "There's no need to talk about it anymore."

Ruth Ann pulled away and ran upstairs into her bedroom where she threw herself on her bed. With her face planted into the pillow she began punching the mattress over and over to try and relieve some of the pressure she felt building up inside her.

When she thought she had contained herself she stood up, only to find herself even more angrier than before. "I hate the Yankees!" She shouted, "I just hate them and I hope they all die!"

Mary Anna tried to get into the room with her, but Ruth Ann refused to open the door. "Leave me alone! I just want to be by myself! I hate this war! I should have let the Yankees kill me too!"

She continued to scream, stomp and yell until all the tears she had cried for her dead husband had made her so tired that she couldn't stand to keep her eyes open any longer. She fell back onto the bed and drifted into a deep sleep where she hoped to awake and realize that this had all been a terrible dream.

But when she awoke she found that her mother had laid out a black dress across a chair for her to wear and she suddenly realized that this was all very real. She stood in front of the mirror and cleaned up her face as best she could before slipping into her mourning dress.

After she had thrown the black garment over her thin body she felt around under her bed for the bottle of brandy that Washington had given her. He had loved the stuff, but Ruth Ann refused to drink anything of the sort.

His exact words to her before he left were, "Ruth Ann, if I don't make it back you drink this brandy. It will make you feel better I promise."

With the bottle in her hand, she stepped back in front of the mirror to watch herself as she drank it. She put the whole bottle up to her mouth and started down the entire drink until it hit her that she needed to breathe and let the sting out.

She stumbled a little bit, but then regained her balance and resumed drinking the brandy, never taking her eyes off of herself. "Here's to you, Washington," she said, "Here's to the Confederates. Here's to the damn war. And here's to me."

After the bottle was empty she left the comfort of her bedroom and stepped down the small set of stairs. Standing on the platform she looked down as everything became hazy and started to spin. She took one step and then found herself hurling down the large staircase into the entry.

Luckily she wasn't hurt too bad and after two days of resting, Johnny took her to Walnut Grove where she told the news of her husband's death to his parents who were completely devastated. He had been their only child and now he was gone with no children of his own to carry on. Before leaving town,

Ruth Ann bought two more bottles of brandy and hid them beneath her black dress as everyone around her looked in her way with sympathy.

The wagon rolled by Polly Hunter and the two other women that had been with Esther near the start of the war when she made the visit to Braymyer Ridge. Polly looked at her with a look that said nothing but, "It serves you right."

Ruth Ann stood up and took one of the bottles of brandy in her hand. She threw it at Polly, "You stupid Yankee!" She shouted. The bottle hit Polly in the upper part of her right leg and shattered.

She sat back down, not caring to see what Polly's reaction was and started sipping on her new bottle. "Johnny," she said.

"Yes, Ruth Ann."

"I done lost one of my bottle's of brandy. You reckon we can go back and get another?"

Johnny looked at her and nearly cried. In all the battles he had fought in and all the friends he had seen killed, seeing his sister like this hurt him the most. But he knew she was suffering and if brandy helped her ease the pain he would get however much of it that he could.

Of course, the only good that came out of the trip to Walnut Grove that day was seeing the look on Mary Anna's face when Johnny told her what Ruth Ann had done to Polly Hunter. Mary Anna stayed up most of the night laughing about it and just pictured the look on poor Polly's face.

Washington's body was retrieved from a field in Mississippi and rather than being buried in an unmarked grave, it was brought back to the home for burial. Rachel had the mason engrave on his stone the same phrase he had said to her in the midst of the terrible storm that had swept through just before their wedding. In beautiful slanted cursive writing it read: "'I love you, Washington. No matter what happens, I'll love you forever.' Rachel became Ruth Ann's best friend during this time as she shared with her the story of her Ralph.

Washington's parents headed west shortly after war towards California and once they were gone, Ruth Ann felt as if she had no connection to her late husband. She would make daily trips down to the cemetery and sit with her husband and their small child and wonder why she wasn't there with them.

"What's a family if we can't all be together," she said to herself as she laid a bundle of roses between the two graves. "What am I suppose to do?"

She stood up and looked toward the western sky as the sun remained halfway visible. She lifted up her bottle of brandy and drank until there was no more to be had. Afterwards, she staggered her way back to the house where her family painfully watched as she headed up to her room, another night without eating. The war was finally over, but Ruth Ann's battle was just beginning.

Dusty Williams

December 13, 1994
Braymyer Ridge

"So did John really kill his own daughter?"

"He had to. It was either that or let his son die and even if he had let Nat get shot, Ben would have probably turned around and shot Will too."

"Wow. I can't believe he had to do that."

"A lot of people don't truly understand how badly the Civil War was and the kind of effect it had on people. Even after it was over, there were still small battles and bushwhacks between the two sides.

You see, at first John and Mary Anna wanted Missouri to stay neutral to avoid these types of things, but soon the union marched in and tried to start taking over everything. It would be like if someone walked into our house and said that they were in charge now. We wouldn't like that very much would we?"

"No, I guess not."

"So was Mary Anna mad that John had killed Esther?"

"She's wasn't mad, but she was sad more than anything. She knew though that John had done what was necessary to protect their small boys. Back then people had to do a lot of things they didn't want to in order to survive. And just think, if John had not shot his daughter and Ben that day…you and I wouldn't be here."

"So is the trap door still under the table?"

"I suppose it is," he said smiling.

"Well… can we go look?"

645

"Sure can, come on."

We went into the dining room just as the sun shone its last ray of light and pulled back some of the chairs that were pushed up to the table. Pappy pulled the rug out from under the table and there before us was a small door in the floor.

I crawled beneath the table and slowly pulled it open, allowing dust and cob webs to float into the room. A narrow staircase was before us and we stepped down into it, using a flashlight that Pappy had brought for light.

It wasn't a very large room, but it was big enough that it must have taken a lot of work to build it with the tools that they had back then. There were a few chairs that were covered in spider webs scattered about the room and some sort of old bullets.

When looking up at the ceiling, little rays of light came down between the cracks from upstairs and I just imagined them down here as they watched the men walk around above them. I felt as though I were actually living in the time of the Civil War and was in hiding below the Braymyer home.

I stepped over to one of the walls where I found carved in perfect handwriting the name, 'Georgia Tennessee Braymyer.' It was amazing to see it still there after all those years and it was as if it had just been done because it had remained so well preserved.

After we had explored the hidden room we headed upstairs to get ready for bed. Pappy cracked the window in our bedroom to allow some cool air in and we were soon fast asleep in the bed that John and Mary Anna had shared all those years before.

January 01, 1867
Braymyer Ridge

The Braymyer home had gained a new member just six days before on Christmas Day. The former Miss Rosalee Burns who had just wed Nat Braymyer was staying with them until her and her husband set up housekeeping on their own.

She was alike with Mary Anna in that she was short, barely standing five foot four, but unlike her she had a golden color of blonde hair on top of her head. She had the same sass and spunk as her new mother in law, but had grown up in Walnut Grove and knew very little about country living.

Mary Anna had taken her under her wing just like Alice had done when she had first married John and was teaching her all she needed to know about how to keep a Braymyer man happy. Rosalee was sixteen and since she was the queen of the city, it was only natural for her to marry to the prince of the country and they truly were happy with each other, just like John and Mary Anna.

Ruth Ann's husband had died during the civil war, leaving her childless and her parents without grandchildren. Ruth Ann didn't figure that she would ever marry again, but she was perfectly happy living in her small cottage at the back of the Braymyer land.

Mary Anna was excited to have Rosalee stay with them, not only because she liked her, but also because she had high hopes that she would give her grandchildren. The two of them spent hours together each day, simply talking about life and what they thought the future might hold for them.

Unlike Mary Anna and Esther, Rosalee favored Ruth Ann more when it came to her dresses. She didn't like wearing the big round dresses, but instead preferred a tighter fitting one. When she moved in, Mary Anna took her into town and bought her several dresses, although given her Georgia plantation lifestyle she couldn't see the thinking in the ones she picked out.

Rosalee's father, Brice Burns, was the Baptist preacher at Walnut Grove, which had kept Rosalee under the spotlight of the town since she was little. She had had a younger brother, but he had died of pneumonia leaving her to be an only child.

"You know," Mary Anna said to Rosalee as they walked along the ridge behind the house, "I think you're going to make my son a fine wife."

"I hope so, Mary Anna."

"You will, darling and call me, Ma Braymyer. You're a part of this family too now. Heck, you'll probably be the only daughter-in-law I ever get to know. Johnny's out riding the cow trails between Texas and Kansas and I doubt if Will will ever settle down with a wife."

"Why do you say that?"

"Oh, I don't know. I just know my boys. Will has always been picky, especially when it comes to women and food. The two things a man can never live without!"

They were laughing as she went on, "If she's not pretty enough, she don't cook well enough. And if she is right near perfect he swallows his tongue and forgets how to talk. But who knows, maybe someday."

"And what about Johnny? You don't think he'll ever settle down? I know my cousin was real sweet on him."

"Honey, only the Lord knows about Johnny. Sometimes I suspect he's got more Indian blood in him than me, and I'm half! He's always been the adventurous one, but like so many others the war changed him."

"Like how?"

"Well, before the war he was a lot like Nat. Always talking to new people, knowing exactly what to say to the girls to steal a kiss from them and then after the war it was as if he was afraid to get too close to anyone. I imagine it has a lot to do with what happened to his sister, Esther."

"Nat told me the story. How terrible it must have been."

"Terrible? No, it wasn't terrible it was down right hurtful. Sometimes I wonder how I was able to give birth to a child that was as far from her father and I as anyone could be. I guess she took after my grandfather Walker in that regard, never caring about anyone but herself. I know this sounds terrible, but what can I do… The day she married she stopped being my responsibility. Did I tell you she had a child?"

"She did? I had not heard that."

"Sure did. A girl they named Polly Anna after me and her other grandmother. Course when they died her other grandmother, Polly took her and ran off to Oregon where she lost all her money. I've tried sending for her to come here and stay with us, but they refuse to let her come. She's the only grandchild I have right now and I doubt if I'll ever see her again. I only hope that she doesn't turn out like her mother, or Polly Hunter for that matter."

"But surely Ruth Ann will marry again someday."

"Honey, Ruth Ann is as wild as her Pa. She doesn't think she needs a man and she was lucky to fall in love for the first time, it'd be a miracle if it happened again which I doubt it will."

"And Georgia?"

"Oh, Georgia, now there's a sight. Out of all my girls she's the most like me. It's hard to believe I was her age when I married. Why if any man tried to take her heart now, John would shoot em' dead in a seconds notice. She's got her Pa all around her finger and I imagine it's because she is most like me and it reminds him of past times.

But eventually even she'll marry and I suspect that she'll have a whole line of eligible bachelors waiting at the front door. A part of me can't wait to see her father's face when that day comes. Ha, he might just have a heart attack."

"Well, I promise you that Nat and I will have children that you are able to see whenever you like."

"Thank you, honey, but you never know where life will take you. I started out on a plantation in Georgia and now I'm living up in the Ozarks trying to survive just like everyone else. Course that's not to say I won't end up somewhere else yet, you just never know."

The two women continued to walk around Braymyer Ridge for the next two months becoming the best of friends when one day in late February Nat came into the house with an announcement to make. Everyone was sitting around the large oak dining room table enjoying their supper when he ran into the house nearly forgetting to hang his hat up.

"Rosie, Ma, Pa. I've got an announcement to make."

"What is it, son?" Mary Anna said looking up from her plate.

"Well, I've decided to move to Texas. Rosie and I will leave in a few weeks."

"Texas!" Mary Anna said.

"Nat," John said, "What are you talking about. Why would you want to leave?"

"Missouri is too crowded, Pa. A man can't make a rightful living staying in the same town he was born in."

"That sounds like Ralph," Rachel whispered to herself.

Rosalee didn't say a word, she had already learned that there was no changing his mind. Her only hope for changing Nat's mind lie in the hands of Mary Anna.

"But, Texas, Nat?" Mary Anna said.

"Yes, Ma. It's full of un-settled land…good farming land."

The family spent all night arguing over the topic, but just like his father before him, Nat got his way. A few weeks after he had made the announcement to his family, Nat and Rosalee headed to Texas.

Dusty Williams

August 14, 1874
Durwood, Indian Territory

Ruth Ann Michaels was thirty-five and found herself living alone in a small log cabin outside the small settlement of Durwood. She had journeyed into the unsettled land to bring education to the children who would eventually become the leaders of America.

She had never remarried and had remained perfectly content in being an independent woman, but today things were going to change. She was strolling down the dusty Main Street when she saw him for the first time. He was riding a brown mare as the western sun gleamed behind him, revealing him to be a tall dark cowboy.

There was something about him that she couldn't resist and there was something about her he knew he had to have. After she had contained herself, she quickly looked away and continued down the road intending to pass him right by. But when she had gotten to where he was sitting on his horse she was startled to find him now standing there, as if he were waiting for her.

"Afternoon, maim." He said tipping his hat.

"Good day, sir." She said trying to avoid him and carry on with her business.

"You know," he said following after her, "You have got to be the prettiest woman I have ever seen in these parts."

"Am I supposed to be flattered, sir? No, I am sure that a man like you would only know this to be true because you have in fact already set your eyes upon every woman around."

"Well, hey now, little missy."

"What did you call me?"

"Little missy. Is that not okay?"

Ruth Ann was taken aback, "Sorry, it's just something my father used to call my Ma."

"I see. So where are you headed?"

"Over to the café to get a bite to eat."

"Well, would you mind if I joined you? I sure could use a decent meal, I've been on the trail for some time."

"Sir, I don't even know your name."

"Oh, my apologies, maim. The name's Eli Bell."

"And where are you from, Mr. Bell."

"Now wait a minute, don't I get to know your name?"

"Ruth Ann Michaels."

"I must say, that is a fine name. I'm from Alabama and you?"

"Missouri."

Eli Bell followed Ruth Ann into the café and joined her for supper. There was something about her that kept his attention and made him eager to learn more. He was quite certain that he could get used to following Ruth Ann around, wherever it is that she may go.

July 4, 1876
Bonham, Texas

Georgia Braymyer had since been married to Seth Williams
and had moved to a small north Texas town called Windom,
which was just outside of Bonham. She was the only one of
the Braymyer children to have inherited her mother's dark
brown hair and she almost always wore it in beautiful curls.

She was twenty-one and was rocking her first born child, a
daughter in her arms after having only been married a little
over a year. She sat on the wagon seat next to her husband as
they headed for Bonham to attend a July Fourth fair. All of
Seth's family had moved to the area and sometimes it made
Georgia feel lonely when she thought of her parents so far
away.

She had turned out to be just an inch taller than her mother
and had the same dark skin. She was in fact, almost the
spitting image of Mary Anna except in place of her brown
eyes, hers were blue like her fathers.

Seth was of average height and everyone knew that Georgia
could have done much better than him, but he was the one she
had fallen in love with. He had light red hair, green eyes and
several freckles scattered across his face. He wasn't bad
looking by any means, but his looks didn't come anywhere
close to comparing with Georgia's.

The wagon rolled into Bonham as people gathered around the
small stores and shared gossip while the children darted across
the streets playing their childhood games. Georgia looked
down at her small child and imagined that someday she would
be out there with the other children living her own life.

She gazed up at the blue sky and thought about the world as
her life slowly started to take off where she was sure, she
thought, to do great things. She had a special calling within
herself to move mountains and build bridges over raging

waters that would enable her to pave the way for future generations.

She thought of her mother and the long journey that she had once made and remembered all the stories that she had told her about her life. She secretly envied her mother for her strength and compassion for living and hoped to one day follow in her footsteps.

The wagon stopped and the two of them stepped out into the courtyard with the baby in her arms. She walked toward the strange faces of a people she didn't know and headed toward the destiny that had been laid out before her.

Some people stopped to admire her divine beauty and the quarter Cherokee that so proudly presented itself about her, while others gazed upon a likeness for life that had they never seen before. The music began to play and shots were fired into the air to celebrate the country's Independence Day as she took a seat among the community that she would become so influential in.

It would in time, run through her veins and become more a part of her than anything she had ever known. This was where she was meant to be and it was here that she would take a stand against all the evils of the world and ensure that her children were able to grow up in a time of peace.

Indeed Georgia had grown to become a lovely young woman and as she grew to call Texas home, she would truly become one of the rare young women to have the capability to turn Texas into a civilized state, just as her mother had done to Missouri. As time went on, she became that independent person who sought to make a better life for herself and in the process she in turn made a better life for all those around her.

June 12, 1880
Braymyer Ridge

Mary Anna was sweeping the front porch when she saw the rider approaching her house from the east. She had only seen him once before and swore that he was from Morrisville.

"Afternoon, maim." He said dismounting his horse and walking up to her.

"Can I help you?"

"Yes, maim I believe you can. I'm the census taker and I've come to get a census of your house."

"Oh yes, come in and I'll make some tea."

The short man was in his mid thirties and had brown hair underneath a top hat he was wearing. He had a fancy gold pocket watch somewhere in his left pocket that had a gold chain stretching up to the top of his suspenders.

He sat down at the table where Rachel and John were already sitting and pulled out a large book and an ink pen. Mary Anna joined them at the table with a cup of tea for everyone.

"Is it only the three of you living here?" He asked.

"Yeah," John said, "Just the three of us."

"Well if you don't mind my saying so, it's an awful big house for only three people isn't it?"

"Well," Mary Anna interrupted, "We used to have a lot more people here but they've scattered with the wind. Johnny, that's my oldest son," she could tell the man was losing interest but she continued anyway. "Well he's over in Kansas with his wife and they go back and forth along the cattle trails.

And my sweet Will went to California. I never imagined any of my family would make it as far as California, but they proved me wrong didn't they?"

The man just nodded his head and acted like he was ready to get this business over with.

"And let's see, Nat's in Texas of course and can you believe it? Ruth Ann moved to Indian Territory to teach school and married a cowboy! Now she is over in Scotland somewhere and is Lady Ruth Ann to everyone over there, oh we are so proud of her. And then our youngest child, Georgia is in Texas as well. And, well you just have to know Georgia, but I imagine she'll have that state turned upside down in no time. Seems like our family has just scattered about. Um, should you be writing this down?"

"No, maim. I am only here to record the names and ages of the people present here."

"Oh, I see. Well do you want mine first?"

"No, I am to start with the head of the family, which will be your husband."

"I don't think so," John said laughing. "Mary Anna's been the head of this family for a long time and nobody has been brave enough to challenge her."

The census taker smiled, "I understand that, but…"

"Mary Anna Braymyer," she said before he could finish, "Aged fifty four."

"And your birth place?"

"Tennessee, but I was raised in Georgia."

The man mumbled to himself as he checked boxes off and Mary Anna stopped him when she heard him say, "White, check."

"Oh no, she interrupted, I'm only half white. The other half is Cherokee."

"Yes, but I shall put you down as white. It looks better."

"Looks better?"

"Well, yes. Aren't you ashamed to be part Indian?"

"Ashamed! Absolutely not! Why would I be ashamed?"

"Well because no one wants to be Indian."

"Well, speak for yourself, but I am quite proud to be half Cherokee. Now, you list me down there as white and Indian."

The man shook his head, but did as he was told. He collected all of John's information and then came to Rachel. "And what is Ms. Lloyd's relation to you."

Mary Anna piped right up, "She's my…"

"Maid," Rachel interrupted. "I'm her maid."

"Okay," he said, "Maid it is. And does anyone here have any kind of illness?"

"Yeah," John said, "Mary Anna's got this thing with her mouth that doesn't allow her to keep it closed for very long amounts of time."

The census taker looked at the group in disbelief while the three of them laughed uncontrollably. So in 1880 on the United States Federal Census is listed, Mary Anna Braymyer, a Indian with a mouth disease; Rachel Lloyd, the maid and poor John Braymyer, may God have mercy on his soul.

December 24, 1882
Braymyer Ridge

The curtains were drawn back in the bedroom and John held
Mary Anna close against his bare chest as they lie in bed and
watch the snow drift down from somewhere up above. The
entire valley was covered in a thick blanket of the winter
miracle and an occasional cardinal could be seen flying down
and landing in the snow. It was still early morning, but the
partial sun reflected off of the snow so powerfully that it
looked to be mid day.

Mary Anna continued her gaze outside as her husband's chest
slowly moved up and down beneath her ear. Melancholy made
its way into her mind as she thought about her children and
their families. She had twelve grandchildren and all of them
were scattered out in different states, one even being in
another country. It would be Christmas tomorrow and she
would be in the company of John and Rachel just as she had
been when she first left Tennessee.

It was almost as if she had come down this long road to
Braymyer Ridge and had nothing to show for it except what
she had started out with. She concluded that she was lucky,
because unlike other people she hadn't lost everything even
though it seemed that way at times.

John had ventured into the woods with their new puppy,
Creek, whom Mary Anna had so aptly named and when they
returned John was dragging a large Christmas tree behind him.
After setting it up in the grand entry, the entire house smelled
of cedar and apple pies and there was no one to share it with
other than themselves. Mary Anna had made paper cutouts for
decorations and strung them all over the large tree.

Beneath the tree were presents for each one of her
grandchildren and although she knew she would have to mail
them all off she left them there. It reminded her that she did

have a family and she was not all alone like how she had felt after Walkie died.

The stair railing had cedar limbs wrapped around it that had been pieced together with thin string and pinecones dotted across it occasionally. Even the front porch had cedar decorations strung about and in each one of the horses stalls hung a single limb with a pinecone as well. Indeed Mary Anna had gone all out this year for Christmas and soon it would be time to take everything down again.

She continued to watch out the window as they became foggy with the rising sun and patiently wondered if she had lived a decent life and had done enough good. Sure there were times she could have done more, but nobody is perfect and she just hoped that in some way she had done the world some good.

John slowly opened his eyes and looked down at his wife's graying hair. "What are you thinking about, darling?" He said putting his arm on her back and running his hand up and down it slowly.

"Life."

"Well I reckon that's a good enough thing to think about and we've lived one helluva one, haven't we?"

"Yes I suppose we have. Sometimes I wonder if it was all real or just certain parts of it."

"We haven't lost our memories yet, darling. It was all real, every bit of it. It's funny where life can take you and how quickly things can change. Take me for example. I went to bed one night with six other siblings, woke up the next day to go offer my help to Grandma Davis and instead I met the love of my life. Now, all these years later I'm still lying next to the most beautiful girl in the whole world."

Mary Anna lifted her head up and kissed him, then returned back to her previous spot only instead of looking away at the windows she looked at John. "I just wish our children could be here is all. Like the census taker said a few years back, it's an awful big house for just three people."

"I know, darling, but we'll see them all again someday, I promise."

"But how, John? We're getting older and everyone else is moving away with the wind. Ruth Ann's letter the other day said she would be spending Christmas in Russia! Now, maybe I'm wrong, but I doubt I'll ever make it to Russia."

John couldn't help but to laugh a little, but was quickly stopped by Mary Anna's glare. "I'm sorry, darling. You've just got to think positive. Remember, you never know where life will take you."

"Do you think our children don't like us?"

"Now, darling. You know that is not true. They are just busy with their own lives. Besides, after we moved here we didn't see my mother or Rachel for nearly ten years."

"But John, that was different. They have trains and better roads than they did back when we moved."

John could see that there was no way he could convince his wife otherwise, so he returned to just comforting her as best he could. Christmas had always been Mary Anna's favorite time of the year and although it wasn't the first one without her children she was taking it the hardest.

"John, do you think Rachel's lived a good life and is truly happy even though she never married?"

"I think she's happy, yes. Rachel never married because she lost her one true love, you know that. I reckon she's just waiting to see him when she gets to Heaven. Ralph always was the jealous type anyhow, I don't think he'd be too happy if she showed up to Heaven with a husband."

Even Mary Anna couldn't help but to laugh. "Oh, John. After all these years you're still full of jokes."

"Jokes? I'm not joking, darling, it's the truth."

Mary Anna playfully slapped him on the chest. "Jokes or no jokes, John Braymyer, you've always had a way of adding light to even the most darkest of times and I love you for it."

"I love you too, darling," he said embracing her in a hug. "Now how about some breakfast?"

They slowly got out of bed and made their way downstairs where Rachel was sitting in a rocker in the front room with a cup of coffee. She slowly rocked back and forth as she watched the snow from inside the window. Mary Anna decided upon looking at her that she was indeed happy.

After John and Mary Anna got their cup, they joined her near the glowing fireplace. The house was quiet, almost too quiet for any of their liking. After six children had been raised inside that house any form of silence had been regarded as an emergency. But even after ten years, the three of them had still not gotten used to the calmness of the home and they expected at any moment for the loud laughter of children to ring out down the hallways…but it never did.

Mary Anna peered out of the window, "Looks like it's going to keep on snowing. Should we go visit the cemetery today instead of tomorrow?"

"That will be fine," John replied, "And if the weather's decent tomorrow we can go then too."

After a light breakfast the three of them bundled up and headed out of the front door, carrying more decorations that Mary Anna had made. The two women stepped to the edge of the ridge and looked at each other as if they had all lost their minds.

"Rachel," Mary Anna said, "How is it that we used to do this?"

"Well, we used to be a lot younger."

"Awe, come on," John said stepping past them toward the ridge.

"John!" Mary Anna said, "If you break your leg again don't expect me to carry you back up!"

John laughed as he sat down on top of the ice-covered rocks. "Here we go!" He shouted giving himself a push.

John went sliding down the ridge at a fast speed, yipping and shouting in excitement the whole way down. Mary Anna and Rachel watched in disbelief as they just knew he was going to kill himself. After he made it down safely and the shock of it all had passed, Mary Anna turned to Rachel. "He's older than us. If he can do it, so can we!"

Before Rachel could convince her otherwise Mary Anna was already sliding towards the bottom of the steep ridge. Rachel sat down at the edge and just before pushing herself down, she said to herself. "I was only going to ask how we'd be getting back up the ridge. But hey, who am I to ask that. Oh, Lord. Here we go…"

Once the three of them were at the bottom, John helped the women up nearly falling on the ice himself. After they were on their feet they began trudging through the thick snow toward the cemetery. Mary Anna had one arm through John's and the other through Rachel's as they walked side by side through the growing snow that was still descending from above.

Once they had reached the cemetery, the three of them brushed away the snow and ice from the monuments and placed the Christmas decorations at their base. They looked down at them and said a silent hello to their loved family members that were resting in the cold ground. There was of course, Alice, Esther and their infant, Mollie. Also buried there were both husbands of the twins and Ruth Ann's small son that had died so young.

They stayed until they could bear the bitter cold no more and then went back to the front room near the fireplace. They drank hot cider and watched as the snow twirled and danced as it fell from the sky, showing no signs of slowing down.

"Rachel," Mary Anna said, "How about we make that fried chicken of yours tonight. I've got a craving something awful for it."

"Lord, Mary Anna. You've always liked your food and I swear you've never gained an inch around your waist," she answered shaking her head as she looked upon her.

Mary Anna was sitting near one of the two front windows as she vaguely spotted a wagon pull up. Because of the thickness of the flurries, it was hard to tell but she was certain someone was out there. "John, I think someone is here."

John looked up from his paper as if he knew something that she didn't, "Are you sure, darling?"

"I'm certain of it," she said wrapping herself in a red shawl and heading for the front door. She stepped out onto the front porch and shielded her eyes from the blinding snow that was being blown up against her as she looked in the direction she had thought she had seen something.

Slowly, emerging from the wind blown snow were the figures of two adults and four children walking towards her. She patiently waited from the comfort of the front porch as they drew nearer and it wasn't until they were right up at the steps that she recognized who they were.

"Nat!" She shouted running after them, nearly sliding right into the group of people. She wrapped her arms around him, "You made it for Christmas! Come inside before the children get sick!"

Thirty-four year old Nat Braymyer stepped into the entry with his wife, Rosalee who was thirty-one and their four children. Nat still looked just like his father had and was just as charming as ever. They were all bundled in coats and blankets, but Mary Anna knew as soon as she saw his blue eyes that it was him.

Rosalee had always managed to maintain her good looks and she still looked just as beautiful as she had on the long days her and Mary Anna had spent together before they had left for Texas. Their oldest child was Cotton who at fifteen looked just like Nat, allowing three generations of Braymyer men to have almost all the exact same physical traits. The three of them walked, talked and acted just alike and now that they were all together it would only be a matter of time before they found themselves getting into trouble.

The next child was Mary Lee who shared traits of both of her parents, but like all Braymyers she had the same set of deep blue eyes. It was obvious that she wouldn't be tall like Nat and Cotton, but she held herself up with grace and smoothness that it made her look much taller than she really was. Her hair was blonde, as was all her siblings and when she unwrapped herself from the blanket it revealed a long river of the blonde hair flowing freely down her back.

Nathan, who was six, struggled out of his thick winter clothing and stayed as close to his father's side as possible. He too would have looked exactly like Nat, but his hair was not quite the same blonde and his skin not as dark. He had freckles on top of his nose and beneath his eyes and Mary Anna knew right away that he would turn out to be a rough little fellow just like her sons had.

Lastly was Addie Leona who was only three. Her hair was blonde, but was so dark that Mary Anna swore she could see small strands of her own brown hair hidden beneath that of Addie's. Rosalee helped her out from beneath her warm blankets and she was the first one to take off running through the house to see what she might get into.

Mary Anna hugged them all as John and Rachel joined them in the entry. One by one, Mary Anna squeezed the cheeks of all her grandchildren and kept them in her sight for as long as she could, but eventually they all took of running through the house with the exception of Cotton. He stayed in the sitting room with his father and grandfather, while Mary Anna, Rosalee and Rachel sat around the dining room table.

Mary Anna nearly cried when she heard the children's laughter flowing freely throughout the house. She could hear the loud footsteps clomp down on the stairs as they went up and down up and down and all across the upstairs halls. It was the most joyous noise she had heard in years and she could feel her heart skip a few beats as she continued to listen to it.

Creek who looked almost exactly like Cherokee chased after them throughout the house, glad to have some younger more able company to keep up with his puppy needs. Mary Anna held Rosalee's hand in hers on top of the table as she listened intently about their journey through the snow to make it here in time for Christmas.

John and Nat continued to sit in the front room with Cotton while they smoked on a pipe. Nat allowed Cotton to try the pipe, but after one drag he had decided that he wanted no part of it. "Cotton," John said, "How many gals do you have chasing after you? You look just like your Pa and I so I know there has to be some after you!"

After joining in on the laughter he answered, "I don't know, sir. I don't pay them much attention really. I've got my cap set on being a sheriff like my Pa."

John smiled and turned to Nat, "You've got a good boy here, son. It makes me proud to sit here and witness it. And speaking of that, how's the life of a sheriff treating you?"

"Oh it's not too bad. I'm still planting cotton as well though, we turned out pretty good this year."

"That's good to hear. I'm thinking about selling all my cattle this spring, getting to be too much for an old man like me, ha!"

"So were you able to keep it a secret from Ma?"

"Oh, yeah, she had no idea you were coming."

"And everyone else?"

"Not a clue."

The three of them laughed as there was a loud knock on the door. Mary Anna rushed out of the dining room toward the door. She had no idea that it might be another one of her children and quite frankly she was still not fully over the shock of her son and his family showing up.

When she swung the door open she was taken aback, for a moment she thought she was looking into a mirror at herself in her younger days. There on the front porch and dressed in a beautiful red coat with fur lining was her sweet Georgia. "Ahh!" Mary Anna shouted. "John, Georgia's here! Georgia's here!"

Georgia smiled and stepped in the house and into her mother's arms as her mother started to cry in excitement. Following closely behind Georgia were three children and her husband who was carrying a baby. Georgia was now twenty-eight and just as Nat looked like John, so did she look like Mary Anna only Georgia continued to keep her hair in beautiful curls that made her look like she was in her late teenage years.

After Seth stepped inside he shut the door behind his family and handed the small baby who was named John after his grandfather to Georgia. He was only a month old, but had already started showing signs of response towards them that most one year olds do. Anna Williams was seven and looked a lot like Georgia with a few of her father's Irish traits. Martha was five and nearly had the same red hair that Alice had had. Her face was covered in freckles and her skin tanned dark from spending too much time outside. Out of all the grandchildren, Martha was the only one who did not have blue eyes, hers were green.

The last of Georgia's children was three year old Allen who was the only one of her children to have blonde hair. Unlike Anna and the baby whose hair was brown and that of Martha's red hair, Allen had hair nearly as blonde as John and Nat's. It was a sight to see something as light complected and fair skinned as him and one couldn't help but laugh when they realized he had came from his mother who carried the Indian heritage more than anyone else in the family.

Mary Anna again took in every detail of her daughter's children and cherished all their faces. But just like Nat's children, they too were soon off and playing, adding more joyous chaos to the large home. Georgia and the baby followed her mother into the dining room with the other women, while Seth joined the men up front.

Mary Anna was so overcome with joy that she found it hard not to quit talking. She covered every little event that had happened over the past ten years since everyone had left and didn't leave out a single detail. She then expected Georgia and Rosalee to do the same where their lives were concerned, so it was going to make for a long talk filled night.

The six playing children continued all around the upstairs portion of the house, playing hide and seek, tag and other childlike games that they had created. Mary Anna, Rachel and John felt like their house had finally been revived of the silence it had endured for so long and enjoyed every bit of the noise that they heard… it was music to their ears.

Rachel left the dining room and began making her fried chicken from the two chickens she had killed the day before. She had also gathered up all kinds of fresh vegetables from the cellar and prepared a rather large loaf of bread. It was going to be one of the biggest feasts any of them had ever seen. Rachel intended to cook every bit of food that was in the house and not even leave behind a crumb for the mice, if they were going to celebrate then they were going to celebrate right.

By now, Rachel had caught on to the plan that John had devised, but Mary Anna had not. Shortly after Georgia and her family had arrived, the front doors flew open and Will stepped into the house with his wife and seven year old daughter. "I'm home!" He shouted.

"Me too!" Another voice followed.

Mary Anna poked around the dining room doorway and peered down the hallway into the entry where she saw them standing there. "Will! Johnny!"

She ran to them and just as she had done with her other children, wrapped them both up in her motherly hug. "And who is this beautiful thing?" she said kneeling down to the blonde headed girl.

"Ma, this is Callie and this here is my wife, Dottie I've written to you about," Will said.

Dottie had the most beautiful auburn hair that Mary Anna had ever seen and she was just about as short as her as well. Her green eyes sparkled as she was taken into Mary Anna's hug. This was the first time the two of them had met one another and right away they knew they would be great friends, just as Mary Anna and Alice had been.

Mary Anna turned toward Johnny who was standing next to his wife, Ellen and their twelve-year-old son, Abram. Ellen was Rosalee's cousin and the two of them looked a lot alike. Abram on the other hand, favored his father and they both looked like younger versions of David Braymyer.

Callie and Abram hugged their grandmother that they had never seen before and politely asked if they may go play with the other children. And so two more laughing children's voices were added to the growing party upstairs and Mary Anna couldn't help but to spin around with her arms stretched out as she savored the moment. And just with the guests before, Will and Johnny went into the sitting room with the men while Ellen and Dottie headed to the dining room where Dottie and Ellen were introduced to more of her husbands family.

Just before Mary Anna left the entry she heard but another light knock on the front door. "Let me guess," she said, "Ruth Ann?"

She stepped to the doors, convinced that she would not overreact this time since she knew exactly who the next company was. When she opened the door she found herself staring at a familiar face that she had not seen in ages, but she still had no idea who the stranger was. The woman had light brown hair and wore it down her back as she held a toddler on her hip.

It was a girl, with brown locks of hair and a pudgy face that smelled of peppermint sticks. "Are you Mrs. Braymyer?"

672

"I am."

"I'm Polly Anna Reynolds, previously Hunter. I believe you are my grandmother."

Mary Anna nearly fell to the floor, she was sure this excitement was too much for her and she would soon die of a heart attack. It suddenly hit her where she had seen this face before, it was the face of her Esther. After all these years without her eldest daughter, she felt certain that she was looking into her eyes at that very moment.

She broke her promise to herself and overreacted, nearly jumping ten feet in the air. "John!" She shouted, "Come quick!"

Mary Anna grabbed Polly Anna by the arm and pulled her inside where she embraced her and the child still attached to her hip.

"What is it, darling?" John said stepping behind her.

"John! It's Polly Anna! Esther's daughter!"

John's eyes welled up with tears as he too thought he was looking at Esther herself. Mary Anna took the small child whose name was Hannah as John hugged his long lost granddaughter.

"Come in," he said, "We've waited a long time to see you."

Mary Anna took her around and showed her to all of her long lost family members. Polly Anna had heard nothing but bad stories about the Braymyer family from her Grandmother Hunter, but she knew what kind of person Polly Hunter was so she believed very little of her stories. Polly had died the year before and now finally, after all these years, Polly Anna was able to reconnect with her mother's family. She was a young widow, her late husband having been killed on a railroad robbery.

The women joined the men in the front room, husbands with wives and children with parents. With the exception of Ruth Ann and her family, all the Braymyers were together at last and it would be the last time that this happened. Mary Anna looked around the room at everyone as she sat in her husband's lap. "I wish Ruth Ann could be here, but I suppose she's in Russia right about now. You know, I hear that's by China, but I've never been so I don't know for certain."

John looked over at Nat and half smiled in his direction. The sun was struggling to stay up now and the snow looked as if it had actually lightened up a little bit. Mary Anna looked out the window into the brightly white covered yard and sighed. But then, as if God had heard her final wish for the day she happened to see the most fanciest buggy she had ever seen in her entire life.

She stood up with a shawl around her shoulders and slowly ventured nearer the window. Never taking her eyes away from it, she side stepped her way out of the room and toward the front doors, leaving everyone else in the sitting room. As she stepped out onto the cold porch, Nat leaned over to his father and said, "Have you ever seen a wagon look as nice as that one?"

"Ha, I can't say that I have son, but she's Lady Ruth Ann to everyone overseas and I reckon they take good care of their ladies."

The wagon was completely enclosed with a driver sitting on top of it. It was stained the darkest brown imaginable and on the side it read, 'Ruth Ann' in green letters. Even the horses who had been put into the barn stomped their feet for although they couldn't see it, they knew there was a buggy out there that they would all love to pull.

674

Mary Anna's hand went up to her mouth as she ventured off of the front porch and in the direction of the buggy. When it came to a stop, the driver hopped down and opened the wooden door on the side of the cart. A long leg stuck out that was covered in the nicest fur coats that Mary Anna had ever seen and it was soon followed by another until the full body of Lady Ruth Ann was standing before her.

Her light brown hair was in a bun beneath a fashionable brown suede hat that matched the long body length fur coat that she was wearing. Her cheeks were rosy red from the Missouri coldness and her hands were covered by satin gloves with the initials 'RAB' written across them.

She looked toward Mary Anna who was now just three feet in front of her, and stopped dead in her tracks by the elegant sight she was now looking upon. "Ma?"

"Ruth Ann?"

Ruth Ann would have ran toward her mother, but being a lady had changed her in that she walked at a fast pace toward her arms outstretched. "Ma, I've missed you so much."

Mary Anna let more tears of joy spill out and land on top of her daughter's expensive coat. They pulled away and turned back to the wagon as a tall man dressed in complete cowboy attire stepped down with a small boy in his arms. They began walking toward them, Mary Anna just barely being able to see his brown eyes beneath his brown cowboy hat.

"Ma," Ruth Ann said as they approached them, "This is my husband, Eli or Cowboy as I call him and this is our son, Harrison, he's three."

Mary Anna stretched out her arms and took the small boy against her. In some ways, he reminded her of her long lost brother from long ago in Georgia. She held him close and kissed him on top of the head. "Ruth Ann, he's a nice looking boy. I knew you would have a child someday."

Not only had Ruth Ann lost her infant son with her first husband, but she had also lost another son with Cowboy. He had been born the year after they had been married and didn't live to see the New Year. This child truly was a blessing to Ruth Ann who had always had a soft spot for children.

Cowboy stepped to the back of the wagon and removed their luggage as the buggy rode off back towards Walnut Grove. He followed the women and his son into the warm house. It was one of the best Christmas Eves that Mary Anna had every witnessed and she would remember it for the rest of her life.

December 25, 1882
Braymyer Ridge
Christmas Day

The next morning everyone gathered in the entry way where the Christmas tree patiently awaited them. A few of the adults stood around, while the rest and all of the children sat on the wide staircase, nearly filling up from top to bottom. John and Mary Anna stood in front of the tree and looked upon all their family members and were the happiest they had ever been.

They handed out gifts to all the children, a doll for the girls and a wooden gun for the boys. Mary Anna had never dreamed that she would see Polly Anna again, so she had not thought to buy her a gift. The night before, she went into Esther's old bedroom and gathered up all of her old dresses and neatly wrapped them up.

Polly Anna was delighted to get them and couldn't help but cry when she sorted through them. For all the rest of the adults, the women got new dresses and matching bonnets and the men got new rifles that John had picked out himself. Shortly after the gifts were opened, all the children took off once again running through the house with Creek not far behind.

After a large Christmas lunch, everyone dressed in their finest clothing and then bundled up. They loaded up onto six wagons and made their way toward Walnut Grove in their own little wagon train. John and Mary Anna's wagon led the way with Rachel, Polly Anna and her daughter, Hannah in their company. Mary Anna watched the sky and smiled willingly at the clearness of the day.

Once in town they marched into Cooks Photography studio and had several family portraits made, including a large one, which had everyone in it. They had so many made that they were there for three hours before heading back down the road to Braymyer Ridge where they all resumed eating again.

677

When the children slowly started to grow tired, Mary Anna rounded all twelve of them into the downstairs bedroom and shut the door behind her. She looked around at them all as they were sprawled out on top of the bed and all across the floor. She sat down right in the middle on top of a rug and took Addie and Harrison in her lap.

"Listen Children, I want to tell you a story."

"Yay! A story!" They all shouted.

"Now let's see. Once upon a time right here in Missouri, in fact not far from where we are now there lived a mean old witch. Now this witch was so ugly that no man would have her as his wife and whenever anyone saw her, it nearly made them sick. Now I suppose you're thinking, what's so different about this witch? Well I'll tell you.

Since this witch was so ugly, she had to find a way to make herself more prettier so every night she would wander the Ozarks looking for young children to take away back to her little log cabin."

The children were completely silent and every one of their eyes was stretched open as wide as they could be.

"When she got the children back to her cabin she would cast a spell on them and wave her hand round and round. She would then move in, real close to them and take in a deep breath from their faces. As she continued to do so, the children's good and young looks slowly started to travel away from them and into her body.

They say that she took more than one hundred children and when the local farmers found them, they looked like little old people wandering through the woods. One day, a bunch of locals got together and set out to get rid of this witch once and for all. There was probably about thirty people or more. It was early in the morning when they set out after her and to this day, none of those brave little townspeople have been seen."

"What happened to the witch?" Anna Williams asked.

"Nobody knows for sure. Some say that she still wanders the woods looking for children, but me. I say she has sucked the beauty out of so many people that now she looks just like you or me. So you never know just who among us might actually be the mean old witch of the Ozarks."

Mary Anna looked around the room where the children continued to stare in her direction, not uttering a sound. "Boo!" She shouted.

The children began screaming at the top of their lungs and burying their faces into pillows and the backs of one another. Addie and Harrison clutched her arms as tightly as they could and looked at her wild-eyed. The screaming went on for what seemed like hours and Mary Anna, who was laughing too hard to try and calm them down, just knew their parents were going to kill her.

Finally after they had settled down to the point where she could stand up without being attacked by frightful arms, she left the room where Ruth Ann was waiting for her. She was smiling as she leaned against the wall next to the door and just shook her head at her mother who was now leaning against the door itself.

"Ma, you're something else. Ha, you know those children won't sleep a wink tonight."

Mary Anna laughed, "You're probably right, darling. Oh, sometimes I wish I could be a child again and have an imagination like theirs."

"Ma, I think you've got imagination enough for the whole family!"

The two of them laughed and just before they had decided to walk away from the children's room, Mary Anna turned back to the door. Ruth Ann watched as she didn't know quite what her mother was up to. Mary Anna slowly turned the knob and poked her head in through a small crack. "Boo!"

Again all the children started screaming at the top of their lungs. By the time their parents made it to the bedroom, Mary Anna and Ruth Ann had already ran up the stairs and were watching them from above. They tried with all their might to contain their laughter as the worried parents stumbled onto the frightened children.

The two of them sat down in the upstairs hallway near where they had shot each other as the other adults tried to calm the children. "Ma," Ruth Ann said, "Do you ever wonder about mistakes of the past?"

"What do you mean, dear?"

"I mean, do you every worry that maybe you've made too many mistakes in the past to fix?"

"Why do you ask?"

"I don't know, sometimes I feel like I'm just a mistake and wonder if maybe I should have died back in the war with Washington. I still miss him you know. Even after all these years. Not that I don't love Cowboy, because I do, but I guess there is just something about your first love that never really goes away."

"Well, I'm not sure how any of that is mistakes, but you're right about your first love. I'm lucky enough to have only loved and been loved once, so I really don't know much about that. But overall, I've buried my fair share of loved ones over the years and it never gets any easier. You just have to be strong, Ruth Ann...or is it Lady Ruth Ann to me?"

Ruth Ann and Mary Anna laughed, "Ma, you know I'll always be your Ruth Ann."

"That's what I thought."

"Do you ever think what happened to Esther was a mistake, Ma?"

"Of course it was a mistake, darling, but some mistakes you just can't avoid. Was it a mistake to shoot her? Absolutely, but it wasn't only your Pa's mistake, it was hers too. Your father made a mistake, but he had to in order to prevent Ben Hunter from making a mistake...shooting your little brother."

"I suppose you're right, but sometimes it just seems that some of the choices we are forced to make are just not rightfully fair."

"I know darling, but in the end all that matters is if you are happy or not. Are you happy?"

"Oh yes, I'm very happy, but I don't think anyone can be as happy as they were before the war."

"Ruth Ann I tried so hard to keep the war away from you and your siblings, course you had already married so there was little I could do in your concern, but I tried just the same. It was a dark spot in our past, but we must remember that it is only one page of our life's book. Now come on, I think the children have gotten quiet again."

The two of them went back downstairs and joined the rest of the adults in the sitting room and acted like they knew nothing about all the commotion. Of course John and Rachel knew better and looked at them with suspecting eyes. Christmas day slowly came to an end beneath the dark Missouri sky and thin lines of smoke arose out of the home's many chimneys.

Over the next week Mary Anna spent time with all her children and grandchildren and slowly said goodbye to them one family at a time. By the end of the next week Ruth Ann, Cowboy and Harrison were the last to leave, heading down to Atlanta to their winter home. Alas the home was quiet again and John, Mary Anna and Rachel resumed their places as they patiently awaited for more excitement to fill the home.

December 14, 1994
Braymyer Ridge

Pappy and I stepped out into the December sun early in the afternoon and walked around the front yard of the Braymyer Home. It had turned out warm for this time of year and I wore only a light jacket over my overalls.

We walked past the old well that was on the opposite side of the house as the barn and walked along a tree line that slowly dripped down cold water from the melting snow. A few birds that had decided to brave the winter weather flew up from the trees as we neared them and found refuge across the drive in other trees.

As we continued to walk I noticed something lying on the ground in front of us. I knelt down and picked up the small piece of metal in my hand as I observed it. "Pappy, what's this?"

Pappy took it from me and then handed it back, "It looks like an old piece of lead son, probably from a bullet."

"Why is it out here?"

"I suspect it's from the battle of Braymyer Ridge."

"The what?"

"The battle that was fought out here."

"What do you mean? There was actually a battle fought here?"

"Sure was, not too long before John died."

"But why was there a battle? I mean what were they fighting over?"

683

"Well, John, Mary Anna and Rachel were fighting for their lives. The outlaws were fighting for the Braymyer's money."

"Their money?"

"That's right. John had gotten too old to work and since his sons had all moved off he was forced to retire. He saved up a bunch of his money and sold off parts of his land that he didn't have any use for anymore. Well, the outlaws found out that he had money and they decided that they wanted it."

"So what happened?"

"Well, they ended up fighting for it. After it was over it became known as the battle of Braymyer Ridge."

"So who won?"

"You sure do have a lot of questions today don't you?"

"Sorry, sir."

"It's okay, I was the same way when I was your age. Now let's see if I can remember how that battle started."

September 02, 1886
Battle of Braymyer Ridge

"Come on, Rachel! Bring me a gun!"

Mary Anna ran from window to window looking out at the intruders who were approaching their home. Her satin dress ruffled as she ran across the rooms and her hair had begun to fall out of its bun, making a mess across her forehead and face.

John was upstairs looking out a window that faced the south as he watched three men try and sneak up to the house. He quickly pulled the window open and stuck the barrel of his rifle outside where he began to fire. At sixty-seven he was still just as good a shot as he had been in his younger days and he brought two of the men down as the third escaped to the front of the house.

He quickly ran down the stairs to join his wife and Rachel at the downstairs windows. "John," Mary Anna said, "Are you okay?"

"I'm fine darling."

"Are you sure? The doctor said we need to watch your heart."

"I'll be okay. Besides, there's not very much we can do if we are under attack."

A bullet was fired from somewhere outside and it flew through the window, right between John and Mary Anna. She quickly jumped in front of the window and fired back, bringing the man down.

"John, did you see how many was out there?" Rachel asked.

"No, but I'd guess at least ten or fifteen."

"Dear God," Mary Anna said. "Rachel, you better go get more bullets."

Rachel ran upstairs to fetch some more bullets, leaving John and Mary Anna alone downstairs. Bullets whizzed through the front windows, planting themselves into the back wall.

John and Mary Anna fell to the floor to avoid being hit and waited for Rachel to return. "John," Mary Anna said as she propped her head on her husband's chest, "We sure have been through some battles haven't we."

"Yes, darling" he said, "We sure have."

John leaned down and kissed his wife and then looked into her aged but beautiful eyes, "You think we got one more battle left in us?"

"I think so, what do you think?"

"I'm ready when you are. It's like your Ma used to say, there comes a point when you just can't run anymore."

"Ha, now if my Ma were here those men out there would have already been running for the hills," John said.

"Isn't that the truth. So let's go, John. Let's go out there and get revenge for Walkie, Grandmother, Aunt Liza, Esther and all the other people that hatred has taken from us. Let's show those men what a little Braymyer willpower looks like."

John leaned down and kissed her one more time as Rachel crawled across the floor to join them. "Let's go, darling," he said.

The three of them busted out of the front doors side by side so hard that the doors nearly flew to the front yard. Mary Anna stood in the middle with John and Rachel on either side of her and the minute they stepped out onto the porch they began firing. A small wind blew against the front of them, causing the women's hair and dresses to flow behind them.

Bullets flew by their heads and hit the large columns as they walked passed them and into the front yard. Slowly, one by one their attackers began to fall to the ground. Gun smoke filled the air around the three of them as they continued their march across the land that they had worked so hard to get. Missouri had become more civilized than it had ever been before, but there would always be the few who broke the law and the Braymyers were not going to stand for it.

The three elderly people continued across the yard, somehow being protected from the bullets of their enemies and they continued to fire, never stopping from their goal. Men shouted and screamed as bullet's found their way to them and an occasional groan could be heard throughout the yard as the outlaws clutched tightly to their wounds.

After Mary Anna had fired the last shot it revealed a total of seventeen men lying dead on the ground and neither John, Mary Anna nor Rachel had a scratch on them. Mary Anna brushed the hair out of her face and looked around her, "Well look's like we've won our last battle you two. Do you think the Lord will let us take it easy now?"

"Shoot," Rachel said, "With you? Nothing will ever be easy."

The three of them laughed as they headed toward the bodies of the dead men that had just tried to take their home away. They drug the bodies over to a tree line and being too old and tired to dig a hole for them, they left them there for the buzzards.

Once they had finished taking care of the bodies they headed back inside just as the sun went down behind the house. They drank tea and shared memories and stories as the night drifted on.

Three years later on April 21, 1888 John walked down the ridge a little more out of breath than usual and wandered down to the cemetery to visit his mother's grave. He used a large stick to assist him in walking and after thirty minutes found himself standing in front of her stone.

He put his hand on top of it and leaned forward a little bit to try and catch his breath. "Ma, I reckon I'll be joining you here soon enough, if that's alright with you."

Just as he finished talking there was a sharp tightening in his chest and he fell to his knees. "Dammit, Ma. I didn't mean today!"

He held his chest tightly with one hand and with the other he still clutched his walking stick that now stood up taller than him. He slowly fell to his side and rolled over onto his back as he looked up into the blue sky he would soon call home.

Mary Anna busied herself around the house as she usually did and after an hour had passed she knew in her gut that something wasn't right with her husband. She took a small drink of water and then followed her husband's footprints in the muddy ground down to the cemetery.

"John!" She shouted running into the cemetery. She knelt down beside him and ran her hand through his hair, taking his head in her lap. "John, talk to me."

"Darling?" He softly said opening his eyes and looking up at her. His eyes continued to shine that brilliant blue that she had fallen in love with so long before.

"I'm here, John. You just rest."

"Ma says to tell you hi."

"John? What are you talking about?"

"Ma… she says to tell you hi and that she's proud of you. Mary Anna, I love you."

"I love you too, darling, now let's try and get you back to the house."

John closed his eyes and then slowly reopened them. Through a dry mouth he said, "No, darling. I think this is it for me. Ma says it's time to come home, Mary Anna. She looks so beautiful."

Mary Anna had tears running down her face as her husband continued to speak. "Darling, did I ever tell you about the first time I ever had Grandma Davis' moonshine?"

Mary Anna let out a laugh through her sobs, "No, honey."

"Me and Ralph we was going to help her harvest her fields. And while we was out there in the autumn sun, surrounded by all the Tennessee trees she brought us something to drink. And, well you can imagine what it was, only we didn't know it at the time. Ralph, he sort of slowly drank at it, but me I was so thirsty that I swigged the whole cup…and it was a large cup.

Boy I fell to the ground kicking and spitting so bad that I darn near knocked Ralph and Grandma Davis both off their feet. Well after I had gotten over the initial first taste I stood up, or tried to anyway. I was so dizzy and I swear I saw two of everything, no fooling. After I had finally managed to get to my feet I saw the most awful sight of my life."

"What was it, John?"

"My mother."

"Your mother? John what are you talking about?"

"It was my mother. She was sitting there atop a horse looking down at us, with no clothing on!"

Mary Anna let another laugh slip, "John I can't see your Ma doing that."

"Well she didn't. You see she was clothed alright, but that moonshine messed with my head so badly that I swear I saw my mother sitting naked on top of that horse. That's when I swore I'd never drink it again."

"Even until the end, John Braymyer, still full of jokes."

John tried to smile and managed to allow a small grin to appear from his quivering lips. "Darling, this is it. I think I'm about to go."

"John," Mary Anna said crying all over again, "Please don't, stay strong. Stay strong for me, please don't leave me."

"Well, you know how persistent my Ma is. She says it's almost suppertime and I best hurry on up there. Darling?"

"Yes, John."

"Kiss me one more time."

Mary Anna leaned down and kissed him romantically where he returned the favor with the last bit of strength he had. He had loved Mary Anna from the day he first laid eyes on her and had done everything he could to show her enough love, even until his last breath.

Mary Anna cried uncontrollably as she held her husband and looked up at the sky. The clouds seemed to be moving faster than normal and a strong gust of wind ripped into her body, blowing her hair in all directions. She watched as the wind that had just attacked her rolled through the small valley and then back up into the sky just above Braymyer Ridge.

They buried him next to his mother and just behind him were Esther and her Yankee husband. Normally, Mary Anna would have died right along with him, but she had an extra thump in her chest that Alice had given her that forced her to go on.

Aside from Ruth Ann and her family, none of the other children were able to make it to his funeral. The three of them wore black dresses as they stood around the rectangular hole in the ground and one by one threw a handful of dirt down on top of his coffin as Cowboy and Harrison watched nearby.

John and Mary Anna had gone through so much together and had nearly conquered the world one state at time, but it was finally time for her to say goodbye to her husband and her best friend. She headed back to the house with her dear friend Rachel whose journey like hers had begun in Georgia nearly fifty years before and just behind them Ruth Ann and her family brought up the rear.

Cowboy and Harrison went inside leaving the three women standing on the ridge alone. They looked down across the Braymyer land and took in every little detail including the small group of stones down in the middle. They could hear the cast iron gate from the cemetery squeak as a September wind pushed against it. Mary Anna looked toward the barn where John had spent so much of his time and thought of how lonely the building would be now without him there to care for it.

The coloring of the late afternoon landscape was filled with warm but cool colors and painted a scene of sadness and also of celebration of one's life. The three of them walked away from the ridge arm in arm back toward the house where they found themselves sitting in rocking chairs on the front porch.

Their black dresses fluttered a bit in the direction the wind was headed and their hair buns held tightly together atop their heads. They slowly rocked back and forth, each one on the same rhythm creating a steady creaking noise as they rocked the rest of the day away.

"Ruth Ann," Mary Anna said. "I don't suppose you have any of that Brandy left do you?"

Ruth Ann smiled in her mother's direction as she reached inside her dress, "Sure do. Just don't get carried away like I did, Ma."

"You know me better than that, darling. I just need something to take the edge off."

691

The three of them took a large gulp of the aged drink and then wiped their mouths with the back of their hands. When they had satisfied their craving they resumed rocking the wooden chairs until the sun had disappeared.

April 21, 1888
Dear Journal,

Earlier today we buried my husband of forty-nine years. It would have been fifty in a few months, but we didn't quite make it. Looking back over everything we went through together, it almost seems as though it was a story written by a famous English author.

Most of the things in my life don't seem or feel real, but then I have to remind myself that it is all indeed very true. Georgia, Tennessee, our first home in Kentucky. Running from the Trail of Tears only to end up in the midst of a Civil War, my goodness the journeys we have been on.

My life hasn't been all bad, sure I've had to fight from time to time, but as I look back now my life was blessed with so much good simply because of the people I allowed myself to be in the company of. They have truly made my life worth living and someday I will join my husband in the ground, but until then I will do what I've always done for my deceased family…I'll live for them.

The road to Braymyer Ridge has finally come to an end as I sit here on a front porch rocker next to Rachel, just as Grandmother and Aunt Liza used to do. The sun will be going down soon and they'll be chores to do in the morning, so I'll put the pen up and head upstairs to my now empty bed.

A grieving widow,
Mary Anna Braymyer

December 14, 1994
Braymyer Ridge

I found myself crying as Pappy ended the story with John's death. I had somehow convinced myself that he would live forever, but just with everything else, it all must come to an end eventually. I felt proud that this story was about my very own family and now that I had heard all there was to know about John, it saddened me that there would be no more stories about him. My childish thoughts made me wish that somehow he could come back and live again so that I might hear more about him, but I knew that wasn't possible.

Pappy and I headed back to the front porch and sat in the rocking chairs that were still there and it was as if they were patiently awaiting our arrival. We sat down and looked out over the Ozarks that John and Mary Anna had called home after their long journey from the east.

It was kind of sad to see that the place had been turned into a bed and breakfast, but at the same time I was glad that it had been so well preserved. I didn't find out until after we left that my Pappy was actually the one who owned it, which is why I guess I didn't get in trouble for punching a hole in the wall.

After sitting in the same rockers that the three women had after John's burial, we headed back inside and down the hallway toward the dining room. All across the wall in the dining room were the pictures that the family had taken on Christmas Day of 1882. Seeing them reminded me of all the children I heard about.

I ran through the entry and into the large guest bedroom. As I walked around it, I pictured all the children screaming in terror as their grandmother told them the story of the witch.

695

How I wished I could have been there to hear it spoken directly from her mouth. She was, I concluded, probably a very good storyteller.

Afterwards I walked out of the bedroom and back towards the kitchen and imagined Rachel making fried chicken for everyone to eat. I could see all the fresh vegetables as they covered the cabinets and chicken feathers on the ground from where she had de-feathered their meal. I could see her standing near the wash basin with a long dress on and her long dark hair resting on her back.

Pulling myself away I ran upstairs and spent time in each of the bedrooms, remembering all those who had called them home so long ago. I slowly walked down the hallway on the right side and laughed at the story of Ruth Ann and Mary Anna shooting each other. I examined the wall at the end, near the front windows and found a small bullet hole. With my finger, I slowly felt the indention and determined it had been the bullet that had hit Ruth Ann.

I stepped into the bedroom where Ruth Ann had killed the Major and by and by, on the headboard directly under the top of it was another bullet hole. This must be the shot she fired that missed, I thought. Boy, I bet that darned ol Yankee was scared to death with Ruth Ann waving a gun around.

I ventured all throughout the house and imagined that I was at the party during the Civil War. Dancing to Mary Anna's song and swinging a pretty girl across the dance floor next to Will, Nat and Georgia as Ruth Ann watched from afar. I could smell the famous apple pies and see both Cherokee and Creek running through the front door in search of the dessert.

I could smell the pipe smoke from John's tobacco pipe and the sweet smell of cedar as Mary Anna strung it about the house in preparation for Christmas. I twirled in the entry, just as she had done when her children finally made it home and just like her I let my arms stretch out and fly around me.

I walked into the sitting room where I found Pappy sitting there and looking out the front window as snow started to fall. The fireplace glowed and threw its warmth out towards us as the windows began to fog over by way of Mr. Frost. "Pappy," I said taking a seat next to him.

"Do you have to die someday too?"

He looked down at me with understanding eyes as if he had asked the same question to someone he loved long ago. "Afraid so, John. It's just a part of life."

"But I don't want you to die."

"I know, son. No one truly wants anyone to die, not deep down anyway. But if we stay here forever then we will never get to see the ones who have gone before us again. I was thinking the other night about your Great Nanny and how much I miss her. You know, I can't wait to get to Heaven and see her, but right now even though I loved her with all I had, I'm glad I'm sitting here with you."

"I'm glad you're here too, Pappy. Will I get to go to Heaven someday?"

"Of course you will, son. And then we'll all be together again."

"So, when you die it will be like we are on vacation from each other? You'll go first and then later when the vacation is over I'll come see you?"

Pappy laughed, "That's right son, life's a vacation."

"So, what became of Rachel and Mary Anna? I mean I know they ended up in Texas because they are buried behind our house, but what made them leave?"

"Well, they were getting older and they didn't have any family in these parts, so they did the only thing they could do, move closer to the family that they did have."

"How come they didn't go live with Ruth Ann?"

"Well, Ruth Ann was always traveling and such, she lived quite an adventurous life you know."

"Well how come Mary Anna wasn't brought back here to be buried?"

"Son, back then it was a long hard journey. And besides, John had his mother here with him and Mary Anna was buried next to Nat and Rosalee. But you know, up until she left for Texas, Mary Anna brought flowers to John's grave everyday. Rain or shine, snow or hail."

"What about Ruth Ann? What became of her?"

"Oh, Ruth Ann. My, my. Son, that's a story in itself and it'll have to wait for another day. Now come on, we best be heading back to Dixie."

September 26, 1925
Dixie Baptist Church
Dixie, Texas

It was a warm September day in Dixie, Texas and the flocks of eager dove could be seen high above in the sky heading south to a warmer climate. Yellow and orange trees filled the peaceful valley and farmers eagerly counted the days until their corn and wheat crops could be harvested.

The Baptist church was a small white building with a tower like structure at its front. It got a fresh coat of paint every year around this time and shone brightly against the morning sunlight as people filed in through its two wooden doors.

Mary Anna had turned 100 the day before and she now sat in a wooden chair at the front of the church as people filled the room for the first Braymyer family reunion. The small petite woman had a head full of gray hair and a smile bigger than the likes that anyone had ever seen before. She wore a blue dress, much like the one she had buried Alice in and held tightly to a blue handkerchief as her hands lie neatly folded in her lap.

Seated beside her were her surviving children, Nat, Georgia and lastly, Lady Ruth Ann and they watched as their great grandchildren gathered in the floor in front of them. As the building continued to fill up, nearly exceeding its max all the children made their way over and sat in front of Granny Braymyer and her children. Also seated in the group of older people and directly beside Mary Anna was Rachel Lloyd.

Nathan Sanders, whom was the grandson of Cotton Braymyer, was in the front row and eagerly awaited to hear what stories they were about to be told. The room fell quiet as the last child took his seat among the anxious children.

699

"Granny Braymyer," Nathan said, "Who's that colored woman next to you?"

"Why child, she's my…"

"House keeper," Rachel interrupted her, "I'm her house keeper."

"Now Rachel, you've kept me quiet all these years and it's time the truth be known. Sweet child," she said looking at Nathan, "She's my aunt."

All of the children's mouths dropped wide open and even a few of the adults who had also gathered to hear the stories she was about to tell. Rachel just started laughing, "Lord, Mary Anna, you just had to do it didn't you?"

"Sure did, darling. Now the whole world knows that my best friend is actually my aunt. Ha, if only Polly Hunter were here now to hear what I had just said."

"Polly who?" Nathan said.

"Oh, never mind her darling," Mary Anna said as she threw a wink in Polly Anna's direction. "Now let's see what story we have. Have you children ever heard the story about the witch from Texas?"

Ruth Ann covered her face with her thin hand and tried to contain her laughter.

"Why Ruth Ann," Mary Anna said, "Witches are nothing to laugh about. Why they are in fact very dangerous people. Now let's see if I can remember correctly.

You see, children, long ago not far from where we are today there lived a witch way up in the woods near the Sandy Creek. Now she lived there in a small log cabin that was well hidden by all the oak trees that surrounded it. Now this was no normal witch, nope, not at all. She was the ugliest thing anyone had ever set his or her eyes upon.

Now every night by the light of the moon, this witch would go out in search of children. You see, she was so ugly that she needed a way to get some beauty into her body and she used children to do it."

All the children stared wide eyed at her.

"She would take the children back to her house and once she was alone with them she would wave her hands all throughout the air and say, 'Child…child…give me your youth!' After saying this spell several times the beauty and youthfulness would slowly leave the child's body and enter into her, causing her to become a little prettier with each child she found.

Now they say that this witch down here in Texas snatched two hundred children, right out of their homes. Finally everyone at Dixie and Sandusky got tired of their children disappearing because there was no one to help them on the farms. So a bunch of them got together one day and decided they were going to catch them this here witch.

That night, they set out for the woods using large torches for light and several hounds at their side. Just before getting to her little cabin they were stopped by a voice. 'Go away… go away or I'll eat you all.

The group almost turned back, but then they realized that they must get the job done or no one would be there to work their farms and then there would be nothing to eat. Well, just before they reached her front door it flew open so hard that it fell right off the hinges. Then suddenly, everyone in that group including the loyal dogs were sucked into the cabin, never to be seen again."

And the usual question came straight from Nathan's mouth, "Well what happened to the Witch?"

Mary Anna looked at them, "Why child, Ruth Ann's the witch."

Ruth Ann calmly stood up and looked out toward them, "Boo!"

All the children shot up off the floor and took off running and screaming like a pack of wild buffalo. They didn't stop until they were out of the building and halfway across the churchyard. Then, they realized they were standing next to the woods and every one of them started shouting again and headed back to the other side of the building that faced the road.

"Ma," Nat said, "You'll never tire of telling that old witch story, will you?"

"Course she won't," Georgia interrupted laughing, "She loves frightening all the little children. I knew she had something to do with our children getting so scared on that Christmas visit at the ridge! Now I know why!"

"That's right, Georgia. You finally figured me out."

"And Ma," Ruth Ann said, "Why did I have to be the witch? I think Georgia would have made a much better one."

In between all the laughter Mary Anna simply said, "Because you're older, *Lady* Ruth Ann and you fit the description much more better than she does."

"Well I declare, Ma," Ruth Ann said still laughing, "You're always full of jokes."

Mary Anna's eyes sparkled as she thought about her husband, "I suppose I am. I get that from your Pa though."

After they had had all the laughing they could handle, Mary Anna stood up with Rachel at her side and headed outside to get some fresh air. Mary Anna's only regret about the whole day was that her John was not here with her to see all their family members.

The two of them walked arm in arm and they watched her descendants run across the churchyard playing games and drinking lemonade. The leaves had started to fall and a few of them floated around the two women as they walked along the end of their long road.

"Rachel, I don't feel old at all. Would you believe me if I told you that?"

"Mary Anna, I've come to believe just about anything you say. Heaven knows you were never a very good liar."

"Well I guess that's why I just chose not to lie. We've come a long way old gal haven't we?"

"Sure have. And to think it all started with us running from the Army. Shoot, if I'd have known all the trouble you were going to get us into I might have just as soon stayed behind with Mr. Walker, beatings and all."

"Grandfather Walker, there's a name I haven't heard in awhile. Rachel, I'm one hundred years old and you're ninety eight and you know, death has never really scared me much."

"Really? I've always been frightened to death of it. Sometimes I wonder if maybe I've made too many mistakes to get into Heaven where I know my Ralph is waiting."

"Honey, mistakes are all a part of life, it's what you do after the mistake has been made that counts. No, I like to think that with every mistake we make the smarter we get and the smarter we get the closer to God we are. I reckon as old as we are Rachel, that we're just about knocking on his front door wouldn't you say?"

"I imagine you're right, Mary Anna, just as you always are."

"Ha, John was always right, not me. I just went along with him most of the times and not once did he lead me astray or have me to want for anything. He was the closest thing to a saint that I ever knew."

"Your husband was a good man, Mary Anna and I will always have fond memories of him over at the ridge. Ha, sliding down that ice covered ridge at his age, what was he thinking!"

"John never lost his sense for adventure, honey. I'm just glad he didn't end up with another broken leg. I don't think I could have handled that Yankee doctor coming up to pay us a visit on Christmas Eve."

"Mary Anna, you're one of the bravest people I know. You never seem to show any sign of fear no matter what the situation is."

"Oh I fear things, I'm sure of it. I just haven't figured out what it is I fear yet. I suppose some day I'll stumble upon something that scares me, then I'll fear."

"Ha, how many more years do you plan on living?"

"Well, I've enjoyed the first one hundred, why not one hundred more? No, I'm a might ready to see John and Alice again. Including my baby, Mollie, I've buried four children and I know they are all up there waiting for me, so when the time comes I'll go willingly."

"Don't suspect it matters if you go willingly or unwillingly, I imagine we'll all go just the same. I hope I die in my sleep."

"Your sleep! Why ever for?"

"That way I won't know that I'm dying. I just simply won't wake up. Isn't that how you want to go?"

"Heaven's no, Rachel! I want my eyes wide open and I want to be fully awake when I head out of here."

"It doesn't scare you? Wait, nothing scares you, never mind. So why with your eyes open?"

"Because, honey I want the last thing I see of this world to be something pretty. Whether it's the blue sky, green grass, the bright sun or one of my children's sweet faces, I want to see a thing of beauty as I go, not the darkness of my sleep."

"I guess that's true enough, but it still don't seem right wanting to go with your eyes wide open. And besides, can you imagine the look on your children's faces if they were watching you die? Ha, I don't think that would be a very pretty thing to see."

The two women laughed as they thought about what their reactions would be if they witnessed Mary Anna croaking.

"Did I ever tell you about John right before his passing?"

"No, and I didn't see it proper to ask."

"You know, Rachel. I honestly think he was in Heaven and then came back to tell me goodbye."

"Oh, Mary Anna."

"I mean it. He told me that Ma Braymyer said hello and that he needed to hurry back up there because supper would be waiting soon. I could see the truth of all of it in his eyes, those oceans of blue so perfectly atop his face. Supper, ha imagine that. I hope they have some left over when I get up there, I could always go for a good meal or two.

705

I suppose John is up there now with his Ma, Pa and all his siblings and if there's any to be had, ha, they're all drinking Grandma Davis' moonshine. Except John of course, I don't reckon he'll ever drink the stuff, not that I blame him."

"My my," Rachel said. "Grandma Davis' moonshine. I'll never forget you soaking Mrs. Walker with the foul smelling stuff or how Walkie liked to have drowned me in it. That's been what, eighty seven years ago?"

"Hard to believe isn't it? I guess we're lucky to have the Walker gene, Rachel. The one that allows us to live so long anyway. Makes me wonder how long my mother would have lived had she not had her heart broken."

"I don't know, Mary Anna. I imagine she would have lived a long time though."

"I reckon she would have, but there's no cause crying over spilled milk. I guess we had better walk back over to the party... or people will start suspecting we're dead."

They continued across the grassy yard arm in arm toward the church, perfectly content with the lives that they had lived and they only hoped that the ones yet to come would have the same sort of adventure that they had had. Mary Anna's three surviving children were now sitting in chairs outside the church waiting for the two of them to return. They took seats beside them and stared out toward the western horizon and talked the rest of the day away.

As the sun went away and Mary Anna grew yet another day older, the heart of the Braymyer family remained just as strong as it ever had, buried deep within her chest. Since Alice had given it to her, she had kept it well protected, but it would soon be time to pass it down to another generation.

December 15, 1994
Braymyer Hill
Dixie, Texas

By the time I turned old blue down the long drive lined with aged cottonwoods at Braymyer Hill, I had gotten quite comfortable with driving. Indeed, I felt as though I could drive anything and go anywhere I pleased. But as we headed down the rock drive, both mine and Pappy's hearts pounded as we saw Grandma Rose on the front porch waiting for us.

We just knew for sure that we'd be in for one helluva ass chewing once that truck was parked. It hadn't snowed at all since we'd been gone, but it was still awful cold out and given my cold nature I just couldn't see how Grandma Rose was standing on the porch with nothing but a light jacket on. I drove right past the house, not daring to look in her direction as I parked the truck in front of the large barn.

I may not have looked at her, but she sure saw me. No sooner had I threw it in park than my door was flung open and I was being pulled out by the ear…the way most grandmothers do to disobedient children. My ear was the last of my worries though. Before I had had a chance to put on my coat, I had already been withdrawn from the vehicle and I thought for sure I was going to freeze to death.

"John! What are you doing driving!" She said screaming and throwing a temper tantrum like a small toyless child would.

"Gra…"

"No! I don't want to hear it! Go inside while I have a word with Daddy! Go on now! Shoo!"

With my head held low I headed in the front door, giving Pappy a look of sympathy as I passed him. I knew only one of two things could happen, either Grandma Rose would smoke enough cigarettes and calm down or I would be heading over to Whitesboro to live with her, but both options included Pappy getting yelled at and I sure hated to see that.

I stepped into the house to find that none of the fireplaces had fires in them. To me, it almost felt colder inside the house than it did outside and I desperately wished we were back at the ridge in the warmth it so willingly offered to us while we were there. I went room to room and lit fires in all the fireplaces and once I had finished I stood in the front room near the fire I had made the biggest.

Soon, Pappy came into the house with his usual no worries big smile on his face. I didn't know whether or not to be relieved or not because Pappy had a way of making the worst of times the most pleasant.

"Ah, I see you got the fires going, son."

"Yes, sir. Is everything ok?"

"Oh yes, everything is fine."

I looked at him with suspecting eyes. "Pappy, where's Grandma Rose?"

"Oh she's headed out to play bingo. Don't you worry none about her."

"Are you sure? I'm not going to have to go live with her am I?"

"No, son. You don't have to go live with her. Don't you fret none over that."

"How come she gets so mad?"

Pappy laughed a little bit. "I suspect it has a lot to do with her husband. I never did care much for him, kind of like John never cared for Esther's husband."

"Pappy, is Grandma Rose like Esther?"

"Well, in some ways I suppose she is, but deep down I don't think she's all that bad. And you know, Esther really wasn't as bad as she sounded to be."

Pappy sat down in one of the antique chairs and I soon followed suit in the one adjacent to his. "But Esther was going to let her brother get shot. That sounds like a pretty bad person to me."

"Well, you haven't heard the whole story and what truly happened to Esther."

"What do you mean? I thought John had to shoot her in order to save Nat?"

"Well, that's the story that has been passed down, but the true story is much different than that. You see, John had everyone believe that he had shot Esther only to hide the truth."

"But why would he want to hide the truth? I mean, why would he want people to think he killed his own daughter."

"Because John, he felt responsible and he didn't want people to think poorly of his Esther, no matter what mistakes she may have made."

"So… what really happened, Pappy?"

"Go to the kitchen and bring us some coffee and I'll tell you all about it."

I ran to the kitchen so anxious to hear this new little detail that I completely forgot how cold it was in the rest of the house. As soon as I came back into the room I took my seat again and just stared at Pappy as I patiently waited for him to take that first sip and begin telling me about Esther.

March 30, 1862
Braymyer Ridge

Esther stood in the kitchen alone as the sun made its way into the clear sky and brightened the house with its rays of light. As she stepped into the dining room with her cup of tea she heard Georgia's familiar voice whispering to Nat down below her feet. She had known all along that her family was hiding beneath the house, but had said nothing. She stomped her foot down onto the floor loudly to shut them up and then went into the front sitting room where she took a seat beside the window.

Lately she had felt a sense of regret over her past decisions, which was a strange thing for her given her uncommonly selfishness. She had gotten her desire for wealth, her nice house, fancy buggy and all the elegant dresses she could ever want for, but she had never fulfilled the desire for love. She had thought Polly loved her, but Polly was so busy trying to be the center of public attention that most of what she did was fake and full of lies.

Ben loved her, she thought, but then she had stumbled into his bedroom on more than one occasion where there was another woman in his bed. She forced herself to get over it and push forward at first, but then as she went into Walnut Grove and noticed that half the children there looked like him she found herself wondering. She had been so jealous of Ruth Ann, not only because her wedding had more guests and was much more enjoyable, but because Ruth Ann was happy and she was not.

They were twins, they were supposed to have everything exactly the same, of course Esther would have never shared her fortune with anyone, including Ruth Ann, but that didn't matter to her. The point was is that she was Esther and she should be able to be happy as well. Since she had become a Hunter her greed and selfishness had only increased and only

711

now did she realize that she had perhaps made a terrible mistake.

But what was she supposed to do? She was married now and there was no backing out of that and her husband only urged her farther and farther away from her family. He wanted Esther all for himself and didn't want to share her with anyone…not even her own family.

No matter how hard she told herself that her family was not her problem anymore, she always found herself wondering back to her childhood where her parents were there for her no matter what. Now, after nearly ten years she barely knew who they were and it was no one's fault but hers.

She quickly jumped to her feet when the first shot was fired outside between the north and the south and ran toward the front door where her husband was standing. Two Yankees stepped into the house behind the two of them and the only look that Ben could give Esther was a look that hinted that she was in the way.

"Here," he said handing her a rifle. "Take this gun, you might need it."

Two shots were fired from behind them and they turned to see that the two Yankees were lying dead and John, Will and Nat were standing next to them. Ben pulled Esther in front of him, holding her right next to the front side of his body, using her shoulder to steady his gun in the direction of Nat.

"Let her go, Ben!" John shouted.

"Pa," Esther said. "I'm sorry, Pa. I know I done wrong and I'm sorry."

Esther was being held so tightly that she could hardly move and the only place she could force the end of the gun was at her own chest. She pushed it against herself as hard as she could, closed her eyes and pulled the trigger. Ben was the first one to fall as the bullet went at an upward angle and hit him in the head.

Esther staggered for a moment and then fell into her father's arms where he gently laid her on the wooden floor. "Pa," she said. "Don't let people know I killed myself."

"Esther, don't talk like that. You'll be fine. Besides what you did was good, you saved your brother's life. I'm proud of you, darling."

"If what I did was good, then let it be between us. No reason letting the world think I am a saint after all the bad I done. Besides, I don't want people thinking that I was coward and shot myself. Please, Pa. Promise me… promise me you won't tell people I shot myself."

"Esther…"

"Pa, they say that a good deed is done only if the person doing the deed does not expect credit. Pa, let me do one good deed in my life and please allow me to do it right. I don't want no credit for this, honest I don't. I suppose I should…I should have tried doing good things a long time ago."

John looked down at her as a tear slipped from both his and hers matching blue eyes and rolled down their cheeks. John watched as the life slowly left his daughter's body and he couldn't have been more proud of any of his children than he was of Esther at that moment. He would honor his daughter's final wish, she was able to use her last act to save a life and her only humble request was that no one know that it was her that did it.

A good deed done with the wrong intent and hopes of gaining approval is only a deed accepted by the devil, but a deed done out of the kindness of one's heart with the intent of improving someone else's life is a miracle within itself. Esther may have spent most of her life doing the wrong things and chasing after everything except what she should have been, but in the end her last heroic act redeemed all the bad she had ever done.

Esther turned out to be a true leader of the people just like her mother had hoped and even if they didn't know it, a lot of things could have been very different had Esther not pulled the trigger that day. Of course, everyone in the family knew the truth about what had happened except for Georgia who didn't find out until she was in her mid twenties. It was kept a secret to honor Esther's humble request and no one else ever heard the true story until Mary Anna told Nathan Sanders just before she died.

December 15, 1994
Braymyer Hill
Dixie, Texas

"So Esther really wasn't a bad person?" I asked.

"That's right," Pappy answered. "Esther was just like the rest of us I suppose. She had done her fair share of wrong things in her life, but what made her different was how she ended everything."

"Wow, she sounds like she really changed a lot from the kind of person she had been."

"Sure did, so you see it was actually her that saved Nat that day and seeing as how Nat was my great grandfather, why she actually saved us as well."

"Well, I wish she didn't have to die anyhow."

"Sometimes life has a way of deciding things for us and although it's not always what we had hoped for, it all turns out alright in the end. Now, let's head upstairs and get some sleep. It's been a long day, but then anytime your Grandma Rose hollers at me it tends to make me sleepy."

We headed up the stairs and went into our bedrooms and slowly drifted off into a deep sleep. I dreamt of nothing but the Braymyer family that night, their long journey, their battles and most of all their sacrifices. A part of me kind of hoped that my vacation of life would soon be over because I was sure anxious to get to Heaven and see them…I had so many questions for them.

Dusty Williams

September 04, 2011
Sherman, Texas

Pappy told me that when Mary Anna died she called him into the room with her and told him that he would now be the carrier of the heart of the Braymyer family. Pappy gave me that same speech a little over a year ago when he died and I have felt an extra thump in my chest ever since.

It's hard to believe that only two people before me, Mary Anna had the special rhythm I now hold within myself. I have thought long and hard about who I will one day hand this special trait down to and often times I find myself awake late at night debating the subject.

It is my hopes that I am able to give the heart of Braymyer to Pappy's stories so that whoever reads them will have a part of it within them. Someday I think, Braymyers heart will beat strongly within us all, paying tribute to not only Pappy and his ancestors, but to all the families of the old west.

It makes me sad to write down all of Pappy's stories. Not because I am remembering him, that brings me much joy. It is because as this book comes to a close, that is one less story for me to put to paper and one book closer to the end.

I am reminded of all those cousins I had growing up and think back on what they said about me not ever amounting to anything. I suppose writing a book really isn't that important, especially since I am only telling of my Pappy's stories, but I wonder if amounting to something extraordinary is even possible in today's world.

I hear of so many people wishing they could live "back in the day," but I wonder if they truly know how hard it was. Sure they had love greater than anything we know, but it was a love of endurance and in order to get it one must first endure. I think one of the greatest things we as people can do is to remember. I firmly believe that we should remember all those who went before us so that we could stand here today not only as a person, but also as a people.

So in the end, if my life amounts to nothing more than the telling of my Pappy's stories, then I suppose that will be just fine with me. It's not half bad for a kid who was raised as far away from the trend of society as me. My only hope is that somewhere up there, my Pappy is looking down and is proud of who I have become.

We stopped having the reunion back in 2005; there just wasn't enough people who would come to it anymore. The few who had cared as my Pappy did, have all passed away and the younger people like myself don't show much interest. I guess that is the price we pay for changing the ways of the past and I am certain it all has to do with how our children are raised.

My children may not grow up being the most popular kids in school, but they will know more truth and meaning than half the others out there ever will. It is my promise to my Pappy that I will instill in them the same values that he taught me in hopes that at least one family line of the Braymyer family will remember the sacrifices that their family made for them.

When Pappy died he left Braymyer Ridge to me. I closed down the bed and breakfast and now use it as a summer home for my family and I. The two holes are still embedded in the wall, one for Alice and one for my Mama and Daddy. All the lavish velvet curtains still hang across all the windows and every room in the house still holds the same special story that was told to me so many years ago.

The cellar is still there as well, neatly tucked away beneath the dining room table under a rug and there are still a few bloodstains in the upstairs carpet from the invading Yankees. I remember Pappy's stories so vividly and can picture not only them in my head, but I can still see myself driving that old blue truck with Pappy at my side as he tells me another story. I remember it had taken him almost a year to tell me about

Ruth Ann's life, but then, that is too much to include in this book.

The End

Dusty Williams

The Braymyer Family Bible
Given to Mary Anna by Alice Braymyer

Births

John Nathaniel Braymyer
April 11, 1819

Mary Anna Walker
September 25, 1825

Esther Alice Braymyer
March 16, 1839

Ruth Ann Braymyer
March 16, 1839

Molly Elizabeth Braymyer
August 14, 1842

John Walker "Johnny" Braymyer
January 08, 1844

William Charles "Will" Braymyer
December 03, 1845

Nathaniel John "Nat" Braymyer
March 25, 1848

Georgia Tennessee Braymyer
November 01, 1854

Deaths

Ralph Morgan Braymyer
November 23, 1838

Molly Elizabeth Braymyer
November 16, 1842

Alice Elizabeth Morgan Braymyer
October 18, 1859

Percey Nathaniel Michaels
March 04, 1861

Esther Alice Hunter
March 30, 1862

Benjamin William Hunter
March 30, 1862

Washington Percey Michaels
1865

John Nathaniel Braymyer
April 21, 1888

William Charles Braymyer
May 01, 1892

John Walker Braymyer
May 14, 1917

Rachel Lloyd
August 03, 1927

Mary Anna Walker Braymyer
November 17, 1928

Nathaniel John Braymyer
September 21, 1932

Lady Ruth Ann Yale
June 24, 1935

Georgia Tennessee Williams
Aug 19, 1957

Esther again pleaded with the king, falling at his feet and weeping. She begged him to put an end to the evil plan of Haman the Agagite, which he had devised against the Jews.
Esther 8:3

About the Author

Dusty Williams, 29, has been writing since his early childhood. What started out as writing short, self-illustrated stories for the Howe Public Library in his elementary years has developed into novels and other works throughout his adult life. With a strong passion for local history, Williams dedicates most of his writings to historical non-fiction. However, he also possess within himself a great story telling skill which combined with his historical knowledge makes, *The Braymyer Saga* a must read book. Williams was born in Sherman, Texas and was raised in Howe and Van Alstyne. All of these towns are within the county of Grayson of which Williams' family have been residents for 9 generations. He is a member of several historical societies as well as the Grayson County Historical Commission. He is married to his wife, J Anna and they have three children. Williams and his family reside in Howe, Texas.

Made in the USA
San Bernardino, CA
19 February 2016